THE LECTURER'S TALE

THE
LECTURER'S
TALE

JAMES HYNES

Picador USA • New York

Library of Congress Cataloging-in-Publication Data

Hynes, James.
    The lecturer's tale / James Hynes.—1st ed.
       p. cm.
   ISBN 0-312-20332-2
   1. English teachers—Fiction. 2. College teachers—Tenure—Fiction. 3. Fingers—Wounds and injuries—Fiction. 4. Control (Psychology)—Fiction. 5. Middle West—Fiction. I. Title.

PS3558.Y55 L43 2001
813'.54—dc21   00-047836

First Edition: January 2001

10 9 8 7 6 5 4 3 2 1

To Glendon Hynes,
my first and best teacher

. . . gladly wolde he lerne, and gladly teche

Is that a' ye ken about the wiles and doings o' the prince o' the air, that rules an' works in the bairns of disobedience? Gin ever he observes a proud professor, who has mae than ordinary pretensions to a divine calling, and that reards and prays till the very howlets learn his preambles, *that's* the man Auld Simmie fixes on to mak a dishclout o'. He canna get rest in hell, if he sees a man, or a set of men o' this stamp, an' when he sets fairly to wark, it is seldom that he disna bring them round till his ain measures by hook or by crook. Then, O it is a grand prize for him, an' a proud deil he is, when he gangs hame to his ain ha', wi' a batch o' the souls o' sic strenuous professors on his back.

—JAMES HOGG, *The Private Memoirs and Confessions of a Justified Sinner*

O cursed synne of alle cursednesse!
O traytours homycide, O wikkednesse!
O glotonye, luxurie, and hasardrye!
Thou blasphemour of Crist with vileynye
And othes grete, of usage and of pride!
Allas! mankynde, how may it bitide
That to thy creatour, which that the wroghte,
And with his precious herte-blood thee boghte,
Thou art so fals and so unkynde, allas?
                    —CHAUCER, *"The Pardoner's Tale"*

CONTENTS

PART ONE

A Man's Reach

Ah, but a man's reach should exceed his grasp,
Or what's a heaven for?

—Robert Browning, "Andrea del Sarto"

1

All Hallow's Eve

Crossing the Quad on a Halloween Friday, as the clock in the library tower tolled thirteen under a windy, dramatic sky, Nelson Humboldt lost his right index finger in a freak accident. Someone called his name three times out of the midday press of students, and as he turned to answer, Nelson stumbled over a young woman stooping to the pavement behind him. Falling backward, he threw his hand out to catch himself, and his finger was severed by the whirring spokes of a passing bicycle.

Only minutes before, in the shadowy office of Victoria Victorinix, the English Department's undergraduate chair, Nelson had lost his job as a visiting adjunct lecturer. He had sat on the far side of Professor Victorinix's severely rectilinear desk, his hands tightly clutching his knees, while she told him with a cool courtesy that the department was forced by budget necessities to terminate his appointment at the end of the semester, only six weeks away.

"You have our gratitude, of course," she said, folding her slim hands in the icy blue light of her desk lamp, "for all your efforts on behalf of the department."

Professor Victorinix was a small, slender, thin-lipped woman with cropped, silvery hair and a bloodless manner barely masked by a disinterested politesse. Even during the day she kept the blinds of her office drawn, and today she sat in the shadows just beyond the direct glare of the lamp. The reflected glow off her desktop emphasized the sharpness of her cheekbones, the deep groove between her eyebrows, the smooth skullcap curve of her forehead. She regarded Nelson with a gaze that seemed to him aristocratic, ancient, bored.

"Under the circumstances," she said, "I realize that our gratitude may not mean much to you."

Nelson swallowed hard and tried not to cry. His own gaze, in order to avoid meeting hers, darted all over the office. His blurry glance took in pale gray walls, rigorously ordered books in steel and glass shelves, a muted etching in a silver frame of the Countess Bathory in her bath. Nelson appreciated that Professor Victorinix looked at him as she fired him, but couldn't she turn away, just for a moment?

"I, I'm sorry." Nelson cleared his throat. "Don't worry about me."

"I'd be happy to write a letter for your dossier." Victorinix began needlessly to adjust her pens and rearrange the papers on her desk. "We'll do what we can for you, Nelson."

Even more than the other senior members of the department, Victoria Victorinix was immune to the self-pity of wounded young men. After twenty-five years of ostracism, and worse, because of her sexual preference, she had outlasted the genteel bigotry of deans, chairmen, and senior colleagues to end up as a tenured full professor at a prestigious research university. Even more remarkably, she had survived three or four paradigm shifts in literary theory. All her books were still in print, from *Rhythm and Metonomy in Coleridge's "Christabel"* to *Daughters of the Night: Clitoral Hegemony in LeFanu's* Carmilla. In the academic world, this approached immortality, and her pitiless gaze told Nelson that in all that time she had seen dozens if not hundreds of young men just like him come and go.

"I-I-I," stammered Nelson, "I'm just grateful you kept me on as long as you did."

Nelson was short of breath. He wished he could retreat to his office and break down in semiprivate. Perhaps Vita Deonne, his office mate and the only person in the department who still talked to him willingly, would turn her attention from her own real and imagined professional terrors and comfort him. But he had a class to teach in ten minutes. He would have to compose himself in public as he crossed the Quad.

"Don't worry about me," he said again. He stood. "Gosh."

Professor Victorinix stood also, and Nelson stooped to pick up his battered leatherette briefcase full of student papers. He straightened to find Professor Victorinix gliding smoothly around the desk, regarding him with her relentlessly indifferent gaze. He backed away, clutching the briefcase to his chest. Nelson was taller even than most of his students, and he towered above the undergraduate chair. But when Professor Victorinix offered him her hand, Nelson felt as if he came only to her knees, looking up at her like a defenseless child. Still, he met her cool, dry palm with his own. No pressure was applied by either party.

Nelson had learned long ago that the handshake of his Iowa upbringing—what his father had called a "manly grip"—was not appropriate in academia. This was a mere brushing of palms, free of any gender typing.

A moment later Professor Victorinix's door closed silently behind him, and Nelson stood in the hall, unable to remember coming out of her office. He felt drained, and he looked woefully down the corridor, wondering if he had the energy to make it to the elevator. This was the highest floor in Harbour Hall, the headquarters of the English Department, where the department's elite had their rooms with a view of the wooded hills surrounding Hamilton Groves, and of the antlike undergraduates on the Quad below. Once upon a time Nelson had aspired to an office on this brightly lit and expensively carpeted hallway. Back when he had been a visiting assistant professor, he had ascended briefly as high as the fifth floor, where he'd had a grand view of the Quad, the Gothic clock tower of Thornfield Library, and the wide, glassy V of the library's underground Annex. Back then, all the secretaries had known his name and had laughed at his mild, self-deprecating jokes. Back then he had traded invitations to lunch with his colleagues while waiting to use the photocopier. Back then Morton Weissmann, his erstwhile mentor, had greeted him every day with a two-fisted handshake and a hearty, "How go the wars this morning, Nelson?"

Now Nelson ascended to the eighth floor only to have another pint of his professional lifeblood drained off. Now the secretaries peered at him warily, watching for the homicidal rage of a disgruntled postal worker. Now the copy machine and its good fellowship were off-limits to him, and he carried his lunch in a paper sack and ate alone in his office. Now he floated above the deep carpeting like a ghost. Colleagues he used to call by their first names didn't even make the effort of averting their eyes. They simply looked right through him, repressing a shudder at the sepulchral chill of failure trailing after him, at the feeling that someone had just stepped on their professional graves.

Nelson swallowed and started down the deep carpet. It always took more effort to walk up here, as if he were treading sand at a very high altitude; the gleaming doors of the elevator seemed to recede the closer he came to them. He heard the whirr of the photocopier and a deep, avuncular laugh coming from the copy room halfway down the hall, some professor deigning to share a joke with a work/study student. Nelson's knees began to tremble, his cheeks began to burn, and he trudged toward the elevators as if ankle deep in the plush pile, ducking his head as he approached the door to the copy room.

5

With a theatrical gust of laughter, Morton Weissmann, almost an emeritus and the man who had brought Nelson to the university and then abandoned him, stepped into the hallway ahead. Weissmann was a large man, once strikingly handsome but possessed now of the sagging good looks of an aging movie star, his tailored suits hanging a little too loosely off his frame. Still smiling, he lifted his eyes from the sheaf of copies in his large, liver-spotted hand and met Nelson's darting gaze. Nelson, rabbit-scared, caught his breath and sank deeper into the carpet. But Weissmann, who had not so much as said good morning to Nelson in a year, gave him a rictus of a smile and a flip of the hand, like Gregory Peck diffidently acknowledging a fan. He shouldered past Nelson and headed down the hall toward his office.

Nelson, flushed and trembling, waded to the elevators, where he stood knee-deep in the carpet and pushed the button. He lifted his eyes desperately to the little red light climbing through the floors, and prayed that he might have the elevator to himself. But someone wafted alongside him and pushed the button again. The elevator climbed slowly, as if it were being hauled by hand, and Nelson was aware of someone scarlet and slender next to him, radiating like heat. Nelson smelled expensive perfume, but if his life had depended upon it, he couldn't have said what it was.

Don't look, he told himself, don't meet her eye; but without lowering his chin, he slid his eyes to one side and glimpsed Miranda DeLaTour, one of the star performers of the department. She was poised and strikingly featured—cheekbones, chin—with an artfully unruly mane of black hair and a red silk suit that showed off her legs and her narrow waist. She ignored Nelson without any effort at all, as if he simply weren't there. She was rumored to be the lover of the department's chair, the flamboyant and forceful Anthony Pescecane; but Nelson, even in his distress, forced himself to remember that rumors of that sort trailed every attractive woman in the academy. She lifted her hand to her hair, brushed a silken strand off her padded shoulder, and sighed. Nelson held his breath.

The bell dinged, number eight burned red, the elevator doors slithered open. Professor DeLaTour stepped into the car, her sharp heels clicking against the floor. Blinking at Nelson without a trace of recognition, she pressed the button for her floor without waiting for him to get on, and the doors slid shut on Miranda DeLaTour regarding her reflection in the elevator's control panel. Nelson breathed out at last and turned to the stairwell.

The stairs at least gave him a few moments' respite from further embarrassment. He descended with heavy, echoing footfalls, drawing in shallow breaths of dead, stairwell air. In eight years at the University of the Midwest in Hamilton Groves, Minnesota, Nelson had fallen from a prestigious postdoctoral fellowship, at the rank of assistant professor, to teaching three sections of composition and one of study skills as a visiting adjunct lecturer on a semester-to-semester contract. Now he was about to become a *former* visiting adjunct lecturer, on his way to failed academic. At times like this, when he was in need of a spiritual buttress, some inspirational line or scene from English literature often came to him unbidden; an unusually thorough memory of the canon was Nelson's chief attribute as a teacher and a scholar. But today the canon let him down, and all he heard in the leaden reverberation of his descending footsteps was "tomorrow, and tomorrow, and tomorrow."

At the foot of the stairs he paused among the dust balls and crumpled candy wrappers. He squeezed the dampness out of the corners of his eyes with thumb and forefinger, lifted his gaze to the concrete ceiling, and sighed once, twice, three times. Losing his position meant that his income would stop on the last day of the year, just after Christmas. His health insurance for himself, his wife, and their two young daughters would be cut off, along with their eligibility to live in university married housing. All this would happen a short six weeks from now. Nelson had no savings and no prospects, and now he was about to have no job, no insurance, and no home. The loss of his finger in a few moments would merely add injury to insult.

He squared his shoulders, adjusted his grip on the briefcase, and thought of having to face his tough-minded wife with the news.

"Screw your courage to the sticking-place," he murmured, and he pushed hard at the battered metal door of the stairwell, swinging it wide into the lobby. It promptly swung back and slammed in his face. As Nelson jumped back, he saw through the square little window the furious, bug-eyed glare of Lionel Grossmaul, the chairperson's administrative assistant. Nelson had swung the door open in Lionel's path.

"I, I'm sorry!" Nelson shouted through the smudged glass. His voice reverberated up the empty stairwell, as high-pitched as a girl's.

But Grossmaul swung the murderous beam of his black-rimmed glasses away from Nelson, and beyond him Nelson saw the leonine head of Anthony Pescecane as he swept by. Grossmaul followed, passing out of sight of the window, and Nelson gingerly pushed the door open and peeked out. Chairperson Pescecane

7

swung into the elevator, shooting his expensive cuffs and clasping his powerful hands before his tailored suit coat, his dark gaze fixed in the middle distance. Nelson stepped into the lobby, his arms wrapped around his briefcase.

"I didn't see you," he said.

But Grossmaul moved between Nelson and Pescecane. Lionel Grossmaul was a pear-shaped little man in discount store khakis and a too-tight polyester shirt, and he stepped backward into the car and viciously punched the button. Lionel was Pescecane's sidekick, bitterly loyal, following in Pescecane's train while the more successful man ascended from department to department. In Nelson's few encounters with Grossmaul, the chairperson's assistant had never yielded a kind answer to Nelson. As the elevator doors clapped shut, Grossmaul glared at Nelson with the open contempt he reserved for his institutional inferiors.

Unnerved, Nelson hurried across the lobby, and the outside door was wrenched out of his grasp by a cold wind blowing out of the north. Nelson was fairly sucked out of the building into the chill, and he staggered to a stop. Ominous, ragged blocks of cloud ground together low over the Quad, trailing wind-blown shreds of gray. The narrow, redbrick clock tower on Thornfield Library, erected not very symmetrically at one corner of the square old building, seemed to glide against the moving clouds, the glaring white face of the clock set against the wind, the ornate black hands pinching together toward twelve. Today was the last day of October, and just as Nelson looked up the clock began to toll noon.

One, tolled the clock, in a long, resonant stroke of the bell, and Nelson was caught in a little dust devil of dry, crackling leaves. The bony fingers of leafless maples were black against the overcast sky, crones swaying to the slow rhythm of the bell all around the Quad.

Two. Nelson put his head down and closed his eyes and clutched his briefcase as the freakish little wind beat around him.

"Professor Humboldt!" someone called.

What an odd thing for someone to call me, Nelson thought. Under the circumstances.

Three. The dust devil pulled at him like a pair of cold, insistent hands. Nelson planted his feet and opened his eyes to see a young man in a hooded black cape just turning away from him in the stream of students moving toward the Quad. Nelson opened his mouth to call after the boy, but he didn't know who it was, and anyway, the kid was walking away, his cape billowing after him. Urged on

8

by the wind, Nelson headed toward his twelve o'clock composition class in the Chemistry Building on the far side of the Quad.

Four, tolled the clock. The tower seemed to sway vertiginously against the rushing clouds, so Nelson kept his eyes down and matched his pace to the rhythm of the bell.

Five. This was the busiest class change of the day, as students entered the Quad from all four corners at once in a slow maelstrom of complex currents and eddies. Out of the eddies little knots formed, students meeting friends or room-mates or lovers, talking loudly in the brisk wind, book packs slung over their shoulders. Today a good many of them were in costume.

Six. In spite of his troubles, Nelson loved this scene. It reminded him that he was looking forward to taking his daughters, Clara and little Abigail, trick-or-treating at dusk tonight, through the cul-de-sacs of married housing. Even in his distress, the gentle riot of students across the Quad seemed to Nelson the epitome of what life at university ought to be: bright, good-humored, energetic young people in a hurry to be somewhere else, chattering happily about their classes, their lives, their loves.

Seven. And on Halloween they were parading their secret faces across the Quad. Some were costumed traditionally, as ghosts, vampires, witches. Some were ironic representations of the working people these students of a prestige university would almost certainly never be: nurses, firemen, cops, carpenters. Some were recognizable to Nelson as movie stars or pop singers; some were made up in abstract masks of red and yellow and green. The Bride of Frankenstein walked beside Marge Simpson, their columns of hair bobbing in counterpoint.

Eight. This was more restorative to Nelson than sobbing in his office. Unlike many of his colleagues—unlike most of them, truth to tell—Nelson liked his students. He believed himself to be a fundamentally cheerful man. He counted another stroke of the great bell—*nine*—and it seemed to him that all of life should have such heedless momentum; all of life should be so full of hope.

"Professor Humboldt!" someone shouted again, a little louder, a little more eagerly. Nelson twisted to see the boy in black, cape flying, beckoning to Nelson from a corner of the Quad between the steps of Thornfield Library and the narrow, glassed-in gully of the library's underground Annex. Or was it a boy? Nelson had already drifted through the densest part of the Quad into a lane of traffic where kids on bicycles, skateboards, and roller blades darted through the fringes of class change; and at this distance, over the heads of the shifting crowd,

9

the caped figure looked like a young woman, with a bosom and hips and shoulder-length hair. The sky was churning overhead; the blocks of cloud were clashing together, drops of cold rain spitting into Nelson's face. As the girl in black turned away, Nelson glimpsed a red, grinning mask with horns, and he was reminded of the undergraduate tradition that the old library was haunted— by the ghost of a suicide, if memory served. *Ten.* Nelson lifted a hand and waved to the figure—boy? girl?—in the cape.

"Professor who?" he called out, uncharacteristically ironic, and stepping backward he tumbled over a young woman in a witch's costume who had stooped just at that moment to pick up a pen. Nelson fell spectacularly, wide-eyed, his long arms thrown out, his briefcase turning slowly above the heads of the crowd. He seemed to fall a very long time, long enough in fact to count off one more slow stroke of the bell—*eleven*—and as he landed on his back the wind was knocked out of him. At the same moment he thrust his right index finger into the spokes of a passing mountain bike, which sliced it cleanly off and sent it flying. The bicyclist skidded, squealing to a stop. The girl rose from where Nelson had knocked her over, her pointed black hat still improbably in place, her kohl-rimmed eyes wide, her hands pressed to her red mouth. Nelson sat up breathlessly at the center of a gawking circle of undergraduates, and he saw his severed finger still rolling in a little arc against the pavement.

Whoa, he thought. He felt no pain, but lifting his right hand, he saw thick blood welling at a slow boil out of the stump of his finger.

Why am I not surprised? he thought. He lay back slowly as if moving through water, until the back of his head rested on the cold, gritty pavement. He knew he was about to pass out, and he blinked up at the clock tower leaning over him, silhouetted against the clouds roiling overhead. *Twelve,* tolled the bell, the hands of the clock stabbing straight up like blades. Why is this happening to me? thought Nelson. Isn't getting fired enough? How will I take care of my family? Won't anybody help me?

Someone was shouting. There was slow movement at the edge of his vision. Then, just before he passed out, Nelson thought he saw, framed by the white clock face of the tower looming against the churning clouds, the figure in the black cape bending over him. The mask was gone, and Nelson saw, or thought he saw, within the hood of the cape, a faceless face, a silvery oblong with no eyes, nose, or mouth. As he blinked up at this apparition, the clock tower tolled one last, impossible beat. *Thirteen.*

"What can I do for *you*, Professor Humboldt?" said the empty face, and then everything went black.

Nelson awoke again briefly, flat on his back, opening his eyes to fluorescent bars of light flashing by above him. Squinting against the glare, he glimpsed uniforms ahead of him and on either side. A black paramedic wearing a white plastic glove held Nelson's injured hand upright by the wrist, while a woman with blonde hair tied in a bun carried his finger in a plastic bag like a leftover, the plastic sagging from the weight and smeared with blood. The black paramedic saw that Nelson's eyes were open.

"Do you want me to call your sister?" he asked.

"My sister?" Nelson said. His mouth was very dry. He didn't have a sister.

"I don't know, man," said the paramedic. "You said something about your weird sister."

"Where am I?" said Nelson, and he passed out again.

Hours later Nelson struggled up out of a narcotic haze, and found himself tucked up to the chin in a hospital bed, wearing a backless gown. His right hand rested on the covers, swathed to the elbow in bandages and a splint. He blinked at the dead gray eye of the television suspended beyond the end of his bed, then turned to the window. There, before a handsome nighttime view of wooded hills and the streaming red-and-white of rush-hour traffic, he saw his wife, Bridget, dozing in a chair. She was nearly as tall as Nelson, but more slender and a good deal more graceful, a former dancer in fact. She had folded herself into the hospital chair with her long legs under her and her head propped up on her hand. Her face was paler than usual, and there were lines in her neck and around her eyes that Nelson had never noticed before. He tried to speak to her, but his mouth was parched. As he watched, her eyelids fluttered, and she shuddered, and Nelson felt another pang of guilt and terror at their future. She opened her eyes and saw he was awake, and she unfolded herself and came to the bed, stooping to kiss his forehead and run her hand over his thinning hair. She poured him a cup of water and held it to his lips.

He swallowed and said, "Where are the girls?"

"With Rachel." She meant their neighbor in married housing, the wife of an Israeli postdoc.

"Are they upset?" He let her give him another drink.

"Oh, honey, they don't even know yet."

11

"Trick or treat."

Bridget widened her eyes, and Nelson wondered if he had been delirious. He struggled to sit up a little higher.

"I was supposed to take them," he said. "Trick-or-treating."

"Shh." Bridget touched his lips. "Rachel took them with her kids. How do you feel?"

He lifted his right hand, swathed like a mummy's, palm flat, fingers together. His right index finger seemed to be in place, though he couldn't feel it at all; in fact his whole body felt as if it were wrapped in cotton. Painkillers, he decided.

"Let me get the doctor." Bridget smoothed his hair and headed for the door.

"Oh, Bridget, we can't afford this," Nelson said weakly, but she only smiled and went into the hall.

She came back a few minutes later with a trim Asian-American man, younger than Nelson. His name tag said DR. GEE. He told Nelson jauntily that they were able to reattach the digit, that Nelson would have some movement in it, not much, but that he would never feel anything in his finger again.

"We'll let you out of here tomorrow," Dr. Gee said. "We can take the bandages off in a week to ten days. The stitches'll come out later. You'll look a little like Frankenstein for a while." The doctor smiled. "From the knuckle down anyway."

"My husband is an English professor." Bridget sat on the edge of the bed, her arm around her Nelson's shoulders. "He teaches *Frankenstein*."

"Really." Dr. Gee's eyes dulled, and Nelson wondered if this young man had read a novel, any novel, since his freshman year. Having heard that his patient taught Frankenstein, Nelson supposed that the doctor had a mental image of a classroom full of enormous, pallid men with flat heads and bolts in their necks, wedged into little classroom desks, with Nelson up front declaiming, "Water *good*. Fire *bad*." As he thought this, Nelson felt something the doctor had just said he shouldn't, a twinge in his reattached finger like a pinprick. He winced, forcing the little fantasy away. Nelson disapproved of sarcasm, especially at the expense of students. No doubt he was affected by the drugs.

"Sweetheart, are you alright?" Bridget moved aside while Dr. Gee peered into each of Nelson's eyes with a penlight and checked his pulse and offered to increase the dosage of his painkillers. Nelson declined, and he thanked the doctor for saving his finger. He offered Dr. Gee his good hand, and they shook awkwardly. As soon as the doctor left, Nelson said, "I have to check out of here tonight. We can't afford this."

12

He sat upright and swung his legs out of the bed, and Bridget tried to gentle him back against the pillow. He didn't struggle, but he wouldn't lie back down either. He took both her hands between the fingers of his good hand. "Bridget, I have to tell you something."

"It can wait."

"No, it can't." Nelson tugged his wife back down on the bed next to him.

"I'm not a professor anymore," he said.

"Okay, a visiting adjunct lecturer," she said, with a bitter smile.

"Listen," Nelson said, and he squeezed her hand and told her about his meeting with Professor Victorinix just before the accident: that he had lost his job today, that they were about to lose their health insurance and their home as well. He kept his eyes on hers as he told her everything, but even in his cottony cocoon of codeine he had never felt so ashamed in his life. In Bridget's eyes her concern for him struggled with her anger at what she saw as his ill-usage by the department. His wife's anger was never far below the surface; she was an Irish girl.

"Sweetheart, please don't say anything just now." He squeezed her fingers with his good hand. "I know I'm still insured, but there's the deductible to consider. What if one of the girls gets sick? Think how much even one night in this room is costing us."

She followed his glance around the bright little room, and he saw that he nearly had her convinced. He squeezed her hand again. "Please help me get dressed, and then you can drive me home."

Bridget opened her mouth to speak, but she kissed him on the cheek instead and helped him to his feet. The light in her eyes withdrew immediately though, and he knew she was enduring their humiliation in silence, worrying it like a sore tooth. She'd never completely understood the life of the young academic: why he taught four classes a semester for a fraction of the salary of professors who taught two, why he was never paid for the articles he published, why he stayed up till all hours of the night writing comments on the papers of students who would only throw them away after looking at the grade. But for now she held her tongue and went to fetch his clothes from the closet. Nelson stood and wobbled away from the bed. He leaned unsteadily against the window, his breath misting on the glass. He watched the cars rushing by in the road below, a white blur of headlights coming one way, a red stream of taillights going the other, and he was grateful for the numbness of the drugs.

2

Curriculum Vitae

Nelson Humboldt was pale of skin and round of face, his thinning hair so fair as to be almost white. He was tall, with big hands and feet and a bit of a belly. He jogged when he could, and wrestled occasionally with the hydraulic weight machines at the university field house. But his limbs remained as round as bowling pins, his muscles without definition. He was powerful but graceless, never good at competitive sports, though he exerted himself mightily.

He was a Midwesterner, the son of a high school English teacher in Maytag, Iowa, who had never finished his Ph.D., and who had spent his career resigned and embittered in equal measure, teaching bowdlerized Shakespeare to the children of farmers and Rotarians. Nelson Senior tried to compensate for his frustration by making his son a prodigy of literary scholarship, reading to Nelson Junior from a very early age the beginnings of the canon in chronological order. *Beowulf* in the bassinet, *Piers Plowman* in the crib, and Chaucer in Middle English just about the time Nelson was learning to walk. Nelson heard *The Faerie Queen* as a very long bedtime story, lasting an appreciable portion of his young life, and Shakespeare all the way through kindergarten and first grade. While other kids were swallowing whole the adventures of the Hardy Boys and Nancy Drew, Nelson was reading "The Rape of the Lock" under his bedcovers with a flashlight. Every week in fifth grade for Show and Tell he declaimed a poem from memory, until the teacher stopped him one week halfway through "To His Coy Mistress." In the hall after school she asked him why he couldn't bring plastic dinosaurs or a G.I. Joe like the other boys.

After this Nelson became self-consciously aware of his difference from other children, but when he tried to explain this to his father, Nelson Senior told his son to "reach me down the Browning." Very solemnly he read Nelson a passage from "Andrea del Sarto," wearing an expression Nelson had never seen on his

14

father's face before. Nelson Senior stopped a couple of times to bite his lip and swallow hard. The book trembled in his hands.

" 'You don't know how the others strive,' " he read, choking. He paused a moment, his mouth working, and Nelson had the very disturbing feeling that his father was about to cry.

But Nelson Senior mastered himself and read a few more lines, ending with something about men who could reach heaven but came back and had not the art to tell the world about it. He closed the book and said, "Do you see, Nelson, what I'm trying to tell you? Do you understand the difference between you and me?"

Nelson Senior favored the Socratic method with his own son, an approach he never tried on the bland, cheerful Iowans he was forced to teach. In this instance, however, Nelson did not have the slightest idea what his father was talking about. Something to do with a painter, was all he got out of it. But he nodded anyway.

"Good," his father said, pushing the book at Nelson, molding his son's hands around the volume.

"A man's reach, Nelson," said Nelson Senior, his voice frighteningly hoarse, "should exceed his grasp." Then, in a whisper, "Or what's a heaven for?"

By junior high Nelson was reading Conrad and Thomas Hardy, and by high school, as other teenaged readers passed dog-eared copies of *The Catcher in the Rye* or *The Fellowship of the Ring* from hand to hand, Nelson was carrying around a copy of the *Cantos.* His first sexual stirrings ran concurrently with his reading of *Ulysses,* and he came to identify Molly Bloom with one Brenda Spack, the strapping daughter of a well-to-do soybean farmer. He sent her anonymous poems, laboriously composed and copied out on his mother's best stationery, then slipped through the vent of Brenda's locker. He stopped after hearing her read them aloud in the cafeteria one lunch period, declaiming his iambic pentameter in mock-breathlessness, as her entourage howled with laughter and stuck their fingers down their throats. He was stung to the heart by the laughter, but also by the embarrassing way Brenda stressed the second syllable in "alabaster" and passed over "integument" in silence.

Worse yet, he and Brenda were in his father's English class together, and, given the assignment to declaim a contemporary poem, she had performed the words to a television theme song. That night his father made Nelson stand up and imitate for his mother the way Brenda had made a sort of curtsey at the refrain, dipping her knees every time she said, *"Petti-coat Junction."* Nelson Se-

15

nior roared at this, saying, "At least it's not Simon and Garfunkel." Nelson flushed with rage at his father, and vowed never again to make fun of a student, even behind her back.

During his senior year, Nelson let his hair grow to his shoulders, and he cultivated a moustache and beard that grew out in patches like the mange. He abandoned the long, teleological march from Chaucer to Hemingway and took up Kerouac and William S. Burroughs; he learned the first half of "Howl" by heart, and trimmed his mangy beard into a goatee. He acquired some "bad" friends for a time, with whom he smoked homegrown dope and listened to Jethro Tull. He'd hold the sweet smoke in his lungs for as long as he could and then comment sagely through the haze that Tull's lyrics were, y'know, written to quite a high poetic standard. To which his doper friends replied, "Aqualung, man. Fuckin' A."

He lost his virginity to a girl named Wendy Walberg in the basement rec room of her parents' house, sound track courtesy of Al Stewart. An exile from Brenda Spack's court, Wendy told him in this intimate setting that she knew Nelson had written the anonymous poems, that Brenda was *such* a bitch, and that she, Wendy, had laughed only because the other girls did. The stereo played "The Year of the Cat," and she pressed herself against him as they lay sprawled in a crackling beanbag chair. She murmured that she'd give anything—*anything*—to have someone send her poems like that. Yes she said yes I will Yes.

Afterward, she told him she was a poet herself and would he care to hear her work?

"Now?" he said, and bare naked she dashed up to her room to fetch her notebook. Pasted to Naugahyde by his own sweat, Nelson felt the first tremors of alarm. The poems turned out to be not quite up to the standard of, say, Jethro Tull, but he told her that they were beautiful, and then, the next day, he avoided her at school. Twenty years later, he was still convinced that it was the worst thing he'd ever done.

The following year Nelson went away to Halcyon College, a small, four-year liberal arts institution in Ohio. Here he abandoned the writing of poetry forever and found his true calling. Having discovered Joyce, Faulkner, and Thomas Wolfe, Nelson embarked upon an epic modernist novel about the coming-of-age of a tall, passionate young Iowan, his struggle for independence and understanding in a provincial small town, and his artistic and sexual awakening in the metropolis. *Theseus,* he called it, after the central metaphor of his hero adrift in the labyrinth of New York, London, or Paris; Nelson couldn't decide which. Nelson likewise couldn't decide whether his hero was a composer or a sculptor. Never a writer, though—Nelson thought that would have been too narcissistic.

After seven hundred single-spaced pages, he had gotten his hero to the fourth grade, and he screwed up his courage and showed the manuscript to Halcyon's creative writing teacher. Walter Midlist was an embittered forty-five year old who, as a young writer, had been cripplingly faint-praised as the new Sherwood Anderson and who hadn't written a word in years. His response to Nelson's novel was succinct and devastating. He dropped the manuscript like a cinder block on his desk and said, "You got something against punctuation, kid? This reads like somebody hit you in the head with a copy of *Absalom, Absalom.* Grow up."

That evening Nelson burned the novel a page at a time in the fireplace of his dormitory's lounge. Then, like the other young men whose literary ambitions Midlist had crushed, he began spending all his free time at the professor's house, where every night Midlist dispensed from the pockets of his leather vest joints as thick as his index finger. Sprawled at the feet of their master, their eyes dilated as wide as olive pits, these acolytes in the cult of failure ripped on the reputation of every published writer since Jonathan Swift. Unlike the rest of them, Nelson had read most of the work they were demolishing, but his talent for quotation impressed them only if he did it with a sneer.

Midlist was busted finally for supplying dope to his students, and went on to write a bestseller about life in the penitentiary ("a new Caryl Chessman," read the blurb). Nelson, meanwhile, was plucked by the hair from his slough of despond when, slouching in the back row of his twentieth-century poetry class, he snidely recited "The Hollow Men" from memory. His classmates were awestruck, and something like pride glowed through Nelson's haze of self-pity and THC. But Professor Gallagher, a gruff man like a fireplug with a buzz cut, glowered at Nelson.

"See me when we're done, kid," he said, and then, after class, marched Nelson into his office. Nelson recited the poem again while Professor Gallagher grunted and shook his head. "More feeling!" he barked. "You're not reading the goddamn Yellow Pages!"

After three tries, Nelson finished to Gallagher's satisfaction, saying, "This is the way the world ends," with the proper degree of existential dread.

"How the hell'd you know that?" asked Gallagher, glowering benignly.

17

"Um, my father?" Nelson said, flattered and embarrassed.

"It's a gift, son." Gallagher leaned back in his chair and linked his beefy fingers behind his head. "But I don't care how many poems you know by heart. You ever read a poem that diffidently in my class again, I'll knock you on your ass." He barked with laughter. "Don't think I can't do it, buster!"

Gallagher was a Midwestern farmboy, a good-humored, hardworking, tough-minded veteran of World War II who had bootstrapped himself up from walking behind a plow into the world of ranch houses, station wagons, and color television. The canon had been new to him in his early twenties, the bounty of the G.I. Bill, and he had something of the autodidact's messianic love of literature. Most of the kids at Halcyon were preprofessional students—"Cattle," Gallagher growled, "goddamn sheep!"—and coming across Nelson was like finding a child raised by wolves. Gallagher drilled Nelson like the master sergeant he'd once been in the Aleutian Islands, and he shamed the doper's diffidence out of Nelson. Twice a week he tutored Nelson in close reading, plucking volumes off his book-shelf and lending Nelson books by Lionel Trilling, Alfred Kazin, and Irving Howe. He taught Nelson prosody, setting him impossible tasks—"Write me a sestina in the style of Emily Dickinson"—just to see if Nelson could explain *why* they were impossible. Sometimes their sessions were like a half-time pep talk or a motivational speech at the Rotary Club.

"My old man was a farmer," Gallagher would say. "The only books we had in the house were the Sears catalog and the Bible, and all he ever used the Bible for was to hit me in the head." He'd lean forward, catching Nelson in his penetrating gaze. "What you've got up here," he'd say, tapping Nelson's broad forehead, "Jesus Christ, son, it's a *treasure.*"

He loved Nelson like a perfect son, the one who read all the books he recommended and laughed at all his jokes. He reawakened Nelson's love of literature and infected him with ambition, urging him on to the glorious career in big-time academia Gallagher himself would never have. Gallagher summed it up in the avuncular fashion of a latter-day Horace Greeley: Go to Graduate School, Young Man.

So Nelson applied to the Ivies and the great state schools in the Midwest and California, and his proud professor wrote him a glowing letter of recommendation. But Nelson's reach exceeded his grasp. The prestige institutions turned him down or put him on waiting lists, and Nelson ended up accepting a teaching assistantship at a brand-new graduate program at a smallish land grant school in north central Indiana. Gallagher mastered his disappointment.

"Scholarship is a meritocracy, Nelson," he said. "A man's worth is judged by the quality of his work, not by the pedigree of his doctorate. Hell," he added, clapping Nelson on the back, "R. P. Blackmur didn't even go to college!"

Nelson spent the summer after graduation back in Maytag, painting houses and fantasizing hopefully about the next few years of his life. Gallagher had painted an idyllic picture of his own grad school days, living in a Quonset hut in East Lansing, Michigan, writing his master's thesis on a card table at one end of the room while his wife and kids watched *Your Show of Shows* at the other. As a going-away present, he had given Nelson a handsome slip-covered edition of Aristotle. This would give him a head start on his literary theory seminar, Gallagher said, and Nelson spent the summer reading it cover to cover, his hands smelling of turpentine.

But on his first day as a graduate student, at the very first meeting of Introduction to Literary Theory, his instructor—a gaunt and entirely hairless man in severe wire rims, a jacket of herringbone tweed, and a white roll-neck sweater— lifted a paperback edition of Aristotle with two fingers and set it on fire with a silvery Zippo. He dropped it in a wastebasket without a word and watched it burn, and when Nelson got up and opened a window to let out the smoke, he spun with a sharp, jerking motion and barked at Nelson to sit down.

"Don't touch that, you!" the professor said, in a vaguely Gallic accent; and then, to everyone, "I want you all to smell that. I want it to penetrate to the back of your nostrils. By the end of the term I want that smell to come to you even in your sleep, to be as familiar to you as the stink of your own pale, oozing bodies."

This struck Nelson as a little extreme on a September morning in Indiana.

"For some of you," the professor went on, "I will be an intellectual *terroriste*, striking *brutally"*—and here he lunged at a young woman in the front row, who cringed and clutched her notebook to her bosom—*"ruthlessly* and *without warning* at the foundation of everything you hold dear. But for those of you with the rigor and the intellectual humility to submit to my will, I will be your guerrilla chieftain, teaching you, disciplining you, driving you with a terrible love to do things you did not think *possible. Some of you will not survive." He fixed Nelson

19

with a fearsome glare, his merciless eyes huge behind his lenses. "But some of you I will lead out of the hills and down into the burning metropole."

He lifted the wastebasket. Aristotle was still smoldering.

"This is just the first step," he said. "We will have to destroy literary theory in order to save it."

Thus Nelson discovered that no one was doing close reading anymore. The professor called himself Jean-Claude Evangeline. Even his colleagues were uncertain of his provenance, although they hadn't examined his *vita* any further than the Collège de France, which was good enough for them. His one published volume, *Les Mortifications,* a book as dense and impenetrable as the man himself, was dedicated equally mysteriously to *"Ma belle guerrière!"* His English was flawlessly idiomatic, but was he French? Flemish? Québecois? Those of his colleagues who envied his cultural cachet and his hypnotic hold over graduate students mimicked his accent behind his back and compared him to Pepe LePew.

Indeed, most of the school's youngish faculty had taken a step down from graduate school to teach here, leaving their cramped apartments in paradisiacal Berkeley or Madison or Ann Arbor to live in large and inexpensive tract homes in the dullest town on the flattest landscape in North America. The State University of Indiana at Edgarville—SUIE, pronounced "Sooey"—had been an agricultural college until recently, and its graduate program in English and comparative literature was brand-new. Most of the English faculty loathed their undergraduates, who were majoring en masse in communications and business administration; and they only barely tolerated their graduate students, who, if they had been any good, would have gone to the same graduate programs their professors had. Nelson's teachers at Halcyon insisted that he address them as "Professor," but would talk to him in the hall for an hour and a half. At Sooey his professors insisted he call them by their first names, and then locked their office doors to him while they furiously wrote articles and books and updated their CVs, desperate to trade up to a better school.

"Call me Judith," Nelson's advisor insisted at their first meeting, "not Professor Engels." But in order to see her he had to book an appointment three days in advance, for a brisk and businesslike meeting lasting all of ten minutes. She kept him longer than that only once that first semester, closing the door and biting her nails and kvetching at length about the flashy, insubstantial work of a friend of hers who had just gotten a job at Princeton. Nelson noted a copy of the friend's book on her desk, the bookstore receipt still stuck in its pages.

Another time, he came upon her weeping, her eyes red and puffy. Her allergies, she insisted. Nelson began to think of Judith as a character from Chekhov, a melancholy exile stuck in the provinces, hopelessly in love with an alcoholic doctor, dreaming of her exciting life long ago in far-off Saint Petersburg.

Nelson himself felt as though he had passed through the looking glass. An innocent and self-evident remark in Evangeline's class about Conrad's jumbled chronologies raised snorts of derision from his classmates. A severe young woman from the Indian subcontinent addressed Nelson without looking at him, telling him painfully, in a posh imperial accent, that Conrad's racism was the *starting* point for any discussion of his work.

"Read Edward Said," she added, in a curt postcolonial sotto voce.

Evangeline himself cut Nelson not *un millimètre* of slack. In his first paper, Nelson manfully tackled Nietzsche, the earliest theorist Professor Evangeline was willing to sanction, and the professor handed the paper back with a failing grade and only one comment; on the first page he'd circled the word "literature" in blood-red felt tip and written in the margin: "When I see this word, I reach for my revolver."

Thus, Nelson's first lesson in graduate school was to keep his mouth shut. Paradoxically his silence, and his status as one of the only male graduate students in central Indiana who wasn't married or gay, led him into the arms of an avid young woman from the East Coast named Lilith. She was the daughter of two psychoanalysts—a mixed marriage, in fact: Dad followed Jung; Mom was a Lacanian. Lilith mistook Nelson's native Midwestern good manners and his liberal pluralist tolerance for acquiescence in the postmodern project, whatever that was.

"I have an agenda," she told him on their first date, after a campus viewing of a scratchy print of *Last Year at Marienbad*. Her master's thesis, she told him, was to be an excavation of the representations of gender in Hallmark cards, but, she added, she hadn't properly theorized it yet. As he listened, Nelson underwent a crisis of conscience: Was Lilith another Wendy Walberg? Was he feigning interest only because he knew she'd go to bed with him? He was still wrestling with this quaint moral dilemma several hours later in her apartment, when Lilith announced that she wanted to investigate with him the interpenetration of power, sexuality, and the pleasures of the text. In practice this meant taking turns tying each other to her futon with an Ace bandage and declaiming "transgressive things" to each other like porn stars. By now Nelson's conscience was burning like a welder's arc, and when it was his turn to tie her down, he shriveled and

21

sat trembling at the edge of the mattress. Lilith turned imperiously maternal, holding his head in her lap (after he'd turned her loose) and telling him it was okay, not everyone could handle transgression.

Under Lilith's thrilling and not unrewarding discipline, Nelson lacerated himself with the bristling prose of Frenchmen whose musical names seemed to have too many vowels, or consonants in all the wrong places: Barthes, Foucault, Baudrillard. He received a passing grade in Professor Evangeline's literary theory class, turning in a paper that he himself didn't entirely understand, a lengthy exegesis on the scripture "Reality is linguistic." For a time Lilith even got him to doubt his patrimony, almost persuading him that his encyclopedic knowledge of English literature was a sort of child abuse, his father's phallogocentric attempt to colonize Nelson's consciousness with the hegemonic discourse. In bed she loved to have him speak a poem from memory and then interrupt him just before the final line. *Logos interruptus,* she called it, laughing at his look of strangled frustration when she wouldn't let him finish the last verse. Under such provocation Nelson often lunged for her, only to be brought up short by the springy grip of the Ace bandage.

"A man's reach should exceed his grasp," she'd cry, fetching him a stinging blow with her riding crop. *"Slave."*

But late at night as she snored beside him, Nelson—his thigh smarting, his feet hanging over the end of her hard futon—dreamed of Professor Gallagher slapping the soles of Nelson's feet with the Sears catalog and crying, "It's a gift!" Even in his sleep Nelson knew that all those words his father had taught him did not form some logocentric matrix in his consciousness. On the contrary, it was literary theory itself that seemed to cage Nelson within his own head, inside a grid as dry and brittle as glass. He could speak the language in class, he could string the jargon together in more or less the right order, but its attractions were as incomprehensible to him as a love of mime.

He broke down in Judith Engels's office just before spring break. In the midst of choosing his courses for the next year, he began to sob. For the first time she turned her distracted gaze from the bookcase full of rivals and looked at him. Nelson confessed to her with all the fervor of an apostate returning to the fold that sometimes he read poetry and novels and plays—literature, in other words—for *pleasure.* He trembled in his chair; tears poured down his cheeks. He could still hear in his head, he told her, every day of his life, his father's voice declaiming

"When in disgrace with fortune and men's eyes," and the words rolled in his heart like a river; they poured through his veins like blood. Judith handed him a Kleenex.

"Good for you, Nelson." She patted him on the knee. "Me too. Who's been telling you otherwise?"

He mentioned Lilith, who had been avoiding him lately, and he managed to mutter the name of Professor Evangeline. Judith gave an unusually lovely laugh and let him in on a little secret: His lit theory professor was really Bobby Evangeline from Bayou Vista, Louisiana, the prodigal son of a long line of Cajun shrimpers.

"So read what you want, Nelson." Judith shimmied in her seat, snapping her fingers over her head. *"Laissez les bontemps roulez!"*

Thus Nelson discovered that even his professors at Sooey had found Professor Evangeline a little—how you say?—*outré*. Indeed, not long after, Evangeline moved to a prestigious private university in the Piedmont; and Lilith, Nelson's own *belle guerrière,* dumped him and followed the *terroriste* to North Carolina, where in time she bore him triplets. Even long after he'd gotten over her, Nelson was vexed with the image of *Monsieur et Madame Professeur en famille,* pushing a triple stroller together under the neo-Gothic arches—*père et mère et les enfants, Roland et Jacques et Michel*—all five in shaved heads, roll-neck sweaters, and matching jackets of herringbone tweed.

Judith Engels took Nelson under her wing. There was nothing Chekhovian about her: She was the veteran of a bad divorce rather than a hopeless love affair and the single mother of a hyperactive five-year-old boy she called "the Change-ling." The nail-biting and the tears and the brisk, ten-minute meetings had come from the stress of providing for Ritalin on a junior professor's salary, as well as teaching and trying to write her book.

"I thought I was going to be Laura Ingalls Wilder," she said, unburdening herself, "raising my golden child on the prairie. Instead, I'm Grendel's mother."

After his brush with bondage, theoretical and otherwise, Judith's playful intelligence kept Nelson from swinging too far in the opposite direction, into a harumphing, defensive conservatism. She got him to read a good deal of feminist criticism, refusing to let him be afraid of it. She taught him to thicken his skin and sharpen his elbows and stick up for himself, so that he could find a way forward in the discipline that was engaged but not intellectually dishonest. In return, Nelson became a pinch baby-sitter for the Changeling, who hit him in the head with a Tonka truck on their first meeting. Nelson, eager not to take offense, smiled against the pain and said, "Good arm."

Naturally Nelson fell in love with Judith, and in an exemplary display of courtly self-sacrifice—for he was a verray, parfit, gentil knyght—vowed not to tell her. But at her New Year's Eve party halfway through his second year, she pulled Nelson onto the crowded dance floor in her huge Midwestern basement and taught him the Elvis Two-Step, culled from repeated viewings of *Viva Las Vegas!*: put your toes in, dangle your hands from your wrists, and chug in place from one foot to the other, lifting the corner of your lip in a sneer. At midnight they brushed shoulders at the rail of her vast redwood deck and looked up at stars as hard as diamonds. She swayed against him and shivered, and Nelson put his arm around her and stooped to kiss her. For a glorious moment she returned it, the warmest, most welcoming kiss Nelson had ever been party to, something indeed out of Chekhov. Then someone yanked open the sliding door behind them, and they sprang apart, steam rising off them in the cold.

After that Judith no longer found time for Nelson. He wrote her a long, passionate letter full of poetry; but thinking of Brenda Spack and Wendy Walberg all those years before, he never mailed it.

Twice brokenhearted, Nelson was at the nadir of his graduate career. His new advisor seemed like a pointed message from the department: Prof. Wilson Blunt was a bald, heavy-lidded old man, perfectly round, the sole survivor of Sooey's days as an ag college. He'd published one book on Longfellow forty years ago, devoting the rest of his career to instructing Indiana's future county agricultural agents in the use of the semicolon and the subordinate clause. Still, even in exile Nelson was conscientious: He tracked down a copy of Blunt's book and read it, blue Hi-Liter poised and ready. But all he highlighted was Blunt's definition of literature in the introduction: "A literary work is any work of imaginative writing—prose, poetry, or drama—that is inherently more *interesting*—rich, complex, mysterious—than anything that could be said *about* it." It was a struggle even to finish the rest of the book.

So Nelson descended with a sinking heart to Blunt's office in the dank, Gothic basement of Mead Hall, Sooey's original building, where Blunt was never seen to go in or come out. Indeed, he seemed to live in his dark cave of an office like some small, podgy animal from *The Wind in the Willows*, scarcely distinguishable from the moldering stacks of books and heaps of yellowing newspaper in the corners. Whenever Nelson visited, Blunt always seemed to be in his chair, pale and immobile, smoking unfiltered Camels and inhaling the dust from bookcases full of ancient, crumbling, orange-backed Penguins. Down here, below ground, as low as you could get at Sooey, Nelson stammered out his proposed dissertation topic, something both safe and obscure—*Guilt and Predestination in the Work of James Hogg, 1770–1835*—and Blunt signed off on it like a somnambulist. Afterward Nelson burst into the open air above ground gasping for breath, fearful that he'd contracted black lung.

Nelson was now one of the shell-shocked and self-effacing white males who made up the lowest ranks of Sooey's graduate English program. Like Nelson, they'd entered the academy because they loved books and the idea of a comfortable, contemplative life. But now they always looked slightly stunned, as if they'd just heard a very loud noise, and were cringingly uncertain when to expect the next one. The loud noise they kept hearing was the impact of very large volumes of cultural studies, queer theory, and postcolonial interventions thudding into the prairie all around them like artillery. Each concussion was an announcement that their race and gender were the root of all evil. That these young men, heirs to a mingled tradition of Calvinism and liberal guilt, already half-believed this themselves only made them more vulnerable; and it slowly dawned on them that the New Order of semioticians, postmodernists, and feminists hated mild-mannered liberal pluralists even more than it hated honest-to-god conservatives. These young men lived in terror of saying the wrong thing, and they were increasingly unable to tell the difference between what they actually believed and what they professed to in public.

Still, Nelson felt comfortable in their good-humored fellowship. They were good husbands and fathers, skilled barbecue chefs, and connoisseurs of Dutch and Canadian beer. They married women only slightly younger than themselves, but never their students—those days were over—and only occasionally other grad students. Instead they married sensible, decent, pretty young women who worked on campus as administrative assistants, librarians, or graphic designers, women who were lively and bright, but not likely to be a threat to a husband's ambition.

Nelson married one of these women himself, a tall, graceful Irish girl named Bridget O'Shea, a daughter of working-class Chicago. She had studied to be a dancer until she was told she was too tall for ballet and not voluptuous enough for show business, and she dropped out of Sooey's Performing Arts program to work in a florist's shop in Edgarville. She claimed to have a bit of "the touch," which she said ran through the women in her family like prematurely gray hair and arthritis. Nelson fell for her one windy October night when she told him she'd heard a banshee the evening her grandmother died, howling over her father's house on a wild, stormy night just like this one.

She also turned out to be surprisingly sharp-tongued in the manner of Irish women. The ideological faction fighting of the English Department only annoyed her, and she didn't understand why Nelson couldn't just work hard and make a success of graduate school. Nelson had begun to wonder that himself. His fellow white male graduate students had become increasingly defensive as their natural sympathy for progressive politics ran up against their thwarted sense of entitlement. They began to whisper among themselves with growing bitterness that the Really Good Jobs were no longer going to Guys Like Us. Some of them resigned themselves to careers at party universities or sprawling suburban community colleges or small church schools in the middle of nowhere, where they'd teach five classes a semester for the rest of their lives. A few of them began to surf the tide of postmodernism, happily so, since it allowed them to ditch their mediocre dissertations on Milton or Pound and do cutting-edge work on Doc Savage novels, the X-Men, or *Star Trek: The Next Generation*.

Nelson resolved to take a middle course. By now he and Bridget had a two-year-old daughter, Clara, but his responsibility for her only made Nelson bolder. Maybe the really good jobs were not going to Guys Like Us, but had they ever? Hadn't "Not fair!" always been the cry of the mediocre? Maybe Professor Gallagher back at Halcyon College had been right, that the academy was a meritocracy. And Judith Engels had taught him not to stand knee-deep in the ocean and command the tide not to come in. He woke up sweating and shaking one night from a dream of himself as Professor Blunt, too weak to rise from his chair, too swollen with inertia to leave his office, too sleepy to finish a sentence. In the morning he went to Blunt to announce that he wanted to change his thesis topic. "I want to do Conrad," he said.

Blunt blinked at him. Nelson swallowed.

"A, a, and colonialism," he added. "I want to do Conrad and colonialism."

At this Blunt began to tremble, his wattles shaking like gelatin, and he gripped the armrests of his chair. What if Blunt objected? The only argument Nelson could give was his nightmare, and he couldn't very well say to the old man, "I want to change my thesis topic so that I don't end up like you."

26

"I, I need to be, that is, I *want* to be, a little more, um, up to date," Nelson stammered, fearful that he was giving the old man a stroke. "I have to admit that some of the, ah, new theory, well, it interests me."

Blunt was pushing on the armrests. He was actually trying to rise. His face glowed red in the dim office.

"Professor Blunt?" Nelson said. "Are you okay?"

But Blunt heaved himself up with a mighty effort, swaying alarmingly on his feet.

"A man's reach . . ." He fumbled for Nelson's hand. His touch was warm and damp, but his grip was firm. "A man's reach . . ." Blunt repeated, tears in his eyes.

By his last year in graduate school, Nelson had come full circle, back to the optimist he'd once been, in love with words and books and stories. But he was no longer quite so naive—along the way he'd picked up a little playful irony and the ability to say "phallocentric" in mixed company without blushing. He did his dissertation on colonialism and Conrad, taking a measured position somewhat to the south of Alfred Kazin and a bit to the north of Edward Said. It was a solid, thoughtful performance, lucidly written, with just enough theory in it to give it some zest, like bits of jalapeño in a brick of Monterey Jack. The Kiplingesque idea he had was that he could be the bridge between the two worlds, the New Order and the Old, that he could walk comfortably among both princes and postmodernists, bringing them together with statesmanlike compassion: Nelson the Peacemaker.

Bridget sank all of her savings from the florist's shop into a tailored suit for Nelson to wear to the MLA convention in the week after Christmas. The annual conference of English professors was held in Chicago that year, and Nelson and Bridget stayed with her family. Nelson had six interviews, and for three days he strode confidently into one elegant suite after another high above Lake Shore Drive, where he sat with his legs crossed and answered every question in a calm, confident basso cantante, making sure to speak in complete sentences. He dropped bits of theory offhandedly to show that he could take it or leave it.

At the end of the week, Nelson, Bridget, Clara, and their new daughter, Abigail, celebrated New Year's Eve at Bridget's father's house on the South Side. At midnight Mr. O'Shea, in the presence of his own large family and of Nelson's widowed mother, lifted a glass of Bushmills and toasted his son-in-law, a few months prematurely, as Prof. Nelson Humboldt, Ph.D. A cheer filled the living room, and tears came to Nelson's eyes. He wished his father could have been there to hear it.

But a month passed, and Nelson heard nothing. Another month passed, and five of the schools sent him form letters thanking him for his interest and wishing him the best of luck. The Guys Like Us began to peel off to lesser schools in Wyoming, Las Vegas, Long Island. The young men behind Nelson in the program began to hold him up behind his back as an example of misplaced confidence in one's marketability. He was only asked to interview at the better schools as the Token White Guy, they whispered, to round out the assortment of candidates presented to the Affirmative Action Office. Even Bridget began to ask him, as March rolled into April and April into May, if he knew what he was doing. She urged him to call the one remaining prospect, the University of the Midwest in Hamilton Groves, Minnesota, to apply a little pressure or just to see if their letter had got lost in the mail.

"That's not how it's done," Nelson would say, as baby Abigail drooled on his shoulder.

"Maybe it *is* how it's done," Bridget said, her Irish rising. She had a working-class girl's practical intelligence for knowing when to cut your losses. "Maybe that's why you don't have a job."

"With a school like Midwest," he said, "you don't want to look desperate."

"Nelson, you are desperate." She lifted Abigail away from him.

But Nelson didn't call. As long as he hadn't heard, he could still hope. Nelson had astonished the other Guys Like Us by getting an interview at Midwest at all; the other schools had at least been within his reach. The town of Hamilton Groves was usually mentioned in the same breath as Madison or Berkeley, a legendary place where the founders of the antiwar movement wrote the famous Hamilton Groves Statement at a picnic table in someone's leafy backyard. On a good day you could draw a deep breath and still smell tear gas or the burning ROTC Building. For his postmodern colleagues, Midwest was the metropole where they might walk the streets like Walter Benjamin, noting everything and writing dense little essays as they sat in coffee bars along Michigan Avenue; for the Guys Like Us, it was as unattainable as Oxford or the Sorbonne. But Nelson was as hopeful as Jude the Obscure watching the glow of Christminster from the roof of a barn. His entree to the English Department there was none other than Professor Blunt, who had exerted himself on Nelson's behalf like the aging

28

Beowulf girding up for one last battle, sending a letter to Morton Weissmann, a senior professor at Midwest and a friend of Blunt's student days.

By the middle of May, Nelson was much in demand for the loading of rental trucks, young academia's answer to barn raising. For ten days straight Nelson wore nothing but shorts and a T-shirt and lived off free beer and pizza, coming home aching and sweaty every night to endure the same tense exchange with Bridget.

"Midwest call?" he'd ask.

"Nope," she'd reply, without looking at him.

Finally, late one Friday evening, as the last yellow truck trundled away across the prairie like a Conestoga bound for Oregon, Nelson and Bridget stood at the gateway of married housing and waved good-bye. Clara clutched her father's leg, and baby Abigail fidgeted in her mother's arms. A radiant Indiana sunset gilded Nelson and his family; the wind lifted Bridget's hair. They looked like noble farmers in a Soviet poster, gazing hopefully into the future of socialism. Bridget handed baby Abigail over to Nelson and told him he'd had two phone calls that day. One was from her father; he'd lined up a job for Nelson on the loading dock at the warehouse in Chicago where he worked—just to tide them over, she added, until Nelson could get a job teaching composition someplace.

"And the other call?"

"A Professor Weissmann," she said, "from Midwest."

"What did he want?" The breeze carried the smell of manure and budding corn.

"For you to call him back."

Nelson kissed his daughter, who gurgled and pulled his hair. Despite what his postmodern colleagues might say, there was such a thing as fate. Epiphanies did happen in real life, and this was one of them. The wind carried the smell of rebirth and fecundity, the golden light fell across his wife and children and turned them into shining, beautiful creatures.

"I'm going to call your father and tell him thanks, but no thanks"—Nelson started back toward their town house, Abigail in his arms, Clara clinging to his belt—"then I'm going to call Professor Weissmann."

"Call Weissmann first." Bridget moved alongside Nelson and took Clara by the hand. "He's probably just calling to say they don't want you."

"They'd have sent a letter for that." Nelson smiled. "I think they want me to come up for an interview."

Bridget touched his arm, and Nelson turned. The fading sunlight shone through her windblown hair. "Nelson, are you good enough for them?" She pushed her hair away from her golden cheek.

Nelson nearly cried at the sight of his tall, beautiful wife. He hefted Abigail in his arms.

"Ah," he said, and swallowed, unable to speak for a moment. He drew a breath and spoke again, in his father's voice.

"Ah," he whispered, "but a man's reach should exceed his grasp. Or what's a heaven for?"

3

The Curse of Fu Manchu

On the morning after his accident, Nelson awoke to the banging of wood against wood. His bed lurched under him, and he bounced against the sagging mattress. In spite of what the doctor had told him, his reattached finger burned slowly as if it were being held over a low flame. Numb with codeine, Nelson opened his gummy eyes. The room shook violently beyond his bare feet; above him his older daughter, Clara, was jumping up and down on the bed. She still wore her Halloween costume from the night before, the skintight uniform of some TV sci-fi dominatrix whose name Nelson could not remember. When she saw his eyes were open, she dropped on her knees next to him.

"All biological entities will be absorbed," Clara growled, in character. "Resistance is futile."

The mattress trembled to a stop, but the slow banging continued a few inches from Nelson's ear. Nelson turned to see his younger daughter, Abigail, grimly hammering Sweetarts into dust against the nightstand, one at a time, with a wooden alphabet block. She too was still in costume, a homemade angel in a sheet and some old lace paper. Her wings hung in shreds from a pair of twisted coat hangers. Her bag of Halloween candy stood next to the bed.

"Not now, girls." Bridget swooped in and snatched Clara off the bed. "Daddy's not feeling well."

"Surrender, human!" Clara wriggled in her mother's arms. "Die, you useless bag of water!"

By the time Bridget came back for her, Abby was mashing candy corn into the nightstand. As she was lifted up, she sprinkled the dust of atomized Sweetarts in her father's eyes. "Fairy dust, Daddy!" screamed his little angel. "Make you *magic!*"

For the rest of the weekend, Nelson alternated between stuporous sleep and the grim effort of grading papers. At meal times he tried to be cheerful, urging Abby to eat another mouthful of fish stick, biting back the pain when Clara grabbed his injured hand. He and Bridget scarcely spoke, and he was unable to look his wife in the eye. After dinner he sat at the kitchen table with his bottle of pain-killers and a cutting board, slicing the pills in half to make them last longer.

After Bridget and the girls had gone to bed, Nelson descended to the cinder-block basement of his town house to go to work. His office consisted of a battered old Steelcase desk, a wobbly office chair rescued from someone's curbside trash, a secondhand, two-drawer filing cabinet, and a bookcase made of stacked plastic milk crates, all wedged into a space beside the hot water heater and across from the furnace. On his desktop Bridget had left his ungraded student papers neatly sorted by class. There was also a large, unopened manila envelope, addressed to Nelson in his own hand, which told him that it was yet another rejected journal article. With a sigh he set aside the envelope and started in on the papers—a thousand words on the topic "Is Lady Macbeth an Enabler?"—working slowly through them as he set his wheezing old PC and his ancient dot matrix printer to grinding out letters of application. It was the same plaintive letter each time, requiring him only to turn away from his grading every few minutes to type a new address from the job listings in *The Chronicle of Higher Education*. It was agony trying to write comments to his students and type with his left hand. Between grading, typing, and ignoring the rejected article, Nelson sat sweating in the clammy basement in the buzzing glare of his desk lamp.

A letter poked up out of the printer, and Nelson lurched forward in his creak-ing chair to tear it off. It was addressed to a search committee at Fricke State College in Fricke, North Dakota. They were offering an adjunct position at fifteen thousand dollars a year to teach four sections a semester of something called "creative nonfiction" at the Fricke Center for Sports Writing. Nelson signed the letter as best he could and addressed the envelope, and as his tongue slid along the gummed seal, he lifted his eyes into the shadows above. The nails poking through the underside of his living room floor all seemed to point at him. The cobwebs dangling from the joists promised to drop spiders in his hair, silverfish down his collar. In the glow of his computer screen he saw his old *National*

Geographic map of literary England on the wall over his desk. He'd taped it to the cinder block to cover a supposedly dormant water stain, but now the stain had darkened much of the map, spreading outward from Stratford-upon-Avon as far north as Wordsworth's Grasmere, as far south as Hardy's Wessex.

He sealed the envelope with the heel of his hand and set it aside with all the others. His fingers lingered above the large manila envelope, and he picked it up. After a moment of struggle with his bandaged hand, he tore the envelope open with his teeth, peered inside, then dumped the contents onto his desk: his latest article accompanied by a form rejection slip from *Clitor/is,* a journal of feminist theory. Nelson's dissertation on Conrad had never received any interest from publishers—the verdict was in, and Conrad turned out to be only a smidgen less vile than Kipling—so Nelson had sought his scholarly niche by returning to his orginal dissertation topic, the Ettrick Shepherd, the Scottish author James Hogg. He had tried to put Hogg to a more up-to-date use, holding the obscure author's major work, *The Private Memoirs and Confessions of a Justified Sinner,* up to various theoretical templates to see if any of them matched the book. The problem was that all of them did, which meant in the end that none of them did. Nelson's delight in finding that the *Confessions* was perfectly suited for a psychoanalytic reading was quickly diminished by his discovery that the text was also perfectly suited to a historicist reading, a postcolonial reading, a queer reading, ad infinitum.

So, doggedly, because he needed to publish and he didn't have any better ideas, Nelson ground out Hogg article after Hogg article, ending up with a book-length manuscript of unpublished and mutually exclusive chapters, each of which proved with equal conviction that James Hogg was a virgin and a libertine; a misogynist and an early feminist; hegemonic and transgressive; imperialist and postcolonial; patriarchal and matriarchal; straight, bisexual, and queer. Hogg's text was scorched earth by now, a plain trammeled by the passage of one army after another. Hogg's prose, in Nelson's split-backed Penguin, no longer made any sense; the words passed before Nelson's eyes as incomprehensibly as cuneiform.

This latest rejected article was "The Transgendered Calvinist: James Hogg in Butlerian Perspective," and in the icy glare of his desk lamp Nelson flipped through it just long enough to note that the two pages he'd covertly taped together near the middle of the article had not been pulled apart. The rejection slip explained the journal's editorial policy, which was that it would accept women writing about women, women writing about men, transgendered persons writing about whatever they wanted to write about, or, very occasionally, men writing about women—but never men writing about men. The note was signed, "In sisterhood, the Clit Collective."

The furnace behind him whooshed to life, and the reflection of a blue line of flame quivered in his computer screen. Hot air rose two floors to the vent in his daughters' bedroom, where the two sisters sprawled half out from under their Teletubby comforters. He filed the article and the rejection slip in his filing cabinet, already crammed with rejected Hogg articles, and let the drawer rattle shut on its casters. Another letter heaved out of the printer, this one asking for Nelson to be considered for a position teaching technical writing at Lamar Community College in Lamar, Texas. No tenure, no benefits, twelve hundred dollars a class. Nelson tore the letter out of the printer with his left hand, awkwardly signed it, and slipped it into an envelope with his CV. Professor Victorinix had fired him on the last day of October, the deadline for most of the better postings. The only jobs left were adjunct positions in places like Alabama and Idaho, at institutions he had never heard of, tiny church schools and technical institutes and vast community colleges like industrial parks. Never mind that James Hogg could be all things to all races, genders, and sexual preferences, never mind his and Nelson's rejection by the Clit Collective—if Nelson failed to get one of these grunt-level jobs, he was only a step away from writing Cliffs Notes or hacking out "research papers" for a term paper service or tutoring frat boys at six bucks an hour. As the children who depended on him slept in their beds above, Nelson fought off nightmares of himself flipping burgers, cleaning toilets, pumping gas.

The furnace clicked off. The tremulous line of flame in his monitor winked out. On the map above his desk the stain inched inexorably toward the inset of literary London, creeping to blot out Bishopsgate, Camden Town, and Blooms-bury.

On Monday morning, still groggy from the pills, his finger aching, Nelson stepped into the predawn gloom of married housing, his briefcase full of graded papers and job applications. He wore a bulky polyester parka, bright orange, that hissed when he walked. In the darkness he stepped carefully through a knee-high litter of abandoned tricycles and toy wagons. He took his place on the university bus among the stressed and weary faces of foreign graduate students—the Indian engineer, the Israeli biochemist, the Taiwanese radiologist—and rode standing up, encased with the others in an icy block of fluorescent light trundling through the gray, November dawn, around the end of the lake, and onto campus.

Nelson got off at the end of Michigan Avenue, clutching his briefcase awkwardly under his left arm. The streetlights were flickering off, and Nelson walked alone past the blank windows of shops that wouldn't open for another two hours: the scholarly bookstore with university press volumes tilted up on wire stands, the convenience mart selling condoms and candy and discount CDs, the darkened deli with its chairs stacked up on tables. Pandemonium, the fashionable café where students sat reading Proust or Foucault all afternoon at small round tables, didn't open until nine. Only a party store was open this early, dispensing coffee in paper cups to early risers.

Nelson knew he couldn't manage a cup with only one hand, so he joined the thin stream of people converging on the campus, the departmental secretaries in pantsuits and running shoes, the maintenance men in jeans and feed caps, the only people abroad at this hour. He kept an eye out for his nemesis, a grizzled, thick-waisted homeless guy with lank red hair who patrolled the sidewalks and doorways of Michigan Avenue. Nelson called him Fu Manchu, because the tips of the man's untrimmed, ginger moustache hung as low as his stubbled chin. Like a junkyard dog, the man could sense Nelson's fear, and there had been a few tense exchanges. Sometimes Nelson wondered whether his orange parka made him a target, but he couldn't afford another coat. Today Nelson thought he was in the clear; but as he came around the corner of the textbook store across from campus, Fu Manchu stepped out from behind a kiosk that was papered with flyers, and he planted himself in Nelson's path, thrusting out his belly and crossing his thick forearms over his chest. This morning he had tied an American flag bandanna over his head. He looked like a WWF wrestler gone to seed.

"Care to help the homeless, *sir?*" Fu Manchu leveled his angry gaze at Nelson. Nelson mumbled and stepped around him, and the angry homeless man turned massively on his axis. "Hey, dickhead!" Fu Manchu called out. "You ain't no better than anyone else!"

At least on this point, Nelson thought, Fu Manchu and Victoria Victorinix are in perfect agreement. His reattached finger began to throb, and Nelson winced and walked faster. The doctor had said he would never feel anything in that finger again, but Nelson was certain of a burning sensation. He tried to shake it off. The clock tower on Thornfield Library rose above the bare limbs of the trees around the Quad, and Nelson tried to remember the story behind the library's alleged ghost. Just who had flung him or herself off the clock tower depended on whom you talked to: Undergraduates said it was a brokenhearted young woman, grad students said it was someone who had failed his prelims, junior professors said it was a lecturer who had failed to get tenure. Nelson himself thought he might have glimpsed, once or twice, a figure behind the mock battlements above the clock face, silhouetted against the sky at dusk. But this morning the tower was empty, and the clock's hands were quivering a fraction away from eight o'clock. Nelson picked up his pace.

Harbour Hall was a tall, narrow slab of a building, and on every floor except the eighth a narrow hall of glazed gray brick and worn linoleum ran the length of the building, with boxlike offices on either side. Even on the brightest days the dimly lit hallway had the sickly look of a high school boiler room. On the third floor, just out of the elevator, Nelson balanced his briefcase on his knee and fed his letters of application one-handed into the mail slot; he heard them slither all the way down the chute. Outside his office door, Nelson wedged his briefcase under his right arm and flipped through his keys. Inside he flicked on the light and perched on the edge of his office chair in the buzzing fluorescent glare, and he pulled his students' papers out of the briefcase with his left hand.

As he passed through the press of students on his way to the classroom building adjoining Harbour Hall, he held his injured hand against his chest and worked out what he would say to his first class about his accident. He'd smile as he walked in and wait a beat for them to notice his bandage. Then he'd wink and say, "Cut myself shaving." But Nelson arrived to find fourteen out of thirty students missing and the remaining sixteen slumped in their desk chairs, gaunt and red-eyed from a weekend of Halloween parties. All four students scheduled to make oral presentations this morning on the topic "My Most Important Personal Epiphany" were absent, so for a few painfully silent minutes Nelson rooted one-handed in the course's modish composition text, looking for an exercise that wasn't too uninteresting. Composition was no longer what it had been when Nelson was an undergraduate; now it was one part writing to two parts twelve-step program. Students were encouraged to mine each literary text in the book for a lesson in their own personal growth, no matter how foreign that text might be to the experiences of a generation of privileged young Minnesotans. They were also encouraged to express their feelings on any topic without fear of contradiction, and Nelson was under orders not to use a red pencil on their papers lest he intimidate them. At last he asked them to read from the textbook Randall Jarrell's poem "Death of the Ball Turret Gunner" and complete the accompanying exercise: "How would *you* feel if *you* had been the ball turret gunner?" He divided them into groups of four to discuss this unlikely scenario, while he gritted his teeth against the pain in his finger.

After class, he paused at the pop machine in the lobby between buildings and considered the expense of a Coke. He gave up at the difficulty of getting change out of his right pocket with his left hand. In his office, he leaned back in his creaking gray office chair, lifted his long legs to his desk, and watched the slow-motion riot of class change on the Quad below. This sight no longer gave him the same pleasure it had last week, so he dropped the blinds. His reattached finger burned; he had half a painkiller in his breast pocket, but it was a long time until he was supposed to take it, and anyway, he had nothing with which to wash it down. He picked up the heavy blue coffee cup Bridget had thrown for him in a pottery class. It was dusty with disuse, and he hefted it in his good palm, wondering how much humiliation he was willing to endure to fill it.

Nelson stood. If he wanted coffee, he'd have to go up to the faculty lounge, where a different imported coffee was dispensed every day from a large, silver urn, as gleaming and immanent as the Holy Grail. He left his office door unlocked so that he wouldn't have to fumble with the key again, and went down the dim hall to the elevator. Nelson had hoped that the car would be empty, and when the doors opened to reveal someone, Nelson almost did not get on. But it was only Stephen Michael Stephens, who was asleep. Nelson stepped into the car and punched his button, and the doors rattled shut. Professor Stephens's eyelids trembled at the sound, but he did not awake.

As the elevator rose, the slow burn in Nelson's finger sharpened into something more painful, and he began to sweat. He looked sidelong at his more successful colleague.

Stephen Michael Stephens slept standing up, his shoulders lightly brushing the rear wall of the car, his chest rising and falling slowly, his hands clasped before him. As always he was impeccably dressed, in a colorful sweater and beautiful wool trousers and a handsome camel-hair overcoat. But, as always, there were bags under his eyes and a sickly gray under the rich brown of his skin. As the department's only senior African American, he made more money than anyone except Chairperson Pescecane. Tenured already on the basis of his prize-winning, semiautobiographical first book, he was not expected ever to write another. Instead, he was expected to chair the university's annual review of its affirmative action policy, to direct every search for African-American candidates, to mentor junior African-American faculty, to be a role model and counselor for African-American graduate and undergraduate students, to teach classes in African-American literature every semester, and generally to explain the ways of black folk to his white colleagues with passion, wit, and intelligence, but without being threatening or inducing guilt. He was expected, in other words, to work like a field hand and be a Credit to His Race, leaving him no time to sleep or have a personal life. He did no work of his own, unless you counted the occasional interviews with black celebrities in *Vanity Fair* and television appearances whenever *Nightline* covered race in America. Consequently he fell into a deep sleep whenever he had the opportunity. As Nelson watched, Professor Stephens sighed in his slumber and mumbled something under his breath.

The elevator stopped at the eighth floor, the doors whooshed open, but Stephen Michael Stephens did not stir. Nelson waited, but when the doors began to shut, he held them back and lightly shook his colleague by his camel-hair shoulder. Professor Stephens started awake.

"Yes, *effendi*," he murmured.

Lately Stephen Michael Stephens had shifted his professional interest to film, in particular the wide-screen colonialist epics of the late fifties and early sixties. Every semester in his large, popular class, Professor Stephens screened films like *Khartoum, The Sand Pebbles,* and *55 Days at Peking* at an old movie palace in downtown Hamilton Groves. Apart from the opportunity these films afforded him to introduce his students to issues of race, imperialism, and postcolonial theory, they were also very long; and sitting in the dark in the plush balcony, Professor Stephens was often able to get two, sometimes three solid hours of sleep. The rumor was that he had never actually seen any of these films all the way to the end, but he seemed to have soaked them up by osmosis, particularly *Lawrence of Arabia.* If you shook him awake, as Nelson had just done, you were liable to be addressed in the whispery, lurching rhythms of Peter O'Toole.

"Um, don't you get off here?" Nelson asked.

Gazing wide-eyed into the distance as if watching for a Turkish train, Professor Stephens sailed out of the elevator with his palms pressed together and his coat billowing behind him like a Bedouin robe. He stopped and turned. "Does it hurt?" whispered Stephen Michael Stephens, nodding toward Nelson's bandaged finger.

"Y-yes," stammered Nelson.

"The trick, William Potter," said Stephens, walking away, "is not *minding* that it hurts."

His finger throbbing, Nelson hurried after Stephens. Luckily, the faculty lounge was close to the elevator, so Nelson didn't have to brave the whole gauntlet of the eighth-floor hallway. He came obliquely into the room in Stephen Michael Stephens's slipstream, and while Stephens crossed straight to the tall, gilded urns of coffee and tea at the end of the room, Nelson glided along the dark wainscoting, hoping no one would notice him. By recent redesign and careful expenditure, the lounge was the very model of a university commons room, with antique library tables and green-shaded lamps and clubby leather easy chairs. Now that it no longer looked like the waiting room of a Medicaid clinic, in fact, it had become so popular that graduate students had been banned; Nelson was not even sure if nontenure-track faculty were welcome any longer. This exclusivity was enforced by all senior members of the department, regardless of ideology; when it comes to academic perquisites, even Marxists and postmodernists are snobs.

Nelson ducked behind a floor lamp when he saw there were other people in the room. On two sofas facing each other across a coffee table were two couples. On the right sat the two senior members of the department's graduate creative writing staff. One was Timothy Coogan, a burly man who perched on the edge of the sofa in a rumpled but expensive wool overcoat, his large shoes planted wide, his face buried in his hands. He was a fifty-year-old American poet who lived the persona of the wild Celtic writer, adopting an Irish accent and referring to himself in the third person as "the Coogan." With his thick head of handsomely tangled iron-gray hair, his twinkling eyes, and red cheekbones, the Coogan looked like a hard-living leprechaun. He had a reputation for sleeping with his female students, and the senior women of the English Department would have preferred to see him gone. But because he still published well, and because the creative writing faculty were not expected to be as evolved as real scholars, he had managed so far to escape sexual harassment proceedings. Today, at nine-fifteen in the morning, and all the way across the room, Nelson could smell Bushmills and sweat. The Coogan massaged his temples with his thick fingers.

"Jaysus, Mary, and Joseph," he groaned. "What day is it?"

"Monday morning, dear," said his companion, a broad-shouldered, white-haired woman whose name Nelson could never remember; he knew her only as the Canadian Lady Novelist. She was reputed to be like Margaret Atwood, only nicer, the department's only likely candidate for a major literary prize. Tall and imperiously maternal, she radiated noblesse oblige and stern compassion, passing through Harbour Hall acknowledging her students and her colleagues with a nod, like Pallas Athena making a personal appearance.

"When was the last time you were home, Timothy?" said the Canadian Lady Novelist.

The Coogan lifted his bloodshot eyes from behind his hands and blew out a sigh Nelson could smell a moment later behind the lamp. The poet started ticking off days on his fingers. "I don't know," he said, looking frightened. "What day were you after sayin' it was?"

Across from them, on the sofa on the left, Marko Kraljević, the department's premier theorist, and his lover, Lorraine Alsace, sat practically in each other's laps, like a pair of ninth graders in love. Kraljević was a short, dark, thick-set Serb, lycanthropically hirsute, with a single black eyebrow and ineradicable five o'clock shadow that climbed nearly to his deep eye sockets. He referred to himself as an intellectual samurai, the Toshiro Mifune of cultural studies, claiming nothing and everything as his speciality. He was a former professor at the University of Belgrade, and a refugee from Slobodan Milosevic, who, for some reason, he called his "evil twin." He had built his reputation on a series of impenetrably recondite essays, on topics ranging from the irreconcilable separation of consciousness from being, to the smell of his fingertips after paring his nails. These, and his vivid if enigmatic presence, made him a star of the international conference circuit, which in turn had led to a tenured position at Midwest. Here he played a game of hide-and-seek with his graduate students (he taught no undergraduates), lecturing on whatever topic took his fancy at the moment. He refused to publish a syllabus, and he refused to use the classroom assigned to him, usually appropriating a classroom already in use because he liked the play of light through the windows. No one ever refused him. When they could find him, his adoring grad students hung on Kraljević's every word. He never showed up for office hours.

He dressed on the same principle of collage under which he wrote, varying his look as the mood took him. Today he was indulging his spiv persona, his feet set wide in a pair of thick-heeled shoes from the disco era, his thighs and genitalia bulging against a pair of tight trousers, his chest hair bursting out of the open collar of a wide-lapeled Hawaiian shirt printed with red and green parrots. He wore, unzipped, a brand-new leather jacket from the Zagreb Hard Rock Café, and he was noisily eating a Sausage McMuffin.

Meanwhile, nibbling at a brioche, Lorraine Alsace clung girlishly to Kraljević's arm with her legs folded sideways under her long skirt. She was a rawboned, straw-haired woman, northern European, with a long jaw, thick-lensed glasses, and reddened knuckles. Her voice was capable of wobbling several octaves in a single sentence; that and a slight speech impediment made her sound like a cross between Elmer Fudd and Aunt Bee from *The Andy Griffith Show.* Nelson had heard her speak at a seminar about the "twansgwessive welease of cwitical theowy," by which she sought the "sacwed viowence" that threatened to burst out of all literature. Her *chef d'oeuvre* was *Das Ding an Sich: A Cultural History of Cultural Histories,* while her current project was, she said, a sort of "bwicolage of Dewwida, Baudwillawd, and Kwisteva."

As yet, however, Lorraine Alsace was not even on the tenure track, but only a visiting lecturer. Kraljević made no secret of his desire to make her a tenured professor. In fact, there was a nasty rumor going around that the two theorists' love affair was the result of a deal: Lorraine was already a United States citizen, and she would marry Kraljević, thus securing him a green card, if he would get her tenure at Midwest. But Nelson did not want to believe this; he preferred to think that their regard for each other was real. Certainly Lorraine Alsace made no secret of her devotion to Kraljević. "My Marko," she had been known to gush, "can talk theowy for eight hours *without a bweak!*"

Nelson slouched behind his lamp, his finger throbbing a little more rhythmically. Stephen Michael Stephens stood with the back of his beautiful overcoat to the room; he was pouring cream and sugar into his cup of coffee. The Coogan had dropped his face into his hands again, while the Canadian Lady Novelist rubbed his shoulders. Professor Alsace pressed herself closer to Professor Kraljević, who pushed the last of his McMuffin between his teeth with the tip of his blunt middle finger.

Nelson drew a breath and stepped out from behind the lamp, lifting his chin to walk boldly between the sofas to the coffee. Stephen Michael Stephens turned, yawning, holding his cup carefully away from his coat. At the same moment the Coogan groaned and hoisted himself to his feet, and Kraljević pushed himself up onto his thick heels. Stephens stepped deftly out of their way, and the poet and the critic simultaneously reached for the last empty cup next to the coffee urn.

Nelson froze. The two women looked up from their respective sofas. The coffee cup swung into the air, suspended by the tension between the Coogan's finger through its handle and Kraljević's finger hooked over its rim. The Coogan's face turned red, his chest swelled. Kraljević bared his teeth in a sneer. Their standoff wasn't just a matter of poet versus critic, literature versus theory—this was the nose-to-nose, eyeball-to-eyeball standoff of Serb and Irishman, the two premier hard-drinking, grudge-carrying, folk-song-mongering, faction-fighting peoples of the earth. Each man tightened his finger on the cup.

"Ye wouldn't be after denyin' a man his mornin' cup of coffee, now would ye?" growled the Coogan.

"There is no 'coffee' here," snarled Kraljević. "There is the urn. It encloses a cylinder of what? We do not know."

The cup trembled between their taut fingers.

"Now, boys," said the Canadian Lady Novelist. Lorraine Alsace beamed at Kraljević in gleeful anticipation, hugging herself tightly on the sofa. Nelson edged backward on tiptoe. Stephens had disappeared.

"*You . . .*" said the Coogan, through gritted teeth.

"*You . . .*" growled Kraljević.

With a little *chink,* the handle snapped off the cup and swung from the Coogan's finger, while the rest of the cup bounced off the carpet and rolled under the table.

All the air seemed to go out of the two men. The Canadian Lady Novelist rose grandly to her feet and turned the Coogan by his shoulders away from Kraljević.

"What you need, Timothy," she said, "is a nice cup of tea."

"I don't want any bloody tay," blustered the Coogan, but he let himself be led around the back of the sofa and out of the room. The two theorists followed a moment later, Alsace stroking Kraljević and kissing the top of his head as she towered over him. As soon as they were gone, Nelson dashed to the table and thrust Bridget's cup under the coffee spigot. But when he pulled the tap, nothing came out. Stephens had drained the urn of the last cup of coffee.

Nelson fled back to the third floor, where he just had time to collect his papers for his ten o'clock class. The pain in his knuckle was really distracting now, but he soldiered on, promising himself a nice cold Coke afterward. As always, the imposing young woman who used the classroom before him was going overtime, making Nelson and his students wait in the hall. Gillian had dispensed with her patriarchal surname, in the spirit of such foremothers as Roseanne, Cher, and Madonna. One of Victoria Victorinix's graduate students, she was applying her mentor's theory of clitoral hegemony to her dissertation about *Buffy the Vampire Slayer*. And indeed, she commanded respect with her weight-lifter's musculature and her military buzz cut, dyed an unnatural shade of blonde. She had a small gold ring through the corner of her lower lip and a pair of mismatched earrings, one the astrological symbol for woman, the other an inverted crucifix. She wore a tank-top T-shirt, a denim miniskirt, torn fishnet stockings, and black, steel-toed Doc Martens. She looked like Irma la Douce played by Arnold Schwarzenegger.

Today Gillian was keeping back a couple of slouching, sleepy-eyed boys, one white and one black. She was explaining the concept of difference to them, with the help of a Venn diagram on the blackboard, a small white circle labeled PATRIARCHY and a much larger circle around it labeled THE OTHER. She was scoring thick chalk arrows across the diagram as she explained.

"You," she said, pointing the chalk at the white kid, "are entirely situated within this discourse." She rapped the chalk against the smaller circle. "While you," she said to the black kid, scoring a line between the circles, "are situated uneasily in both discourses because of the nexus of your race and your phallicity."

The two boys shot glances at each other and pursed their lips. Nelson stepped into the room, looking significantly at his watch. Gillian glared at him; Nelson raised his eyebrows at her. They had perfected this exchange over the course of the semester, as ritualized as a mating dance, by which they negotiated the transfer of the room at ten o'clock every Monday, Wednesday, and Friday.

By looking at his watch, Nelson was saying, "It's time for my class."

Gillian's glare said, "I'm not done yet. You're not entitled to this room just because you're a white male."

"I appreciate your devotion to your students," said Nelson's raised eyebrows, "no matter how far afield it may lead you from what I would consider the appropriate subject matter of an introductory literature class. But be that as it may, I need the classroom now."

At last Gillian drew an even larger circle around the two original circles, using up most of the board, and wrote SAVE in huge block letters. Then she snatched up her papers and shouldered Nelson aside, glaring back at him all the way down the hall. Nelson stood back to let his own students in. Gillian's two students shuffled away in the other direction.

"What's 'phallicity,' anyway?" the black kid said.

"She's talking about dick," said the white kid.

"Fuck," said the black kid, in a long diminuendo.

"She's hot for you, homes," said the white kid, flaring his fingers like a gangsta.

"How many times do I have to tell you?" said the black kid as they vanished around the corner. "Don't call me 'homes.' "

Nelson went in. Attendance was a little better at this hour, and two of the students with personal epiphanies had actually shown up. The first presentation, by a frighteningly earnest young woman named Melanie, was titled "Holocaust on the Highway: The Tragedy of Roadkill." Tears squeezed from the corners of Melanie's eyes as she read of an early epiphanic encounter with a flattened racoon. Nelson, sitting behind her, glared at the rest of the class to keep them from snickering. He cut the discussion short, allowing Melanie to leave early and compose herself, and proceeded with the other presenter, a sorority girl who declared that her most important personal epiphany had been the day she found out her high school boyfriend was also sleeping with her mom. Nelson wasn't quite sure this counted as an epiphany, but it certainly brought the class out of its hungover lethargy. It was all Nelson could do to keep the discussion from turning into *Jerry Springer*. The pain in his knuckle burned now, making him sweat, and he caught students smirking behind their hands at what they thought was his embarrassment at the topic under discussion.

Afterward he was wild for a Coke, not just to help swallow the pill, but for the stinging cold of it. At the pop machine in the crowded lobby he clutched his papers with his good hand and tried to wedge his bandage into his pocket, hoping to pluck out three quarters with the unwrapped tips of his third and fourth fingers. But the bandage wouldn't fit into his khakis, so he shifted his papers under his right arm and tried to twist his left hand into his right pocket.

"Do you need some help, Professor?"

Nelson looked up to see the girl whose mother had stolen her boyfriend. She was watching him with a helpful expression.

"Would you like me to get some change out of your pocket?" She stepped forward, and Nelson wrenched his hand free of his pocket, nearly dropping his papers. He started back, blushing, and blundered into the students behind him.

"That's okay! I have to, uh, I really ought to . . ." He gestured vaguely over his shoulder, letting himself be swept away by the stream of students.

"I cut myself shaving!" he added desperately, as he was carried out of sight.

In his office he dropped the papers on his desk, closed the door, and shut the blinds. He was trembling now, craving Coca-Cola with all the palsied fervor of an addict. He kicked off his shoes without untying them, undid his belt and zipper, and dropped his pants. Then he stepped out of them, lifted the limp trousers from the floor, and rooted in the pockets for a handful of change. Just then, of course, he heard the click of a key in the lock, and he dropped the change all over the floor. He turned to meet the astonished gaze of his office mate, Vita, who stared openmouthed at Nelson as he stood in the middle of their office in his socks, briefs, and shirttails. Coins rang against the linoleum. He snatched up his trousers and pressed them against his chest.

"Vita!" he cried. "Don't come in!"

She jumped back and slammed the door. Nelson could see her silhouette hovering tensely beyond the pebbled glass. He arranged his pants on the floor and stepped into them, hauling them up one-handed.

"It's okay!" he said at last, shoving his shirttails inside his belt as best he could. "I'm decent!"

Vita opened the door a crack and peered in, warily taking in Nelson's state of dress, the drawn shades, the quarters, dimes, and pennies all over the linoleum. Nelson stammered something that included cold pop, loose change, and pain-killers, but at last he collapsed into his chair and held up his bandaged arm.

"Vita," he said, nearly in tears, "I only have one hand!"

Vita came in and shut the door. She was a short, shy, roundish woman whose fashion sense was based on the principle of self-effacement. She wore loose trousers and bulky sweaters and flat-heeled, round-toed shoes, all of them shades of brown or gray. Her brown bangs and tortoiseshell glasses fit her like a mask; she looked like Joan of Arc traveling incognito. From time to time Nelson had come upon her in their office clutching the top of her head with both hands, as if twisting her hair into place.

"What did you do?" She hovered near the door, clutching her satchel to her coat.

Vita Deonne was, by default, the only friend Nelson had left in the department. As his office mate she was obligated to hold some conversation with him, but she went beyond that, relying on him as her sole confidante and regularly

45

accepting the hospitality of his home and family. Indeed, he seemed to be her only friend in the department as well.

Vita puzzled Nelson because she was simultaneously the most gender-conscious and the least sexual person Nelson had ever met. On the one hand, her scholarly obsession with the body, gender, and sexuality was nothing short of astounding. Her work was full of more than Nelson ever wanted to know about breast enlargement, breast reduction, penis enhancement, face lifts, nose jobs, hair plugs, leg waxing, depilatories, and electrolysis. She wrote icily clinical accounts of circumcision, castration, clitorectomies, hysterectomies, and mastectomies. There were gruesome descriptions of tatoos, ritual scarification, and piercings of the eyebrow, lip, navel, tongue, nipple, clitoris, and penis. And when she wasn't writing of various ritual and medical forms of bodily mutilation, she wrote in astonishing detail about sexual acts Nelson would blush to mention to his wife, and a few he'd never even heard of, acts he couldn't even picture in his imagination: bondage, sadomasochism, golden showers, coprophilia, and necrophilia. Sex with household pets, farm animals, stuffed toys, and fruit; sex in airliners, Amtrak trains, and submarines; public sex, Satanic sex, Tantric sex. Fetishization of shoes, wigs, underwear, small household appliances, and hand-held power tools. Sex with poultry, alive, dead, plucked, unplucked, canned, and frozen.

Yet on the other hand, Vita adopted measures just short of purdah to obscure her own sexuality, and she blushed like a virgin on those rare occasions when Nelson or Bridget had gingerly asked about any romantic interest in Vita's life. Indeed, whenever Vita came to Nelson's house to watch videos with his daughters, any hint of eroticism, no matter how innocent—Julie Andrews making calf eyes at Captain von Trapp, Lady and the Tramp nibbling at opposite ends of a strand of spaghetti—sent her bounding from the room on the feeblest pretext.

"I'm getting the girls some more juice!" she'd cry, puttering around in the kitchen until the scene was over.

The only hint of romance in Vita's life that Nelson had ever heard of had been a rumor about a kiss Vita had impetuously and awkwardly planted on the lips of a graduate history student named Virginia Dunning, a member of a theory reading group Vita had once belonged to. The kiss was not reciprocated, according to the rumor, and Vita had quit the group immediately afterward. Sometime later Dunning had graduated and moved to Texas. Nelson himself had never heard Vita speak of her. And the only man Vita had ever mentioned in Nelson's presence was her brother, Robin, who lived in Orlando, Florida. When Vita was first assigned to share an office with Nelson, she had placed on her desk a photo of a trim, smiling young man in a T-shirt and khakis, leaning against a palm tree. His short hair and carefully tended moustache and goatee suggested to Nelson that he was gay; but when he asked Vita, in one of their first conversations, if the man in the picture was her twin, he ran up against Vita's hair-trigger paranoia for the first time.

"Why would you think that?" she'd cried, tensing immediately in her office chair. "Do you think I look like a man?"

"No!" protested Nelson. "It's just that there's a family resemblance."

"That's Robin Bravetype," she'd said, snatching the photo off the desk, "my brother."

But before Nelson could ask about the difference in surname—was he her half-brother? Had she been married?—she ended the conversation.

"I don't look anything like him," she'd declared, slamming the photo in a drawer. The next day it was replaced by an old photograph of Oscar Wilde as Salome. Nelson had never asked her about her brother again.

Still, the fact that she seemed relatively comfortable around Nelson most of the time was due to the likelihood, Nelson suspected, that her only affectionate relationship of any kind with a man had been with her brother, and that Nelson himself—married and a father and manifestly harmless—now filled that role. Just now, however, he was afraid he had lost her goodwill forever.

"I had an accident," he said, swallowing, and he told her of his mishap on Friday and his weekend of pain. He told her about losing his job, his home, and his health insurance. Vita seemed to relax, and by the end of his story she had set her satchel on her desk and turned her chair toward Nelson, her knees primly together.

"Why didn't you call me?" she asked. "This must make extra work for Bridget."

Nelson repressed a sigh. This, too, was typical of Vita; he sometimes wondered if she liked him only for his family. Still, he'd seen a side of his office mate that no one else in the department had—Vita giddy and unselfconscious, rolling about on the carpet with his daughters, laughing and squealing like a girl. At a time when everyone else in the department ducked into doorways at his approach or pretended not to see him, he was grateful that she was still willing to be seen in his company.

"Are you in pain?" she asked.

"A little. That's why I wanted a Coke. To take my pill with."

This brought out Vita's maternal side, and she scooped up a handful of his change and escorted him back downstairs to the Coke machine. The lobby was empty now, and they sat on one of the concrete benches. Vita held the pop can while Nelson fished out his half of a painkiller and popped it in his mouth. He drank most of the Coke in one long, blissful swallow.

"What are you going to do?" she asked him.

"I don't know." He wiped his mouth with the back of his hand. "The job market right now . . ."

"You should talk to the Housing Office," Vita interrupted. "I'm sure they'd let you stay on through the end of the school year."

Vita was never interested in anyone else's job prospects, especially Nelson's. This in spite of the fact that Nelson had listened to hours and hours of Vita's paranoia about her own future in the department. In a low, conspiratorial whisper, she would parse with a cabalist's attention to detail the meaning and motives of every offhand remark made to her by a tenured faculty member.

"I was coming up in the elevator with Weissmann this morning," she'd say, meaning Nelson's former mentor, "and he said it was 'awfully wet out.'" Here Vita would peer at Nelson through the wide lenses of her glasses. "What do you think that means?"

"Well," Nelson would say, "it's raining pretty hard today."

"Yes, but that's not what he said," Vita would whisper. "He said, '*It's awfully wet out.*'" Then she'd peer through her glasses as though she suspected Nelson of knowing the code and not telling her.

Now, in the lobby of Harbour Hall, she sat erect suddenly, as if coming to attention. Nelson looked up to see the department's high command surge out of the elevator and march briskly across the empty lobby in a flying wedge. At point was Chairperson Pescecane, a short, tanned, barrel-chested man in an Armani suit, silk shirt, and paisley tie. His handmade Italian shoes clicked briskly across the floor, his cashmere overcoat hung loose across his shoulders. He looked like a mob boss, and he knew it. He had short legs, but he managed to look as though he were setting the pace with long, confident strides. At his heels trotted his executive assistant—"my consigliere," the chair liked to call him—the pop-eyed Lionel Grossmaul. Grossmaul clutched a handful of memos, and he murmured into the chair's ear from behind as they walked.

A few steps back to Pescecane's left glided Victoria Victorinix, pale and thin lipped; she was wearing little, round sunglasses indoors, even on this cloudy November day. She was accompanied by Gillian, Nelson's rival for classroom space, who towered above Professor Victorinix but managed to look less imposing. To the chair's right, Morton Weissmann marched heavily, determined to keep up. His smile was set, but his eyes were hung with bluish bags, and he tread on the cuffs of his tailored trousers. After him trailed three identical brown-haired, white male grad students named Vic, Bob, and Dan, who were known by the other graduate students as "the Lost Boys." They loped at Weissmann's heels, hoping no one would notice them.

The three professors and their retainers were on their way to an informal session at Pandemonium, where the Big Three could negotiate the business of the department without the trouble of an agenda or minutes. Waves of tension radiated from this procession; it was an open secret that none of the three professors trusted either of the others. Sitting on the bench Nelson felt as if he and Vita were adrift in a violently rocking rowboat as an armada churned by. Vita actually clutched the sides of the bench, as though she might fall off. She was smiling fearfully, unable to make up her mind whether it was better to be noticed or unnoticed by the high command. Nelson no longer even expected to be seen.

As the trio of personages and their entourage passed, Nelson felt a slash of pain, as if someone had run a flame along his injured finger from the suture to the tip, precisely where the doctor had said he wasn't supposed to feel anything. Nelson groaned aloud and waved his bandaged hand, trying to cool his burning finger.

Vita glanced wildly at him, her eyes wide with fear that he had drawn attention to the two of them. Chairperson Pescecane halted in midstride and looked across the lobby; Lionel danced on his tiptoes to keep from running into him. Professor Victorinix paused, and Gillian halted behind her on the toes of her combat boots. Weissmann actually held up his hand like a cavalry captain, and the three Lost Boys blundered into one another. They followed Weissmann's glance across the lobby and, perhaps apprehensive at the fate of a Guy Like Them, glanced away again, a school of fish turning in unison. Nelson could hear them murmuring to each other.

"Uh-oh," said Vic.

"Look out," said Bob.

"It's him," said Dan.

Professor Victorinix's gaze was unreadable behind her sunglasses, but Weissmann met Nelson's eye. He opened his mouth to speak and closed it again. The chair, meanwhile, kept his gaze on Nelson and inclined his head ever so slightly toward Lionel. "Humboldt, Nelson," Lionel whispered. "Adjunct."

Pescecane smiled wolfishly and drew himself up. "Humboldt," he said loudly. "The fuck happened to your hand?"

Anthony Pescecane was a son of the docklands of New Jersey. His longshore-man father had served as an extra in *On the Waterfront,* as Chairperson Pescecane was fond of telling everyone. Other academics of similar backgrounds had worked long and hard to lose their accents, but Pescecane had labored to keep his, so that by now it had a theatrical ring to it.

Nelson was surprised at his own response. His finger burned, he felt himself sweating from the pain, but his mind was suddenly clear. The feeble joke he'd been repeating all morning didn't even occur to him. "Freak accident," he said. "My finger was severed on the Quad."

Pescecane blinked. Lionel's pop-eyed stare did not waver. Weissmann winced. Gillian glared at Nelson as if he were trying to take her classroom, and Professor Victorinix directed the blank gaze of her sunglasses away from him. Vita chuckled nervously, a series of wheezes that made her sound as if she were hyperventilating. The Lost Boys whispered among themselves.

"This could happen to you," said Dan.

"But for the grace of God," said Vic.

"Who stepped on my grave?" said Bob.

Weissmann cleared his throat. "My goodness, Nelson. How are you getting on?"

Coming from him, that question had a lot of resonances, and Nelson surprised himself again by leveling his gaze at Professor Victorinix, who had fired him only three days before. But there was no way to tell if she was looking back at him, and Nelson realized that his profile was so low in the department that Morton Weissmann, his old champion, didn't even know he'd been sacked.

"They sewed my finger back on." Nelson gritted his teeth against the searing pain, but his mind was still cool. "It'll be good as new, they said." He looked at Pescecane. "Maybe even better."

Pescecane flatly returned Nelson's gaze. At times he really did have the blank, threatening look of a hoodlum. Suddenly he laughed, an explosive snort, and he twisted his massive torso to take in the others behind him. "Sue the fucks," he said.

"I beg your pardon?" said Weissmann.

"Sue the fucking university." Pescecane's silk, wool, and cashmere-clad shoulders shook with mirth. "Huh? Am I right?"

Weissmann lifted the corners of his lips in a reluctant smile; he found Pescecane insufferably vulgar. Professor Victorinix's thin mouth remained set in a perfect line below the black discs of her lenses. Only bug-eyed Lionel joined in the chair's laughter. He snorted once through his nose, his expression otherwise unchanged.

"Sue the fucks," said Lionel, in a strangled voice. He always sounded as if he were trying to talk and swallow at the same time.

"Yeah," said Pescecane, "sue the rat bastards."

He swung away and started across the lobby again, and the others followed. The Lost Boys wheeled to keep as many people as possible between them and Nelson. Only Weissmann gave Nelson a nod in parting. As they passed out of earshot, Vita sagged and breathed out heavily.

"What do you think he meant by that?" She clutched her elbows and watched the figures recede down the hall. " 'Sue the rat bastards.' What do you think that means?"

The pain in Nelson's finger continued, but his clarity of mind was fading. He doubled over, clutching his bandaged hand by the wrist.

"Oh, my gosh," he murmured, "it's not supposed to hurt like this."

"Nelson?" For nearly the first time in their friendship, Vita lay her hand on his shoulder.

"The nerves are severed." Nelson sat up, sweating and pale. "I'm not supposed to feel anything."

"You look awful. Maybe you should go home."

"I can't do that." Nelson managed to stand. "I have office hours this afternoon. I have my three o'clock section."

He staggered, and Vita caught him under the elbow. She was surprisingly sturdy under his weight, and she steered him toward the elevator. "Cancel your office hours," she said firmly, her maternal side returning. "I'll take over your three o'clock." She glanced about the lobby and lowered her voice. "What possessed you to talk to Anthony like that? You looked right at him."

Nelson felt his finger throb, and he laughed. "What's he going to do," he said, "fire me?"

Vita stopped dead and, still gripping his elbow, looked up at him. It was very unlike Nelson to be sarcastic, and Nelson felt himself blush. "Did I say that?" he asked.

Vita looked away and pressed the button for the elevator.

At home Nelson took two halves of a painkiller, and slept through dinner. Bridget tried to keep the girls away from him, but he was awakened by Abigail, who pounded on his forehead with the heel of her hand.

"Alive, Daddy?" she shouted. "Are you alive?"

Nelson blinked back at her, unable to answer.

He helped with baths and bedtime stories, and then Nelson let his wife cradle his head in her lap as he sobbed quietly, so as not to waken the girls.

"You pushed yourself too hard today," Bridget murmured.

"No." Nelson sniffled. "I don't push myself nearly hard enough."

This was an old argument. Having given up in an instant her own dream of being a dancer, Bridget expected Nelson to be equally unsentimental about his own prospects. With a degree from a former agricultural college in Indiana, she often asked him, did he really expect to keep a job at a Big Ten school?

"Vita's right." She stroked his hair. "I think you should talk to the Housing Office about letting us stay till the end of the school year." She paused. "I'll do it, if you don't want to."

Nelson sat up, rubbing his eyes. As a modern academic he was feminist by default, but even so his Iowa upbringing wouldn't allow him to let his wife do his dirty work for him. Her solicitousness stung. This was his failure. If anyone should grovel, it should be him.

"No, I'll do it," he said, and he started to cry again. Bridget folded him in her arms.

A week after the accident, Dr. Gee took off the bandages. The rest of Nelson's hand was pale and wrinkled from a week under wraps, but the reattached finger itself was ruddy and warm.

"Look at that," said the doctor, turning Nelson's hand slowly from side to side. "I've never seen anyone heal so fast."

"Is that unusual?" said Nelson.

Dr. Gee shrugged and said, "Can you feel anything in it?"

Nelson hadn't even told Bridget how his finger burned from time to time. It was not her pain, and he felt oddly proprietary of it. Now he was afraid if he mentioned it, they might end up paying for even more expensive procedures.

"Not really. I mean, I get twinges, but I suppose that's just my imagination."

"Well, there're no nerves in it." The doctor flicked Nelson's finger hard with his own fingernail. "Feel that?"

"No," Nelson said, and he didn't. His finger felt cold.

"There you go," said Dr. Gee. "I guess we can take out the stitches."

That night Bridget treated Nelson to a movie, their first night out in months. Nelson protested that they couldn't afford it, but she brooked no objection. She even took him to a film she knew he'd like, a cartoonishly postmodern western, a cynical remake of *Shane*. It was a busy Friday night in the multiplex, but the only other people in the theater where the western was showing were a middle-aged couple a few rows forward. The man, a pudgy fellow with strands of hair plastered across his bare scalp, insisted on talking to his spouse even after the credits had rolled. Bridget glared at them.

"In Asia," Nelson whispered, "the audience is *supposed* to talk during the film. It's their way of participating in the narrative."

"Fine," Bridget said. "Let him go watch it in Singapore. Right now, I want him to shut up."

Nelson got up and moved down the aisle of the darkened theater toward the pale, striated circle of the man's bald spot. Nelson's finger, newly released to the air, began to burn again; and he flexed it as he slid up the empty row behind the talking man. The man glanced back and bent closer to his partner, lowering his voice to a husky whisper. Nelson's finger seared him, and he stooped and lay his right hand on the man's shoulder, the injured finger brushing the man's neck.

"Please don't talk during the film," Nelson said, and the pain vanished. Indeed, Nelson felt a kind of balm in his reattached finger, as if he had plunged it into ice water.

The man stiffened and started to rise. His hand still on the man's shoulder, Nelson said, "Oh please, don't get up. I'd just appreciate it if you wouldn't talk."

The woman stirred in her seat, and Nelson brushed her shoulder with his right hand. "Really, stay where you are," he said. "I didn't mean to disturb you."

Nelson returned to his seat. Normally he didn't like revisionist westerns, preferring the uncomplicated, unironic classics of the forties and fifties. And this film was revisionist with a vengeance: The gunfighter began by helping the local farmers, killing the henchmen of the local cattle baron in self-defense one by one. But by the end the gunfighter had turned into the thing he was fighting, killing the cattle baron in a climactic gunfight and taking his place as de facto dictator of the little valley. But this was Nelson's night out, and he resolved to take from the film only the simpler pleasures of his childhood: laconic men on horseback; wide-open landscapes; sudden, redemptive violence.

As the lights came up after the movie, Nelson noticed that the middle-aged couple were glancing anxiously back at him. The man had his hands on his throat, and was making choking sounds. Nelson hurried down the aisle.

"Are you folks okay?" he asked.

The woman, her eyes wide with fear, threw her arms around her husband as if to protect him. The man rubbed his throat and moved his mouth, but all he could do was grunt.

"What did you do to him?" the woman hissed.

Nelson's finger began to burn again. He gripped the man by the shoulder.

"Can you breathe?" he said. "Say something, if you can."

The man gave a shout, a wordless cry. Nelson felt that ice-water shock along his finger again, and he jerked his hand away.

"Holy Mother of God, mister," the man gasped. "What do you want from us?"

Nelson stepped back. "Nuh, nothing," he stammered.

"Can we go now?" said the woman, her voice trembling.

"Can you go?" Nelson was bewildered. "Of course. The movie's over. I simply . . ."

The man and woman both jumped up, clutching each other, and then halted. Nelson was in the aisle, blocking their way.

"I'm sorry." He backed up, but they clambered over the seats into the row behind, then into the row behind that, and then ran up the aisle, banging the swinging door and disappearing into the lobby.

"What was that all about?" Bridget asked as Nelson came slowly up the aisle.

"I have no idea," Nelson said, but his finger burned with an icy fire.

4

Nelson in the Underworld

As Nelson hurried up Michigan Avenue on the following Monday morning, Fu Manchu followed him for a block. "It's fuckin' November, man," he declared loudly. "I don't have a coat, and it's fuckin' cold out."

He marched a few paces behind Nelson, swinging his massive bare arms in a filthy, sleeveless denim vest. His hair was tied back in the red, white, and blue bandanna.

"Some people, they *got* a coat," said Fu Manchu. "They got someplace to go. Maybe they should, like, share a little of what they got with the less fortunate."

Nelson hurried on, his finger throbbing. He had used up the painkillers; the doctor had said he didn't need them any longer. At the corner across from the campus, Fu Manchu halted.

"Hey, thanks for listening," he called out, "faggot."

Between classes, Nelson sat in a plasterboard cubicle at the Housing Office while a plump, soft-spoken African-American woman peered through the lower half of her bifocals at a computer screen. "Your appointment's been terminated," she said.

"I know, but . . ."

"I'm afraid that ends your housing eligibility." The woman glanced at the screen and added, "Professor."

"I was hoping," Nelson said, "that is to say, I was wondering if there was any sort of grace period. . . ."

The woman peered gravely over the tops of her lenses. "I'm afraid not, sir. You have to be out of the unit by the first of the year."

"That's only six weeks from now."

Nelson's finger smoldered. He should have let Bridget do this. She was a big city girl, much less likely than Nelson to be self-conscious about the clerk's race and gender and much more likely to let the woman have both sides of her tongue.

"Maybe there's no one scheduled to take over our town house," Nelson said brightly, "and we could just stay until . . ."

"Sir." The woman lifted her hands off the keyboard. "We have a six-month waiting list on these units."

Nelson's finger was on fire.

"Is there any way I could reinstate my eligibility?" he said, wincing at the pain.

The woman sighed. "Sign up for classes?" she said.

Suddenly Nelson lay his right hand on the woman's hand, his burning finger along her wrist. What am I doing? he thought. She tried to pull her hand away, but he tightened his grip on her hand and said, "I want you to check again. Maybe you read the screen wrong. I don't think my housing eligibility is up until next May."

He felt the pleasant shock of coolness in his finger, and he let go of the woman's hand. Her eyes were glazed; she stared at nothing. What have I done? he thought. He was about to jump up and flee, but now the woman was blinking at him oddly.

"Are you alright?" Nelson asked.

The woman turned silently to her computer screen and lifted her hands to the keyboard. Nelson slid to the edge of his seat, a stammering apology rising to his lips.

"This is wrong." The woman lifted her chin.

"I, I'm sorry . . ." Nelson was halfway out of his chair. "I shouldn't have . . ."

"Somebody put this in wrong." The keyboard clattered. "You're not due to be out of the unit until May first."

Nelson froze, his heart beating hard. "Are you sure?" he said. He lowered himself to his seat.

"Oh, yes." The woman turned the screen toward him and pointed to a glowing line in blue. "Your eligibility is good through the winter semester."

Nelson blinked at the date on the screen. He felt ashamed and elated all at once. His finger hummed.

"Thank you," he said, blushing.

"Wasn't me." The woman shrugged. "I just go by what it says on the screen."

"How'd you manage that?" Bridget said when he got home. Abigail was screaming in circles around the living room. Nelson danced in a little circle of his own, stepping lightly over broken-backed dolls, splintered blocks, crayon-defaced picture books. Bridget watched them both, arms akimbo.

"Just made them do it," Nelson said. Abigail ran into him at full force, but he swung her up lightly onto his back.

"You *made* them do it?" Bridget widened her eyes.

"Well, talked them into it." His finger was cool now, but he had a vivid memory of its flaring heat, and how it had cooled against the skin of the housing clerk. Nelson pushed the memory away. It can't be, he thought.

Abigail was clawing her way up her father, pulling on his hair and trying to haul herself up on his shoulders.

"Daddy be a ladder!" she shouted.

"Well, if it was that easy," Bridget said, "you might have asked them to lower the rent as well."

Nelson turned abruptly away, Abigail swinging from him like a monkey. He looked out the sliding-glass door into the scrubby woods behind the town house so that Bridget couldn't see his expression. Heat was rising to his face: He hadn't even thought of asking the woman at Housing for something more. Maybe my finger has a little something . . . extra now, he thought, but it would have been wrong to take unfair advantage, to make the woman lower their rent. He even felt a little angry that Bridget should suggest it. Abigail lost her grip and slid off his shoulders, and he caught her.

"Nap time," Bridget said, reaching for Abigail.

"I'll take her." Holding his daughter horizontally like a battering ram, Nelson started up the stairs.

"Nelson," said Bridget, and he paused, Abigail wriggling in his arms. Bridget came halfway up the steps and kissed her daughter.

"God knows we need some good news in this household, don't we, pumpkin?" She kissed Nelson too, and he smiled and started up again.

"But next time, sweetheart?" Bridget called after him. "When you've got them on the run? Press your advantage." Bridget's voice followed Nelson around the corner at the top of the stairs. "Life doesn't look out for people like us, Nelson. We have to look out for ourselves."

The following morning, between classes, Nelson left his office without his coat and trotted across the Quad to Thornfield Library with his hands in his pockets and his shoulders hunched against the cold. In the circulation department in the

57

Annex he picked up the key to the Poole Collection, then worked his way up into the old library, through the stacks and into the clock tower, in search of yet another volume by James Hogg.

The university library's active collection had been shifted to the new underground Annex, a bright, vast, climate-controlled atrium that plunged six stories into the earth. The old library had been saved from demolition only because its image was still imprinted on sweatshirts, letterhead stationery, the university's web site, and the hearts of well-to-do alumni all over the world. The old stacks, with their stamped metal flooring, low ceilings, and flickering fluorescent fixtures, were nearly empty now, holding only ancient encyclopedias and bound volumes of long-extinct journals. The abandoned card catalog had been moved into the old library's dank subbasement, the long drawers like coffins full of carefully typed cards rotting away. As Nelson climbed the clanging flights of the narrow, cast-iron staircase, past one darkened floor after another, he fancied that if he lost everything—his family, his career, his place in the world—he could come live here, among the useless books, like the Phantom of the Opera. *He* could be the ghost of Thornfield Library.

At last Nelson came breathlessly up a narrow iron stair into the tower itself. The Poole Collection was not a real collection at all, but the library's repository of withdrawn books—duplicate copies, obsolete texts, superseded scholarship, and novels and volumes of poetry that had been tumbled from the canon like outcast angels. Any book deemed worthless was pulled from the shelves in the gleaming subterranean Annex and hoisted into the tower by a creaking old dumbwaiter. Thornfield Library was being filled from the top down with a purgatory of books, where they would wait until they were lowered down the dumbwaiter again to be sold, given away, or trucked off to the landfill. The depository was named ironically after the placid librarian in the Circulation Department who dispensed the key, a square-set, red-haired woman who spent all day doing needlepoint behind her desk.

In the tower, Nelson climbed through several large, square, empty rooms where the gray November light glowed through arched windows of warped and unclean glass until he came to the lowest floor of the collection. Here, discarded books were stuffed at random into rough wooden shelves and caged off behind a fence of unpainted steel mesh. He fitted the key into the lock and opened the enclosure's gate on its shrieking hinges, then closed it with a clang and a click, as it locked behind him. He started up the stairs within the cage, climbing past a couple of more floors crammed with books. The old shelves reached nearly to the ceiling. Some books stood upright, spine out, but others had been shoved in on their sides, backward, upside down, with their boards bent back, or their deckled pages exposed to the weak sunlight. At the end of each row of shelves a midden of books was heaped on the cold, wooden floor. More books were heaped against the wall, under the dirty windows. Halfway up the last flight of stairs, Nelson rubbed a clean patch in one of the windows and peered out. Each window was caged behind rusty bars, presumably because of the suicide years before; below him, through the bars, Nelson saw the wide, bright, inverted V of the Annex cut into the lawn. Through the bright skylight he could see six stories straight down into the atrium. It was a sight out of an Escher print, with little round-headed, foreshortened figures of indeterminate gender strolling back and forth along the sharp edge of each floor.

On the next-to-last floor of the tower a narrow passage ran along the windows to a small spiral stair that led, through a padlocked grating, to the bells and gears of the giant clock on the floor above. Nelson heard a giant, resonant *chunk* from above and felt the vibration through his feet as a counterweight dropped or a gear lurched one fraction of a revolution. He flicked the switch on a square, gunmetal junction box, and slivers of light pierced the narrow gaps between the shelves, from the bare bulbs hung in each aisle. He threaded his way between the heaps of books on the floor, into the cold reek of mold and rotting paper and swollen leather, until he came to the deepest aisle of the room, where the collected works of James Hogg had been rudely stuffed into a shelf just under the bulb, higher than Nelson's head.

Nelson pulled volumes off the shelf and peered at the titles in the harsh light. *The Three Perils of Man,* read one; *The Three Perils of Woman,* read another. *Man,* according to the slip in the back of the book, had not been checked out since 1922, and *Woman,* not since 1908. This suited Nelson perfectly: Since *The Private Memoirs and Confessions of a Justified Sinner* was Hogg's only real claim on the canon, perhaps it was overworked. Perhaps the way to get an article published was to find work by Hogg that had been overlooked. Since yesterday afternoon, his wife's admonition—"Life doesn't look out for people like us, Nelson"—had been circling endlessly in his brain like an ineradicable snatch of song, chasing a line from Hogg himself: "*Man mind yoursel* is the first commandment," said the Justified Sinner's servant near the end of the *Confessions.* "An' wha's to blame?"

Nelson found a fairly steady stack of old books and sat, a volume of Hogg in each hand. He set *Man* on his knee and began to leaf through *Woman*. Most of the pages of the old volume had never even been cut. This was, from the scholarly point of view, virgin territory, something he could use to get into print, to leverage himself up into a job at some out-of-the-way school. He only hoped it wasn't too late: Just after grad school, when jobs had been plentiful, he could have easily secured a position at some small liberal arts college. He'd have gotten tenure by now, teaching bright kids in some leafy small town, with summers off to write and tend his lawn. Classmates of his had mortgages already on houses with two and a half baths and a bedroom for every child. They had car loans on Volvos in which they drove their daughters to dance lessons and gymnastics practice, and second loans on tanklike minivans that could hold an entire soccer team of twelve year olds. They had enormous side-by-side fridges and thirty-inch TVs and brand-new PCs with hard drives measured in gigabytes. And each of his classmates had a real study of his own, with paneling and bookshelves and a reading chair, not a second-hand Steelcase desk and books stuffed into plastic milk crates and a dented two-drawer filing cabinet full of an unpublishable book on James Hogg. The best lack all conviction, though Nelson, while the worst get sport utility vehicles.

What's the difference between those guys and me? he wondered. What have they got that I haven't got? Luck, he answered himself, shifting uncomfortably on the unsteady stack of books—luck and a clear-eyed acceptance of their place in the academic universe. They hadn't aimed as high as Nelson, and they had thrived. It's my own fault, Nelson thought, following a well-worn path in his imagination, thinking I could make it at a place like Midwest. Hubris brought me here.

There was another muffled clunk from above, and Nelson looked up. He often heard strange noises here, usually from above. There could be no one up there, of course: You'd have to pass through the locked gate to the Poole Collection and the locked trap door to the bell chamber, and at the moment Nelson had the only key to the enclosure. Yet he sat very still for a moment, with the books in his hands, distracted from his self-flagellation by the legend of the ghost of Thornfield Library. The apparition was mentioned to each undergraduate during orientation and to each new faculty member, wryly, at his or her first faculty function—*Have you heard about the Thornfield ghost yet?* At the moment, his skin tightening, his heart beating a little faster, Nelson reminded himself that every version of the story he'd been told was different from every other version. He reminded himself that he could not recall ever hearing of anyone actually seeing the ghost. And yet, what, or who, had he seen on the Quad the day of his accident? Had each of the three sightings he'd made that day even been of the same person? If not, why had there been three different figures, each wearing a cape and a devil's mask and each calling his name? And why had they, or it, or whatever, singled him out? The faceless silvery face had clearly been a hallucination, but just as clearly someone had spoken to him just before he passed out. *What can I do for* you, *Professor Humboldt?*

Nelson stood suddenly; a few books slid off the stack he'd been sitting on and thumped to the floor. This is crazy, he told himself. It's this room, this putatively haunted place; it's getting to me. Somebody was playing a Halloween prank on me that day on the Quad, probably a disgruntled student, some frat boy pissed off about a grade, and it went badly awry. The rest—the silvery face, the clock striking thirteen—was delirium, from shock and loss of blood. He clutched the books together before him with both hands as if they were one volume, *The Three Perils of Man and Woman.* Nobody would mind if he took them; the books were doomed to the landfill anyway. He edged down the crowded aisle between the abandoned books bulging from the tall cases on either side. Still, he told himself, something has changed since my finger was reattached. Something out of the ordinary happened between me and the housing clerk yesterday—just like something odd happened with that guy and his wife in the movie theater last weekend. Maybe the apparition passed something to me that manifests itself in my finger.

"This is nuts," he said aloud, pausing in the aisle between the tall shelves, the spines of useless books pointing at him. This has nothing to do with magic, he told himself, it's just time to put my courage to the sticking place. His little victory today at the Housing Office proved he could do just that. If the ghost wanted to relive its moment of despair and fling itself forever from the top of the clock tower, then live and let live—so to speak. Whether his finger had anything to do with it or not, for the first time in a long while he felt a glimmer of pride, that at last he had done something for his wife and his little girls, that they weren't just clinging to him as he dragged them down to live in a trailer park, or worse. He was smart, he was hardworking, he was personable. He'd fallen on hard times, but now his luck had changed. If he wanted to ascribe that to his finger, to use his finger as a metaphor or a talisman for the change in his luck, why not? All he wanted was a chance to prove himself on his merits again, to show the department what he could do. His wife was right; no one looked out for people like them. He'd have to do it himself. He'd have to press his advantage. He drew himself up and stepped out of the aisle.

Something scraped on the far side of the room. Nelson froze. His knees went rubbery. The hair stood up on the back of his neck. He heard a soft, rapid padding as of footsteps, and against the weak glare of the windows he saw—or thought he saw—a pale figure gliding rapidly toward the stairs. "Hey!" Nelson started to say, but the word caught in his throat. He crouched in the aisle, his heart pounding. His finger was suddenly burning again. Even if there were no ghost in Thornfield Library, even if his newly empowered touch was all in his imagination, it wouldn't hurt to act as if it were real, would it? What if his mere touch brought him anything he wanted? Think of what I could do for my family, for my department, he thought, recalling the tormented comic book heroes of his youth—Spiderman, Johnny Storm, the Incredible Hulk—using their miraculous and unasked for powers *only for good*. It wouldn't hurt to try, would it? Would it?

He peered around the end of the bookcase. The figure was gone—if it had ever been there at all, he told himself, sighing. He drew a deep breath, hefted his books, and headed for the stairway.

"I'll show you," he told the ghost, under his breath. "I'll show you all. I'm not dead yet."

Back in his office, Nelson found signs of Vita's recent presence: her coat tossed over the back of her chair, her satchel listing to one side on her desk. But she was nowhere to be seen, so Nelson left the two volumes of Hogg on his desk, locked the office, and headed for the elevator. As the car sank, his injured finger throbbed. Why not try it and see? Why not try to get his job back? My God, he thought, cradling his injured hand in his uninjured one, what have I got to lose?

There were nine floors in Harbour Hall, but only eight of them were above ground. During the fifties a windowless underground bunker had been sunk as a hideaway from nuclear war, with walls of reinforced concrete sixteen inches thick. The elevator sank below ground level and lurched to a stop, nearly buckling Nelson's knees. The doors rattled open to the harsh, unnatural light of the bunker's airlock, between two doorways that used to be sealed with massive steel doors. Nelson hesitated in the car, holding the automatic doors open with his good hand. A motto had been lettered over the inner doorway, in indelible Magic Marker. The motto had been painted over since, but still shone dimly through the whitewash, making it even more ghostly and macabre. ABANDON ALL HOPE, it said, YE WHO ENTER HERE. This was the portal to the Bomb Shelter, home of the Department of English's Composition Program.

Nelson stepped out. The elevator door hissed shut, and the car whined away upward. He passed through the steel doorway into a vast, white room of plasterboard cubicles, where the muffled rumble of the ventilators and the constant fluorescent buzz gave the place the feel of a sweatshop. Above the industrial hum rose the steady murmur of lonely women in their thirties and forties, their cubicles lined up like sewing machines in a shirtwaist factory. Nelson started down the aisle between the cubicles; he was already beginning to sweat. He always hoped when he came here that no one would notice him, but everyone always did. In each cubicle a thin woman in thrift shop couture sat earnestly tutoring some groggy student in a point of grammar or the construction of an argument, and each woman looked up at Nelson as he passed with the hollow-eyed, pitiless gaze of the damned. A few composition teachers lived in hope: faculty wives making a little extra money, the department's own recent Ph.D.s teaching a year of comp as they played the job market, MFA students treading water as they finished their novels. But most of the comp teachers were divorced moms and single women with cats who taught eight classes a year and earned a thousand dollars per class, who clung to their semester-to-semester contracts with the desperate devotion of anchoresses. They combined the bitter esprit de corps of assembly-line workers with the literate wit of the overeducated: They were the steerage of the English Department, the first to drown if the budget sprang a leak. They were the Morlocks to the Eloi of the eighth floor. *Pace* Wallerstein, they were the colonial periphery, harvesting for pennies a day the department's raw material—undergraduates—and shipping these processed students farther up the hierarchy, thus creating the leisure for the professors at the imperial center to pursue their interests in feminist theory and postcolonial literature.

Passing among them, Nelson knew he stood out like some dissolute white beachcomber in Robert Louis Stevenson. Even though his appointment was in the Comp Program, he was not *of* them. Not necessarily because he was a man, but because he was a failure: Like colonial peoples everywhere, the women of the Composition Program despised any overlord who had sunk to their level even more than they hated overlords in general. Every gaze in the place was pointed at his back like a spear.

In the Comp Office Nelson took a moment to compose himself, and then, eyes straight, back erect, he strode past the grimy Mr. Coffee and the ancient hand-cranked mimeograph machine. He stepped into the doorway of the small, private office of Linda Proserpina, the director of the Comp Program, a petite, wide-eyed woman with prematurely gray hair and skin as pale as moonlight. She sat at her cluttered desk reading through teacher evaluations, gripping the top of her head with one pale, bony hand, and clutching a smoldering cigarette in the other. She regarded the computer forms with wide-eyed boredom, as if there were nothing in this life or her former life among the living that she hadn't already seen a thousand times. Without looking she tapped ash into a tin ashtray heaped with butts. Smoking was prohibited in all university buildings, but down here, where not even night or day mattered, the director of the Composition Program could do anything she wanted.

"Linda!" Nelson said heartily. "A moment of your time!"

Very slowly, Linda lifted her cool, pale gaze. "Nelson," she said after a moment. "I hear you'll be leaving us."

This was a euphemism for, "I hear you've been fired." Even in the underworld, they observed the proprieties. Nelson held his smile, momentarily flustered.

"We'll be needing your cubicle," Linda went on. "When do you think you can have it emptied out?"

Nelson's finger burned. They may observe the proprieties down here, but there were no illusions. "Well, Linda, actually," Nelson said, "I don't have a cubicle. I still have my office on, you know, the third floor."

"Oh." Linda blinked. Nelson's office was still in the world of the living, so it held no interest for her. She dragged on her cigarette and said, "What happened to your hand?"

Nelson tried out the witticism he'd been working on. "Cut myself shaving." He widened his smile. His finger throbbed.

"Oh." Linda exhaled a gray cloud. "I thought maybe you crossed Anthony somehow." Like the department chair, Linda was Sicilian.

"So how's winter enrollment shaping up?" Nelson's voice cracked like a teenager's.

Linda took another drag and balanced the cigarette in the ashtray. The little office reeked of old tobacco. "Pardon my bluntness, Nelson, but what concern is that of yours?"

"I was hoping you might give me a couple of sections of 101." Nelson's smile was getting difficult to maintain.

Linda sighed and leaned back in her creaking chair, wreathed in smoke. She spoke slowly, as if to a child. "Well, Nelson, your appointment isn't with us, strictly speaking. We only gave you classes because the department proper told us to." She lifted her gaze to the eighth floor, nine floors above. She spoke with all the disdain of the Queen of the Underworld for the spoiled and capricious residents of Olympus.

"I understand." Nelson edged into the room, his smile collapsing. "I was hoping you might recommend me for an appointment in the Comp Program itself. Now that I'm . . . now that I can accept one. My evaluations . . ." He gestured feebly at the forms on her desk.

"Are no better or worse than anyone else's." Linda picked up her cigarette, leaned forward, and lowered her gaze to the evaluations. "Have a nice day, Nelson. Remember me to the world of the living."

Nelson's finger burned, but even so, this was going to be harder than he had hoped. He put his hand in his pocket. "Linda, you know my situation." He lowered his voice. "I need the job."

Linda looked up again. She emphatically stubbed out her cigarette and folded her hands on the desk.

"You know, Nelson, I've got a list," she said, keeping her voice level, "of fifty women in this town, all of them wonderful teachers, *dedicated* teachers, and most of them, Nelson, most of them are waiting tables. Or clerking in bookstores. Or doing freelance copyediting. Or living off welfare, for God's sake."

"It's not fair, I know."

"Fair?" Linda raised her eyebrows. "It's a goddamn crime is what it is. Now you've got a *doctorate,* Nelson . . ."

Nelson balled his hand in his pocket into a fist. He dug his nails into his palm.

"That means you have options that most of us don't," Linda went on. "You're only teaching composition because you have to. Meanwhile, those of us who love to teach . . ."

She trailed off. Linda had only a master's degree, and she herself subsisted on a renewable three-year contract with no hope of tenure. She was the head of the

Composition Program because no one else, tenured or otherwise, was willing to do it. Who wanted to teach nothing but writing to nothing but undergraduates for the rest of one's professional life? Still, Nelson thought, I don't deserve her contempt. His finger seared him, and he felt himself starting to get angry. Don't tell me what to *do,* he wanted to tell it.

"I'm sorry, Nelson." Linda cast about for her cigarettes and found the pack under a quilted heap of papers. She tapped one free. "It's not your fault." She balanced the cigarette between her lips and felt about with both hands for her lighter.

Nelson stepped up to the desk and pulled his hand out of his pocket. "That's alright, Linda." He offered her his hand. "Thank you for your time."

She looked startled, as if no one had ever offered to shake hands with her before. She grimaced and took his hand loosely. Nelson tightened his grip.

"I know you're a good woman, Linda." His voice was low and urgent. "I know you do the best you can every day with an impossible job. I know you deserve better than this."

Nelson's finger throbbed. Would it work? Linda blinked rapidly at Nelson. The unlit cigarette dropped from her lips. Nelson loomed over her, clutching her hand.

"But I have to have a job. I have to feed my children. I'm not begging you, Linda, I'm telling you. *You have to give me two sections of 101.*"

His finger cooled suddenly, and he tried to let go, but to his surprise Linda hung onto him, her mouth working. "I cah, I cah, I cah . . ." She was breathless, her eyes widening in panic.

Nelson jerked his hand free and backed away from the desk. Linda Proserpina slumped back in her chair as if all the air had gone out of her. Her smooth, pale face was pink and wrinkled suddenly; her usually impassive eyes were liquid and rimmed with red. A tear trickled down her cheek. "I *can't,* Nelson," she said in a tiny voice. "God help me, I'd like more than anything else in the world to give you the work, but I *can't.*"

Linda's shoulders shook; she started to sob. Nelson glanced into the main office. It was empty, thank God. He closed the door and reached across Linda's desk, plucking a tissue out of a box and offering it to her.

"Oh, God," she said, copiously blowing her nose, "I'd give you my own job if I could, Nelson, really I would; but I can't offer you anything, don't you see?" She looked up at him as if she were pleading for her life. "Victoria herself terminated your appointment. If I rehired you behind her back, she'd, she'd, she'd . . ."

"It's alright," Nelson said nervously. His finger was warming up again.

"She'd bleed me *dry,* Nelson," Linda said in a quavering, husky whisper. "I love my job, Nelson. It's all I've got."

She looked up at him, biting her lip.

"God help me, Nelson," she sobbed, "but I love teaching composition!"

Nelson came around the desk and squatted down next to Linda. He touched her, very lightly, on the arm, careful not to use his warming finger again. "What if I got Victoria to sign off on it?" he was astonished to hear himself say.

Linda whirled in her chair, her gray hair flying.

"Oh, *could* you?" Her eyes were full of light, as if she were about to kiss him. "Oh, Nelson, that would be *wonderful.* Oh, if you could do that . . ."

Nelson nodded, and he touched her again with his finger, as lightly as he could. "Draw up a contract for two classes. I'll bring you a note from Victoria." His finger cooled again.

"Oh, yes, absolutely, right away!" Linda's hands quivered over the desk as she tried to recall where the contracts were. At the same time, he could tell, she was looking for her cigarettes. Nelson pushed himself up, hesitated; I'm here to do good, he thought, and he touched her lightly on the arm again. She looked up at him hopefully. It was a frightening expression on a woman so pale and so thin.

"Why don't you give up the cigarettes, Linda," he said. "They'll kill you."

She blinked rapidly, and he let go of her. On his way out the door he saw her plucking a contract out of a drawer with one hand as she dropped her cigarettes into the trash with the other.

Alone in the elevator, Nelson let out his breath in a long, shuddering gasp. His elation at what he had just done was quickly overwhelmed by terror at what he had to do next. He had hoped never to have to speak to Professor Victorinix again. The momentum of the elevator pushed at his knees, and he quailed at the almost physical impossibility of reaching into the shadows across the surface of her desk to take Professor Victorinix by the hand. Last time he'd met with her, he'd nearly lost his finger. This time she'd tear his throat out.

The elevator stopped on the first floor. The door rattled open to reveal Professor Victorinix and Gillian waiting in the lobby. Nelson blushed, and his lips moved, as if they'd caught him talking to himself. Gillian instantly stiffened and glared at him, but Professor Victorinix's face was an immovable mask, her eyes hidden behind the round lenses of her tinted glasses.

Nelson's first impulse was to flee, but there was no way past them. So he stepped back against the rear wall of the elevator, trembling. Professor Victorinix glided in and turned on the ball of her foot with eerie precision. Gillian stepped in after her and hit a couple of buttons. The elevator doors closed, and the car began to rise.

No one spoke. Nelson's finger began to burn. The little car radiated with reflected emotion—Nelson's fear, Gillian's hostility, Victorinix's uncanny indifference. Gillian stared at Nelson sidelong, trying to pierce him with her eyes without turning her head, the inverted crucifix quivering from her ear. Nelson's face burned nearly as hot as his finger, and he fixed his gaze straight ahead at his own blurred reflection in the burnished metal of the elevator door. Because of the dim light, perhaps, or Victorinix's pale complexion, Nelson could make out only himself and Gillian in the door; the two round, black discs of Victorinix's glasses seemed to hang unsupported in empty, gray space.

The elevator lurched to a stop at the second floor, where the graduate student offices were. The door opened, but no one moved. Gillian's glance shifted to Victorinix. The professor inclined her head slightly, and Gillian stepped into the dim hallway, glaring at Nelson as the door closed.

The elevator started up again, and Professor Victorinix took a step to the side, closer to the buttons. Nelson's heart hammered. He moved his lips, silently trying out conversational openers.

"Nice day," he mouthed, though it wasn't. "Nice to see you," though it wasn't. "Fancy meeting you here," he nearly said, and he winced. This is it, he thought. If I wait until the eighth floor, it'll be too late. But already Nelson's resolve was draining away. It was one thing to persuade a housing clerk or even Linda Proserpina to cut him a break, but this woman was too powerful, too imperious, too frightening. His finger throbbed.

"Nelson?"

Nelson blinked and looked down. Professor Victorinix was looking up at him through her impenetrable round lenses. "Isn't this your floor?" she said.

The elevator had stopped, the doors had opened. Nelson jerked his gaze into the dim, empty hallway, then up to the glowing yellow 3 above the door. Professor Victorinix held down the "open" button with her slender thumb.

"Muh, Muh, Madame Chairman," Nelson said. He shook his head violently.

"Woman," he gasped. "I mean, Chair*person.*"

Professor Victorinix's lips puckered slightly. Good Lord, Nelson thought, I sound like I'm making a toast. He shriveled inside, but his finger burned.

"Linda Proserpina," he began.

Professor Victorinix's bemusement faded. "Are you getting off or not, Nelson?" she said.

Nelson shifted to face her. "Linda Proserpina would like to offer me two sections of 101 next semester," he said breathlessly.

Professor Victorinix released the button. The doors shut, the car rose. Her mouth narrowed to a line again. She looked up at the numbers over the door.

"Only with your approval, of course." Nelson moved to the other side of the door, angling into her line of sight. The stinging heat in his finger was making him sweat.

"I thought we understood each other, Professor." Victorinix would not look at him.

Nelson shoved his hand in his pocket, afraid he might lunge for her like a rapist. If she sensed his anxiety, she gave no sign, watching the numbers light up one after another above the door. They passed the fifth floor.

"We do!" Nelson protested, a little too loudly. "It's just that Linda feels she can make room for me."

"It's not up to Linda." Victorinix leveled the blank gaze of her glasses at him. "It's up to me, Nelson. And I can't do it." She looked away. "I'm sorry."

She doesn't mean *can't,* Nelson thought, she means *won't.* He pulled his hand out of his pocket, ran it through his thinning hair. His finger burned, burned, and he bit his lip against the pain.

"How's your finger?" she said.

"It hurts," Nelson said, grimacing.

The elevator stopped at the eighth floor before Professor Victorinix could make her diffident profession of sympathy. The door opened, and the Lost Boys began crowding into the car like frat boys until they saw Victorinix. Then they bumped into each other backing up.

"Whoa," said Bob.

"Pardon me," said Vic.

"My mistake," said Dan.

"Boys," said Victorinix drily. The Lost Boys leaped back as the petite, pale woman moved through them and glided down the hall. They turned to the elevator and jumped back again at the sight of Nelson, catching their breath in unison.

"Aieee," said Vic.

"The Living Dead," said Dan.

"Going *down,*" said Bob.

Nelson pushed past them, after Victorinix. "Professor," he said, his voice trembling.

Victorinix turned on her axis as if she were floating an inch or two above the ground. Up here on the eighth floor of Harbour Hall, the corridor was wider and airier. The clear, bright November light streaming through the window at the far end of the hall made Victorinix look older and frailer, her skin dry and papery, her cropped hair almost dingy. There were crow's feet at the corner of her eyes, as if, even behind her sunglasses, she was squinting.

Nelson started up the hall toward her. The walk seemed less strenuous, the carpet less deep than when he had fled her office in humiliation only ten days or so before. Behind him the Lost Boys watched his progress from the elevator as the doors rattled shut.

"He's screwed," said Bob.

"He's fucked," said Dan.

"He's dead," said Vic, as the doors closed.

It was the lunch hour. There was no one else in the hall. Nelson's blood pounded as he came up to Victorinix, and his heart surged at the way she had to lift her chin to look up at him. "I'm sorry to have bothered you," he said, and he offered her his hand.

It hung in the air for a long, awful moment. Nelson's courage began to drain quickly away, and his hand began to tremble. I'm a fool, he thought. She looked as if she might turn away without taking his hand, and Nelson began to feel relieved. It wouldn't work anyway, he thought, not with her. She could destroy me in a heartbeat; she could shrivel my soul to its roots. The trembling began to move up Nelson's arm.

Victorinix met his grasp just as he was about to drop his hand. Again she intended just a brushing of palms, but before she could pull away, Nelson folded his hand around her dry, smooth palm and squeezed. "I'd like you to reconsider," he murmured.

He felt that icy release in his burning finger, but it was slower this time.

70

Professor Victorinix's thin lips tightened. Her free hand jerked galvanically at her side. I should let go, Nelson thought, this is dangerous. But he hung on. She lifted her free hand to her temple and slowly unhooked her glasses, lowering the dark lenses. She was blinking rhythmically, but something was struggling up through the haze over her gray eyes.

"I'd appreciate it if you could write Linda a note," Nelson tightened his grip for dear life and dropped his voice an octave, "telling her she has your approval to give me a job."

Professor Victorinix's eyelids fluttered rapidly. The corners of her lips twitched. Something was coming through her eyes, and suddenly Nelson released his grip. Victorinix jerked her hand away and stumbled back a step, her gaze sharpening again. They both stood swaying in the hall, Nelson speechless, Victorinix breathing hard through her nose. Then she rotated on her heel and glided silently up the carpet.

Nelson's heart pounded so hard he was afraid he might faint. He turned unsteadily and fled back to the elevator and pressed the down button, hoping he could remain standing at least until the car arrived. He sneaked a glance back down the hall. Victorinix clutched the knob of her office door as if she were holding herself up. She fumbled her keys out of her coat and after three tries fitted the right one into the lock. She opened the door but did not go in, leaning against the door in the clear light from the far end of the hall. The elevator came at last, and Nelson staggered into the car, slumping against the rear wall as Professor Victorinix watched him disappear behind the sliding doors.

In his office Nelson sagged into his chair. Even now, he was certain, Victorinix was adding a scathing letter of reprimand to his file, driving a stake through his professional heart. He froze when he heard someone pause outside his door, afraid that Victorinix had sent Gillian to break his spine and fling his lifeless body out the window. A key rattled in the lock, and Nelson nearly overturned himself in his chair. But it was only Vita, peering around the door with her satchel clutched to her chest, making sure her office mate was fully clothed. She was panic-stricken herself, it seemed: She had good news.

"Anthony wants me to do a Seminar Luncheon!" she wailed, closing the door and pressing her back against it, as if hounds were on her scent. The Seminar Luncheon was a prestigious, invitation-only session hosted once a month by Chairperson Pescecane.

71

Nelson tried to muster sympathy for this harrowing turn of events. "That's wonderful, Vita." He managed a smile. "Congratulations!"

"It's a disaster!" she cried. "He wants me to present my paper on Oscar Wilde and the lesbian phallus! Anthony's actually read it! He told me he thought it was 'nice work.' What do you think he means?"

Vita's latest paper, now under review at several major journals, was "The Lesbian Phallus of Dorian Gray," in which she applied gender theory to the works and life of Oscar Wilde. While the author might have seemed a natural subject for gender theory, Nelson thought Wilde seemed an odd subject for Vita. Among the qualities that Vita did not share with Oscar Wilde were wit, irony, flamboyance in dress, and an ability to believe in two mutually contradictory ideas simultaneously. What they did share, Nelson supposed, was a love of the *bios theoretikos,* but even there, what Wilde took to mean "contemplation" meant something else again to a modern literary theorist.

"Maybe Anthony liked the paper," Nelson said absently. He was thinking it might not be too late to apologize to Professor Victorinix. Perhaps he could offer to throw himself from the roof of Harbour Hall and save Gillian the trouble.

"Those were his exact words." Vita sat across from Nelson and clutched her knees. " 'Nice work.' What do you think he *means* by that?"

Nelson silenced Vita's paranoia by inviting her home for dinner, where he knew she would be distracted from the terrors of her success by rolling around on the floor with Clara and Abigail. Perhaps Nelson himself would be distracted from the imminent collapse of his academic career. The distraction worked, too, at least as far as Vita was concerned: In Nelson's living room that evening she was girlish and giddy, singing old sitcom theme songs with Clara, who knew them from Nickelodeon. The two of them made it only halfway through the song from *The Patty Duke Show* before they collapsed into hysteria. For a time Vita sat patiently with Abby too, as the two of them tried to put Barbie's head back on. Bridget looked on happily from the kitchen, grateful for the temporary release from parental duties.

Once, early in their friendship with Vita, Nelson had watched Vita getting on famously with Clara, and he had innocently suggested that Vita might want children of her own someday. This had been a mistake: As a rising star of the department, every bit of good fortune—a successful interim tenure review, a grant won, a paper enthusiastically received—was the scripture for one of Vita's sermonettes on how difficult it was to be a woman in academia. On this occasion

Nelson's casual remark resulted in a forty-minute treatise on the politics of the woman's body, with particular attention to the essentialist, heterosexist construction of woman as breeder. Passionately and at great length, she explained how patriarchy uses the myth of motherhood to phallically inscribe its text on the blank page of the womb, how penis can be read as pen/is, the very reification of the ontological claim of phallogocentrism, and how impossible it is to maintain one's credibility in an academic environment as a mother. She finished with a horrific story about a comatose pregnant woman whose husband kept her on life support just long enough to bear the child she was carrying. "Don't you see?" insisted Vita. "That woman was just a brood mare."

Vita's concern for the Rights of Women did not extend to the feelings of Bridget, brood mare of two, but Bridget took it in stride. After Vita had left, Bridget had explained to Nelson his mistake. "Vita doesn't want a child," she had said. "Vita wants a playmate."

Tonight the evening concluded with a long, energetic game of Monkey in the Middle. Vita insisted that she be the monkey, and she drove the two little girls to hysteria, pretending that the foam ball the girls tossed over her head was always just out of her reach. Bridget joined in, holding Abigail between her knees and helping her youngest daughter throw the ball higher. Clara leaped from side to side, snatching the ball out of the air just beyond Vita's grasp, jumping excitedly on the furniture.

Nelson excused himself to do the dishes. He watched through the kitchen doorway as Vita pretended to be unable to reach the ball. She can grab the prize anytime she wants to, he thought, anytime she works up the nerve. Not like me: It doesn't matter how high I reach, they just toss the ball higher. He attacked the pans in the sink roughly, scrubbing hard, furious at himself for the way he had bungled his approach to Professor Victorinix that afternoon. He had heard from neither Victorinix nor Linda Proserpina about the sections of 101, and now his injured finger, on which he had stupidly pinned his hopes, was gray and wrinkled in the hot water. A lot of good *you* did me, he thought. What a screwy fantasy, to think that my *magic touch,* for God's sake, would turn my life around.

"A man's reach should exceed his grasp," he muttered, up to his elbows in suds, his dead finger shriveling in the dishwater. "Or what's a heaven for?"

5

The Seminar Luncheon

In the morning, Linda Proserpina called and offered Nelson two sections of Composition 101 for the winter semester. She was eating as she spoke to him over the phone.

"Victoria sent a note down with Gillian," she said, smacking her lips, "twenty minutes after you left my office." She swallowed noisily. "I had to take the sections away from someone else."

Nelson caught his breath, his enormous relief briefly punctured by guilt.

"But that's not your problem." Linda sounded like her old self: dry, brittle, unimpressed. "I only follow orders. If Victoria says jump," she went on, and something crunched in Nelson's ear.

"Linda?" Nelson said.

Linda swallowed again. "Sorry," she said. "I quit smoking yesterday, and I can't stop eating."

She hung up, but Nelson stood a full minute longer with the phone in his hand. His finger felt numb. He tried to muster some feeling for the poor comp teacher who had lost her job so he could keep his, but all he could think was, *the finger works.*

Nelson tried calling Vita to tell her the good news, but heard only his own voice when the answering machine picked up. To disguise her gender, Vita was listed as "V. Deonne" in the phone book, even though Nelson had told her that every pervert and breather in the world knew that only women used their first initials. So to reinforce the disguise, she had asked Nelson to record the outgoing message on her machine. She brought the machine to their office rather than invite him to her apartment, and she told him what to say and how to say it. He recorded the message six times before she was happy. Now he listened to his own robotic and emotionless voice speaking Vita's phone number with no mention of her name.

"Leave a message after the beep," he heard himself say, and he answered himself jauntily.

"Vita!" he said. "I have some good news for a change! Please call me!"

But she did not call him, and she did not come to their office all that week. Nelson knew what the problem was: Vita was fretting about her appearance at the Seminar Luncheon. He knew that she was sitting in her apartment screening her calls, afraid to pick up the phone.

Late Sunday night, Nelson was at his computer, reading the on-line job postings in the *Chronicle of Higher Education* when a little beep announced an incoming e-mail. He clicked to a message from Vita.

"I'm terrified," it read. "The seminar is Wednesday. Anthony wants me dead. I'm terrified."

Isn't that just like Vita, Nelson thought, to turn a triumph into an ordeal? He would have killed for an invitation to present his work at one of the chairperson's monthly luncheons, or simply even to attend. The Seminar Luncheons, held on the third Wednesday of every month, offered the members of the department's elite the chance to shine, or gave someone promising a chance to demonstrate his or her worth. The luncheon was catered by Osterman's, Hamilton Groves' fashionable New York–style delicatessen. The Friday before the luncheon, the seminar's invitees were allowed to select a massive, expensive sandwich from the deli's precious, hand-lettered menu, to be paid for by the university. As a local celebrity, the chair had his own entry on the menu, the Anthony Pescecane "I Coulda Been a Contendah" roast beef sandwich, or the Contendah for short: a half-pound of extra-tender brisket and a slab of sharp cheddar, topped with horseradish and a thick slice of raw onion and lots of sinus-clearing English mustard, on the darkest, most pungent rye bread on the market. The chair described it as the very definition of lunch, according to Samuel Johnson—as much food as a man can hold in his hand—and the sort of sandwich Pescecane's stevedore father ate every weekday of his life on the New Jersey docks. Chairperson Pescecane's version was garnished with half a slice of crisp, raw cucumber, shaved like a shark's fin and stuck on edge in the back of the sandwich. Vita, Nelson knew, would order the cheapest thing on the menu—a side salad with no dressing—and then not eat it, rushing to the women's room afterward with the dry heaves. He sighed and lifted his hands to the keyboard to reply to her e-mail. His injured finger was beginning to burn a little.

"Are you permitted to bring a guest?" he wrote. "Perhaps it would help to have a friendly face in the room."

He sent the message. There was a thread of flame in his finger like a burning vein, and Nelson could no longer concentrate. Now that he had gotten what he wanted—his job back, his housing eligibility restored—he had hoped to ignore his injured finger. But the pain troubled him, so he shut off the computer and started upstairs in search of an ice cube to rub along it. The phone began to ring in the living room, and he took the steps two at a time, afraid the ringing might wake Bridget and the girls.

It was Vita. "But who could I ask?" she wailed as soon as Nelson picked up the phone. "I don't *have* any friends in the department."

Nelson's finger burned, but she was right. Certainly he scarcely counted as a colleague anymore, and Vita was even more right about her own standing in the department. She had not been the first choice for her position, but a compromise between Pescecane and Victorinix. As a result, Vita belonged in no one's camp. She continued to rise because neither Victorinix nor Pescecane could force the other to advance junior members of her or his own circle. Having suspected that Victorinix might actually be warming to Vita, perhaps Pescecane was now wooing her himself. Step by step, Vita was advancing to tenure by default.

At the moment she was pouring into Nelson's earpiece a torrent of woe that would have embarrassed Job. Her paper for the seminar had already been distributed, and she was convinced that the other luncheoneers were reading it *right this moment* and writing vicious marginalia in bold red ink. Nelson glanced at the kitchen clock; it was three o'clock in the morning.

"Vita, I don't think anybody's actually reading it at the moment," he said.

"What should I wear?" she wailed. "Anthony likes women who know how to play their gender roles"—a reference to Miranda DeLaTour—"so maybe I should wear a dress. But Victoria will be there! She'll think I'm pandering to Anthony!"

"Vita?" Nelson's finger burned. "Why don't we get together tomorrow and talk about this?"

"What should I eat?" Vita cried. "If I eat when I'm stressed, I get gas. But if I don't eat anything, my stomach rumbles."

"Vita, it's very late."

"Should I wear my glasses or my contacts? Heels or flats? Should I get my hair cut?"

"*Vita!*"

She caught her breath.

"If you can't think of anyone else to ask," Nelson said, "I'd be happy to come with you on Wednesday."

Vita's silence was charged. Nelson knew she was calculating the advantage of having someone she trusted in the room against the risk of admitting that the biggest loser in the department was her only friend.

"Think about it," Nelson said. "I have to go to sleep now, Vita. I have to be in class in five hours."

He listened a moment longer, heard nothing, and gently hung up the phone. The pain in his finger had receded, but it still bothered him enough to make him toss and turn in bed and threaten to wake Bridget. So he went back downstairs, shifted the gutted stuffed animals and stray Legos off the narrow, procrustean couch, and stretched out to sleep, his feet dangling off the end.

On Wednesday morning Nelson slogged to the bus stop through wet snow in leaky rubbers. He rode all the way to campus with freezing snow melt soaking into his shoes. Trotting along Michigan Avenue in the narrow track made by even earlier risers, he was thinking that *at least the weather has kept Fu Manchu out of sight* when a snowball slammed into the wall a foot from his head. He whirled, his finger flaring, and saw only secretaries in moon boots and comp teachers in thin coats tiptoeing through the slush. All morning his shoes squished with every step. Gillian glared at him as always at the ten o'clock class change, but today he glared back, his finger throbbing, until Gillian turned away. He managed to distract himself from Vita's problems by focusing on his classes that morning, where he gave his kids a choice of paper topics debating the pros and cons of the Middle Ages: Feudalism—blessing or curse? Chivalry—worth keeping or obsolete? Magna Carta—major advance or major mistake?

Fifteen minutes before the Seminar Luncheon was due to begin, Nelson sat in his office and opened his bag lunch—carrot sticks, raisins, a homemade brownie. The sandwich was one of last night's fishsticks between two slices of store-brand white bread smeared with cocktail sauce. He had splurged on a Coke from the lobby. He was sitting with the pop unopened and his lunch untouched on his desk when Vita burst breathlessly into the office.

"There you are!" She shut the door quickly and backed up against it as if someone were after her. "I've been looking all over for you!"

Vita had spruced up for the seminar. She'd decided on a dress and stockings, and Nelson thought she looked good, in a prim, spinster librarian sort of way. The dress was a muddy paisley that came to her calves, belted at the waist. It was buttoned up to her neck and down to her wrists, and she wore a scarf around her shoulders that made her look like a Girl Scout. He managed to avoid looking her up and down, but he noted that she had not cut her hair, that she was wearing her glasses, and that the heels of her shoes were neither flat nor high, but judiciously in between.

"Vita," he said, "you look very nice."

Vita caught her breath sharply. "What's wrong with it?"

"Nothing," insisted Nelson. "You look very professional."

"Is it the hair?" She brushed at her bangs.

"Vita, you look great." He glanced at his watch. "It's almost twelve, shouldn't you be . . ."

To Nelson's astonishment, Vita launched herself across the office and hauled him bodily out of his chair.

"You've got to come!" She clutched his arms; her voice trembled. "I couldn't find anybody else!"

Nelson bit his lip. Visions of a Contendah danced in his head.

"I can come for the first hour," he said. "I have a one o'clock class."

"You can't cancel it?"

"*Vita.*"

"Fine," snapped Vita, turning to the door. "Come for an hour then, if that's the best you can do."

She paused at the door. "You'd better bring your lunch," she said. "I didn't order you a sandwich."

Anthony Pescecane had come to academic superstardom by way of advertising. Though he had started out as a son of Hoboken, he had moonlighted during graduate school as a very successful copywriter on Madison Avenue. His work was admired for its swaggering, urban quality; his first big success had been a campaign for a vegetable oil spread that he had christened "I Can't Believe It's Not 'I Can't Believe It's Not Butter!' " His best-known campaign had been for a hamburger chain; his Clio-winning spot showed a brawny, ducktailed ethnic in

78

a tight T-shirt—looking a lot like the teenaged Anthony Pescecane—standing in coiled, working-class fury at the counter of the chain's competitor, nodding his head in barely contained rage at a hamburger the size of a half-dollar. "Call *that* a hamburger?" was the wildly successful catchphrase.

But Pescecane realized that even successful copywriters lived at the whim of the client, and in the academy he found an arena where his talent for words and the heedless momentum of his ambition could bring him absolute power. So while one generation of scholars fought a desperate rear-guard action on behalf of truth and beauty, and the next lacerated its own flesh with the thorny switches of French theory, Pescecane wrote a forcefully argued dissertation on Milton called *To Reign in Hell: The Will to Power in* Paradise Lost. *Pace* William Blake, Pescecane argued that Milton was really rooting for Satan, only the poet just couldn't admit it to himself. Satan, wrote Pescecane, was the best thing that ever happened to Adam and Eve. Adam was simply a bland suburban Baptist in polyester and Eve his drippy wife, and Satan represented rough trade for this bored couple, the swarthy Other full of mystery and erotic danger. God's grumpy pieties were a snooze, argued Pescecane; only Satan told the truth, which was that there is no justice, compassion, truth. There is only power. Appeals to moral authority do not settle questions; rather, in the struggle over moral questions, authority is won by the victor. "Better to reign in Hell than serve in Heaven," said Anthony Pescecane, was the truest line in *Paradise Lost.*

The junkyard collage of postmodernism and its utter lack of moral and polit- ical content were second nature to an advertising man, and Pescecane was a postmodern Pangloss, with a touch of the Elizabethan: "Why this is hell, nor am I out of it," wrote Marlowe, to which Pescecane added, why not make the best of it? The hegemonic world system is what it is, there is no outside to it, and so, as the only possible world, it is the *best* of all possible worlds. An advertising man understands even more viscerally than an academic that the world is made of discourse, Pescecane argued; he understands in his bones that true power resides in the infinite manipulability of signs. "Advertising is postmodernism as praxis," wrote Pescecane, and the fact that Milton did not understand that Satan was his true protagonist was reified in the mediocrity of *Paradise Regained,* and in the utter political collapse of the utopian revolution Milton had supported. It took an advertising man to free Milton's poem from Milton's own blindness.

"Indeed," wrote Anthony Pescecane, "in the most important sense, *I* am the author of *Paradise Lost."*

So by virtue of his own indomitable will and his gift for punchy salesmanship, Pescecane became a star of the profession and an influential public intellectual. His book *Screw Free Speech,* an aggressive defense of campus speech codes, led to appearances on *Charlie Rose* and *Politically Incorrect* whenever the subject was the culture wars or political correctness. In his Gucci suit and his silk tie, he sat across from Arianna Huffington and Dennis Miller and let America know what literary scholarship was all about at the turn of the millennium.

"It's not about truth anymore, Bill," he'd say, making it pithy. "It's not about beauty. It's about the etiology of *powah,*" he concluded, inflecting the word the way they did back in Hoboken.

As the elevator doors opened to the eighth floor, Vita gestured for Nelson to keep back while she peered down the empty hallway. The coast seemed clear, so Vita and Nelson tread silently down the carpet. Vita didn't know what to do with her hands. She wrung them, she dropped them to her sides, she clasped them before her like a novitiate on her way to see the mother superior. Nelson didn't know what to do with his lunch, which was wrapped in a crackling plastic bag from the supermarket. He shifted it from one hand to the other in a futile attempt to find a dignified way of carrying it. With the bag swinging awkwardly from his hand, he followed Vita as she squared her shoulders and marched into the seminar room.

One of Pescecane's first acts as chair was to have the department's seminar room remodeled at great expense. Formerly the decor had been Formica under Fluorescent Light, but now the room was paneled with dark oak wainscoting like a solicitor's office out of Trollope, and furnished with a long, oaken table lined with stout, leather-upholstered chairs that filled the room from end to end. Eighteenth-century portraits of wealthy directors of the East India Company lined the walls, on permanent loan from the university art museum. The men in the portraits were shameless slave traders and colonialists, but Chairperson Pescecane couldn't help but admire their drive and their managerial expertise.

Vita and Nelson were the first to arrive, except for the delivery guy from Osterman's, a wiry postadolescent with a shaved head and a ring through his eyebrow. Vita froze at the sight of him laying out the sandwiches, and Nelson nearly ran into her. The kid grinned at them over his shoulder and finished stacking the wrapped sandwiches on a silver tray on the oaken sideboard.

"Dig in," he said. He stepped back for a running start, and then dived onto the table, gliding down the polished surface on his chest. Vita lurched into a corner and pulled Nelson in front of her. At the end of the table near the door the kid somersaulted off and landed on his feet.

"My time among you is through." He bounced on the balls of his feet. "And now I take my leave." He did a cartwheel out the door and down the hall.

"Oh, my God," whimpered Vita, behind Nelson. She sagged into a seat along the wall, under the darkened portrait of some periwigged colonialist. Nelson sat down next to her and pushed his lunch bag under his chair with his foot.

"Do you want something to drink?" he said. Vita shook her head, but he rose anyway and walked around the table to the sideboard. There was a silver urn each of tea and coffee, but he poured Vita a glass of ice water from a cut-glass carafe. He paused to survey the artful stack of sandwiches in their paper wrappers, each labeled with a pair of initials in felt tip marker. AP was right on the top, and Nelson glanced toward the door and lifted the edge of it to see who was underneath.

"Nelson!" hissed Vita. "Don't you dare!"

"I'm just counting them," he whispered back, "so we can see how many people are coming."

He hefted one of the sandwiches. It was warm, and it weighed more than Nelson's entire lunch. Without warning, Nelson's finger turned to flame. Vita made a sort of strangled cry, and Nelson, still holding the sandwich, turned to see Morton Weissmann and the Lost Boys slide into the room. Weissmann wore his widest, most collegial smile. He clutched Vita's paper rolled up in his left hand and offered her his right as he angled around the table.

"My dear!" he cried. Vita jerked her hand up to meet his. She smiled desperately. The Lost Boys pulled up short at the sight of Nelson, and Weissmann stopped just out of Vita's reach. He turned to see Nelson across the table, hefting a sandwich that didn't belong to him.

"Uh-oh," said Dan.

"Him again," said Vic.

"Bad penny," said Bob.

Weissmann opened his mouth and closed it again. Then he turned to Vita and grasped her hand, which was trembling in the air.

"My dear." He held her hand much too long. "I'm so looking forward to today's luncheon. A *fascinating* essay. Though I believe you call them 'interventions' these days, isn't that right?"

Vita squeaked, and tightened her smile. Under the blank gaze of the Lost

81

Boys, Nelson smiled weakly and set the sandwich back on the stack, giving it a little pat.

"Yes, well." Nelson backed the long way around the table. "Vita, perhaps I ought to go."

But Nelson's exit was blocked as Marko Kraljević and Lorraine Alsace came into the doorway arm in arm. Professor Alsace, as always, wore a long print skirt and a baggy cableknit sweater, but today Professor Kraljević was favoring his Hong Kong action star look, with a loose, shiny silk suit, a cotton T-shirt, and a pair of flat black slippers. Alsace was nearly a head taller, and she clutched him tightly, nuzzling her cheek against the stubble of his close-cropped hair. Lorraine was not even tenure track and had no right to be here, but no one was liable to tell that to Kraljević this morning. Nelson glanced at Vita, to see if she noticed their arrival. If a tenured position were to open, Lorraine Alsace would be Vita's chief rival. But at the moment, Vita sat with her eyes squeezed shut. Together the two theorists sauntered to the sideboard, each picking up a sandwich without reading the label.

Nelson edged toward the door again, but now he ran into Penelope O, a petite, high-strung Brit who was the Hugh M. Hefner Chair in Sexuality Studies. She had been hired, and the chair endowed, as it were, on the basis of her book *Reading with My Pussy: I Gang-Bang the Canon,* which featured her fantasies of sex with famous canonical authors—adopting the missionary position with Rudyard Kipling, enjoying mutual cunnilingus with Virginia Woolf, letting Plato do her doggy style like a boy. As a result, all over North America, young academics were doing "pussy readings" of canonical authors, dragging hapless dead authors into increasingly elaborate fantasies: fisting Henry James; Emily Dickinson in leather; and three-ways between W. H. Auden, Ernest Hemingway, and Edna St. Vincent Millay.

Penelope O often had one of her undergraduates in tow, some beautiful boy or girl, but today she was alone, in three-inch heels, patterned black leggings, and an off-the-shoulder sweater that revealed a lacy black strap over her pale, bony shoulder. She seemed to live on cigarettes and coffee, and the air around her vibrated at the wavelength of nicotine. The Lost Boys took one look at her and stepped back against the wall at the end of the table, wheeling out of her way with drill team precision. Professor O looked Nelson up and down, and then stepped up briskly to Weissmann and offered her hand.

"Morton," she said, in her brittle accent, "how lovely to see you."

"Your servant, Penelope," said Weissmann, half again as tall and nearly twice as big. He took her hand in both of his and dipped his head. On every basis imaginable—cultural, ideological, sexual—they loathed each other.

At last Nelson saw an opportunity for escape. But as he edged past Vita, she dug her fingers painfully into his forearm and dragged him into the seat next to her. She was still smiling desperately, though no one was paying her the slightest attention. He offered her the glass of water he was carrying, but she didn't even see it. He drank it off himself in one long gulp.

Stephen Michael Stephens slouched in, looking stylish but exhausted. Behind him were the Coogan and the Canadian Lady Novelist, to Nelson's surprise: The creative writing faculty were almost never invited to functions like the Seminar Luncheon; it was considered embarrassing to have living writers in the room whenever literature was being discussed. The Coogan, at least, made the most of it. Under the novelist's maternal glower, he made a beeline for the sandwiches, trailing the scent of Bushmills.

Through the press of glad-handing just inside the door, Nelson glimpsed Miranda DeLaTour standing very still in the hall, clutching her hands before her with her eyes closed like an actress preparing for her entrance. She was from the comparative literature side of the department, where, Nelson had heard, she was sometimes referred to as a vulture. Nelson had a hard time seeing such a beautiful woman as a carrion bird, but she was known for appropriating the insights of other, less flamboyant scholars and making them distinctively her own. Her latest project was her attempt to demolish brick by brick the reputation of Franz Kafka, condemning him as sexist and derivative; "Kafka understood cockroaches," she had famously written in a paper published in *Clitor/is,* "because he *was* a cock-roach." Still, she was best known around the department for her stunning presence; today she wore a tight, green velvet jacket and a miniskirt and little suede boots. As Nelson watched, she opened her eyes, and her countenance brightened suddenly as if she had switched herself on. She stepped into the room blinking prettily, waiting for someone to notice her.

Weissmann straightened his sagging shoulders and spread his large hands wide. "Miranda," he intoned, drawing everyone's glance to her.

She tilted her head and lifted her chin. "Morton!" she said with bright insincerity. "I hadn't known you were coming today." Miranda spoke with the plummy, charm school graciousness of a thirties movie star, Claudette Colbert on the tenure track.

Weissmann raised a finger to his lips. "Well, you know," he said in a loud stage whisper, "I wasn't actually invited, but I couldn't keep away. So mum's the word."

The next to last to arrive was Professor Victorinix, who slipped in as silvery and silent as a ghost, her eyes hidden behind the dark round discs of her sunglasses. She nodded briskly to everyone as she came in and started along the table. She stopped short when her blank gaze met Nelson's. His finger throbbed, and he was on the verge of rising from his chair. Then she looked away and walked along the far side of the table, taking a seat near the head. Nelson glanced at Vita; she was gazing into her lap and tearing fiercely at her fingernails.

Finally Chairperson Pescecane swept into the room, his blunt chin lifted. His leonine sweep of black hair was carefully coiffed; his trousers broke just so over his handmade shoes. He was not wearing his suit jacket, but the sleeves of his shirt were rolled down; he wore gold cufflinks and a gold tiepin and another gold pin holding the tabs of his collar together. He trailed the scent of a musky cologne. At his heels was his pop-eyed assistant, Lionel Grossmaul, whose own clothes, a shirt a size too small and a pair of polyester blend slacks, unfortunately emphasized the steep slope of his shoulders and the breadth of his backside. He trotted in the chair's wake like a particularly annoying little dog, carrying a pen and a notepad in his tight grip.

Pescecane settled into his chair at the head of the table, under the portrait of a director of the East India Company preening in his silk breeches and stockings, one hand poised on the golden lion's head of an ebony cane. The chairperson began a whispered conversation with Professor Victorinix at his right hand, while Lionel stood behind Pescecane and surveyed the room with his lighthouse glare. His bug-eyed gaze fell across Nelson, then shifted balefully to the Lost Boys, who stood with their backs pressed to the wall at the far end of the room. Weissmann, meanwhile, having let his beefy hands trail lightly down Miranda's back as he took his leave of her, settled heavily in the chair at the far end of the table. Lionel stooped over Pescecane and waited until the chairperson had finished his exchange with Victorinix, then he whispered something in Pescecane's ear. Pescecane leaned back, one hand poised on the armrest of his chair, the other resting lightly on the table, fingers curled.

"So, Mort." His voice cut through the murmur around the table. "The fuck are you doing here?"

The small talk halted, though people continued to unwrap their sandwiches.

All eyes turned down the table, where Weissmann sat back in his chair smiling, his hands folded loosely on the table.

"A fair cop, guvnor," he said brightly. "It's just that a copy of Vita's paper—may I call you Vita, my dear?—a copy of her fascinating essay came into my hands and I couldn't help myself. I simply had to come." He leaned forward and whispered loudly. "I'll be as quiet as a mouse."

"Want a sandwich?" Pescecane lifted a thick eyebrow.

"I've eaten, thank you." Weissmann spread his hands. "Please, all of you, enjoy your luncheon. Don't mind me. Really, my good friends, you won't even know I'm here."

"I already know you're here," Pescecane said.

Everyone along the table shifted their gaze back and forth between the two men, except for Professor Victorinix, who folded her hands in her lap and gazed through her sunglasses at the table before her. She wasn't eating anything; her lunch consisted of a small glass of blood-red tomato juice. From his angle behind her and to the side, she looked to Nelson as if she were meditating.

Pescecane tilted his head toward his assistant. "Give him a sandwich," he said.

Lionel, glowering, left his station behind Pescecane's seat and went around the table to pick through the remaining sandwiches.

"Really, Anthony," Weissmann said, "that won't be necessary."

"Give him mine." Pescecane smiled down the table at Weissmann.

Lionel lifted a large sandwich—a Pescecane Contendah, Nelson noticed—and sent it sliding like a hockey puck down the length of the table. Weissmann lifted one palm and stopped it as deftly as a goalie.

"You're too kind, Anthony, but I'm really not hungry."

He pushed the hulking sandwich to one side. The Lost Boys leaned forward along the wall behind Weissmann, their eyes wide.

"Look at that," said Dan.

"That's big," said Vic.

"Whoa, momma," said Bob.

Weissmann shot them a sidelong glance, and they snapped back against the wall.

All eyes swiveled back to Pescecane, who sat absolutely still, saying nothing. Nelson had the impression of hoodlum rage, Robert De Niro beating some minion to death with a baseball bat, but at last Pescecane smiled and glanced about the room. "So," he said, "who's the entertainment this afternoon?"

Vita sat bolt upright, her eyes wide with alarm. She looked as though she'd been shot through with electricity. There was a ripple of laughter around the table, but the object of the joke didn't get it. Nelson touched her on the wrist and felt her terror as if it was his own. He had a vivid image of Vita leaping out of a cake wearing her glasses, a Girl Scout scarf, and nothing else.

"Vita," Pescecane said with a seignorial pity, "don't be a wallflower. Come sit up here where we can see you."

Pescecane gestured to the chair at his left, where Lionel was sitting. Lionel rose immediately, his face red, and stepped backward to one of the chairs along the wall. Across the room Vita shot to her feet, smoothed down her skirt twice, then marched ramrod straight around the table to take the seat next to Pescecane. All around the table people were masticating with varying degrees of savoir-faire: Penelope O was stabbing at her salad with a plastic fork, briskly eating little mouthfuls, looking alertly around the room. The Coogan had brought a silver saltshaker with him to the table from the sideboard, and he opened up his massive corned beef sandwich and coated each layer of meat in salt. He took massive bites, chewing openmouthed like a ruminant. Professors Kraljević and Alsace sat nearly in each other's laps. They were deconstructing their sandwiches, taking them apart and popping pieces of turkey breast and pastrami into each other's mouths like newlyweds, licking smears of mayonnaise and mustard off each other's fingers, ignoring all the while the sour glances of Stephen Michael Stephens and Lionel Grossmaul, whose sandwiches they had taken. The Canadian Lady Novelist was eating, with great delicacy, a club sandwich neatly cut in four. Miranda ate nothing, but sat back in her chair looking bored, twirling a raven curl of her hair around her slender finger.

"Vita," Pescecane said, "we've all read your paper, but why don't you start us off with a few remarks?"

"Yes." Professor Victorinix roused herself from her private study. She took off her sunglasses and lowered them into her lap, and she lifted her head to level her cool gray eyes at Vita directly across the table. "Why don't you tell us what led you to the lesbian phallus?"

Professor Weissmann sighed heavily and lifted his eyes. Behind him the Lost Boys bit their lips and turned red in the face, struggling not to laugh out loud. Nelson was close enough to hear them whispering to each other.

"A seminal work," said Vic.

"A penetrating study," said Bob.

"The thrust of her argument," said Dan.

Nelson's finger burned, and he wanted to go make them be quiet. Vita hadn't even noticed; she was quailing under the icy gaze of Professor Victorinix. With her primary interest in feminist theory, Vita should have been welcome in Victorinix's camp, but there had been some sort of incident not long after Vita arrived at Midwest. Vita had never told Nelson the details, or even the names of the parties involved. All he could gather was that there had been an approach of an intimate nature that had caused a paralyzing panic in Vita and bristling embarrassment in whoever had approached her. Nelson wasn't sure if Victorinix had been personally involved, but ever since, Vita had been treated coolly by the other feminist theorists in the department. Nelson guessed that they were dumbfounded, as he was, at how someone could write so graphically about sexuality and yet have no apparent desire for the act itself. Nelson could only conclude that Vita's excavation—her "archaeology," as she called it—of every variety of sex known to man, woman, and everything in between was intended to render all sex, even the most common practices, equally disgusting.

Now Vita drew herself up to begin, and Nelson tensed himself. Her habit of speaking mostly in questions was exacerbated when she spoke as a scholar; it was worst of all in her prose, in which Nelson often searched for pages at a time for a straightforward declarative sentence. After wading through the thickets of Isn't-it-the-case's and Could-we-not-assume-that's, Nelson would often make the mistake of asking Vita exactly what she'd intended to say.

"So gender is a kind of playacting?" he had asked her once. "We're all in drag?"

"No, no, *no!*" Vita had cried. "You don't understand at all! That's a gross oversimplification!" This outburst had culminated in a rather huffy exhortation to review, if he hadn't already, all the sources cited in her bibliography, and then to read her article again more carefully. Nelson, trying to be clever, dredged his memory of Professor Evangeline's literary theory class at Sooey and quoted Adorno's critique of Heidegger to Vita, that "he lays around himself the taboo that any understanding would simultaneously be falsification." But Vita only flattened him with another Adorno quote, that "retention of strangeness is the only antidote to estrangement."

"So I can only understand your argument if I don't understand it?" Nelson had said, trying to understand.

"You're missing the point," Vita had said, as if to a child. "If you agree with my analysis, then you understand."

"What if I *understand* but I don't *agree?*"

"That's not possible." Vita had reached the peak of her exasperation. Nelson could tell because she spoke in declarative sentences.

"If you understand, you'll agree," she had said. "If you don't agree, then you don't understand."

So Nelson had tried reading her article again, but the jargon pulled at his ankles like swamp mud, and the question marks bristled at him like scythes waved by angry villagers. Indeed, her ability to retreat into the infinite regress of "That's not what I meant" and claim that the reader was too patriarchal or too phallogocentric or just plain too stupid to follow her argument was Vita's main defense as a scholar. But Nelson knew that she couldn't play that game here, at the Seminar Luncheon, and he clutched the arms of his chair tightly to brace himself for Vita's humiliation. Vita herself drew a deep breath.

"Could we not say," she said, scarcely breathing out, "that whenever one considers the phallus, one naturally begins with Lacan, by way of Butler?"

"Naturellement," murmured Weissmann, just loud enough to be heard. Behind him the Lost Boys, slouching against the wall, nearly doubled over with repressed mirth.

"Mais oui," said Dan.

"Certainement," said Bob.

"But of course," said Vic.

"Believe it or not, I've heard of Lacan," said Weissmann, his eyes focused on the ceiling, "but who is this fellow Butler when he's at home?"

"She, Morton," snapped Penelope O. "When *she's* at home." She addressed Pescecane at the far end of the table. "Even my undergraduates know Judith Butler as the discoverer of the lesbian phallus."

"Discoverer?" Weissmann's eyes widened. "She discovered it as one might discover the source of the Nile?"

"No," said Penelope, still not looking at Weissmann. "More like Cleopatra's Needle."

A murmur of laughter relieved the tension. Weissmann inclined his head, as if to say, touché. Miranda blinked her long lashes and pursed her lips. Lionel Grossmaul, who hovered tensely even when he was seated, glanced at Pescecane; but the chair merely tightened his smile, and Lionel, after looking daggers at

Weissmann, settled back slightly in his seat. Vita continued as if she hadn't heard. She was too busy fighting off the relentless gaze of Professor Victorinix from across the table.

"Isn't it the case," Vita went on, "that Lacan positions the phallus as a privileged signifier, that is to say, as the structuring and centering principle of muh, muh, 'man's' "—Vita gestured quotation marks with her fingers—"epistemological relation to the 'world'?" She made the quotation marks again. "And doesn't Lacan narrate the phallus not as an anatomical puh, penis, nor as an imaginary relation, but as the ordering principle of the symbolic, by which, during the mirror stage, the decentered buh, 'body' is transformed morphologically into the specular buh, buh, 'body'?"

Vita's hands, bent into little two-fingered claws for indicating quotes, hung self-consciously in the air until she whisked them under the table. Nelson shifted in his seat; he could tell that Vita was losing her nerve. He glanced about the table. Stephen Michael Stephens was grimly chewing the sandwich he'd ended up with. The Canadian Lady Novelist was beaming motherly support at Vita, but she was on the same side of the table, and Vita couldn't see it. The Coogan was like a rugby player at a dinner party, smacking his lips and licking his fingers. Miranda continued to twirl a length of her glossy hair around her finger, gazing into the distance as if regarding herself in a mirror. Waiting for Vita to continue, Penelope O nodded slowly, while Weissmann silently drummed his fingers on the table. Lorraine Alsace, her thigh pressed against Marko Kraljević's, made a great show of eating a kosher dill pickle from one end to the other, nibble by nibble, while Kraljević pursed his lips lubriciously.

"Isn't it possible," Vita resumed, "considered from a position of radical and enforced alterity, that this use of the phuh, phuh, phallus is unsatisfactory?"

"The phallus often is," Professor Victorinix said evenly.

"Speak for yoursewf, Victowia," said Alsace, popping the last of the pickle between her lips. She let her hand drop into the lap of Professor Kraljević, who started violently.

There was subdued mirth about the table; Pescecane limited himself to a vulpine smile, while Weissmann laughed loudly and insincerely. Vita blushed. Nelson shifted in his seat again, wondering if he was the only man in the room with the urge to cross his legs.

The Coogan swallowed and paused in his attack on his sandwich. "Jaysus, Mary, and Joseph," he said. "Are yez after talkin' about what I think you're talkin' about?" His accent sounded like Sean O'Casey read aloud by Scotty from *Star Trek.*

"Indeed, my friend," said Weissmann, "I believe it gets more interesting." He smiled down the table to Vita. "Or should I say, more pointed?"

Weissmann acted as if he were running the seminar, and at the far end of the table Pescecane's smile tightened. Along the paneled wall Lionel wrote something furiously on his notepad, glancing heatedly at Weissmann. Vita went bravely on, her voice quavering.

"Is it possible that Butler's conception of the lesbian phuh, phallus," she said, looking anxiously about, everywhere but at Professor Victorinix, "represents an intervention against the valorization of the phuh, phuh, phallus as the central structuring metaphor of the semiological schema? Couldn't we read it as a sort of critical miming of the hegemonic pah, patriarchal phallus, reifying the contradictions inherent in . . . ?"

Weissmann rather theatrically cleared his throat, covering his mouth with his fist, and the Lost Boys erupted in a fit of coughing. Once again Penelope O shot Weissmann an angry glance, and Pescecane pointed his blunt chin down the table at him. Victorinix did not shift her penetrating gaze from Vita.

"If I may," Weissmann said through his fist, with mock sheepishness.

"Got a question, Mort?" Pescecane said.

"Perhaps it's not my place," said Weissmann.

"Mort's got a question, everybody," Pescecane said.

"I don't mean to interrupt." Weissmann spread his large, pale hands.

"Ask the fuckin' question," Pescecane said.

The seminar participants shifted in their chairs and murmured; something was unsettled in the room, like the surface of a pond when something is about to come up from below. No one said anything, but Lionel looked as if he were about to launch himself out of his chair and across the table.

"You may all rest easy," Weissmann said, pursing his lips in a smile. "I am not going to belabor the obvious, to wit, what does the lesbian phallus, whatever that may or may not be, have to do with Dorian Gray, let alone with poor, old, sainted Oscar Wilde. Indeed, it might surprise you to know, I have a *theoretical* question."

There was more murmuring. Penelope O twisted in her chair and glanced sharply at Pescecane, as if imploring him to do something. But he ignored her, keeping his gaze leveled at Weissmann at the far end of the table.

"My dear." Weissmann turned to Vita. "I may call you that, mayn't I?"

Vita stammered something, and Weissmann smiled.

"I am not quite as unsophisticated and old-fashioned as you might think," he said, with warm insincerity. "I am not entirely a babe in the woods, 'theory' wise." He mimicked Vita's air quotation marks. "Indeed, I might be said to appreciate the, ah, meat of your argument, so to speak, to follow the, um, the ins and outs of it, as it were."

He worked his lips to keep from laughing. Behind him the Lost Boys looked at the ceiling. No one else in the room laughed. Vita blushed bright red.

"But be that as it may," Weissmann went on, "I was simply wondering . . . well, it's a sort of foundational question I have, an inquiry into first principles, as it were."

Penelope O gave Pescecane another long, meaningful look down the table. Alsace murmured something rapidly into Kraljević's tufted ear, punctuating her remarks with little licks of her long, pointed tongue. Stephen Michael Stephens yawned mightily. Lionel glowered murderously at Weissmann, clutching his pen in his fist like a dirk. Vita painfully maintained an expression of eager attentiveness; she looked as if she expected someone to hit her.

Weissmann licked his finger and paged through Vita's paper as he talked, smiling down the table at her.

"If," he said, "as you seem to take for granted, gender is a sort of performance, if, indeed, 'materiality' itself, by which I assume you mean one's physical existence, is some sort of linguistic construction . . ."

Kraljević swung his piercing eyes to Weissmann and growled in his throat like a wolfhound. Even Professor Victorinix sighed and closed her eyes.

"My question is simply this," insisted Weissmann loudly, scoring the air energetically with quotation marks. "If everything is 'constructed,' if there is nothing 'essential' about 'gender,' or indeed about our actual physical 'bodies,' then who's to say that any particular 'construction' is better than any other?"

There was a wordless groan around the table.

"Do you have to do this every time, Mort?" said Professor Victorinix.

"Christ, Mort," snapped Penelope O, "that's the sort of stupid question my undergraduates ask me."

"I'm friggin' lost," said the Coogan. "Are we still after talkin' about penises?"

"Perhaps," insisted Weissmann over the hubbub, "perhaps if we let the author simply answer the question . . ."

Alone among the people in the room, Nelson watched Vita's reaction. She followed the conversational ball wherever it bounced with a hopeful expression, hoping that it wouldn't end up again in her lap. She was reprieved for the moment from the gaze of Professor Victorinix, who was leaning across the corner of the table in urgent conference with Chairperson Pescecane. Alsace nuzzled Kraljević, stroking his thigh as he breathed angrily through his flared nostrils. Stephen Michael Stephens sat with his head propped in his hand, his eyes blinking as he struggled to stay awake. Against the wall Lionel was writing so violently that Nelson could hear the rapid tap of pen against notepad. The Lost Boys were glancing at each other and eyeing the door.

"I have a question," declared Penelope, "one that is rather more to the point."

"I believe, *Professor O*," Weissmann insisted, "that I have the floor."

"What about *jouissance?*" Penelope asked, ignoring him. She leaned across the table and caught Vita's eye, giving her a sisterly smile. "Vita, I'm not sure you are entirely clear about its infinite displacement as language."

A silence fell, and everyone turned to Vita. She opened her mouth and gasped, mortified to be the center of attention again.

"That's a good question," said Pescecane, settling back in his chair as Professor Victorinix settled back into hers. "Dontcha think that's a good question, Mort?"

Weissmann, his face flushed red, dipped his head.

Penelope smiled again across the table at Vita and asked urgently, "What about *jouissance,* Vita?"

Vita's mouth opened and closed, and Nelson felt his finger burn. This very situation was at the heart of his ambition as an intellectual, his desire to bridge the gap between the Weissmanns and the Vitas of the academic world. He was cursed with the liberal's ability to see every side of every argument, and he wanted to step in like some sort of jet-set peacemaker, the Jesse Jackson of the seminar room, and get each side at least to shake hands with the other.

"Well, *jouissance* is problematical for me," Vita managed to say. "I've been struggling with *jouissance.*"

"*Hah!*" cried Kraljević, startling everyone. He was sitting bolt upright in his chair, his eyes rolled white in their deep sockets. Alsace smiled knowingly, lifting her hand out of his lap.

"While you've been stwuggling with *jouissance,*" she said, "some of us have been enjoying it."

"If we could get back to *my* question," Weissmann said.

Several conversations were in progress at once, and Nelson detected something riotous in the air; he half-expected to see chairs thrown at any moment or at least pieces of food. His finger burned with his desire to enforce a little collegial decorum, and he looked down the table at Pescecane, shocked at the chair's lack of control over the situation. This was the man, after all, who had once been quoted in *The New York Times Magazine*—in an article titled "Anthony Pescecane Has a Cold"—as saying that "the finest thing in life is to take an academic department and bend it to one's will." Now he sat back with his legs crossed and his hands draped over the carven arms of his chair, and it wasn't until Nelson saw the light in his eye and the smile playing about Pescecane's lips that he realized that the chair was *enjoying* this. A voice in Nelson's head said, "Havoc and spoil and ruin are my gain."

Somehow Vita had found her voice again.

"Is the claim that reality is luh, luh, linguistic re, reductive?" she stammered. "Is it not possible that you cannot separate discursive practice from the sed, sed, sedimented production of materiality?"

" 'We are such stuff as dreams are made of,' " said Weissmann slyly. "Is that it, my dear?"

"Yes!" gasped Vita. Then she blinked and said, "No! I mean . . ."

"Anthony," said Penelope loudly, "can't you see what Morton is doing? There's a sort of rape in progress here . . ."

"A *rape?*" said Weissmann. "Is the lesbian phallus up to the job?"

"Bloody hell!" Penelope whirled on Weissmann. "What's your bloody problem, mate? Zeitgeist passed you by?"

"Oh-ho!" cried Weissmann, and suddenly everyone was talking at once—Penelope, Weissmann, Victorinix, Alsace—everyone, that is, but Vita, who had gone white, and Stephen Michael Stephens, who was deeply asleep in his chair, his head canted over his shoulder. Across the table from Nelson, Lionel Grossmaul looked like a pit bull strangling itself at the end of its chain; he gripped the arms of his chair so hard he looked as though he might wrench them free. Nelson's own finger burned, and he winced against the pain, shoving his hand into his armpit.

"Alright, alright." Pescecane lifted his palm majestically. "Calm the fuck down."

Suddenly the Coogan slammed his palm against the table. "Balls!" he shouted, startling everyone to silence.

"Balls!" he cried again, pushing himself unsteadily to his feet, drawing the gaze of everyone in the room. He was a big fellow who wore faded jeans a size too small, a denim workshirt, and a leather vest, haut couture for poets, circa 1975.

"We're a fuckin' English department, aren't we?" cried the Coogan. "So what's all this shite about penises, and what's it got to do with literature?"

He wobbled in place from side to side, clenching and unclenching his fists, ready for a shindy. Miranda, on one side of him, pushed back her mane of hair and regarded him warily, while on the other side of him, the Canadian Lady Novelist touched his arm and cooed soothingly. Stephen Michael Stephens had started awake at the noise, and he blinked wide-eyed around the room with the bright gaze of Lieutenant Lawrence surveying the Turkish defenses at Aqaba.

"Oh, sit down, you silly bugger," said Penelope, directly across the table.

"Listen, you mad cow." The Coogan flinched away from the novelist and poked a thick finger at Penelope. "Since when did you have anything useful to say on the subject of penises?"

"Since when did you have one worth talking about?" said Penelope.

"If you were a man," he said, turning red, "I'd ask you to step outside."

"If you were a man," said Penelope O, "I would."

"That's it!" The Coogan put one knee on the tabletop, while the Canadian Lady Novelist clung to him with both hands, murmuring, "Timothy dear, *please* behave."

Suddenly Stephen Michael Stephens was on his feet, shoulders squared, hands quivering, eyes blazing as bright as the Arabian sun at noon.

"Sherif Ali," he said in a whispery, quavering voice, "so long as the Arabs fight, tribe against tribe, so long will they be a little people, a silly people, greedy, barbarous, and cruel."

He swiveled his angry gaze across the table to the Coogan, and added vehemently, "As *you* are."

Roaring wordlessly like a Celtic berserker, the Coogan wrenched free of the Canadian Lady Novelist and clambered up onto the table. Penelope O reared back wide-eyed in her seat, and Weissmann struggled to get out of his chair. Stephen Michael Stephens fairly quivered. The Lost Boys pressed themselves even harder against the wall. Miranda slipped out of her seat to the doorway. The Coogan swayed above them all, balling his fists and roaring like a bull. No one else moved, no one else breathed. No one, that is, except Professor Kraljević, who sprang suddenly to the tabletop in his elegant black slippers and began to pirouette slowly in a series of martial arts moves, making enigmatic gestures with his palms.

"You must give me *face*," he growled, and suddenly, faster than Nelson's eye could register, Kraljević's foot lashed out in a shoulder-high kick that caught the Coogan along the side of the head and dropped him to the table like a sack of malt barley.

In the aftershock of this moment no one spoke, all eyes on Kraljević. He stood hunched with his head lowered, his eyes squeezed shut, his palms pressed tightly together. He drew a deep breath, held it, and let it out slowly. Then he opened his eyes, stepped over the Coogan in the middle of the table, and leveled his gaze at Weissmann. The Lost Boys clutched each other, knocking one of the portraits askew. Weissmann himself was half out of his chair, his hands pressed to the tabletop.

Kraljević suddenly lifted his left hand in a gesture like a benediction, and Weissmann froze. Kraljević reached inside his silk jacket, pulled out a slim, pearl-handled object, and raised it as high as his ear. Nelson's finger burned, but he couldn't move. There was a sharp click, a blade sprang out of the handle, and with lightning speed Kraljević flung the switchblade into the table at his feet. The knife quivered back and forth, a foot or two from Weissmann.

"Thus I refute logocentrism," said Kraljević.

The Lost Boys jumped a foot off the ground and bolted from the room, banging the door. Weissmann sagged into his seat and sighed. Kraljević stooped quickly, plucked his knife out of the table, and turned away.

Everyone breathed out again, and for a moment everything happened at once. The Canadian Lady Novelist, her face a mask of pained compassion, came around the table and shook awake Stephen Michael Stephens, who had begun to doze in his chair again, and together they hoisted the Coogan by his armpits and dragged him off the table and out of the room. Penelope trotted out after them with quick little steps. Lorraine Alsace rose slowly from her chair, her thick glasses steamed up. She removed them and gazed up at Kraljević, her curiously diminished eyes brimming with tears.

"*Schatz!*" she breathed.

"*Mon amour!*" replied Kraljević, springing lightly to the carpet. They exchanged a long, moist, openmouthed kiss; Kraljević murmured something guttural in her long white ear, and she beamed. They hurried from the room, clutching each other tightly.

Nelson's finger was reduced to a dull ache. Weissmann slumped in his chair, drumming his fingers, staring pensively at the knife cut in the tabletop. Lionel was furiously writing on his notepad. Victorinix had replaced her sunglasses, and she and Pescecane passed along the far side of the table and out the door, murmuring to each other. As the chair stepped out the door, the light went out in Miranda's face. Weissmann blinked at her, and Nelson could see the effort in his old mentor's face as he tried to muster his wit.

"O brave new world," Weissmann said, managing a feeble smile, "that has such people in it."

"Tis new to you, Mort," said Miranda, and she wheeled elegantly on her sharp heel and passed out the door, the backs of her thighs flashing. Weissmann sagged again, looking old, and he put his spotted hands on the arms of his chair and pushed himself wearily up. He turned his head slightly, and Nelson thought Weissmann was actually going to say something to him. The pain in Nelson's finger returned at full force. He wasn't sure what he'd say if Weissmann spoke to him. But Weissmann sighed and slouched out of the conference room without saying anything.

Vita was nowhere to be seen, and Nelson bent to look under the table. She wasn't there. He sat up to find himself fixed in the pop-eyed glare of Lionel Grossmaul, who stood across the table, clutching his notepad tightly.

"Your friend fucked up," said Lionel, swallowing his words.

"She didn't really get a chance to . . ." Nelson began.

"She got more of a chance than most people do." Lionel made as if to lunge across the table at Nelson, but he came up against his invisible chain. "Some people would kill for a chance to present a paper in front of Anthony Pescecane."

And I'm one of them, Nelson thought, his finger searing him, but he didn't say it. He knew Lionel didn't mean him anyway; the story went that Grossmaul and Pescecane had actually been peers in graduate school together, and that Grossmaul had even been considered the more incisive theorist. The rumor was, in fact, that Lionel Grossmaul had taught Pescecane everything he knew about theory. But Grossmaul's complete lack of personal appeal had been exacerbated by a crippling and unending case of writer's block when the time came to write his dissertation, and he fell into a vicious spiral, the nightmare of any academic: The more frustrated he felt in his attempts to write, the angrier he became; and

96

the angrier he became, the harder it was for him to write. In the end, he had never published so much as a paper in a journal, and his career, such as it was, consisted entirely in following his grad school friend from triumph to triumph in a series of dead-end administrative jobs.

Nelson said nothing.

"What's that under your chair?" Lionel said in his strangled voice.

Nelson reached under his chair and pulled up the plastic bag with his sorry meal in it.

"My lunch," he said.

"Take it with you when you go," Lionel said, and he went to the end of the table behind Weissmann's chair and straightened the skewed portrait. Nelson stood, his lunch swinging from his hand, and his eyes fell on the last remaining sandwich, the Contendah that Pescecane had offered Weissmann; somehow it had survived the dust-up on the table top. Before he could step toward it, Lionel came back into the room, leaned across the table, and snatched up the sandwich. Then he left. A moment later Nelson followed in search of Vita.

6

Professor Weissmann Explains

But Vita was nowhere to be found. Nelson hovered outside the women's room on the eighth floor until it was clear she wasn't there. In their office he found signs of her hasty departure: her chair rolled away from her desk, a fan of spilled pens from her overturned penholder, a limp glove on the linoleum just inside the door. He called her answering machine and left a message for her to call him.

Meanwhile he tried as best he could to concentrate on his classes. He ended up doing what he often did when he was fatigued or stressed or simply needed relief from the daily tsunami of student papers: He broke his classes into discussion groups. He gave each of his remaining classes that day a different topic from an unusually therapeutic chapter of the comp text: Is Rip Van Winkle a victim of a sleep disorder? Discuss. Role-play psychiatrists and treat Captain Ahab for monomania. Consider whether Roderick Usher would be helped by Prozac. As a paper topic over the weekend, he asked all three classes to consider whether literature could be cured by antidepressants.

By the end of the day Nelson still had not heard from Vita, and he stuffed his latest batch of student papers into his briefcase and pulled on his loud parka. He stooped to turn off his desk lamp, and the instant the reflection of his office and his own oval face disappeared in the glass, the window was filled with a luminous blue twilight. The spherical lamps around the Quad were just flickering on, and there was a silvery glow from the narrow V of the library Annex, as if from a crack in the earth. Above the Annex, the tower atop Thornfield Library was printed against the darkening sky. Nelson was about to turn away when he saw someone moving behind the crenellations at the top of the tower. He stooped over his desk again and watched a small, pale figure silhouetted against the deepening blue of the sky, moving in the gaps of the tower's battlements. Not just moving, in fact, but dancing: The figure was shooting its arms straight out and

98

bobbing. Nelson blinked, his finger throbbed, he tingled all over with fright. The figure leaped and kicked high in the air, and Nelson flinched away from the window—it was the same move he'd seen Marko Kraljević execute on the Coogan that afternoon. The pale figure on the tower wasn't dancing—it was practicing a martial art.

Nelson's briefcase fell from his grip, and the thump made him start, with a little, childish squeal. He bent to pick up his briefcase, and when he stood again, the top of the tower was empty in the swelling darkness. The figure was gone.

The image of the figure on the tower chilled him all the way across campus to the bus stop—was it the figure he had seen that day on the Quad? Was it a ghost or a living person?—but once Nelson was on the bus the memory of it was overwhelmed by the all-too-human smell of sweat and bad breath and wet winter clothing. Nelson was forced to stand in the packed aisle near the front. The metal bar he clung to overhead was actually warm to his touch. He tried to undo the zipper of his parka with his free hand, but he was squeezed up against the other standees fore and aft. He closed his eyes and tried to think of the wide-open spaces of the western he'd seen a couple of weeks ago, but instead he saw Weissmann smirking down the conference table at Vita like a riverboat gambler leering at the virgin schoolmarm. His finger came alight, as if he'd gotten a current off the metal bar.

The argument at the Seminar Luncheon today between his friend and his former mentor was between two people who no longer spoke the same language. Weissmann, *pace* Cleanth Brooks, still believed in beauty and truth and all ye need know. Vita believed that the ode, the urn, and even the Greeks whose representations were posed around it all had the same ontological value, that they were all nodes of a vast, sticky web of signifiers, none of them any more important or "real" than any other. Nelson himself was torn between his affection for his office mate and his grudging agreement with Weissmann's position. Even though he disapproved of Weissmann's Olympian arrogance, Vita's paper represented thirty pages of the ugliest prose Nelson had ever read in his life. The jargon set his teeth on edge, like fingernails down a blackboard.

Yet he had to admire its ruthless honesty. What Vita's work lacked in elegance was made up for by the way that Vita nakedly struggled with the strangeness of her own presence in the world, with her own fleshly reality—what she would call, in her bristling prose, her own radical alterity. It made the sort of canon maintenance that Weissmann was famous for—the magisterial sorting of novels, plays, and poems into major and minor, into the "literary" and the merely "popular"—seem pedantic and inconsequential. Vita's work was a quest for the truth of her own life, though Vita would deny to the death that it had anything to do with her personally, let alone that there was anything as essentialist, reductive, and old-fashioned as "truth." She wasn't simply obsessed about the various constrictive representations of her gender; she seemed stymied by the very existence of her body itself. Even Nelson's grad school lover Lilith shut it off once in a while, lounging in bed and watching Judy Garland movies for fun; yet like some hapless mortal cursed by a capricious god, Vita seemed locked in an eternal struggle with herself. Still, Nelson admired the sheer courage of Vita's attempt to arm wrestle with her own existence.

Nelson shifted hands on the overhead bar, garnering irritated looks from the people pressed around him. The dusky grad student behind him glared, looking weary and crumpled in his heavy overcoat, but Nelson didn't notice. In spite of Weissmann's treatment of Vita today, Nelson could not help feeling sorry for his old mentor. The academic zeitgeist *had* passed him by, and Weissmann knew it. Nelson thought of something his father had said once about an aging prizefighter: He's dead, but he won't lie down. Weissmann had been at his professional and personal peak in the early seventies when he had edited and written the commentary for a major, multivolume anthology of English literature, in which he had passed judgment on the entire canon from "The Dream of the Rood" to *On the Road*. He'd been at the height of his erotic powers as well, with his matinee idol looks and the Dudley Do-Right wave in his hair, the very model of a modern literary heartthrob. While his wives, each of whom had been one of his students once herself, raised their children and looked the other way, Weissmann seduced a long procession of what used to be known as coeds. No one seemed to object much or even notice: Weissmann was Zeus come down among the mortals to have a little harmless fun. He grew his sideburns fashionably long, smoked a little discreet reefer at department parties, and signed petitions against the Vietnam War, pleased to see his name alongside Alfred Kazin's in the *New York Review of Books*. And with the same magisterial evenhandedness with which he divided Alexander Pope's poems into major and minor, he allowed that he approved of the political and cultural passions of the younger generation and particularly of their freedom in intimate relations.

"The kids have something to teach us," he announced with seignorial graciousness at one smoky party, his large hand comfortably around the waist of a braless twenty year old with silky blonde hair hanging to the middle of her back. He wasn't just pleasuring himself, he declared if anyone objected; he was doing this girl a service, liberating her from the oppressive suburban morality of her parents, relieving her of her burdensome virginity. Who better to do that than someone calm, experienced, and, one might almost say, paternal? Afterward, with no regrets and just a hint of *tristesse,* he would pat her on her firm young backside and send her on her way, having turned her from a coed into a woman.

"What I'm doing," he concluded, settling back in someone's deep leather couch, wreathing himself with pipe smoke, "is teaching these girls how to fend for themselves."

Then the times changed more abruptly than anyone expected. *Of Grammatology* landed in academia like a Molotov cocktail. Jacques the Ripper, Weissmann called the new critical superstar, pleased at his own joke, but the rising tide of French theory paradoxically left Weissmann high and dry. His massive anthology, meant to stand as the final word on the canon until his retirement or the turn of the century, whichever came first, was remaindered while disco was still king. His younger colleagues began to speak in a code, regarding those who did not understand them with the blank, cultish condescension of Moonies. Worse still, they seduced away from Weissmann the best and the brightest graduate students, initiating them into their hermetic mysteries. Meanwhile Weissmann was left with bland young men of mediocre intelligence who wanted to do their dissertations on spy thrillers and baseball novels.

Nelson's bus heaved to a stop at the university hospital, and the momentum forced everybody in the aisle forward against each other. The man in the overcoat behind Nelson pressed right up against him. Nelson grimaced and shifted hands on the overhead bar again, his finger throbbing, as a dozen more people squeezed on. This was the last stop before the bus began its long, wobbling run around the end of the lake and up the hill to married housing. The bus ground forward, and everybody tipped back against each other.

By rights he should have been thinking of Weissmann bitterly—when was the last time Weissmann had ridden a crowded bus?—but instead he thought of Weissmann's long march through the eighties, as he watched his grad students and younger colleagues turn into pod people. His own books and articles continued to be published, but by smaller, less prestigious journals and university presses. He began to drink too much. Standing in a doorway at one department function, he had surveyed the room with eyes swimming in scotch, turned to a bored younger colleague, and said, "You know, I believe I've slept with every woman in this room." The colleague walked away in disgust. It was a pathetic thing to say, not only because it was craven and sexist, but also because it was no longer true. The young women of the department had turned puritanical, no longer desirous of Weissmann's firm guidance toward womanhood, and he escaped sexual harassment proceedings a couple of times only by the skin of his teeth. And now he was turning from leading man into character actor. His face had begun to sag, liver spots had appeared on the backs of his carefully manicured hands. His hair had retained its impressive wave but had turned a dirty white.

(The bus raced down the hill alongside the lake, swaying frighteningly. Nelson fought back the image of some awful, Third World public transportation disaster, the bus pitching through the crumbling concrete railing, bodies tumbled on top of each other as the freezing water rose, his own body floating facedown in the lake. The man in the overcoat behind him grunted and pushed a little against Nelson.)

But after a few years in the slough of despond, Weissmann pulled himself out. He was fighting for higher stakes now than just his professional reputation: He had become by default the champion of literature itself, and he mounted an aggressive counterattack on behalf of the canon. He sought out and took over the corners of the department's administration that were of no interest to the New Order—director of undergraduate advising, chair of the Academic Grievance Committee—and turned them into a power base, biding his time. His biggest coup had been to become head of the department's endowment fund, a moribund post that he resuscitated, raising money for fellowships and scholarships from conservative businessmen around the state—sausage magnates and wealthy dairy farmers—on behalf of the preservation of Western civilization. Meanwhile, he swallowed his pride and accepted the fact the the brightest young people would be attracted to the gaudier pleasures of postmodernism, and went trolling for grad students and junior colleagues from small, conservative colleges and second-string state schools, scouring the lists of dissertations in the *PMLA* for anyone, anywhere, who might be sympathetic to his cause. They may not have been the best minds of their generation, but then the goal at hand was not brilliant scholarship, but the preservation of the cultural tradition from Plato to Norman Mailer. They were to be the new Irish monks, rough and semiliterate perhaps, but dogged in their determination to preserve the treasures with which they had been entrusted.

Nelson himself had been one of these, a plain, blushing maiden seduced by a god in the form of a bull. Even though Weissmann had learned to keep his hands off coeds—learned, indeed, not to call them coeds anymore—his powers of persuasion were as potent as ever, and Nelson accepted a three-year postdoctoral fellowship with no guarantee of a position afterward.

"This isn't about our own professional survival, Professor," Weissmann had said the day he offered Nelson a fellowship. They had been walking slowly across the Quad, and Nelson had tried to show respectful attention to his new boss even as he noted the bemused glances of passing students at the sight of this late-middle-aged matinee idol ranting in public.

"They want to teach our children that Africans invented the airplane!" he had cried, spittle flying from his lips. "I ask you! Who's the Tolstoy of the Zulus? Show me the Shakespeare of the Hottentots, and I'll put him in my syllabus!"

Bridget had been suspicious from the start, but Nelson won her over by admitting that the fellowship was a gamble, but that if it paid off, he would be assured of a long and illustrious career at one of the premier institutions of higher learning in the nation. What he didn't tell her was that the fellowship at Midwest squared with his dream of bringing balm and sweet reason to the culture wars, of black, lesbian, queer theorists laughing uproariously at Alexander Pope, of sixty-year-old white men identifying with the heroine of *Beloved*. In the world of his dreams, in other words, there was no rancor on the one hand, and no guilt on the other. He was self-aware enough to recognize his dream as the white liberal's fondest fantasy; but even so, whatever his personal motivations, surely a dream of a department in which every member recognized every other member's humanity wasn't such a dishonorable hope?

(The four-lane road along the lake narrowed to two where it crossed a narrow bridge, and the bus picked up speed, shooting out the other side like a watermelon seed. The driver noisily shifted gears, grinding a little more speed out of the bus. Everybody on the bus heaved backward under the momentum, and the man in the overcoat grunted under Nelson's weight, putting his hands firmly in the small of Nelson's back.)

After years in the wilderness, doing the jobs no one else wanted to do, advising undergrads, bringing in sympathetic junior faculty on sausage and cheese money—the Cholesterol Fund, some wit called it—Weissmann had risen from the dead and made a credible bid for the chair of the department. This posed a direct challenge to Professor Victorinix, the New Order's candidate, who had also been toiling for years toward the same goal. Nearly everyone took a perverse pleasure in the coming battle. It was more than an election for department chair; it was a referendum on the state of the discipline. Victorinix's followers saw a chance to drive a stake through the heart of phallogocentrism, while Weissmann saw a chance to reerect the pedestal of Western culture. The only people uncomfortable with the situation were Weissmann's junior faculty, especially Nelson. His chance of a lifetime turned out to be mortgaged; his future at Midwest depended on Weissmann winning the election. It was bad enough that he turned out to mean no more to Weissmann than some wino paid off by a ward heeler, but it was worse to discover that no one had ever taken him seriously as a peacemaker between the factions. His postmodern friends, who now found excuses not to talk to him anymore, thought of him only as Weissmann's man, bought and paid for.

Then the unexpected happened. Department chairs were technically appointed by the dean, a tall, bushy-browed man who affected shabbily genteel corduroy suits, and the dean was not necessarily bound by the vote of the department. On the day of the election, Nelson waited until the last moment to enter the lecture hall where the department was meeting. Weissmann and Victorinix were not present, waiting like Roman generals alone in their offices to find out if they were going to command the legions or be exiled to the Caucasus. At the last moment, before Nelson could decide which side of the room to sit on, the dean entered, followed by Anthony Pescecane, who was instantly recognized by everyone.

"I've saved you all the trouble of voting," said the dean, which was his idea of a joke. "I'm sure you'll offer a warm Minnesota welcome to the new chair of Midwest's English Department."

Rage and despair from all quarters. Weissmann was publicly gracious. Victorinix, who had long practice at it, bit back her anger and resigned herself to another five years of silence, exile, and cunning. She accepted a vice chairmanship, and Weissmann accepted a sort of ministership without portfolio. Privately, each of them considered the battle to be in abeyance merely, not over. Only Nelson was happy—the solution was ideal from his point of view, everyone forced to work together—but his happiness only lasted until he received a memo from Morton Weissmann, regretfully announcing that Nelson could not be guaranteed a position beyond the end of his fellowship. We had hoped, the memo continued, that your publications record would warrant further consideration of your position, but, etc. etc. "Perhaps something could be found for you," the memo went on, in an ominously passive voice, "in the Composition Department until you secure a more permanent position elsewhere."

Nelson had felt positively Anglo-Saxon, like a lonely *scop* whose liege lord had died, whose *wierd* it was to plough the icy waves in search of a new mead hall. Other evils had passed; this might also. But his liege lord hadn't died, Nelson was forced to remind himself; his liege lord had given Nelson the push. Bridget, an unsentimental Celt, had been right all along about that.

"In other words," she had said, folding the memo briskly in two between her long fingers, "here's your hat, what's your hurry?"

The bus heaved up the hill, toward the first stop at married housing. The driver shifted down and stepped on the brakes. Everyone lurched forward, including the man in the overcoat, pressing hard with his hands in Nelson's back. The bus stopped, and Nelson twisted around and put his hand on the man's shoulder. His finger blazed.

"I'm very sorry," he said through clenched teeth, "but would you mind *very much* stepping back *just a bit?*"

Nelson's finger sparked. The man in the overcoat blinked and lurched back. Every one behind him, the entire length of the bus, toppled back on top of each other like dominoes, until the last person, an immense woman in a nurse's uniform, flattened two girls on the seat along the back. Nelson felt glee and dismay all at once. The folks tumbling in the aisle shouted and waved their arms, and the girls under the large nurse in the back positively shrieked. The driver jumped up and heaved the few people still standing roughly out of his way.

"Jesus H. Christ," he said, jerking Nelson to one side, and though it wasn't his stop, Nelson hurried off the bus into the cold November evening. He slipped through the maze of town houses, crossing parking lots, avoiding street lamps, enjoying the dark. He trembled a little, ashamed at the pleasure it had given him to see all those people toppling on the bus. I should be angry at Weissmann, he thought. I should be angry at the man who seduced and abandoned me. After the aborted election, all of Weissmann's other young men had fled the department, but in spite of Bridget's advice to do likewise, Nelson had hung on for five years, hoping to claw his way back to the tenure track. But Weissmann shifted his attention to his graduate students, hoping to manufacture from scratch a tough-minded, militant, canon-defending professoriate in his own image, who might spread out from Midwest like Jesuits disappearing into the wilderness. As far as Weissmann was concerned, Nelson was a mistake, a once-promising fellow who now lived on the scraps the department threw him out of embarrassment.

Nelson began to run, his parka hissing, his big feet thumping on the frozen lawns and cracking on the frosty pavement. His finger burned again, and he swung into his own courtyard through the trees, breathing hard and running in long strides. A pair of neighbor children screamed and fled at the sight of the tall orange beast charging out of the dark. He leaped Abigail's Big Wheel and took the three steps up to his front door in one stride, gasping happily, blowing clouds of steam like a plow horse. But I'm not a plow horse, he thought, with his hand on the doorknob; they might work me like one, but I'm a thoroughbred, a racer, with speed and power and intelligence. He threw open the door, proclaiming as heartily as Ward Cleaver, "Honey, I'm home!"

Bridget was on the phone, Abigail wrapped around her leg, and she lifted a finger to silence her husband.

"Speak of the devil," she said into the phone, fixing Nelson with a glance, "he just walked in."

She covered the phone with her palm and swung one leg toward Nelson, the other anchored by her clinging daughter.

"Catch your breath, sweetheart," she whispered. "It's Morton Weissmann. He wants to meet you for lunch on Friday."

In a brisk, offhand fashion, Weissmann suggested Peregrine, a fashionable bar and grill on Michigan Avenue, across from the campus, and Nelson agreed, too stunned to suggest a cheaper place. After his ten o'clock class on Friday, Nelson paced up and down the sidewalk outside the grill at eleven-thirty; Weissmann had suggested an early lunch to avoid the line. Then Nelson saw Fu Manchu slouching in a doorway a few shops down, his red bandanna like a flag. Nelson turned the other way and saw Linda Proserpina coming toward him, pale and blinking; she was eating cookies out of a bag as she walked. Nelson ducked into the grill.

The hostess seated him in a deep, paneled booth along the wall, and a lanky young waiter with moussed hair struck a pose and asked what Nelson would like to drink. Nelson would like to have had one of Peregrine's wide assortment of imported beers, but he asked for water. He wasn't sure that Weissmann was going to show, and he didn't want to spend four dollars on a glass of beer before he retreated to his office and the cheese sandwich he'd left there, just in case. He had eaten at Peregrine before, in happier times, but not since his fall in the department. On the extremely rare occasions when he and Bridget and the girls ate out—usually when his mother-in-law in Chicago sent them a check—it was at some noisy, overlit, family steak house where they waited on a glacially slow line for gristly four-ounce ribeyes and a salad bar that tasted like government surplus, while Muzak oozed over the room like syrup. By comparison, Peregrine seemed like paradise, with its springy hardwood floor and its ornately carved antique bar. The food was elegant and fresh, and the diffident young wait staff sidled with athletic grace between the tables. Blues and jazz and the better sort of singer/songwriter played at just the right volume over a custom-designed sound system.

The waiter came back with Nelson's water. Nelson looked at the glass without drinking from it, wondering if he'd have to pay for it if he decided to leave. He did not even open the menu. There was no point in teasing himself with a lunch he couldn't afford, especially if Weissmann didn't show. Instead, Nelson looked about the restaurant and noted star performers from a variety of departments: the lanky pomo anthropology professor brushing back his blond hair and lifting his stubbled chin to see who else was in the room. A tableful of bantam poli sci professors whose throats worked against their knotted ties while they plotted their way onto the National Security Council. The firebrand feminist law professor, with her unruly mane of hair, holding forth to a table of adoring acolytes with identically unruly hair, gesturing sharply over her untouched crabmeat salad as she repeated the incendiary argument she'd made to Ted Koppel the night before.

Nelson glanced at his watch. Weissmann was ten minutes late. Any moment now the hostess would ask Nelson to order something or leave, or at least move him to a table back near the toilet.

"Nelson, my good friend!"

Nelson looked up. Morton Weissmann was hanging his expensive overcoat on the hook at the edge of the booth. Smiling, Weissmann took the younger man's hand firmly in both of his, shaking it vigorously.

"What a pleasure to see you!" he cried. "It's been much, much too long, my friend!"

"Good to see you," Nelson said, adding weakly, "Professor Weissmann."

Weissmann slid into the booth, across from Nelson. "What's this? 'Professor Weissmann?' Surely we know each other better than that."

Before Nelson could reply, the lanky waiter sidled up and posed. Weissmann made him repeat, slowly, the entire list of imported beers before deciding on a Belgian brand at six dollars a bottle.

"What are you having, Nelson?" Weissmann held the waiter back with a large hand.

"It's a little early for me." Nelson reached for his water. Weissmann released the waiter.

"My God, Nelson." Weissmann snapped open his menu. "You're not turning into one of these postmodernist puritans, are you? Drinking only designer water?"

"Um, I don't think so." Nelson wondered if the waiter had brought him mineral water, something he'd have to pay for. He nudged the glass away.

"I take my graduate students out these days, and they only want to drink those appalling 'lite' beers." Weissmann held his menu out at arm's length in a sort of grand gesture, to disguise the fact that he was too vain to wear glasses. "Or sickly sweet drinks that taste like soda pop. It makes my teeth ache just to contemplate it."

"It's just a little early for me." Nelson opened his menu, peering at Weissmann over the top of it. He didn't know if Weissmann was paying for lunch or not, so he read only the prices, looking for the cheapest thing on the menu. He remembered the burgers here with great pleasure—Peregrine ground its own beef—but they were expensive. Nelson knew that with tip he could easily spend ten dollars on lunch. He browsed through the appetizers and the side salads, not even allowing himself a look at the recto page of the menu.

"I will try something a little different this afternoon," Weissmann said, as the waiter set the Belgian beer before him. "I will have the Long Island duckling with balsamic vinaigrette. Now the baby red potatoes—promise me they don't come out of a *can*." He uttered the last word with a broadly nasal, midwestern inflection.

"As if." The waiter tossed his head.

"Excellent!" Weissmann handed his menu to the young man with a flourish. The waiter raised his eyebrows at Nelson.

"Um." Nelson cleared his throat. "The house salad?"

The waiter blinked. Nelson handed him the menu.

"Do you want bread with that?" The waiter tucked the two menus under his arm.

Nelson wished he could snatch back the menu. Did the bread come with the salad, or would he have to pay extra? If he said no, would he be giving up something that came with the price of the salad? The silence stretched out, and the waiter and Weissmann exchanged a glance.

"No!" Nelson gasped. "No thank you. No bread, please." There was always the cheese sandwich back in his office.

The waiter went away. Weissmann clapped his hands together, rubbed his palms, and leaned forward.

"Well, Nelson." He lowered his voice, his eyes alight. "I can't tell you how pleased I was to see you at our little luncheon yesterday. What a relief it was to have at least one other reasonable man in the room. Or perhaps I should say, reasonable 'person.' "

"I was pleased to be there," Nelson said. "Mort," he added.

"The 'lesbian phallus.' " Weissmann lowered his voice further. "Have you ever heard such nonsense? Just suppose I presented a paper about the male vagina. Can you imagine the uproar from the PC Brigade? Oh, brave new world," he added, as if Nelson hadn't heard him say it yesterday, "that has such people in it."

Nelson shrugged. He ought to have leaped to the defense of Vita. But he didn't know yet why Weissmann had invited him to lunch after all this time, and he wanted to find out.

"I don't need to tell you, Nelson," Weissmann was saying, his face a mask of gravity, "that we live in difficult times, *desperate* times. I don't mean merely the rising tide of vulgarity all around us, Nelson, but something much closer to our hearts. As members of the same department. As colleagues."

Nelson blinked at him in astonishment—*colleagues?* When was the last time Weissmann had taught composition?—but Weissmann seemed to be looking hard at something just above Nelson's head.

"The very foundation of our culture is under attack, my friend, on all sides. Yesterday you heard the sort of . . . well, claptrap is too mild a word for it . . . the sort of dreck, the sort of *merde* that passes for scholarly debate these days."

Weissmann paused as if he expected an answer, and his gaze flickered in Nelson's direction.

"Well, you know, Mort," Nelson began, "Vita . . ." Is my office mate, he wanted to say, is a friend of mine, but Weissmann shook his head.

"A pleasant enough young woman, I have no doubt. These plain girls often are, of course." He leaned forward, lowering his voice to a lubricious murmur.

"But really, Nelson, do you really think she'd be speaking such useless *quatsch* about the phallus if she'd ever actually been on the business end of one?"

Nelson felt himself blushing, partly from embarrassment, partly from anger on Vita's behalf.

The waiter arrived at that moment, balancing on his sculpted forearm Weissmann's duckling on a long platter, gleaming with sauce, surrounded by little red-skinned potatoes dripping with butter, garnished artfully with a slice of vine-ripened tomato and a sprig of fresh parsley. He slid it expertly down his arm onto the table before Weissmann. Then he rather abruptly deposited Nelson's salad, in a little round bowl, next to Nelson's glass of water. Weissmann sat up and shook out his napkin, pursing his lips at his steaming lunch.

"Believe me, Nelson," he said, brandishing his knife and fork like a surgeon looking for a place to make the first cut, "thirty-year-old virgins are not at all uncommon in academia these days."

He sliced into the duckling, and a little juice squirted beyond the edge of his platter and onto the table. Nelson lowered his eyes to his tiny bowl of romaine lettuce and croutons. He thought he might swoon from the smell of roasted fowl. He looked away from the booth and saw Anthony Pescecane and Miranda DeLaTour following the hostess to a table at the center of the room; with Pescecane's proprietary hand on her elbow, Miranda looked about her with little birdlike movements of her lovely neck, taking in the covert appraisal of the postmodern anthropologist, the short, sharp glance of the feminist lawyer, and the beetling stares of the bantam poli sci guys.

"Nelson?" Weissmann's gleaming cutlery was poised to descend upon the duckling. He followed Nelson's glance and smiled.

"I'm sorry." Nelson picked up his fork and speared a piece of lettuce. "You were saying."

"Pray don't apologize." Weissmann wrenched the duckling apart between the tip of his knife and the tines of his fork. "There was a time, of course, when a gentleman could openly admire a handsome woman." He shot a glance toward the center of the room. Pescecane was settling into his seat and shooting his cuffs. Miranda smoothed her tight skirt under her while the hostess held her chair.

"To the victor belong the spoils," said Weissmann, forking up a pink piece of duckling.

Nelson chewed his salad as if it were gristle. His finger was beginning to burn.

110

"Of course, our noteworthy chairman—I beg your pardon, chair*person*—is illustrative of my point."

Weissmann paused only to chew rapidly, keeping his voice to a sotto voce roar.

"Consider the function of an English department, Nelson. There are several, of course, but I would not be amiss in saying that its central function, the purpose at its very heart, is to hand down the tradition of prose, poetry, and drama in the English language from one generation to the next. Would you agree?"

Nelson swallowed his mouthful of salad and dabbed at his lips with the linen napkin and opened his mouth to speak.

"Indulge me a moment, Nelson." Weissmann held up his hand. "If that is the case, and I believe it is, then the heart of our department is and ought to be the upper-level *under*graduate courses, the purpose of which is, and ought to be, to introduce the canon to our more advanced young people."

Weissmann rested his wrists on the edge of the table, pointing his knife and fork at Nelson.

"But here's the perverse element in our present situation: Since the very idea of a canon is under attack, this puts our postmodern friends in the awkward position of giving with one hand and taking away with the other. Do you see the irony of it, Nelson? It would almost be funny were it not so tragic. Bright, impressionable young people are introduced to important books and authors whom they most likely would never have read on their own, only to be told that these books are *not to be trusted*, that the authors' motives are impure and political and—what's the word?—hegemonic. They introduce their students to Jane Austen, say, they invite them to appreciate her ironic wit and the elegant precision of her prose and then—" he waved the knife and fork about—"hey, presto! You were wrong to like her! She's a racist and an imperialist because she never mentioned the poor oppressed Jamaicans!"

The tips of his utensils descended on the duck like dive bombers.

"And what do our poor students take from this? That you must read these works, children, but *you may not enjoy them.* These trusting youths are told that books—great books, Nelson, the jewels of our civilization—have value only as cultural artifacts or as evidence of some ideological failing. My God, Nelson, students are being told that the language itself is corrupted and untrustworthy! In *English* classes!"

His voice had risen. Sweat appeared on his forehead and upper lip. His cutlery trembled in his hands. He drew a breath to calm himself and stabbed a red-skinned potato.

"Unless, of course," Weissmann went on in an energetic whisper, "the work in question was written by a woman or a member of an oppressed race or sexual preference, in which case the book is subversive and *counter*hegemonic and to be trusted implicitly as a work of art of the highest order."

Nelson glanced nervously about. Weissmann smiled.

"I suppose you're wondering what this has to do with our illustrious chairman," he said, watching Nelson. "I don't believe I saw you at the MLA convention last year, did I, Nelson?"

"I didn't make it." What Nelson didn't say was that he hadn't gone to the MLA meeting in the vain hope that his job at Midwest might continue. He avoided Weissmann's gaze and forked up another leafy bite.

"It was brutally hot," said Weissmann. "Unseasonably so, I'm told, even for Miami. Well, you were spared the spectacle of our worthy chairman, attended by his paramour and that brutish little man who trots at his heels, *Grrrros*maul," Weissmann said, rolling the r's. "At any rate, our Anthony gave the keynote address at the opening session, with the euphonious title of—and you must forgive me, my dear fellow, I'm only reporting what I heard with my own ears—the title was, and I quote, 'The Fuck Cares about Edmund Spenser?' Unquote. The argument of this groundbreaking essay was, as I recall, that the new criterion for determining what is worth reading and what is not—God forbid the word 'literature' should pass our chairman's lips—the criterion for literary merit is something Anthony defines, and I quote again, as 'street cred.' "

He grimaced as he spoke, as if he were spitting up the words.

"It's a pity you weren't there, Nelson. I wish you could have seen this shameless spectacle." He pushed his dissected but only partially eaten duckling aside with the tips of his cutlery. "There was something approaching a riot. Evidently 'street cred' is such a fundamental and ineffable conception that it does not require definition. Our esteemed chair was forced to fall back on the declaration that he could not tell us what street cred was, but that he knew it when he saw it. In other words, the ultimate arbiter of literature at the turn of the millennium is—wait for it—Anthony Pescecane." Weissmann beat the air lightly with his knife and fork, as if conducting an orchestra, then sighed and set them aside, lifting his napkin to dab at his lips.

"Evidently, someone called Kathy Acker has street cred in spades, Toni

Morrison had it until she won the Nobel, Virginia Woolf still has enough to keep her afloat, ha ha, but poor Edmund Spenser is utterly bereft of credit. *The Faerie Queen* may have possessed street cred once upon a time, but apparently it doesn't anymore. Anthony was in his glory, of course, but it was an appalling spectacle, I can tell you, appalling."

With a glance across the room at Pescecane, Weissmann leaned across the table. "I swore I smelled brimstone that day, Nelson." He lowered his voice. *"Vexilla regis prodeunt Inferni."* He wadded up his napkin and tossed it to the table, settling back against the dark upholstery of the booth.

"There was a rather spirited exchange at that point in the proceedings, from which I recused myself, of course, as a loyal member of Chairperson Pescecane's department. As you're well aware, Nelson, I hold collegiality as dear as life itself. I believe it extends even as far as the Grand Ballroom of the Fontainbleu Hotel."

Nelson said nothing. It clearly didn't extend eight stories down to the Composition Department. He pushed his salad bowl aside and took a long drink of water. It was tap water, thank God. His finger throbbed with a burning pain, on and off with the rhythm of a siren, and he decided to pluck up his courage and ask Weissmann—collegially, of course—just why he had been asked to lunch. But Weissmann was twisting about in his side of the booth and half rising to his feet.

"Anthony," he was saying, "how good of you . . ."

"Easy." Pescecane had appeared at the side of the booth. He gestured with his palms for Weissmann to stay seated. He did not look at Nelson.

"To what do I owe the pleasure . . . ," Weissmann began, but Pescecane waved it away. He had taken his coat off, but his cuffs were secured with gold links, and his tie was knotted up and pinned to his shirt with just the right amount of bulge to it. His biceps pressed through his shirtsleeves, and his powerful chest strained against his suspenders. Beneath Pescecane's aftershave Nelson detected the strong but not unpleasant musk of the chairman himself. His finger burned steadily now.

"You get that memo?" Pescecane rested his fingertips lightly on the edge of the table.

Weissmann shot a glance at Nelson. "The memo," he said, "about our, ah, ongoing situation?"

"Yeah."

"Ah. Yes. Yes, I did."

"There's no question of our pen pal going quietly." Pescecane flexed his fingers on the tabletop. "He denies everything."

"You spoke to him?" Weissmann leaned forward. "To, ah, our mutual friend?"

Pescecane swiveled his massive head slowly toward Nelson and then back again to Weissmann. "I shouldn't say anything more."

"Of course." Weissmann glanced at Nelson. "I beg your pardon."

"Check your schedule," Pescecane said. "Make some time this afternoon. We need to talk."

"Naturally. Of course. As soon as possible."

Pescecane lifted his hands and stepped back. "Set something up with Lionel. I told him to clear my afternoon."

"Immediately." Weissmann licked his lips and gestured to Nelson. "Anthony, no doubt you've met my good friend Nelson Humboldt?"

Pescecane shifted his dark gaze to Nelson. Nelson's finger burned a bit hotter. He attempted to smile.

"With the severed finger," said Pescecane. "How is that?"

"Much better, thank you," said Nelson.

Pescecane swung his hand up as if offering to shake with Nelson, and Nelson pulled his hand out from under the table. His finger seared him all along the length of his arm, and he bit his lip to keep from crying out. But Pescecane made a gun with his forefinger and thumb, clicking his thumb at Nelson as if shooting him.

"Sue the rat bastards. Am I right?"

He gave a wolfish smile, turned on his expensive heel, and walked away. Beyond him, Miranda toyed with a large salad and looked bored.

"My apologies, Nelson," Weissmann murmured. "A bit of departmental business. Something of a crisis really."

"Is everything alright?" Nelson rubbed his finger under the table. The pain had abated somewhat.

"Nothing you need concern yourself with." Weissmann smiled. "You understand."

There was a moment of silence as each man considered his lunch. Weissmann's was largely untouched, while Nelson's bowl of greens and croutons was emptied down to the little pool of dressing at the bottom. Nelson thought the lunch was over, without his ever having found out what it was about.

"Nelson." Weissmann leaned forward and clasped his hands on the tabletop. "You know, I regret that we have not been as close this last year or two as we were formerly. Naturally, I blame myself, but the press of events and my responsibilities . . ."

He trailed off, leaving space for Nelson to protest that no, it was his fault as well. But Nelson waited a beat too long, and they ended up speaking at the same time.

"Please." Weissmann held up his hand. "If I may. The fact of the matter, Nelson, is that I have felt your absence dearly. May I speak frankly, at the risk of embarrassing us both?"

"Um . . ."

"What I miss most of all," Weissmann began, leaning back in his seat and fixing his gaze above Nelson's head, "is intelligent conversation. Like the good talk we've been having today. My difficulty these days—and believe me, Nelson, I'm the first to admit this—my difficulty is that I don't get the best graduate students anymore. No, really, I'm afraid you cannot contest the truth of that." He lifted his hand and closed his eyes, though Nelson had not said anything.

"To be laceratingly honest," he continued, opening his eyes and actually looking at Nelson now, "I am left with the halt and the lame, intellectually speaking. Even the best of the younger generation are no longer interested in the preservation of"—Weissmann actually placed his hand on his breast—"the preservation of the best that has been thought and said. And I understand that, really I do. Scholarship is sacrifice, Nelson, I'm sure I don't need to tell you. It is the willing act of yoking oneself to the greater minds and finer sensibilities that came before. You must abase yourself before them; you must give your life to them, as I have." He lifted his eyes to the ceiling and intoned, "I listen only to the eternal being, the principle of beauty—and the memory of great men." Weissmann squeezed his eyes shut again, as if in the grip of a deep emotion, then opened them on Nelson.

"But we live in a narcissistic age, my friend. Why shouldn't the brightest young people among us be drawn to a critical regime that, as they themselves might put it, foregrounds the critic, indeed puts the critic ahead of the artist? Who can blame them, when the model for individual achievement in our debauched culture is no longer the solitary artist toiling in obscurity in the service of truth and beauty—and I am not ashamed, Nelson, *not ashamed,* to use those words unironically—but pop singers and film stars and even criminals. My God, Nelson, all you need to do these days is murder someone spectacularly, and you are rewarded with a book contract and a film deal and chat show appearances. I'm not a religious man—not in any conventional sense, that is—but if I were, Nelson, if I were"—Weismann drew a deep breath and let it out—"I'd be convinced that this is the endtime. Surely postmodern scholarship and celebrity murder trials are signs of the Apocalypse."

"I've missed you too, Mort," said Nelson.

"Indeed," said Weissmann, brightening. "Which was why I was surprised and frankly a little relieved to see that Victorinix had taken you under her wing."

Weissmann peered at Nelson, but Nelson said nothing. Understanding dawned behind his eyeballs, momentarily blinding him.

"I exempt Victorinix from my general disapprobation, of course," he heard Weissmann say. "We've had our differences over the years, God knows, but her Sapphic propagandism apart, I don't believe her heart is with the postmodernists. Once upon a time the woman did some very competent work on the Romantics and the Victorians."

Nelson blinked, and Weissmann swam into focus again. *This* was the reason for lunch at Peregrine: Weissmann was under the impression that Nelson had attended the Seminar Luncheon yesterday as the guest of the undergraduate chair. No doubt he had heard that Victorinix had reprieved Nelson and conjured another couple of classes for him, an uncharacteristically warm-blooded act. No doubt the Lost Boys, having seen Nelson and Victorinix speaking in the eighth-floor hallway a week ago, had reported this unusual activity to their chieftain. Weissmann was not interested in Nelson qua Nelson; he simply wanted to know what Victorinix's interest was.

"Of course, I shouldn't tell you this," Weissmann said, dipping his gaze modestly, "but I had a brief word on your behalf with *la belle dame sans merci,* oh, when was it, a week or so ago. I can't claim that it did the trick, of course—I'm the first to confess that the female mind, let alone the lesbian phallus, is a mystery to me—but whether I had anything to do with it or not is irrelevant. It was gracious of Victoria to find something for you in these, ah, budget-restricted, ah, belt-tightening . . ."

Nelson's finger was searingly hot again. Weissmann was lying, and Nelson knew it. The only mystery was if Weissmann knew that Nelson knew and simply didn't care.

"Thank you." Nelson folded his hands tightly.

"I only wish the department could have done more for you," Weissmann said.

"Perhaps it can," said Nelson.

The waiter reappeared with their check. Weissmann slipped a credit card onto the tray without even looking at the bill.

"Let's let the department pick up the tab, shall we?" Weissmann winked. "I know how it is to be a young married fellow. Every penny counts."

After the bill was settled, Nelson helped Weissmann on with his overcoat. His finger felt red hot as it passed within a fraction of an inch of Weissmann's neck. With a jaunty wave at Pescecane and Miranda, Weissmann worked his way between the tables and then through the press of people waiting in the vestibule. Nelson followed close behind.

"Professor Humboldt!" Weissmann proclaimed when they were out on the sidewalk in the cold. "We mustn't let so much time pass between lunches. I greatly enjoyed your company." His leather gloves clutched loosely in one hand, Weissmann offered his other hand to Nelson.

"Tell me," Nelson said, meeting his grip firmly, "that matter that Pescecane mentioned, when he came up to the table. The department crisis?"

Weissmann blinked at Nelson and smiled.

"What's that all about?" asked Nelson. His finger burned.

Weissmann tried to withdraw his hand. "I'm really not at liberty," he began.

"I appreciate that." Nelson hung on tightly. "But I'd really like to know."

Weissmann blinked and worked his mouth. Passersby parted around the two men clutching hands in the middle of the sidewalk.

"Tell me, Mort," Nelson said. "Please."

His finger cooled suddenly, as though dipped in ice water. Weissmann, who was nearly as tall as Nelson, began to wobble alarmingly from side to side, as though his knees were buckling. His eyes rolled back into his head, and his eyelids fluttered, and Nelson, still clutching Weissmann's hand, slipped his other arm under the older man's armpits and propped him up.

"Mort," he whispered, "are you alright?"

Perhaps he'd gone too far. What if he'd given Weissmann a heart attack? After all, the man wasn't as young as he used to be, and he'd been living on scotch and duckling for years. But then Weissmann stood bolt upright, opened his eyes wide, and turned to Nelson. Nelson let go of him and stepped back.

"Never better!" Weissmann said heartily. He caught Nelson by the arm and turned him toward the campus. "If you promise not to breathe a word of it," he said in a husky whisper, "I'll tell you. But not a word to another living soul. Do I have your promise?"

"I promise."

"Well, then." Weissmann glanced theatrically about. "Someone in the department has been sending poison-pen letters."

7

Enter a Murderer

After his last class, in the late afternoon twilight, Nelson entered the student ghetto near campus in search of Vita. In his parka and leaky rubbers he moved up narrow streets past eighty-year-old frame houses full to bursting, like overripe seed pods, with undergraduates. On each sagging porch a moist, swaybacked sofa moldered into humus and a wheel-less bicycle rusted, chained to the railing. A row of trash cans overflowed in each narrow gap between houses. Threadbare little lawns were littered with crushed beer cans and crumbling Styrofoam cups. The gutters were clotted with a mash of rotting leaves, hamburger wrappers, and dirty snow melt. The sidewalk was a glassy archipelago of packed ice. Nelson wondered if he should have tied a string to a tree before he entered this labyrinth of undergraduate squalor.

Nelson was worried about Vita, but now he had another reason to track her to her lair. After lunch, on the way back to Harbour Hall, Morton Weissmann had told Nelson that someone had been sending an anonymous and obliquely threatening letter to the gay and Jewish members of the department. No one knew how long this had been going on because none of the first recipients had told anyone else about the letter. It wasn't until Weissmann received one himself and showed it to Pescecane that others began to come forward. No overt threats were made, but the letter implied that the barbarians were at the gates, that Western literature and Christian civilization were being undermined by feminism; queer theory; and the political, cultural, and sexual relativism of Jewish intellectuals. There was a certain literary flair to the letter, a certain wit, Weissmann allowed, dropping his voice so low that Nelson had to strain to hear it. The letter alluded approvingly to famous literary anti-Semites—Pound, Eliot, Christopher Marlowe—bespeaking a level of sophistication beyond your garden variety neo-Nazi.

As a Jew, Weissmann was clearly alarmed and offended by the letters. "Vile missives," he called them, and he seemed to mean it. But he was also alarmed and offended to be lumped with the likes of queer theorists, and he was certainly shrewd enough to realize that the letter was making a similar argument, minus the anti-Semitism and overt homophobia, to the one he'd made to Nelson at lunch. He pulled Nelson to a stop just outside Harbour Hall, his gloved hand in the crook of Nelson's arm.

"We have an idea who it is," whispered Weissmann, his eyes bright with the excitement of knowing a secret. "The difficulty, of course, is how to force a tenured colleague to go without damaging the department. Though I say too much."

Weissmann released Nelson to pull off his gloves. Nelson's finger burned. His only thought was an intense, almost prurient interest in the suspect's name. He took off his own gloves, in order to grasp Weissmann by the hand again, to press his burning finger into Weissmann's palm.

"Professor!" someone barked.

Weissmann and Nelson turned, and Nelson blushed at his mistake. No one was calling *him*.

"Anthony wants to see you." Lionel Grossmaul steamed out of Harbour Hall in his shirtsleeves, nearly bowling over an undergraduate boy, who then gave him the finger behind his back.

"Enter Caliban," Weissmann whispered, "a savage and deformed slave."

"He wants to see you *right now.*" Lionel stepped between Nelson and Weissmann.

Grossmaul was lying, Nelson knew; they had just left Chairperson Pescecane with Miranda DeLaTour at the restaurant. Lionel had no doubt seen Weissmann arm in arm with Nelson from his eyrie on the eighth floor and had swooped down to separate them.

"Duty calls!" Weissmann moved away from Nelson, out of his reach. Lionel trotted at Weissmann's heels, glaring murderously back at Nelson over his shoulder. Nelson was left standing stupidly, his finger burning, the name of the suspected letter writer snatched from his grasp. As he pulled on his gloves, he had the uneasy feeling he was being watched, and he turned suddenly. A few students hurried by, their breath misting after them. Nelson glanced up at the clock tower on the corner of the library, expecting to see someone moving behind the battlements. But no one was there, only the wide, white clock face, reminding Nelson of his next class.

120

In his three o'clock session, Nelson handed back papers on the topic "Lord and Lady Macbeth: Can This Marriage Be Saved?" In order to give himself time to think, he directed his students to expand their paper topics into a role-playing exercise, a daytime talk show on the topic "Is Your Man Ambitious Enough?" What the kids didn't know about Shakespeare they made up for with an intimate familiarity with *Jerry Springer* and *Jenny Jones*. Lord and Lady Macbeth were played by volunteers from the class, who clearly knew the talk show drill: The Thane of Cawdor was sullen and defensive, slouching in his seat and speaking in monosyllables, while his lady taunted him, to the laughing encouragement of the rest of the class. Members of the "studio audience" suggested makeovers.

Meanwhile Nelson sat at the back of the room, rubbing his smoldering finger and trying to think of an excuse to show up on Vita's doorstep. The instant Weissmann had said "poison pen," Nelson knew that he needed to see one of the letters, so he could figure out who was writing them. He was certain Vita would have received one, and equally certain she'd have told no one about it. Whether Vita was gay or not, the sort of person who wrote anonymous homophobic letters would think she was. But Vita wasn't responding to his messages, and Nelson had never been asked inside her apartment, let alone shown up uninvited.

After class Nelson had ascended to the eighth floor and pried two days' worth of academic junk out of Vita's mailbox: a flyer from a local copy shop, a review copy in a padded envelope (*Where's Waldo? The Representation of Everyman in Emerson,* by J. O. Schmeaux), a glossy call-for-papers ("Anal/yzing the Father: Penetrating Patriarchy from Behind"). Flipping through the stack under the raptorish gaze of the department secretary, he found nothing urgent enough to justify showing up on Vita's doorstep. But back in their office he stepped on the glove she'd dropped inside the door yesterday. His finger flared. He'd put the glove in the pocket of his parka, pulled on his rubbers, and headed out for her apartment.

Now, as the streetlights flickered on over the narrow street, Nelson stumped up the steps of Vita's front porch. Vita lived on the second floor of an old frame house. She had her own outside entrance, a solid old door that led to a dark staircase. Nelson paced the creaking porch in the garish porch light searching his conscience and concluding that he had her welfare at heart, that he was only helping to put her mind at ease. He pressed the doorbell and counted to ten, knowing Vita wouldn't come at the first ring, and then pressed the bell again.

Through the door he heard the stairway inside creak with a tentative step, so he pressed the doorbell once more. Immediately he heard a frantic thump.

"Go away!" Vita cried, muffled by the door. "I won't talk to you!"

"Vita, I . . ."

"I left your book inside the storm door! Please go away!"

What book? Nelson wondered, and he opened Vita's aluminum storm door. A brand-new copy of the *Book of Mormon* leaned against the scuffed footplate of the inner door.

"It's me, Vita," he called out. "It's Nelson."

A silence. Then Vita called out, "What do you want?"

"I brought your glove," he said. "Vita, open the door."

There was another long pause.

"Let me see you," Vita said, and Nelson stepped back into the sickly glow of her porch light, which she left on twenty-four hours a day. Someone who had given her a ride home once referred to her as Vita of the Seven Locks, and now Nelson heard the snap of a dead bolt, then another, then another. He lost count. With a grinding, sepulchral scrape, the door swung back a few inches and thumped against its chain, not wide enough to let the *Book of Mormon* fall over. Vita's ghostly face peered out of the darkness. She insinuated her pale hand through the crack for the glove. "Thank you," she whispered.

Nelson closed his hand around the glove in his pocket. His finger smoldered.

"How are you, Vita?" he said. "Are you alright?"

"I'm fine," Vita sniffed.

"May I come in?" Nelson spoke as if he were trying to coax a sleepy daughter into her pajamas. "Just for a moment? It's freezing out here."

Vita blinked at him out of the darkness. Then she jerked her hand inside and slammed the door, making Nelson jump back. He heard the chain slithering like a drawbridge being raised, then the door cracked open a little wider, and Vita snatched Nelson inside by the sleeve of his parka. Nelson could scarcely see in the stairwell. The only light was a line of yellow under a door at the top of the stairs.

"Did you see any Mormons?" Vita hissed, invisibly.

"Mormons?"

The door slammed, the chain slithered, the dead bolts snapped home one by one. "They left me their book last week," Vita whispered, "and they said they'd be back today to talk about it."

122

Vita shifted sibilantly in the dark. "Nelson, what do you think that means?"

"I just came to see how you are," he said.

He felt a firm tug on his parka. "Be quiet coming up the steps. They may be talking to my downstairs neighbor."

Nelson tread the stairs as lightly as he could. Vita moved silently to the top and waited; then she pulled him through another door into a harshly lit vestibule like an airlock, where three closed doors stood at an angle to each other. She squeezed past him, her shoulders hunched under an immense, fluffy blue bathrobe that hung to her ankles; she looked like a nun in terrycloth. She opened the door to the right, and Nelson followed her into her living room. There was a round-backed blue love seat against one wall, an overstuffed blue chair in one corner, and, at the far end of the room, an old wooden desk with a computer on it. A tall, gray filing cabinet stood in the corner. Two windows were completely covered with heavy blue drapes; between them were three tall, deep, impeccably ordered metal bookcases of industrial gray. A pair of floor lamps at their highest intensity lit the room like a sound stage.

Vita shut the door and motioned him to sit. The room was stuffy, but she didn't offer to take his parka, so Nelson only unzipped it and sat on the springy love seat. He saw no decorative touches: no prints on the wall, no postcards taped above the desk, no tchotchkes on the bookshelves, not even a photograph of her brother, Robin. He had always figured Vita for a cat lover, but there was no cat hair on the blue upholstery, no cat toys underfoot, no litter box odor. The only hint of Vita's inner life were three carefully ordered stacks of periodicals on the coffee table at his knees: *Critical Inquiry,* the *PMLA,* and *Seventeen.*

Vita sat across from him in the overstuffed chair, perched on the edge of the cushion with her knees together, her hands clutched in her lap. Under the hem of her enormous robe Nelson saw big, fluffy slippers. The robe's belt was cinched with a knot the size of a baseball, and between its lapels Nelson glimpsed a high-necked Lanz of Salzburg nightgown, little red hearts against a blue background. When Vita saw where Nelson was looking, she pinched her lapels shut with a hand at her throat, clenching her other hand in her lap.

"How are you, Vita?" he said.

"Fine," she said in a small voice. She looked in his direction, but not at him.

"You haven't answered any of my messages, Vita. Folks have been worried about you."

Vita's eyes flickered. The corners of her mouth twitched. "Fuh, folks? Like, who?"

"Well, you know," he said. "Like me."

"Anybody else?" she said. "Anthony, maybe? Victoria? Wuh, Wuh, Weissmann?"

Nelson's finger began to heat up again.

"C'mon Vita, nobody blames you." He ventured a chuckle. "It was kind of funny, when you think about it. What happened."

Almost mechanically, Vita started to laugh. Her shoulders shook, her page boy bangs flopped. She rapped her knee with the back of her hand. In spite of the heat Nelson was chilled under his parka. Suddenly she opened her eyes wide and mimed throwing a knife.

"Zwip!" she cried. "Brrrrrr!" she added, mimicking the hum of a blade vibrating in a tabletop. Her laughter dropped in pitch until it was almost guttural. Nelson shuddered on the love seat. Vita threw herself back in her chair and bared her throat and howled with laughter until she started to cry. She drew her legs up under her, slippers and all, and clutched her elbows. Her shoulders shook with sobs.

"Aw, Vita." Nelson knew that if he crossed the room to comfort her she'd scramble up the bookcase behind her like a cat.

"Vita," Nelson said gently, "is there something else that might have upset you?"

There was a catch in Vita's sobbing, a sharp intake of breath. She looked up sharply. "What have you heard?" She curled tightly in her chair, one hand at her throat, the other clutched across her middle. Her eyes were red, her cheeks shiny with tears. She narrowed her gaze.

"I heard about the letters," he said.

Either Vita knew about the letters, or she didn't. If she didn't, she'd be frantic to know what he was talking about. If she had received one herself, she'd be frantic to know how he knew. And if she had heard about them, but hadn't gotten one, she'd be frantic to know why not. I'm doing her a favor, Nelson told himself. He looked down at his hands. His finger was on fire, but above the suture it looked paler than the rest of his hand, like a parasite.

"Did *you* get a letter?" she said sharply.

"No."

"Then how did you know?"

"Vita, it's common knowledge in the department."

Nelson's finger throbbed. His throat was very dry. She had no way of knowing that he was lying. He met Vita's gaze fitfully, his eyes shifting from her to the bookcase and back again. He couldn't tell her that Weissmann had told him; that would end the conversation. But perhaps he didn't really need to explain: It was an article of faith with Vita that the common knowledge of the department was common to everyone except her.

Vita wiped away her tears with the back of her hand. Behind her reddened eyes, Nelson could see the finely tuned engine of her paranoia humming at full throttle. Vita was the Lamborghini of conspiracy mongering; she could go from 0 to 120 in nothing flat.

"You!" She clapped her hand over her mouth. *"You* sent me the letter!"

Nelson gasped. The pain in his finger soared. He hadn't expected this.

"Who else?" Vita coiled herself tighter in her chair. "Who else would know about me and Vic, Vic, Victoria?"

"You and Victoria?" Nelson sat slack jawed. "Know *what* about you and Victoria?"

Even in his astonishment, his mind was racing. He'd often wondered if something had happened between Victorinix and Vita, and now Vita had practically admitted it. But asking her outright would only lead him deeper into the labyrinth of Vita's paranoia; she'd freeze finally and never show him the letter. But if he didn't ask her what had happened, she'd assume he already knew.

"How would I know?" he protested.

Vita gasped again. Her eyes got even wider. "She told you, didn't she? She told you, and then had you send the letter!"

His finger burning, Nelson struggled to follow Vita's reasoning: Victoria had given him another semester's work, and so, in Vita's hothouse universe, Nelson was now Victoria's stooge.

"Victoria told me nothing," he insisted, rubbing his finger. He was beginning to sweat. "I came on my own. Nobody sent me."

Vita shot up out of her chair and glided as soundlessly as a geisha across the room until she stood across the coffee table from Nelson. Her eyes were wide, her mouth was a perfect O. With the robe hanging to her toes and both her hands pinching her lapels, she looked like a Christmas candle.

"Then how did you know I got a letter?" Vita whispered. "I didn't tell a *soul.*"

Nelson wished he could manage this better. He wanted to reach across the table and grab her by the wrist and say, *"Show me the letter."* But he knew that if he did, she would trip over her robe trying to back away from him. He crossed his arms and thrust his burning finger into his armpit.

"Vita, please listen to me. Whatever happened between you and Victoria, believe me, I'm the last person she'd tell. For heaven's sake, she tried to *fire* me." Nelson swallowed. The pain in his finger was searing. He looked up at Vita, trying to control his anger.

"Nobody knows you got one. *I* didn't know for sure you had one until just this minute. I thought you might have because gay members of the department are getting them. I don't know whether you're gay or not, Vita, but everybody else in the department thinks you are."

Vita was pale. She didn't seem to be breathing.

"All I know is that your peace of mind matters to me, Vita," Nelson said, getting angry now. "You're the only friend I've got. I knew that if you *had* gotten one of these letters, you'd keep it to yourself, like you do everything else, and drive yourself crazy, just like you always do. I came over here to see if I might offer you my help."

He jumped to his feet suddenly, and Vita took a long step backward, still wide-eyed, still clutching her lapels. "I think I'd better go," Nelson muttered, and he fumbled at the zipper of his parka.

"Wait!"

Vita held her hand out, her eyes pleading with him. He stopped with his parka halfway zipped.

"Sit," she said, in a tiny voice. "Please."

Nelson unzipped his parka and sat on the edge of the love seat. Vita pivoted and glided soundlessly toward the tall filing cabinet at the end of the room. She turned. "Don't look," she said.

Nelson looked away. He heard Vita unlock the cabinet, slide open a drawer, rummage in it, close the drawer, and lock the cabinet again. What would Vita file hate mail under? he wondered. Was the whole drawer devoted to plots against her, broken down into individual files by conspirator? Pescecane, Weissmann, Victorinix, the department in general, the dean's office, the university at large, the entire profession? Maybe the whole filing cabinet was devoted to it.

Stop, Nelson scolded himself, Vita is your friend. His finger hummed at a steady temperature now, but the heat was no longer searing. It wasn't comfortable exactly, but he was aware that it came from him, that he was doing it, that if the lights went out his finger would glow in the dark like a heating coil.

"You can look now."

Vita stood just across the coffee table, holding out a plain white, letter-sized envelope. Nelson took it, his finger burning. To his surprise, Vita came around the coffee table and sat beside him on the love seat, her robe rustling. She watched his face as he turned the envelope over. There was nothing on it, no address, no postmark, not even Vita's name.

"That's how it came," she whispered, peering at him.

The pain in Nelson's finger receded somewhat now that he had the letter in his hands. Vita sat very close to him. Nelson fought the urge to stand and cross the room.

"Go ahead and open it," Vita said.

He slipped his finger under the flap of the envelope and pulled out the letter. It was a plain sheet of white paper, with no date or signature. The layout mimicked a seventeenth-century broadsheet, but instead the lurching type had the effect of an anonymous note made up of letters cut from magazines.

"Is it like the others?" Vita was close enough for Nelson to smell her Ivory soap. Nelson slid an inch or two away from her on the love seat.

"Yes," he murmured, although this was the only one he had seen.

Dear colleague, the letter began.

The **JEW** squats on the windowsill, the **QUEER** comes **OUT**
to snigger in the woodpile.
THE QUEERS ARE UNDERNEATH THE PILINGS
(the **Prisoner of Reading Gaol**—*Virginia and Vita,* the **QUEENS** of
silence, exile, and *cunnilingus*—
the **Bard** of *Avon calling!* loves the Dark Laddie of the Sonnets
—Kit Marlowe gives good Edward II—
little *Lottie Bronte* longs to cry across the moors, *Reader* I married **HER!**)
AND THE JEW IS UNDERNEATH THE LOT . . .

There was more after that, which Nelson, as a scholar of modernism, recognized as quotes or paraphrases from the anti-Semitic writings of Pound and Eliot. This only made it more difficult to detect the hand of the author.

"Why would she send this to me?" Vita had edged closer to Nelson again on the love seat. Their knees touched.

"Why would who send it to you?" he murmured, still distracted. Whoever had written it was no mere prankish undergraduate, and probably not even a graduate student—they didn't read Pound or Eliot much anymore. For an instant, Nelson wondered if Weissmann himself had written the letters to stir things up. But he doubted it: Ethnicity aside, Weissmann loved the sound of his own voice too much ever to do anything anonymously.

"Look." Vita brushed shoulders with Nelson, pointing at the letter. "Victoria mentions us both, together."

"Where?" He edged away from her.

"*Here.*" Vita pointed again. She peered at him from very close.

"Come on, Vita." Nelson slid away from her, holding the letter between them. "It says Virginia, not Victoria."

"She's talking about Virginia Dunning," Vita said, referring to the history graduate student she was reputed to have kissed. "I'm sure you know all about it. Everyone else does."

Nelson was taken aback; Vita had never mentioned the incident to him before.

"It's got nothing to do with you," he said, not entirely sure it didn't. "Haven't you ever read *Orlando*?"

"Why would you ask me that?" Vita gasped, her eyes wide. She clutched her throat. "Why would you ask me if I've read *Orlando*?"

"Because the letter's not talking about you and . . . whoever. It's talking about Virginia Woolf and Vita Sackville-West."

"Why would you mention *Orlando* to me?" Vita said in a quavering voice. "What has Victoria told you?"

Nelson pushed himself off the love seat and stepped over the coffee table to put some distance between Vita and himself. Vita clasped her hands tightly in her lap, the lapels of her robe parted slightly to reveal the little hearts on her nightgown.

"Look, Vita," he said, "will you let me look into this for you? I can take care of this."

"Oh, don't tell her!" Vita clapped her hands over her mouth.

"Victoria didn't send this." Nelson waved the letter in the air. "Pardon me, Vita, but it's crazy to think that she did." He licked his lips. "But I won't tell her about it. Or anybody else. I promise."

He crouched down across the coffee table from Vita. She sat wringing her hands like the beleaguered heroine of a Victorian romance, a maiden about to be taken vile advantage of.

"Will you trust me to take care of this for you?" Nelson caught her gaze. "No one will know where I got the letter. I'll find out who it is, and I'll make them stop. Okay?"

Vita watched him with her liquid gaze, her mouth working silently, and Nelson was afraid she might lunge across the table and throw her arms around him. He was afraid he'd have to run for it.

"Okay," she said at last, very meekly.

"Alright." Nelson nodded and refolded the letter. He stuck it back in the envelope, and slid the envelope inside his parka.

"Thank you." Vita was scarcely audible, her eyes welling with tears.

Nelson stammered something and started shuffling toward the door. As nervous as Vita was, he'd never seen her like this, and it embarrassed him.

"I'll let myself out," he murmured, fumbling for the doorknob behind him and opening the door. Vita sniffled on the love seat.

In the vestibule he couldn't remember which of the three doors led to the stairs, so he reached for the middle one. It was scarcely open a crack when Vita lunged past him from behind and slammed the door, splaying herself against it like a silent movie heroine barring the way to the landlord.

"Not that door," she barked, her tears drying, her eyes wide. "The one on your left."

Vita's door slammed behind him as Nelson came out onto the porch, and he stumbled over the *Book of Mormon,* neatly punting it down the steps and into the hands of one of a pair of two strapping, neatly scrubbed boys in dark overcoats. "Elder Chip" and "Elder Dale," read their plastic name tags, and when they stripped off their gloves and eagerly offered their hands to Nelson, he pressed his sparking finger into each of their palms and told them to go away and leave people alone. They blushed and backed down the steps.

"Geez, what were we thinking?" said Elder Chip.

"Yeah, where do we get off?" said Elder Dale. They hurried away into the dark, and Nelson hurried in the other direction, back toward campus.

Vita's letter was a lead weight in his pocket. He wanted to take it out and look at it, but he waited until he came to the streetlights of Michigan Avenue.

He stopped in the glare of a Chinese fast-food place called Wok'n'Roll and took out the letter. He held it close to his chest, afraid that the people hurrying by would glimpse its bilious erudition over his shoulder; it was like reading pornography in public. It's okay, he wanted to tell passersby, I'm a trained literary critic.

He read the letter once more, quickly, trying to consider it not just as a pastiche of quotes, but as a text in its own right, with particular attention to its use of rhythm and parallel structure and alliteration. But the aggressive typefaces bristled at him like spikes. There was no point in trying to follow its "argument" or determine its literary provenance. His finger burned, and he refolded the letter roughly with trembling hands, jamming it into the envelope and stuffing it angrily back inside his parka. He marched through the vivid gloom up Michigan Avenue toward his bus stop.

Someone bumped into him, and Nelson spun, his finger blazing. A student mumbled an apology as he hurried away. Nelson drew a deep breath. He was standing before Pandemonium, the coffee shop that served as Anthony Pescecane's storefront, where the real decisions of the department were made over expensive lattes and ethnic pastries, where Pescecane and Victorinix and Weissmann cut deals and negotiated spheres of influence like the Big Three at Yalta.

Nelson peered through the steamy window, his breath misting red in the glow of the neon CAPPUCCINO sign. The tables just inside the glass were taken by self-consciously intense students sitting with their books and notebooks splayed open, their legs tightly crossed, heavy cups of café mocha cooling before them. In a happier time Nelson had stopped here often, but a cup of coffee here cost more than Bridget budgeted for his lunch every day. All he could afford to do was stand with his nose pressed to the window like Tiny Tim.

He started to turn away, but beyond the students on display in the window, through the steam and the glare of fluorescent lighting, Nelson glimpsed Anthony Pescecane sitting alone in the back. From his class this afternoon he heard Lady Macbeth speaking to her husband in the therapeutic tropes of talk TV: My lord, you're just not working up to your potential. Press your advantage. Screw your courage to the sticking-place. *Life doesn't look out for people like us.* Vita's letter pressed against Nelson's heart, his finger burned, and before he knew it, he was through the door and into the chattering racket of the café.

The interior of Pandemonium was glossy and bright, with a blond parquet floor and white walls. The air was humid with breath and wet woolen clothing, but under the damp was the dry, desert aroma of coffee. Behind the counter were a tropical array of bright syrup bottles, a hissing, polished espresso machine, and tall steel samovars of hot water, gleaming like hospital equipment. Young men dangled backpacks, and young women threw their dark coats off their shoulders, and they crowded in a sort of line at the cash register, while pairs, trios, and quartets of graduate students slouched knee to knee in black bentwood chairs around wobbly little tables. The stark walls were hung with vivid opera posters, most of them variations of red and black—Gounod's *Faust,* Verdi's *Macbeth,* an opera called *Mefistofele.*

Over the undergraduate heads all around, Nelson glimpsed Anthony Pescecane sitting at a large table in the back, his tie knotted to a creamy bulge, his cashmere coat draped over a chair next to him. His legs were crossed, and his trouser cuff was lifted just enough to display a reach of pale silk sock. The knuckles of one hand rested on the tabletop beside a tiny, gold-rimmed cup of espresso.

Nelson edged through the crowd in his garishly middle-class, unnaturally orange parka, trying on a collegial smile. But as he came around a wide, square pillar hung with a poster for Penderecki's *Paradise Lost,* he saw that Pescecane was not alone, and his smile seized up. Behind the pillar, seated a little way back from the table, drinking nothing, was Marko Kraljević. Today he was wearing a brand-new suit of western wear: a red-and-black-checked shirt with buttoned pockets and piping around the seams, a string tie with a cattle skull clasp, and a pair of brand-new snakeskin cowboy boots with pointed silver toes. His blunt fingers clutched the knees of a pair of tight black jeans, and he wore a big silver belt buckle shaped like the state of Texas. He wore a brand-new black Resistol hat tipped low over his forehead and a long, black duster that hung from his shoulders and puddled on the parquet floor. With his single black eyebrow and cropped hair and a length of straw between his teeth—not an easy thing to find in Minnesota in November—he looked like a Balkan version of Garth Brooks.

Nelson balanced on the balls of his feet, ready to flee. It wasn't as if he'd known what he was going to say to Pescecane, and whatever it was, he certainly hadn't intended to say it in front of Marko Kraljević. But as he started to pivot away, Pescecane lifted his little cup to his lips, and his eye caught Nelson's. Nelson froze, but his finger burned. Kraljević stared at a point over the middle of the table, rhythmically working his piece of straw. Pescecane lowered the cup to the exact center of the saucer without taking his gaze off Nelson. He lay his knuckles against the table again and said nothing, and Nelson smiled and gasped and gestured.

"Anthony," he began, then winced and said, "Professor Pescecane."

The chairperson sat perfectly still. "How's the hand?" he asked.

"Um, great." Nelson swallowed. "Never better." He shot a glance at Kraljević.

"Whaddaya want?" Pescecane said.

"Puh, pardon me?"

"The fuck do you want, Professor?" Pescecane flexed his fingers, once, on the tabletop.

Nelson shuffled in place. He stole a glance at Kraljević, but the theorist only shifted the straw from one corner of his lips to the other, his eyes dull. Vita's letter felt like a lead bar in Nelson's parka. Pescecane flexed his hand again, and Nelson heard his wife's voice. *Press your advantage,* she said. *Screw your courage . . .*

"I can help you," Nelson blurted. "I mean, the department." He drew a sharp breath. "I can help the department."

"You can help the department," Pescecane said in a monotone.

"Yes."

"Do what?" Pescecane lifted his knuckles off the table and folded his hands over the expensive knee of his trousers.

"I can make the letters stop," Nelson said.

Pescecane breathed out slowly, as if he were disappointed in Nelson. "What letters?"

Nelson reached into his parka, but the corners of Pescecane's lips dipped slightly, and he shook his head once, briskly. Nelson jerked his hand, empty, out of his coat.

Pescecane unclasped his fingers, and he ran one powerful hand just above the glossy ridges of his hair. At the same time Kraljević pulled the piece of straw out of his mouth. "Yippie. Yo. Ki. Yay," he said, without looking at either Nelson or Pescecane.

Pescecane dipped his chin and closed his eyes as if in some minor discomfort, precisely scratching his forehead with his middle finger. "Sit." He opened his eyes and gestured to Nelson.

Nelson pulled back a chair and perched on the edge of the seat. He glanced at Kraljević, but the cowboy theorist was chewing the straw again, his eyes dull.

From across the table, Pescecane fixed Nelson with a cold stare. "You write these fucking things?"

"No!" Nelson glanced back at the crowd behind him. He hunched forward in his chair and dropped his voice. "Of course not!" he said with a glance at Kraljević. He hesitated, then assumed that Kraljević was in the chairperson's confidence. "But I . . ."

"You what?"

"I-I-I," Nelson stammered, "I know who did."

Where had that come from? Nelson had no idea who was writing the letters. "That is," he began, intending to take it back, but Pescecane lifted his hand.

"Who told you? Weissmann?"

"No. I mean, I don't *really* know who . . ."

Pescecane held up his hand again. "You're Nelson, right?"

Nelson nodded.

"You don't think I can handle this?"

"No!" Nelson protested. "I mean, yes! I mean, I think . . ."

"You think I need your help to deal with this?"

Nelson gasped wordlessly.

Pescecane curled his manicured fingers around his cup. Kraljević turned to one side and spat out the straw. His Serbian accent waxed and waned with the circumstances, but this evening it was at high tide. "My wild Irish rose," he said, but it came out, "My vile Iresh russ."

Pescecane glanced at him, then fixed his gaze on Nelson. "So you know our friend," he said.

"Who?" Nelson was trying hard not to look at Kraljević.

"Our literary friend," said Chairperson Pescecane. "Our anonymous author. The guy who wrote the letters."

Nelson fully intended to say, I have no idea who it is; I'm sorry to have wasted your time, but Pescecane cut him off with a gesture.

"That's okay, don't mention his name." Pescecane lifted his cup and took a delicate sip. Over the cup he glanced at Kraljević. "Some people got a big fucking mouth."

He lowered the cup. Kraljević sighed heavily. He pushed back his hat and lifted his eyes to the ceiling.

"Or did Mort already tell you?" Pescecane asked, his eyes brightening.

"Professor Weissmann didn't tell me anything."

"I'll bet Mort told you."

"Really, Weissmann didn't . . ."

"Mort tell you what I said to the son of a bitch?"

"No." Nelson's heart pounded. His finger burned.

Pescecane smiled to himself, remembering, then included Nelson in the smile, a seignorial gesture. "Listen. You'll like this."

Pescecane shot his cuffs. He settled in his chair and worked his neck in his high collar. He laid his hands on the tabletop. "I call him into my office. It's just me and You Know Who."

"I don't actually," Nelson said.

"No names," said Pescecane, warming to his story. "So this putz sits across the desk from me. No farther from me than you are right now. I lift one of these piece of shit letters off my desk—like he hasn't seen one before, the fuck—and I say, 'What's up with this? What are you, Ezra fucking Pound?' "

Pescecane looked away and laughed, exposing his wolfish incisors. Kraljević scrunched up his lips and worked them from side to side.

"So then this jamoke says to me, 'I didn't do it. It's not me.' " Pescecane laughed again, then fixed Nelson with a murderous glare. "So I say to him, 'You think I'm an idiot? You think I just fell off the fucking potato truck, you mick asshole? Maybe you've had a bit too much Bushmills, my friend. Maybe you got warm Guinness where your brains oughtta be.' "

The Coogan? Nelson thought, astonished.

"So he says to me, 'Jaysus, Mary, and Joseph.' " Pescecane did a better Irish accent than the Coogan did. " 'I swear to yez, Anthony, by my dear sainted mother, by the Holy Mother of God, I didn't do it. T'isn't me you're after.' "

The Coogan? Nelson hardly believed it. Sure the poet was loud and buffoonish, but he wasn't mean. He wasn't a bigot.

" 'Listen to me, you paddy bastard.' " Pescecane uncrossed his legs and leaned forward, his hands flat on the tabletop as if he meant to come across at Nelson. For the first time Kraljević looked at Nelson, his hands twitching on his knees.

" 'Nobody fucks with Anthony Pescecane. Especially not some boozed up, constipated little bigot. Shut *up,*' " he said vehemently, though neither Nelson nor Kraljević had said anything. " 'You got two choices. You can do the right thing and resign the department, in which case you can keep your retirement. Or you can get a lawyer. What's it gonna be, Ezra? You tell me.' "

Pescecane pushed himself back from the table and sighed heavily. He plucked a creamy handkerchief, matching his tie, out of the breast pocket of his coat and gestured with it.

"So I let him go on for a while. 'This is unfair, I didn't do it,' yadda yadda yadda. Then I tell him, 'Cut to the chase, pal. What's it gonna be?' "

Pescecane dabbed at his lips, looked at the handkerchief, folded it, and tucked it carefully back in his pocket. "You know what he says to me? This is rich. He says, 'I'll see you in court.' And you know what I said, Nelson? Mort tell you that much?"

Nelson shook his head. Kraljević rested his hands on his bulging thighs.

"You'll love this." Pescecane crossed his legs, folded his hands over his knee, and smiled. " 'Make my day,' " he said.

Nelson just blinked at him.

"Make my day," Pescecane said again.

"Wow," Nelson said.

Pescecane dipped his eyes and gave an insincerely self-deprecating shrug. Kraljević reached up and unbuttoned the breast pocket of his shirt, and with two fingers he pulled out a little cloth bag. "This town," he said, "ain't big enough for the two of us." *Dis tun ent beg enough vor de tooeevus.*

The pain in Nelson's finger flared. "Let me talk to him," he whispered.

Pescecane fixed Nelson with a skeptical eye. With makings from the little bag, Kraljević started to roll a cigarette.

"You think you can do better than that?" Pescecane said.

"No," murmured Nelson, "but I, I know him pretty well."

This was untrue. Nelson had spoken to the Coogan exactly once, to say, "Mind your head," when he had helped the poet into a taxi at the end of a faculty party. Just before the door closed, the Coogan had leaned out and vomited on Nelson's shoes.

"I can make him stop writing the letters," he said.

"He send you to talk to me?" Pescecane said.

"No!" Nelson was shocked. But then why shouldn't Pescecane think that he, Nelson, was the Coogan's emissary?

"No," he said again, a little more equivocally. Maybe it wouldn't hurt to let Pescecane think so. "He doesn't know I'm here. I just thought I could help the department."

"You thought you could help the department."

"I promise you," Nelson said, "he won't do it again."

"No." Pescecane lifted a blunt, admonitory finger. "Uh-uh. Wrong. He's out. He's history. He either jumps, or he gets pushed. It's up to him. You tell him I said so."

Nelson opened his mouth and closed it again. This was happening too fast; he wasn't good at this. All he wanted to do was set Vita's mind at ease, and now he had allowed himself to be cast as a player in this little drama. He glanced at Kraljević as the cowpoke deconstructionist licked his cigarette paper and folded it over a wad of tobacco.

"I'll take the dickless wonder to court if I have to," Pescecane said. "But since you're a friend of his, tell him this. It would be better for everyone if he just went. You understand what I'm saying to you, Nelson?"

"Um, well, I." Leave now, Nelson thought. You're getting in too deep. Say you're sorry to have intruded, get up, and leave.

"I'll tell you something else." Pescecane folded his hands over his knee again. "Whoever makes our friend go quietly will have rendered the department an invaluable service, *capiche?* Isn't that what you wanted to do, Nelson? Help the department?"

Nelson blinked. The pain in his finger was almost unbearable. This was Anthony Pescecane's idea of collegiality. Nelson was nothing to him. Less than a grad student really, because he had no future. If he had the chair's attention, it was only because suddenly the chair saw a brief use for him. But Nelson couldn't budge; Pescecane had fixed him in an angry glare.

Kraljević held up his fat new cigarette and crumpled it between his fingers, dropping shreds of paper and tobacco to the floor. For the first time he turned to Nelson. His accent abated somewhat. "Will no one rid me of this turbulent priest?" he said.

The pain in his finger made Nelson wince. He blinked at Kraljević, then he blinked at Pescecane. Without meaning to he now had a role in this drama, but only as a bit player with no name of his own. *Enter a Murderer,* read the stage direction.

"I don't . . ." Nelson said. "I mean, I can't . . ."

"Whoever helps me out with this is a friend of mine, Nelson. Think about it." Pescecane picked up his espresso. "Thanks for stopping by."

Nelson stood, clumsily, nearly knocking over the little bentwood chair. Kraljević gave him a broad, Balkan grin and waved his palm in a slow semicircle. "Howdy, pardner," he said.

Nelson blinked at him, speechless.

"Howdy is aloha," said Marko Kraljević. "Sometimes it means good-bye."

Out in the lamplit cold, Nelson was breathless and dizzy. His pulse was racing. The fire in his finger had receded, but it hadn't gone away altogether. Snow had begun to fall at a slant through the streetlight. Cars hissed by in the slush, their red taillights mirrored in the street. Couples arm in arm hurried past Nelson on their way to the art movie theater around the corner. Nelson looked at his watch and cursed; he should have been on the bus two hours ago, on his way home for macaroni and cheese or tuna casserole. Bridget would be angry at having to feed the girls and put them to bed without his help. He zipped up his parka and started for the bus stop, and then remembered his briefcase back in his office, full of another ninety papers he had to grade by Monday morning. He groaned and turned back, trotting across the street and up the sidewalk toward the Quad, between twin rows of bright lamps. He'd call Bridget from the office and tell her that he'd had an important meeting with the chair of the department, that he had an opportunity for—what? Advancement? Professional salvation? He wasn't even sure how far Pescecane's gratitude would go. All Nelson had to do was destroy another man's career.

His breath came short, and he stopped to lean against a kiosk papered with flyers. He splayed his hand against a weather-stained poster for a band called No Radio and tried to draw a deep breath into his tight chest. He moved slowly around the kiosk, steadying himself with his hand. If dirty work needed to be done, why not get Kraljević to do it? He'd enjoy it. He already had the outfit for it. Nelson shuddered, thinking of the switchblade at the Seminar Luncheon. But even then, the Coogan had started it. Don't waste your sympathy on the Coogan, Nelson told himself. If he wrote the letters, he thought, certainly the Coogan deserves to go. You can't have someone like that teaching young, impressionable minds. And he's not even that good a poet anymore, Nelson thought. It's not as if he's working at the peak of his powers.

Nelson found himself facing the shops and cafés on Michigan Avenue again, their bright lights blurred by the falling snow. He was as winded as a distance runner, his hand trailing across posters and broadsides for every imaginable position—Brits out of Ireland, Israelis out of Gaza, Serbs out of everywhere but Serbia. How did they all *know* it was the Coogan? Nelson asked himself. What if they were wrong? And even if they were right, what did academic freedom mean, what did tenure mean, if a man could lose his job for an opinion? Even a vile one?

Snow caught on his eyelashes and made him blink. It's none of my business, he thought. Let them fire the Coogan, let Pescecane take him to court, let Kraljević gun him down in the street at high noon. The letters will stop whether I make him quit or not. It won't be on my hands, the ruin of a man's livelihood.

Nelson swung around the kiosk and came face to face with Timothy Coogan, coming up the sidewalk between the lamps. The poet was as startled as Nelson, and both men stepped back. The Coogan was draped from shoulders to knees in a huge black overcoat dusted with snow, his face swaddled to his upper lip in a long black muffler. The two men shuffled from side to side in an Alfonse and Gaston routine, until the Coogan grunted and lunged around the other side of the kiosk. The heat in Nelson's finger focused like a welder's arc, and he bit his lip to keep from crying out loud, jigging on the sidewalk as he waved his hand in the air. The poet's steps hurried away toward Michigan Avenue, and Nelson danced in indecision. Wouldn't hurt to talk to the man, Nelson thought. Maybe he hadn't written the letters, and Chairperson Pescecane would be just as grateful to know that. Nelson wheeled around the kiosk and ran after the poet. "Professor Coogan!" he called as cheerfully as he could.

The poet's pace stuttered a few steps, and he turned, his hands in his pockets, his head sunk to the ears in the muffler. Nelson trotted up to him smiling. "Listen," he said, "could I buy you a drink?"

The Coogan watched Nelson with a liquid gaze. Nelson could almost hear the poet's already overlubricated mind slipping gears as it translated the request.

"Sure." The Coogan shrugged, and Nelson fell into step with him. They waited at the curb for a shoal of cars to hiss past on the wet street. Snow fell between them like a veil. The Coogan gave Nelson a quizzical, sideways glance.

"Who are you?" he said, through his muffler.

"A friend," said Nelson Humboldt.

138

8

Nelson in Nighttown

Up an alley, hours later, Nelson and the Coogan are pissing against a wall.

"Ahhhhhh," sighs the Coogan. The bricks before him steam pungently. "The simple pleasures of the poor."

Nelson stares drunkenly at a spray-painted slogan on the wall, inches from his nose, a long-standing leftover bit of collegiate radicalism. UP THE IRA! it reads.

"Did I mention," Nelson says, "that my wife is Irish?"

There's something Nelson wants to ask the Coogan, something he's meant to ask him all evening, but his mind keeps slipping gears, and he can't remember what it is. The Coogan's turned out to be lashings of fun, a stout fellow, a gentleman and a fuckin' scholar. Nelson sways, his stream of piss playing from side to side like the stream of a fire hose. He pretends he's trying to put something out.

"Mind yer aim, Kinch!" The Coogan punches Nelson in the arm. "I've been baptized, ye fearful Jesuit!"

Other things Nelson can't remember: What time it is. What day it is. Where he is at the moment, exactly.

"Ow!" Nelson says, when the pain reaches him.

The Coogan steps back and tucks himself up with a ritualistic formality. "Button up, Kinch," he says. "The night is young."

Out of the alley and up the street, the Coogan before, Nelson a few steps behind. They're a long way from campus, along the dowdy, gentrifying main street of Hamilton Groves, where gutted department stores and boarded-up shoe shops stand dark between neon-lit sports bars and yuppie bistros. Nelson turns slowly on his own axis as he walks, trying to get his bearings, a tricky little dance of one foot over the other, and he catches himself just before he falls over. There's the Coogan a few paces away, before the dark woodwork and beveled glass of a pricey saloon. Just beyond the glass a couple of smooth-faced yuppies, a man and a woman, are eating barbecue buffalo wings and drinking margaritas. The Coogan has veered from his progress up the pavement, drawn as a moth to the flame by their bourgeois barbarity: The young couple are daintily eating finger food off the ends of forks.

"The world's turned upside down, Kinch," the Coogan calls over his shoulder. "I'll wager this idjit eats lasagne with his bare hands."

The man and woman exchange a glance at his approach. They've driven all the way up from Minneapolis just for this, to see some colorful Hamilton Groves eccentric in his native habitat. The Coogan does not disappoint. He leans one hand against the glass, fixes the young woman with his gaze, and declaims loudly:

> *"There was a young lady from Cork*
> *Who squealed, when you poked her, like pork.*
> *But the tang of her meat*
> *Was the tastiest treat,*
> *And it came very neat off the fork."*

Señor yuppie leaps to his feet, brandishing a crusty bit of chicken at the Coogan, but yuppie señorita restrains him with a hand on his arm. The Coogan has already wheeled away from the window.

"Jot that one down for posterity, won't ye, Kinch?" he says. "I'm after compiling my collected works."

Nelson and the Coogan are drinking pitchers of dark, bitter Guinness in Slieve Bloom, an Irish bar, under the sign of crossed keys. The Coogan's known here, but they serve him anyway. There's music on a Friday night, a gaunt man on guitar and a bony, big-nosed woman on fiddle; and without leaving the booth he shares with Nelson, the Coogan shouts out a request. He sings along with the first stanza of "The Wild Colonial Boy," then weeps through the next seven verses as Gaunt the Guitar and Bony Big Nose harmonize.

"He dies in the end," the Coogan whispers wetly, halfway through the song, "but he takes the bastards with him."

Numb Nelson is chiefly aware of the room reeling. Out of the booth and off to the jakes for a piss, and the uneven, creaking floorboards rock from side to side like a rough passage from Larne to Stranraer. At the urinal Nelson's nose directs him to a pair of graffiti.

Juneau, Alaska, reads the first.

No, reads the reply, *but if you hum a few bars, I can fake it.*

Nelson considers the Unanswered Question, the one he means to ask the Coogan. If he can only remember what it is.

"Why am I here?" he asks the greasy, clammy, snot-bespeckled wall.

Back at the booth, sliding in with a hiss of polyester parka, he asks it again, "Why am I here?"

The Coogan does a classic spit take, spraying a fan of Guinness warmed to 98.6 degrees Fahrenheit. Christ, thinks Nelson, did I say that out loud?

"Well, there's an intelligent fuckin' question." The Coogan belches. "I'll bet ye keep yer students in stitches, a sharp-witted fella like yerself."

"But why *am* I here?" gasps Nelson, his parka glazed in imported beer. "I can't remember."

"It's existential doubt now, is it?" The Coogan wipes his mouth with his palm. "If that's what ye want, I'll give ye existential doubt."

The Coogan lifts his glass and leans forward.

"I should've been an Elizabethan, Kinch," he whispers. "Even if it meant being a bloody Englishman. *There* were poets, by Christ. Ben Jonson laid bricks and soldiered some and went to fuckin' prison. Kit Marlowe spied and whored and died in a barroom, stabbed to death in the forehead. They were after fighting over the check, don't ye know. Now *that's* a poet's death."

He drinks, swallows, smacks his lips.

"Whereas the worst that'll happen to me," he gasps, "is I'll lose my fuckin' tenure. It's a pusillanimous time to be a poet, Kinch. I ought to be ashamed of myself."

Nelson hears a little crystalline *ping!* like the chime of a wineglass, but there're only two foamy beer glasses and an empty plastic pitcher on the table. You *ought* to be ashamed, thinks Nelson, meaning the Coogan, then claps his hand over his mouth. Did I say that out loud?

The Coogan bangs on the table with the pitcher.

"Molly!" he bellows. "Molly Molly Molly!"

The music stopped some time ago; Gaunt and Big Nose are nowhere to be seen. When did that happen? A waitress is standing a step back from the end of the table, arms akimbo.

141

"Who's Molly?" she says.

Good question, thinks Nelson. She doesn't look Irish; she looks Hispanic, with black hair and dark eyes and olive skin. She stands with her lips pursed, her hip canted, her little apron across her darling lap like a loincloth. Darling lap. Nelson claps his hand over his mouth. Did I say that?

"He's Kinch," says the Coogan, pointing at Nelson. "Sharp as a fuckin' knife is Kinch." He adds, in a hoarse stage whisper, "But don't ask him about his mother."

The waitress swings her level gaze to Nelson. "Mum's the word," she says.

A breathless pause. Nelson and the Coogan catch each other's eye and erupt into laughter. Nelson laughs so hard he snorts Guinness through his nose.

"And how's that Hebrew husband of yours?" the Coogan says to the waitress.

Ping! Something swims up out of the sea of beer behind Nelson's eyes, and for a moment he can almost glimpse what it is. It's something to do with Hebrews. That and the Coogan's shame.

"Maybe you guys have had enough," the waitress says.

"Not lately," says the Coogan, and he leans out of the booth to make a feeble lunge for the waitress's ass. She steps nimbly back, and the Coogan catches himself, barely, by the edge of the table. She glances back at the bar.

"Oh, Jaysus." The Coogan is nearly prone on his seat, peering one-eyed over the edge of the table. "Is he after watching us, Kinch?"

"Who?"

"The barman, ye jejune Jesuit," hisses the Coogan. "Stately, plump whatsisname."

Nelson turns to look, and the Coogan hisses at him again. "Don't be so bloody obvious about it!"

So Nelson looks at the ceiling. He looks in his glass. He looks at his watch. He looks at the empty stage. Then, with a wide yawn, he looks at the bartender standing at the end of the bar, his hands on the bartop. A big fellow, and he's watching.

"Well?" The Coogan is nearly under the table.

"Yes," whispers Nelson. "He's watching us."

The Coogan lifts his head and ducks down again.

"O shite and onions, Kinch, it's Blazes Boylan! The man himself!"

The Coogan propels himself out of the booth, nearly horizontal. He's all elbows and knees, bulging at all angles through his vast black overcoat like two weasels fighting in a sack. Nelson manages a more graceful, polyester-hissing exit, but once upright Nelson dare not take a step because every direction from where he stands is *down*. The room wheels around him on a pivot, and the Coogan passes him once, roaring, then the bartender passes, cracking his knuckles. Nelson is lifted and propelled down the slope of the barroom floor on his toes. He sails out the door into the snow, skidding sideways like a hockey player.

"K.M.R.I.A.!" howls the Coogan, sailing out after him. "Kiss my royal Irish arse!"

In the bitter, frosty cold, they clutch each other for support, their single blue shadow staggering in the streetlight along the pavement, a rough beast, a hunchbacked, two-headed, four-legged thing. The freezing haze roughens Nelson's throat and tightens his skin. Is the Coogan holding him up, or is he holding up the Coogan? Is there a difference?

"Irish women," the Coogan pants. "They'll cut ye so quick yer half drained before ye know yer bleeding."

"Funny," Nelson says, trying to master the use of his feet, "she didn't look Irish."

"Black Irish." The Coogan peels himself off Nelson a finger at a time. "The worst kind. Daughter of a fair Limerick colleen and some dusky Spanish sailor washed up from the Armada, a commingling of bloodlines ye can trace all the way back to fuckin' Morocco."

"Did I mention," says Nelson, "that my wife is Irish?"

"I had a wee Jewish girl once." The Coogan stands free at last. "Speaking of Mediterraneans. A mouth like velvet she had, so. She could suck a billiard ball through thirty feet of garden hose."

Nelson's ears are pinging again, or is it just the cold?

"Why did you say she was Jewish?" he says.

"Because she *was*." The Coogan staggers up the sidewalk. "She was of the Hebraic persuasion. She was Judeo but not Christian. The fuck difference does it make?"

In slow motion, in the misting cold, the Coogan turns and swings his ham fist at Nelson. Nelson ducks in slow motion. He finds himself propped against a wall, his parka caught on the rough red brick at his back.

"There was a time, Kinch," the Coogan is saying, waving his finger at Nelson from inches away, "when teaching poetry was a license to fornicate."

He wobbles, an inflatable clown who cannot fall over.

"Every semester, another crop of virgins." He lifts his eyes to a golden past. "I'd look out over that classroom full of sweet young faces, and I'd pick one out like I was picking a chocolate out of a box. It was a perquisite of the job. Like free books. Like summers off. Like a fuckin' parking space."

He sighs heavily, and even in the freezing air, Nelson can feel the brewery blast of the poet's breath.

"Nobody complained. Nobody noticed. Nobody got hurt. Twas a fair exchange. Good value on the dollar. The young ladies could tell their grandkids that they lost their cherry to a real Irish poet, and I got more pussy than Mick Jagger."

The Coogan digs his thick fingers deep into Nelson's parka. "There once was a poet named Tim," he says,

> "Who whored all his life after quim.
> But the feminist crowd
> Said, 'Tim, that's not allowed.'
> Now Tim's chances for quim are quite slim."

The Coogan's eyes have a pleading, liquid gleam, but he isn't seeing Nelson at all. Waves of the Coogan's murderous breath wash against Nelson's face, while behind Nelson's eyeballs there's a steady pulse that goes *ping! ping! ping!*

"I have two daughters, sir," Nelson manages to say, and an alarm goes off in his head. What time *is* it? Where am I? Bridget will want to know. Talk about your sharp Irish women.

"Then ye'll want to be keeping them from the likes of me." The Coogan focuses at last on Nelson. "Don't teach yer daughters poetry, Kinch, that's my advice."

He turns away, but reaches back one-handed and peels Nelson away from the wall.

"No lollygagging, Kinch!" he cries. "Off we go, slouching toward Bethlehem! March or die, Kinch, march or die."

Down darker streets away from the student bars and yuppie saloons, where gloomy industrial buildings stand behind cyclone fence and razor wire. Streetlights are half as frequent as before, and half of those are smashed. Breathlessly they enter the sickly yellow light of a nameless workingman's bar, a squat, clammy, windowless box of cinder block. Flickering neon signs advertise blue collar beers with blunt Teutonic names—Hamm's, Schlitz, Pabst. The only heat's a roaring gas burner over the door. Gray-faced men of indeterminate age slump in shapeless flannel coats at the bar. Nelson and the Coogan slump as well in one of the two booths at the back under an undusted Stroh's sign that hasn't been lit since Nixon was president.

The flinty bartender brooks no brouhaha from anybody.

"Glenfiddich?" inquires the Coogan, not sounding too sure about it.

"Jim Beam," says the barkeep, and the Coogan buys the bottle entire to keep on the man's exceedingly narrow good side.

A bottle and two chipped glasses on the sticky, beer-ringed tabletop. No more undergraduate friskiness. The giddiness of beer is over. It's time for serious drinking, when a man can crawl up his own fundament and vanish quietly without a trace. In keeping with the dress code, the Coogan sits red-faced in his coat, stewing in Kentucky bourbon and his own sweat.

"You hate me, don'tcha, Kinch?"

His deadened gaze. His murderous breath across the table.

"But I *don't*," protests Nelson, pretty sweaty himself in his lurid parka. "It's the truth."

He just doesn't want this man near his daughters, and that's the truth too. The distant pinging in his brain.

"The truth," says the Coogan, his accent a good deal less distinct than before, "that's rich."

He erupts into a wheezing laugh, which ends only when he downs the contents of his glass.

"Easy," says Nelson. He lifts the bourbon and tries to top up his glass, the Coogan's glass, both their glasses, the mouth of the bottle turning and turning in a widening gyre about the lip of his tumbler. At last bottle meets tumbler with a clink, and bourbon splashes out, some of it in the glass.

"But you do," the Coogan insists, "hate me. That's why you're here, init? It's your nature, as the frog said to the scorpion. Not just you, Kinch, but the whole useless, Jesuitical lot of ya. Morons. Vermin. Curates. Cretins. *Crrritics.*"

The Coogan begins a wet, hacking cough that goes on for some time. Some small figure in Nelson's brain sits before a greenish sonar screen, which goes steadily *ping . . . ping . . . ping* while the figure searches the depths for an echo. He should have approached the Coogan that first moment on the curb, when Nelson could have taken the poet by the hand, man to man, and said to him . . . what? Something surfaces for a moment, then dives again into the darkness.

"Plato was the first," the Coogan wheezes. "To hate poets, I mean. Showed us to the border of his tinpot republic and told us to *piss off.* Unless, of course, we wrote him hymns to the gods and songs of praise to famous men. Otherwise, it's on yer bike, paddy. No poets need apply."

Ping! Is that an echo? Something down there in the deep?

"Nobody trusts *Plato* anymore," Nelson insists, his gullet burning. Whoever said bourbon was smooth was a fucking liar. "He's phallo . . . he's phallogo . . . he's . . ."

Nelson reaches for the bottle and misses.

"But you're still after reading the bastard, aren't ya?" The Coogan lurches forward. "It's the same fucking argument; you've just tarted it up with new jargon. A poem can't ever just be a poem, it has to *enlighten,* it has to *empower.* It must represent the Hottentots in the most flattering fucking light. It must transgress the hegemonific fucking discourse. In other words, a poem must do *fuck all,"* shouts the Coogan, "but what it does best!"

His rising voice catches the unforgiving eye of the barman, but the Coogan falls deflated back in his seat.

"Beauty and truth, Kinch," the Coogan says. "Beauty and truth. All the rest is bumper stickers."

The Coogan lifts the bourbon and gauges the level against the sickly light. He holds his glass to the light as well and unerringly aims the bottle into it.

"Bugger Plato," he mutters, and giggles like a schoolboy. "But then he'd've enjoyed that, wouldn't he? The old sod."

Ping! That's something! Up she rises!

"To the ould sod," Nelson says, lifting his glass, trying to change the subject.

But the Coogan's not listening. He's swirling Jim Beam against the light, Dr. Jekyll judging the proportions.

"I'm your tamed poet," he says, "your artist in captivity. Old Ezra was the last poet in the wild, and you put him in a fuckin' cage. After which we poets learned our lesson and found ourselves a nice cage each and handed the likes of you the bloody key. In exchange for what? Lifetime employment and summers off."

He drinks, one burning gulp. Winces, eyes watering.

Ping! Ping! Ping! goes Nelson's sonar. Something the Coogan said has set it off, and this time Nelson thinks he catches the shape of it swimming up out of the waves behind his eyeballs. It's Pound. The Coogan mentioned that old anti-Semite, Ezra Pound.

"The pure products of America used to go crazy." The Coogan belches. "Now they do committee work."

Not to mention, thinks sobering Nelson, that crack about that old bugger, Plato.

The Coogan pours another, holds the glass between himself and Nelson, and closes one eye.

"I had a member of my tenure committee tell me I was a minor poet. A minor poet."

He peers through the amber glass with one liquid eye.

"To my *face*," roars the Coogan, slamming the glass on the table. Bourbon erupts volcanically out of his glass. The bottle and Nelson's tumbler thump on the tabletop like clog dancers.

Thar she blows! Ahoy the great white whale! Nelson presses himself back in his seat, shocked another quarter inch toward sobriety. The barrel-chested bartender, his face set like old concrete, comes around the bar. The shapeless men scarcely turn to watch.

"You two." The bartender twists a rag between his massive hands like he's killing a chicken. "Get out."

The Coogan slides halfway out of the booth, stops, and reaches for the bottle. The bartender clamps him by the wrist and squeezes until the Coogan lets go.

"I paid for that bottle," the Coogan says, rubbing his wrist.

"You paid for the booth." The barman's eyes are like gun slits. "I let you drink from the bottle."

The Coogan stands, barely. Nelson hisses out and edges all the way around the massive bartender. The Coogan's eyes are full of need and self-pity, and Nelson can tell he's considering a grab for the bourbon.

"Come on," Nelson says, trying to turn him away by his shoulder.

"Take your hands off me!" The Coogan leaps back, putting the bartender between himself and Nelson. "Murderer!"

Now Nelson's stone sober. He remembers why he's here. Vita's letter is still nestled inside his parka, and for the first time since they started drinking this evening—or was it last evening?—he feels the weight of it against his heart. His finger throbs.

147

"That man's my executioner!" The Coogan clutches the bartender from behind, turning him toward Nelson. "He's been sent to kill me!"

"I-I-I," stammers Nelson.

The bartender flips his rag over his shoulder, freeing his hands. Nelson backs
away.

And the Coogan, with no one watching, snatches the bourbon from the table,
breaks surprisingly nimbly around the bartender, and dashes for the door.

The barman lunges, knocking Nelson sideways and breathless. He catches the
Coogan by his coat and reels him in, the Coogan's feet scrabbling against the
gritty linoleum, the bottle clutched to his chest. The barman turns the poet and
slams a fist into the Coogan's gut. The bottle drops and smashes. The Coogan
doubles over silently and nearly falls, except that Nelson catches him under the
arms and hauls him, gasping and groaning, backward toward the door.

A fine, steady snow hisses through the freezing air. A rubbled lot under a single
harsh light, bordered by water-stained brick wall on one side, by darkness on the
other three. Shattered concrete, broken glass, shards of tin, twisted lengths of re-
bar, all blurred and blunted by a thick layer of snow. Two men, one holding the
other, furrow the drifts, lurching and twisting as broken bricks shift under their
feet. The man in the slippery parka breathes hard, supporting his companion, his
breath misting steadily. The man doubled over in the overcoat blows out pale
clouds at irregular intervals. He clutches his gut with one hand, and he flails feebly
with his other at the one holding him up. At last, almost by accident, he catches the
man in the parka in the face with the back of his hand, and the parka lets him go.
The overcoat falls heavily to his knees, threatens to topple over, rights himself with
his knuckles in the snow. On all fours, hunched almost like a runner at the block,
he retches, a thin, clear stream that plunges steaming through the snow.

He wipes his mouth with the back of his hand, then pushes himself back on
his knees, breathing out clouds of vapor. He looks up. The man above him is
lost in the glare of the overhead light.

"Murderer," gasps the Coogan.

Nelson stands steady and clearheaded above him. Nelson's skin, clammy from
sitting in bars with his parka on, is tightening around him in the cold like a black
leather glove. Only his finger is warm. In the glaring overhead light, the snow all
around, in the air, on the ground, sparkles like diamonds.

"That little wop sent you to do me in, didn't he?" The Coogan's accent is

148

gone now. His voice is thin; he can't manage anything more than a whisper. "You're here to *make my day*, isn't that right?"

Did he? thinks Nelson. Am I? He says nothing.

"Nobody ever expects the Spanish Inquisition," the Coogan says, laughing hoarsely. He looks up at Nelson.

"You're my judge, jury, and executioner." He smiles. "Don't be so surprised. You've the soul of a Jesuit torturer, every fucking one of you. It's the hallmark of your parasitical profession. Blindness and insight, isn't that it? We're the blind bastards, and you've got all the insight. You set yourself up as little paper gods, and you judge *everybody*. You judge your students. You judge your colleagues. You judge each other's useless fucking books."

He coughs, a feeble honk lost in the cold.

"But most of all you judge *us*," the Coogan says, watching Nelson sidelong, "the poor artists, the idiot savants who create the grist for your fucking mill."

"Everybody's innocent," says Nelson, "until proven guilty."

The grip of the cold tightens around Nelson, and he can feel it squeezing his heart. He has little pity left for this poor, sodden, foul-mouthed, lustful, bigoted drunk. This man kneeling in the snow is a threat—to the department, to his colleagues, to his students, to Nelson's innocent young daughters. The Coogan watches Nelson's hand with a narrow interest as Nelson's reaches into his parka and produces Vita's letter. He unfolds it, crisp and crackling in the frozen air.

"Did you write this?" His finger burns.

The Coogan glances wearily at the letter. He pinches his lapels together with pale fingers and looks away through the snow glittering through the lamplight.

"It's Pound's fate turned on its head, isn't it? You're going to drag me out of my cage and let me die in the wild. Where I've forgotten how to live." He's breathing hard, blurring his face with his own steam. "Same conniving crew of murderers, though. Pound was done in by the Italians and the Jews, and so am I. Victorinix is in on it too, isn't she? Our own little road company Gertrude Stein. It's the one thing all three of them can agree on. Screw the poet."

His shoulders start to shake under the vast coat. He expels little chugging clouds of steam. He's laughing.

"There was an unfortunate mick," he wheezes,

> "Who made much too free with his dick.
> An Italian and Jew

149

The Coogan's hacking with laughter. Nelson refolds the letter along its knife-edge creases, slides it silently into his parka again. He can't feel his hands, or rather, he seems to manipulate them from a distance. His burning finger seems to float entirely free of him of its own accord. Distantly, he's aware of the action of every muscle, the cold charge of every nerve impulse. He steps toward the Coogan. The snow crunches under his boot.

The Coogan starts violently at the sound, tumbling sideways onto his backside. He crawls crabwise away from Nelson through the snow, backward across the broken field, gasping.

"You think we're arrogant," pants the Coogan, "but we're not. We're the humble ones. Always have been. Right from the start, from Caedmon on. The first poem in English, and it's all about how God creates everything. We create nothing. Especially poetry. We're only stewards. Vessels for the Word of God. That's what you can't stand. Proof that there's a higher authority than literary critics. *Agh!*"

The Coogan yelps, yanks a hand out of the snow, collapses onto his back. He looks at his hand, holds it up for Nelson to see. He's cut himself on something sharp under the snow. His blood is as bright as a flower.

Nelson pauses, looming over the poet.

"You're full of passionate intensity, Kinch, I can see that." The Coogan closes his palm, clutches it to his chest. "But hold on for a moment. Listen."

His chest heaves under his coat. He closes his eyes. He speaks.

> *"Loss of our learning brought darkness, weakness and woe*
> *on me and mine, amid these unrighteous hordes.*
> *Oafs have entered the places of the poets*
> *and taken the light of the schools from everyone."*

He opens his eyes. Tears are squeezing down his cheeks. Nelson is crouching over him now on one knee. The Coogan begins to tremble.

"Where's your humility, Kinch? Only the arrogant look at all of creation and see nothing but words, words, words. The worst tragedy in life, don't you know. We are all of us in the gutter, Kinch, but some of us are looking at the stars."

He heaves himself up one last time out of the snow and digs his fingers into Nelson's parka.

"Lift your eyes, you Jesuits!" he cries. "And ask yourselves the question, what is the stars? What is the stars?"

Nelson takes him by the wrists and squeezes until the Coogan releases his grip. There's a stain of blood on Nelson's parka. The Coogan collapses full length, head to toe, as though he intends to make an angel in the snow. He's staring up into the sky, but there are no stars to be seen in the glare of the lamp, only the flakes, silver and dark, falling obliquely against the lamplight.

"Out of key with my time," murmurs the Coogan, "I strove to resuscitate the dead art of poetry." His blue lips work soundlessly for a moment. "Wrong from the start."

Nelson's on one knee beside him, head bowed. He might be praying, or administering final unction, but he looks over his shoulder and sees nothing through the faintly falling snow, nothing beyond the thick drifts over the wreckage in the yard, only darkness all around. The blows and buffets of the world, Nelson thinks, have so incensed me, I am reckless what I do to spite the world. The flame in his finger soars, and he takes the Coogan by the hand, flesh against flesh, neither man feeling the other's touch, and tells the poet what he has to do.

9

The Morning After

Nelson awoke with the worst hangover of his life. He cracked an aching eyelid to find himself looking up at pipes and wiring and the cobwebbed underside of his living room floor. He was in the cold basement of his town house, lying on the bare mattress of their rollaway bed. His daughter Abigail stood a few paces away in the dim subterranean light, watching him with narrow eyes and clutching some headless Sesame Street character upside down.

"Daddy smell bad," she said, and dashed up the stairs.

Nelson sat, very slowly, and swung his enormous feet to the floor. He still wore his rubbers. He was still in his parka as well, with a brownish stain of dried blood on its left lapel. He could smell himself, a mingling of liquor and sweat and bad breath. His mouth was parched and furry.

He climbed the stairs, squinting in the light, rubbing his stubbled cheeks. His head pounded with each step, and he had to rest when he got to the top, clutching both sides of the doorway. Bridget was in the kitchen, cooking eggs and bacon and furiously ignoring him. He knew he didn't even dare speak to her, and he laboriously swung his gaze to daughter Clara, who sat at the dining table, reading the color funnies and ignoring her father with the same furious tilt to her neck as her mother's. The smell of simmering fat made Nelson nauseous, and he wondered distantly if he could make it upstairs to the bathroom in time on his trembling knees. His vision had narrowed to a small circle like a pin spot, and he swung his head slowly, looking for the clock. He couldn't remember where it was.

"What time is it?" he heard himself say, without meaning to speak. He wasn't sure he was intelligible to anybody but himself.

"It's *Sunday morning*, Daddy," said Clara, without lifting her gaze from the funnies, a perfect simulacrum of her mother, only an octave higher.

Nelson staggered upstairs, where he showered and shaved and stuffed his reeking clothes into the bottom of the hamper. Standing at the sink in a clean pair of briefs, he dabbed at the front of his parka with a washcloth. Some of the blood flaked off, but a brown, ineradicable stain remained deep in the polyester. Pulling on a clean pair of trousers and a shirt in the bedroom, he remembered the papers he needed to grade by Monday, still sitting on his office desk on campus. So he pulled on the parka again, bent with a throbbing head to pull on his boots, and went downstairs. A plate of cold bacon and eggs sat at his place as Bridget and the girls silently ate their breakfast, and Nelson's gorge rose again. Only Abigail watched him as he passed, and he kept his eyes on the floor all the way out the door.

Under a pale blue November sky, the campus was empty on a Sunday morning, buried under the thick quilt of another snowfall Saturday night. Sunlight glittered painfully off the fallen snow. The maintenance crews had not even ploughed the sidewalks yet, and Nelson, squinting against the snow glare, trudged through the silence, making the first deep tracks across the Quad. He looked blearily up at the clock tower, its battlements and window ledges heaped with white. A wind high up blew some snow against the sky in a little dry mist—like a ghost—and Nelson felt a chill. He wondered if the tower had attracted another suicide in the last twenty-four hours, and he just didn't know it yet. The last he had seen of the Coogan was on the poet's front porch, while a yawning cabbie waited in a taxi at the curb. Nelson peered nervously into the snow-filled gully of the library Annex, its sloping glass heaped with drifts; he half expected to see a poet-sized hole punched in the snow. But the skylight of the Annex was a smooth curve of white, and Nelson lifted his face to the tower, meeting the wide, white gaze of the clock face without fear. It was too cold for ghosts.

Nelson let himself into Harbour Hall with his key and stamped his feet just inside the door to shake the snow loose, the slap of his rubbers reverberating off the walls of the lobby. On the poet's porch last night, propped up in his own front door, the Coogan had dug his fingers into Nelson's parka and wept down the front of it.

"Where will I go?" he sobbed. "What will I do?"

"Frankly, my dear . . ." Nelson had nearly said, but instead he left the Coogan just inside the door, slumped against the wall of his foyer, his legs splayed in front of him, his hands palm up in his lap, snot dripping off his chin. Nelson did not remember the cab ride back to married housing.

He climbed the stairs to the third floor slowly. In his office he took Vita's letter out of his parka without looking at it, stuck it in a campus mail envelope, and left it on her desk. His finger burned a little as he handled it, disgusting him. He almost wished he could just cut it off again.

He tried to work for a while, but the lines of type of his students' papers seemed to slide and strobe across the page, and finally he pushed them away. Without really thinking about where he was going, he got up from his desk and opened the door and turned right down the hall. All the creative writing faculty, even the tenured ones, had their offices on the third floor, with the visiting professors and the adjunct lecturers, and Nelson edged along the gray brick past one office door after another until he came in sight of Timothy Coogan's office. He stopped. The door was not just ajar, it was wide open.

Nelson licked his lips and glanced back down the hall, toward his own office, toward the elevators. Apart from a few caffeine-crazed comp teachers in the Bomb Shelter, he thought, I'm probably the only living soul in the building. Which was an unfortunate turn of phrase: His heart began to pound and his knees to tremble, and he felt himself drawn against his will toward the open doorway, expecting at any moment to see someone sprawled across the linoleum. Or worse: What if someone were hanging from the suspended ceiling, someone massive and limp and dark against the sparkle of the snowlight from the Quad, dangling perfectly still in the dead air? Nelson's finger turned to ice. He could scarcely breathe.

But the office was empty. More than that, it was stripped bare. All that remained was the university-issue furniture: an office chair worn in the seat, a battered Steelcase desk, gray metal bookcases. All of the Coogan's effects were gone: the books crammed into the bookcases, the piles of old copies of the *Irish Times* and *American Poetry Review* in the corners, his threadbare Turkish rug. For the first time in two decades, his desk was cleared down to the black matte desktop, and even the pushpins had been removed from the crumbling corkboard glued to the wall. Nelson crept in as quietly as he could, as if afraid of waking something. There was not a scrap of paper or a dropped paper clip on the floor, not a shred of Scotch tape left on the walls. The Coogan's Bord Failte poster, reading "Come back to Innisfree!" in English and Gaelic, which he had placed over the pebbled glass of his door to give himself a measure of privacy for whatever it was he got up to in his office, was gone. The only traces of his existence were the pale rectangles where his Easter Rebellion proclamation and magazine photos of famous poets used to be affixed to the walls. The office didn't even smell like the Coogan any longer, but was unheated and dank, almost sepulchral. Nelson's shoulders were hunched, and his neck was tight, as if he were afraid of being struck from behind. He was tempted to open the drawers of the desk, but he was afraid of the noise and afraid of what he might find.

A footstep scraped behind him. Nelson whirled. Lionel Grossmaul stood in the doorway, wearing a sagging sweater that emphasized the narrowness of his shoulders and the breadth of his backside. He stood very still and watched Nelson with his angry, bug-eyed glare, his thick lenses magnifying his pale eyeballs. He looked to Nelson like Gollum.

"Your wife told me you were in your office," he said in his strangled voice. The way he said *"your* office" sounded like an accusation.

"I-I-I saw the door open," Nelson stammered. "I just came down to, um . . ."

"Professor Coogan is no longer with the university," said Lionel. "He resigned yesterday, effective immediately."

Lionel swallowed, and his Adam's apple jerked almost audibly under his skin, in a way that made Nelson's stomach twist. *Gollum.*

"He resigned on a *weekend,*" Lionel went on, the note of accusation sharpening. *"Somebody* had to clean out his office. I suppose he couldn't wait until Monday."

Nelson didn't dare move. The empty office seemed to tighten around him. "I don't know anything about it," he said.

"Chairperson Pescecane would like to see you tomorrow," Lionel said, "at your earliest convenience."

Nelson blinked, and Lionel was gone from the doorway. Nelson stood paralyzed for a moment, listening to the crunch of Lionel's footsteps against the grit in the hallway; then he dashed out the door and down the hall. He glimpsed Lionel stepping into the elevator, and Nelson skidded to a stop just outside the doors.

"Wait!" Nelson cried.

The doors were already closing on Lionel's furious glare.

"Do you know what he wants to see me about?" Nelson blurted, twisting to peer through the narrowing gap of the elevator doors.

"Yes," said Lionel Grossmaul, as the doors slid shut.

After another night on the rollaway in the basement, Nelson arrived on campus to find his two morning classes nearly empty. It was the week of Thanksgiving, and most of his students had left already. He handed back two or three papers in each class and sent the stragglers home; then he plucked up his nerve and took the elevator to the eighth floor.

Lionel was at his post before the door to Pescecane's office, hammering violently at his computer keyboard. He took his eyes away from the screen only to look very significantly at his watch. "You're too late," he said. "He's on his way to Switzerland."

"You didn't tell me a time," Nelson protested, breathlessly.

Lionel's lips twitched. "He just left." His fingers never left the keyboard. "If you run very fast, like a little bunny, you might catch him on the way to his car."

Nelson took the stairs and bolted out of Harbour Hall without his coat. He raced through the stretches of melting snow on the Quad in his street shoes, trying to leap the puddles and landing neatly in the middle of every one. Luckily the Quad was virtually deserted, all the students and many of the faculty having already left for the holiday. The only person in sight was Fu Manchu, who stood straddling the top of a cement trash can in his sleeveless vest like the Colossus of Rhodes. "Run, motherfucker!" he howled, as Nelson passed. Then, in the distance, Nelson saw the retreating figures of Anthony Pescecane and Miranda DeLaTour in their sweeping, expensive overcoats, halfway down the mall on their way to the faculty parking structure.

Nelson caught up to them on the first level of the structure. The chairperson was holding the passenger door of his Jaguar, and Miranda was swinging her well-turned calves into the car. Nelson only caught a glimpse as she folded her overcoat over her legs and Pescecane shut the door. Nelson called out breathlessly as he trotted forward, ducking his head under the low concrete beams.

"Anthony!" he gasped, and Pescecane turned, the skirts of his coat swirling.

"Prah, Professor Pescecane," Nelson said, stammering to the rhythm of his pounding heart.

Pescecane looked Nelson up and down as he approached. Miranda stared blankly through the windshield into space. Nelson stumbled to a stop on the other side of the car from the chair.

"There's blood upon thy face," said Pescecane.

Nelson's hand flew to his cheek, and the chairperson laughed, exposing his wolfish incisors. He unlocked his door and opened it, standing in the gap with his forearms on top of the sports car and his keys dangling from his thick forefinger.

"You wanted to see me?" Nelson blushed.

"It's a funny thing, Nelson," said Pescecane. "Somebody quit the department all of a sudden. Suddenly the budget's loosened up a little, and we have a little extra money. Can you fucking beat that?"

Nelson coughed and cleared his throat.

"So, miraculously, I'm in a position to offer you a three-year lectureship. For services rendered." He smiled. "Unless you have another opportunity you'd like to pursue."

Nelson caught himself staring at Miranda in the passenger seat, shaking back her hair and looking bored.

"Nelson?"

"No!" he burst out. "I mean, yes! I mean, yes, I'll take the lectureship. I don't have any other, um . . ."

"It's not much money," Pescecane said, "but it's more than you're making now. There's some committee work involved." Pescecane pulled his door wider and started to slide behind the wheel. He paused, his powerful hand on the top of the Jaguar.

"It's a hiring committee." He lifted a corner of his lips in a lupine grin. "Suddenly I've got a budget line to fill. Come see me after I get back from Gstaad." He got in and slammed the door.

"Thank you," murmured Nelson, feeling limp and light-headed. But the car roared to life, lurched back out of its space, and swerved around Nelson. Nelson jumped back, and the car jerked to a stop. Pescecane's window rolled down with a little electric whine.

"I hope you can handle it, Nelson," the chairperson said, and next to him, out of sight of Nelson under the low, pearl gray roof of the sports car, Miranda DeLaTour let out a peal of glittering laughter. The window whined up again. Pescecane laughed behind the tinted glass. The car roared out of the structure and into the street with the shriek of tires against pavement.

Nelson arrived home that evening with the biggest turkey he could find at the supermarket near married housing. Bridget, he knew, had planned on having meatloaf for Thanksgiving dinner; but Nelson, feeling flush, had taken fifty dollars out of the ATM and bought the turkey—a fresh one too, not frozen. In the checkout line he brushed the cashier's wrist with his finger and got the bird for half price. He also bought a half-dozen red roses at a considerable discount from

157

the florist's shop in the same strip mall, and arrived on his own doorstep like a gawky and solicitous Bob Cratchit, the bulging turkey cradled in one arm, the flowers in the other.

"A *lectureship?*" Bridget said, her first words to him in three days. "What on earth for?"

Nelson stood in his parka, grinning happily. Abigail edged around him and barricaded herself behind her mother. In her young life she had never seen her father so full of energy and hope, and it frightened her. Bridget reached behind her to stroke her daughter's head. "I mean," she said, blushing, "what's changed?"

Nelson stood with his mouth opened to speak, and nothing came out. Bridget peered at him, suspicion and incipient forgiveness passing in waves over her face.

"They need me," Nelson said at last. "They're shorthanded all of a sudden, and they need me to . . . to . . . pick up the slack."

"I don't understand this at all," Bridget said, but her body was looser; she wasn't holding herself in rigid refusal of him any longer. Nelson shifted the turkey in his arms and stepped closer to her.

"Things are going to get better," he started to say, but he was interrupted by an escalating shriek from his daughter, which made both parents look down. Abigail was staring with round, enormous eyes at a large blister inside the turkey's plastic wrapping. Blood dripped rapidly from the blister to the floor, splashing Nelson's rubbers.

"Daddy!" she cried. "What have you done?"

PART TWO

The Rope Dance

These Diversions are often attended with fatal Accidents, whereof great Numbers are on Record. I my self have seen two or three Candidates break a Limb. But the Danger is much greater, when the Ministers themselves are commanded to shew their Dexterity: For, by contending to excel themselves and their Fellows, they strain so far, that there is hardly one of them who hath not received a Fall; and some of them two or three.

—Jonathan Swift, *Gulliver's Travels*

10

The Story of O

A week before Christmas, an hour after he turned in grades for the fall semester, Nelson treated himself to lunch at Peregrine. After the turn of the year he was going to be making nearly twice what he was bringing home now, so he reckoned he could afford a celebratory meal. Indeed, after the semester he'd had, he believed he was entitled to one of the fashionable grill's hamburgers. He had been constructing one in his imagination for weeks now: eight ounces of ground round, medium rare, on one of Peregrine's toasted Kaiser rolls, with aged Swiss cheese and tart honey mustard and a slice of full-bodied, vine-ripened tomato from Peregrine's own greenhouse. There would be fries as well, real ones, a large handful of big, crisp wedges of Idaho potato with the skin on, dusted with seasoning salt. The burger would be garnished with a little moist heap of pickle slices, a long wedge of kosher dill across the lettuce, and a firm, cool, thick slice of sweet Vidalia onion, the tang of which Nelson could feel in his sinuses even before he got to the restaurant. And an imported beer, he thought as he crossed the Quad, or maybe even a really good domestic one, one of Peregrine's own blends perhaps, from the microbrewery in their basement. . . .

Nelson winced at the thought of beer. At odd moments he thought he could still smell the Coogan's breath, as if the poet were standing just over his shoulder. Depending on who one talked to, the Coogan had either exiled himself to the Irish enclave of Chicago or New York or to Ireland itself. One story had it that he had been offered tenured positions by half the small liberal arts colleges in the Midwest—including Halcyon, Nelson's alma mater—but that the Coogan, even now, was too proud to step down to a less prestigious school. Better to live off of his friends than teach undergraduates who couldn't get into Harvard, Stanford, or Midwest. Nelson decided he'd be perfectly happy with a big, cold glass of Coke.

He stopped at Paideia, the little scholarly bookshop across the street from the grill, and bought a brand-new, ink-smelling copy of the *New York Review of Books*. For the longest time he had resigned himself to reading badly disheveled, incomplete, two-month-old copies of the magazine in the Annex, when he had time to read it at all; a new copy was another luxury, like lunch at Peregrine. At the cash register he pretended to cast a knowing eye across the two-tone cover, where the headlines were stacked up in the intellectual equivalent of a boxing card, decipherable only to the cognoscenti: "Dworkin on Fish," "Wills on MacKinnon," "Gordon on Gordon."

Coming out of the bookstore, Nelson hung back with his hand on the door to wait for Linda Proserpina to pass. He had almost not recognized her—thickened under a huge serape, her sharp face rounded and smooth, her salt-and-pepper hair pulled back in a tight bun. She had just come out of the student discount store next door with a box of Little Debbie snack cakes, and she had stopped on the sidewalk just outside the bookstore to tear the end off the box. Nelson pretended to read a flyer taped to the door—for a performance poetry group called Haskell, It's Real—and waited as the director of the composition program pulled a single Little Debbie out of the box, tore open the cellophane wrapper with her teeth, and extruded the entire cake from the wrapper into her mouth. Nelson averted his eyes.

In the crowded vestibule of Peregrine Nelson arranged the magazine under his arm so that the title was prominently displayed. He'd hoped for one of the small booths along the rear wall, but the hostess seated him at a central table in the smoking section, making him a little more conspicuous than he wanted to be. But he folded his parka out of sight onto a chair and confidently flipped open the *New York Review*. With a snap he presented to his fellow diners the front cover, hoping to give the impression that he already knew what "Gordon on Gordon" meant. He scanned the table of contents for something engrossing but not too difficult to read. He would be the successful professor at his luncheon, if only for an hour.

His waitress, a pale, wide-eyed young woman, clasped her hands behind her back and committed his order to memory. She fetched him a Coke, and Nelson sipped it as he turned at last to the two Gordons—something to do with the search for the Garden of Eden and a nineteenth-century British imperial martyr—and began to read as he waited for his hamburger. For the first time in years

Nelson felt as if he had the leisure simply to read—and eat—for pleasure. Although he had not yet received the first paycheck at his new salary, the paperwork was winding its way through the coils of the university's Human Resources Department. His family would continue to be covered under the university's health plan, and they might even be able to move out of university housing and rent a small house in town, with a yard and trees and separate bedrooms for the girls. Nelson could be the paterfamilias again; yuletide visions of new shoes, new clothes, and new toys danced in his head. Maybe they could even afford dance lessons for Clara and painting lessons for little Abigail. He saw himself taking Bridget out to dinner—to someplace with a waiter and a wine list and tablecloths—and then to a movie at the mall, her choice. He saw them walking hand in hand past all the bright shops, saw himself waiting self-consciously in Victoria's Secret while his wife wriggled into something in the fitting room. . . .

Nelson blushed behind his *New York Review*. It had been a long time since he'd been stirred by the thought of his wife. She was relieved at his sudden good fortune, but even now she was still skeptical of the reprieve from his professional death sentence. Without quite saying so, she was clearly wondering if Nelson wasn't setting himself up for a fall again, if the department simply hadn't found a new way to take advantage of him.

"Sweetheart," he'd protested, "they put me on the search committee for the poetry position. They don't ask just anyone to do that."

"Great." Bridget had narrowed her eyes. "They won't make you tenure track, but they'll ask you to slog through the process of hiring someone who will be."

But Nelson replied that the committee work paid an extra thousand dollars, and Bridget's suspicion was deflected into the effort of calculating that the extra money was just enough to bring their ancient automobile up to a minimal standard of safety and performance. Count on my working-class wife, Nelson thought gratefully, to know to the penny the cost of new brakes, a new starter, and a new radiator for a ten-year-old Toyota.

His lunch arrived, the hamburger oozing blood into the toasted bun. Nelson closed his eyes: The smell of the cooked meat was intoxicating. He set aside the magazine to assemble his hamburger from top to bottom: mayo, lettuce, burger, pickles, onion, tomato, and a single knife swipe of honey mustard. He poured a chunky little pool of spicy ketchup for his fries. He breathed in the fatty aroma of his meal once more and carefully propped his magazine open before him. He lifted his burger with both hands, opening his mouth wide. His uvula glistened, his tongue bulged pinkly, and just at that moment his gaze met the gorgeous hazel eyes of Miranda DeLaTour.

Nelson froze, the burger poised between his teeth. The hostess was seating Miranda, Penelope O, and Penelope's latest young person at the next table. Miranda gave Nelson only the barest of nods, as if she knew she'd seen him someplace before but wasn't sure where. Ever since the Coogan's resignation, Nelson had detected a slight repolarization of the electromagnetic field of the department—colleagues who had previously ignored him now acknowledged him, just barely, with a curt nod of the head, or ignored him even more aggressively than before. Nelson wondered if the different responses depended on just how securely each colleague felt he or she belonged in Anthony Pescecane's affections. Timothy Coogan had been a tenured professor after all.

Then Miranda looked away from him, smoothing her skirt under her bottom as the hostess held her chair. Professor O's chair was held by a stunned-looking but handsome young man in undergraduate kit—threadbare sweater, billed cap, goatee—and she sat, twining her calves together in their tight black leggings and gesturing for the boy to sit next to her.

"Does anyone mind if I smoke?" Penelope's red fingernails twitched before her as she lit a cigarette.

Nelson's face burned, and he narrowed his focus on the burger before him. He'd intended a big, manly first bite, filling his mouth with soft, warm, bleeding meat, making his nose clench under the sharp incitement of onion and mustard, squirting hot juice down his throat. Instead he just nipped delicately at the burger with his front teeth, tugging loose a pickle, some toasted bun, and a shred of bitter lettuce. At the same moment a plume of Penelope O's smoke drifted across his table, and all Nelson tasted was tobacco.

"Lunch is on me, James," Penelope gasped, clutching the young man's wrist. "You may order anything you like."

"Um, it's Jake." The boy scratched his head under his cap.

"Whatever, studmuffin, you've earned it." Penelope dragged on her cigarette. As the current holder of the department's chair in Sexuality Studies, Penelope taught a wildly popular class called "Lord Rochester to Larry Flynt: A Cultural History of Fucking," which featured showings of grainy stag films, European snuff videos, and regular guest appearances by a porn star turned performance artist who encouraged the students to view her vulva through a jeweler's loupe.

The reading list alternated between impenetrable theory and smudgy old copies of *Hustler* and *Oui,* on reserve in the graduate library; students were encouraged to masturbate if they got aroused while reading the assignments or even if they got aroused during class. The course drew more students than Introduction to Chemistry, and the vast lecture hall, the largest on campus, was usually standing room only, an improbable mix of earnest young lesbians and awe-struck fraternity boys. Every semester, once she had worked her way through the graduate assistants who taught her discussion sections—"my bitches," Penelope called them—she began to sample her students one at a time, alternating genders. "My sexual preference is undergraduate," she had been known to say. One poor boy had had the temerity to bring her up on charges; and in her appearance before the university's sexual harassment panel, Penelope had delivered a passionate explication of the erotics of pedagogy.

"Teaching *is* seduction," she'd declared, climaxing her presentation with the argument that since sexual harassment was an instrumentality of the oppression of women, no woman could be guilty of it.

"And ain't I a woman?" she had declared to the harassment panel in her posh accent, fingering the laces of her leather bustier. The chair of the panel, a blushing, matronly classics professor in her sixties, had abruptly declared the matter closed.

Now Penelope cocked her wrist and expertly blew another stream of smoke straight at Nelson. I should move, he thought, just slide one seat over, out of the jet stream of Professor O's exhaust.

"Who does Anthony have in mind for the poetry position?" Penelope said.

With his backside lifted a quarter inch off his seat, Nelson froze. The poetry position was his position. That is, he was responsible for the vacancy. That is, he was on the hiring committee for the position, to replace . . . the poet who had quit.

"The poetry position?" said Miranda, in her plummy, movie star manner. "What poetry position?"

Nelson lowered himself to his seat and stole a glance at the next table. Miranda was shaking out her napkin. Penelope was coughing with surprising force into her fist. The boy slouched in his seat with his cap pushed back, staring slack-jawed at Penelope. If I move now, Nelson thought, it would be obvious that I'm listening.

Penelope continued to cough, and the boy gingerly patted her on the back.

"Not *now,* Jason," barked Penelope, recovering. She stubbed out her cigarette and lit another. "Bloody hell, can't you think about *anything* else?"

"It's Jake," he said, and then the waitress came. Penelope dithered, quizzing the waitress on the exact amount of oils and fat in every salad on the menu. Miranda ordered a club sandwich, while the boy ordered a bowl of clam chowder.

Nelson took the opportunity to take a couple of huge bites of hamburger and swallow a couple of thick french fries. The first blush of heat was off the burger, and the fries were just a tad cooler than he'd have liked. Still, he thought with his mouth full, it's best to look as if I'm not paying attention to a word they say.

"Anthony's throwing the position open, isn't he?" Penelope asked, in a low, urgent voice as the waitress went away.

"Hm." Miranda arranged her napkin across her lap.

"Well, thank God for that. The last thing the literature department needs is another poet."

A thread of acrid smoke drifted between Nelson's nose and the burger in his hands. He'd already hit the ground running on his committee assignment, spending every afternoon for the last three weeks carefully reading the dossier of each applicant. It seemed as if every poet in North America had applied: straight poets, gay poets, bisexual poets; male, female, and transgendered poets; poets of every age, race, religion, and place of national origin; poets with national reputations; poets who hadn't published a thing since 1973; twenty-two-year-old poets who hadn't finished their MFAs yet. The dossiers were thick with yellowing small press books whose author photos showed, like prehistoric mosquitoes preserved in amber, young men with bushy sideburns or young women with granny glasses and ironed blonde hair. There were chapbooks with stapled spines, handprinted broadsides, offprints from little magazines. There were typescripts of sonnets; ballads; terza rima; heroic couplets; free verse; concrete verse; syllabic verse; villanelles; chansons; aubades; odes and palinodes; single, double, and triple sestinas; and one author's epic philosophical poem on the tree. In the incestuous world of the academic poet, some applicants had written letters of recommendation for other applicants, who had written letters of recommendation for them, praising each other in mutually contradictory terms and canceling each other out like matter and antimatter. Every single applicant, Nelson discovered, had won an award, from the Yale Younger Poets to the Pushcart Prize to a competition sponsored by a tiny magazine at a community college in Oklahoma, where the prize was four contributor's copies and a gift certificate for two to the International House of Pancakes.

Nelson took a bite of his burger without tasting the meat, the mustard, or even the onion. The hiring committee wasn't even supposed to meet until after the first of the year, to narrow the poetry candidates down to three and invite the survivors to Midwest for a campus visit. His finger began to ache.

"Anthony's decided," Miranda was saying, "to take the position in a more scholarly direction."

Nelson forced himself to swallow his mouthful of burger as if it were sand. Everything he'd done on the poetry search to this point, reading stacks of letters, reams of CVs, and poetry by the gross, had just been rendered useless. He thought of the careful list he'd been keeping on a legal pad of all the candidates he'd read so far. Not judging them—God forbid he should ever judge a poet again—but just ranking them. The sheet was full of cross outs and emendations and arrows moving poets up or down the list as he changed his mind. Now the list was only a detailed record of his own wasted time.

"Too bloody right," said Penelope, gasping out smoke. "They're all pigs anyway, poets."

The women's lunches arrived. Penelope stubbed out her cigarette and began to stab at her salad, as if the tomatoes and cucumber were trying to get away from her. Miranda picked up a neat quarter of her club sandwich and took a delicate bite. The undergraduate boy shot glances to either side and began to slurp up his chowder as quickly as Oliver Twist, as if afraid that it might be whisked away at any moment. Nelson took advantage of the sudden absence of smoke to wolf down as much of his burger as he could before Penelope exterminated her salad and lit up again. He kept his eyes lowered on the *New York Review* article before him, carefully turning the page even though he hadn't read a word.

"So who does Anthony have in mind?" Penelope asked between mouthfuls.

"Anthony's entered into a sort of tactical alliance with Victoria," Miranda said. "She wants another queer theorist, naturally."

"And Anthony has a problem with that?"

"Of course not." Miranda tossed back her hair. "It's just that Anthony has to think of the broader needs of the department. We don't really have a postcolonialist, unless you count Steve Stephens, and we haven't got *anyone* in Celebrity Studies."

167

"What about Maggie Wong at Michigan?" Penelope pointed the tines of her fork at Miranda. "Have you read her book about the brooding male actor? She's done some *spectacular* work on Lance Henriksen and Patrick McGoohan. Or Gretchen Wahl at Chicago? Did you read her on Keanu Reeves? Absolutely fabulous. Surely either of them cover all the bases."

The undergraduate was finishing the last of his chowder with flashing strokes of his spoon. Penelope pinched his arm. "*Must* you eat like a beast, cuddle bear?" she said, smiling ferociously.

"Sorry," gulped the boy.

"I can't talk names at this point, you know that," said Miranda, "but rest assured that Anthony and Victoria will come up with a list of possibles we all can live with."

"What about Weissmann?"

"What about him?"

"Vita Deonne?" Penelope gave a humorless bark of a laugh. "The Seminar Luncheon?"

"Oh, please, Penny." Miranda dabbed at her lips with her napkin. "Mort's a spent force."

"But he still has the capacity to create mischief, doesn't he?" Penelope pushed her salad away with the tips of her fingers and picked up her cigarettes. "I mean, there's his bloody Valentine's Day party to get through."

Miranda laughed, and Nelson winced on Weissmann's behalf. His annual party in celebration of amour ran the risk every year of becoming a joke—yet everyone in the department went.

"We'll just have to place him *sous rature*," said Miranda, and both women laughed.

The boy glanced from side to side and chuckled tentatively.

"Oh, Johnny," said Penelope sweetly. "You haven't the slightest idea what we're saying, do you, love bunny?" She applied a match to the end of her cigarette and wreathed herself in a toxic cloud of smoke.

"It's *Jake*," said the boy, slumping in his seat and crossing his arms.

"Has Anthony given any thought," gasped Penelope, "to opening the position to someone who's already tenure track in the department?"

"Did you have someone in mind?" said Miranda, as if she knew the answer and didn't want to say.

"Well, we'll have to do something for Lorraine Alsace if we want to keep Kraljević. And there's Vita."

At that moment Nelson was lifting his Coke to his lips, and all that kept him from dropping the glass was the thought of Vita passing out cold at the very idea of getting tenure. Penelope's smoke drifted across his table. He stared at the cold remnants of his hamburger, at the grease congealing on the plate, and tried to remember the last time he'd seen Vita. Her copy of the Coogan's letter had disappeared a day after he'd left it on her desk in their office. With Bridget's permission, he had left a message on Vita's machine inviting her to Thanksgiving dinner, but she had never called back. She had not held her office hours in weeks, leaving Nelson to turn her students away. Once he had glimpsed her down the hall from the elevator; she had been unlocking their office door. Then the elevator doors slid shut, and by the time he'd ridden back to the third floor, she was gone. The only trace of her in the office was a slight disturbance in the air, a hint of bath powder.

"You have to admit, tenuring Vita has its appeal," Penelope O was saying. "If Mort Weissmann were dead, this would make him spin in his grave."

"No doubt," said Miranda, "but there's Victoria to reckon with. I've heard that there's some *personal* tension between Victoria and Vita."

"Oh, *Christ,*" barked Penelope. "Victoria probably had her hand in poor Vita's knickers, and Vita was too thick to realize that it was just what she needed. You're all bloody Puritans, you Americans." Penelope sucked on her cigarette, then spoke while trying to keep the smoke in, her voice diminishing with her air. "Vita's not a little girl anymore. It's not as if sticking your hand up some dolly's skirt was a *crime . . .*" She gasped and expelled a gray cloud.

"But I can't help wondering," said Miranda, "the Victoria situation aside, is Vita up to the *job?*" Miranda's voice had lost its thirties movie star inflection. Now it sounded sharper, faster, more Ida Lupino than Claudette Colbert. "Anthony says that Vita is someone who seriously needs to grow a pair of balls."

Jake the Undergraduate, his arms clenched across his chest, glared at the two women and gave a little grunt of a laugh. Penelope sucked in her breath, and Nelson was afraid she was going to choke on her own secondhand smoke.

"Think of it as gender construction, darling," Miranda said.

The undergraduate grunted again, glaring at Penelope. She blew smoke in his face. "You can be replaced," she said with cruel good humor. *"Boy toy."*

They must know I'm here, Nelson thought. How could they talk about this four feet away and not care that he heard every word? Miranda must know that I'm on the search committee. It wasn't that Miranda spoke as if she didn't care what he heard—it was that she spoke as if he *wasn't even there.* His finger smoldered.

"Anyway, if you knew the external candidates Anthony was considering," Miranda continued, "you wouldn't even mention Vita or Lorraine in the same breath."

"That's just too cruel, Miranda." Penelope leaned avidly across the table. "Surely you can tell me a name."

"I know what *sous rature* means," grumbled the undergraduate. "I'm not just a piece of meat."

Nelson could hardly breathe. He wanted to hear the name, but he didn't dare give the slightest indication that he was listening.

"Please, Miranda," said Penelope.

Miranda was flushed with her secret knowledge, glowing like a noblewoman in a Renaissance painting. Her listeners at both tables counted their heartbeats like courtly lovers postponing ecstasy. The undergraduate sulked, scowling at his empty chowder bowl.

"Lester Antilles," Miranda said at last, shaking back her glossy mane of black hair.

Penelope gave a little cry. Nelson swallowed very loudly. Jake the Undergraduate sighed and looked away. Lester Antilles was one of the biggest names in the profession, current occupant of the Cecil Rhodes Chair in Postcolonial Studies at Columbia.

"My, God," said Penelope in a hushed voice. "Would he come? Can we afford him?"

"Well," said Miranda conspiratorially, "Anthony says we could always increase the size of undergraduate classes and let some lecturers go."

Penelope was so caught up she had lost track of her current cigarette. A full inch of burning ash dangled, giving off smoke like burning tires. The undergraduate screwed up his face and waved at the smoke.

"I'm having a *conversation,* Jerry," said Penelope. Then, to Miranda, "What would Victoria say?"

"Well," said Miranda, "surely even she can see that Lester Antilles is worth fifteen or twenty composition instructors."

Nelson's finger burned at the thought of Linda Proserpina waddling through the cubicles of the Bomb Shelter, dispensing pink slips like Little Debbies.

"And where does that leave Vita? Or Lorraine, for that matter?" Penelope said. "You introduce someone of that *stature* into the department, and he rather sucks up all the oxygen, doesn't he?"

Miranda elegantly performed a vulgar gesture, gracefully turning up her palms and curling her fingers, as if she were offering Penelope a pair of plums.

"Use them or lose them," said Miranda.

"Fuck. This. Shit." Jake reached forward and snatched the cigarette from Penelope's fingers, dropping ash all over her salad and tossing the butt into the heaping ashtray.

The air over the women's table went very still, and they both turned, astonished, to see Jake the Undergraduate on his feet, quivering and red faced with anger. Nelson dove into his magazine, and then peeked up. Jake flung his napkin to the table. Tears were squeezing out of the corners of his eyes.

"I am a *person,* lady." His voice trembled. "I have *feelings.* Do you think you can just *use* me and throw me away? Do you care about me at *all?*"

A hush fell over the restaurant. Penelope sighed and canted her head to one side, giving the boy a look of puppy dog condescension.

"Now, Josh," she said. "You wouldn't want to *fail* my course, would you?"

"It's *Jake!*" cried the boy, nearly weeping. "J.A.K.E.! Jake!" He snatched his coat off the back of his chair and hurried away, his slim hips switching between the tables. As every head in the restaurant turned to watch him go, Penelope lit another cigarette.

"Jake." She pursed her lips. "Rhymes with cake."

At this moment the waitress arrived with their check, and Miranda snapped her upturned palms shut, a gesture that made Nelson wince. Miranda handed the waitress a departmental credit card—"I think we can call this a professional lunch," she said—and as the two women rose and shifted into their coats, Nelson quickly flipped the flimsy pages of his magazine, as if he were looking for something in particular. He found himself gazing intently at a personal ad in the back, someone seeking the *New York Review* version of a May-December romance ("Hannah Arendt seeks her Martin Heidegger. Must be passionately intellectual, politically engaged, and hold the highest cultural standards. Must also like kitties; no smokers."). When he looked up again, Miranda and Penelope were edging through the crowded restaurant toward the door.

Nelson twisted in his seat, looking for the waitress. He awkwardly refolded the *New York Review* and pulled his parka off the chair next to him. With the waitress nowhere in sight and his two colleagues disappearing out the door, he tossed a ten dollar bill on the table and bolted after them in his bright parka, squeezing through the crowd by the door with a polyester hiss. Pushing out into a cold, gray Minnesota noon he nearly blundered into them as they stood on the sidewalk taking their leave of each other. Professor DeLaTour was tightening the belt of her coat around her narrow waist; Professor O was crushing her cigarette on the sidewalk under the sharp toe of her boot.

"Oh, I never read Deleuze unless I'm out of the country," Penelope was saying.

Miranda laughed, and Nelson tried to look inconspicuous as he towered over the women in his orange parka with the bloodstain on the front. He looked up at the sky, he dug in his pocket for his gloves, he pulled up the parka's zipper with intense concentration.

"So," Penelope said, dropping her voice girlishly, *"are* you going to Mort's party this year?"

Miranda shrugged. "Anthony always puts in an appearance, out of pity," she said, tossing her hair. "So I suppose I'm going."

The two women giggled like a pair of sorority sisters; then they kissed each other lightly and departed in opposite directions. Penelope lit up again and trailed smoke like a locomotive, while Miranda walked up Michigan Avenue, the sharp heels of her boots clicking against the sidewalk.

Nelson hesitated a moment and then followed twenty paces behind Miranda, his rubbers squeaking, the arms of his parka hissing against the coat. He felt like a ten year old in a snowsuit again, following some imperious, pink-cheeked Iowa farm maid home from school. He had no idea what he wanted from Miranda or even if he could work up the nerve to speak to her. But they were not only colleagues, they were serving on the same hiring committee, and he had every right to know how the search was progressing and what exactly they were searching for. And didn't he owe it to Vita to find out? Vita's tenuring hung in the balance, after all.

For a moment Miranda seemed as if she might veer into Pandemonium, the coffeehouse where her lover held court, but she was only stepping nimbly around some slouching undergrad. Nelson stumbled a bit when he saw it was Jake, weeping and lightly beating his head against the wall. Miranda picked up her pace again, thrusting her hands into her coat pockets and shaking back her hair.

Nelson shambled after her, admiring her slender, belted waist and her rhythmic, runway walk. He licked his lips and considered how to address her: Miranda? Professor DeLaTour? And how would he introduce himself? Hi, you might remember me, I'm . . . a member of the hiring committee? Professor Humboldt? Nelson? First Murderer?

"Check it out," said a harsh voice next to Nelson. "Poontang on the hoof."

Nelson whirled. Fu Manchu was walking in step alongside him, his reddened eyes gliding up and down Miranda DeLaTour's retreating figure. His massive arms were bare in the cold under his denim vest; stretched across his belly was a black T-shirt that read, in bold white block letters, FUCK YOU, I'M FROM TEXAS.

Nelson staggered back against a shopfront. Fu Manchu had never been this close to him before. The homeless man stood and smiled, revealing missing teeth and a metallic incisor like a silver fang. "You can't afford her, dude," he said. "So you might as well give your money to me."

Nelson's finger seared him, and he spun on his rubber heel and marched quickly away, the heat rising to his cheeks and reddening his ears. He listened for the homeless man's footsteps coming after him, but Fu Manchu stayed where he was, chuckling deep in his throat, an obscenely liquid sound halfway between a hacking cough and a death rattle. Miranda, meanwhile, had disappeared from sight ahead. Nelson thought he could still hear the sharp tattoo of her heels, but all he saw before him were strangers on the sidewalk in the gray light.

"You'll never catch up to her, motherfucker!" cried Fu Manchu, laughing.

Christmas morning was as shrill and happy as it should have been. The fact that Nelson and Bridget could actually afford the girls' gifts this year did not make the slightest bit of difference to Clara and little Abigail. They still trampolined on their parents' bed at five in the morning. They still tore through the wrapping of each package with no concern for whose gift it was. And by eight o'clock the end result was the same: All of Abigail's gifts were either broken or missing crucial pieces, and most of Clara's gifts—the expensive ones, generally—were heaped in a corner while she played obsessively with some cheap stocking stuffer. This year it was a plastic Irish pennywhistle, upon which she played the same piercing, tuneless, repetitive air while her younger sister defaced every page of *Where the Wild Things Are* with a black crayon. Their parents meanwhile sorted through the crumpled paper a shredded piece at a time, looking for the head of Native American Princess Barbie.

In earlier years, even the lean ones, Nelson had gloried in the holiday chaos, but this morning he was brooding about the hiring committee and his snub by Miranda DeLaTour and Penelope O. In another moment he was going to twitch the pennywhistle away from his daughter and snap it in two. You'd think (he thought) that she'd get better with practice; you'd think if only on the statistical principle of the monkey at a typewriter eventually pounding out *King Lear,* that Clara would at least once stumble upon a variation that actually sounded like a tune. But each rendition was somehow more halting and wandering than the last, and as the shrieking notes penetrated deeper into his brain, Nelson began to suspect that his daughter had leapfrogged the first two thousand years of Western melody and progressed straight to Karlheinz Stockhausen.

"Found it!"

Bridget was flat on her stomach in her nightgown, prying something out from under the couch with her long fingers. She held up Barbie's dusky, raven-haired head.

"How did it get under there?" Nelson asked.

"You're asking me?"

Bridget gave him the happiest smile he had seen from her in months, maybe even in years, and he tried to smile back. The night before, at his wife's instigation, Nelson and Bridget had made love for the first time in months.

"What about the girls?" Nelson had protested, meaning that Christmas Eve was the least likely night of the year they could expect their daughters to leave them alone. And Nelson was afraid he might hurt his wife, that he might touch her with his finger and do something to her that he'd regret. But Bridget had hushed him with her fingers to his lips and lifted her nightgown over her head.

Nelson did the best he could, keeping his right hand away from his wife as much as possible. They were both self-conscious and awkward, and Nelson was distracted—by the fear of their daughters walking in on them, by the memory of all that poetry he'd read for no reason, by the image of Miranda DeLaTour shaking back her raven hair and striding away from him on her sharp heels. This last image angered him, and in an unguarded moment he gripped his wife with both hands, his finger smoldering. Bridget's eyes, which she had closed in earnest concentration, flew open; every muscle in her body pulled taut, and she cried out hoarsely, as if in pain.

"Oh, my God," Nelson gasped. What have I done? he thought.

He started to pull back, but Bridget shuddered and sighed and folded her long arms around her husband, pulling him close. She held him tightly for a long moment, her heart hammering, her breath rasping in his ear. Nelson lay atop his wife stiffly, eyes wide, his mouth dry. Then she loosened her grasp, and he rolled onto his back. Bridget loomed above him, her eyes shining in the dark, sweat and sex rising off her like steam.

"*Nelson*," she gasped happily, "where did you learn to do *that?*"

In the morning, Bridget seemed ten years younger, and she left off her bathrobe and did not brush her hair and sat on the living room floor with her nightgown up around her knees. She held Abigail in her lap as they opened gifts, making eyes at Nelson over Abby's head like a love-struck teenager. Every time she moved about the room, cleaning up or passing in and out of the kitchen, she trailed her hand through his hair, or brushed him with her hip, or, once, licked him lightly on the back of his neck. Nelson was stirred, even as he cringed in shame.

"Daddy's turning red!" shouted Abigail, pointing.

"Oh, sweetie," Bridget had said, her chin on top of Nelson's head, her hand inside his T-shirt, "Daddy's got *nothing* to be ashamed about."

Now Bridget knelt and twirled Barbie's Native American head around her index finger. "Think you can fix this?" she said.

Nelson took the head from her, and he retreated to a corner of the swaybacked couch with the head and Barbie's sexless body—already stripped of its fringed deerskin sheath—and tried to figure out how to put the two together again. Clara brought her pennywhistle across the room and sat crosslegged on the couch next to him, her forehead knotted as she concentrated on shrilling out the same tune one more time. But Nelson scarcely noticed. As he gazed down at the doll's wide-eyed face and impossibly glossy black hair, his finger began to burn, and he was distracted again by a tumble of memories—the avid grimace on Abby's face as she'd decapitated the doll; Vita stammering about Barbie's lack of nuh, nuh, nipples as the reification of the objectifying male gaze; the joyous abandon on his wife's face when he'd held her in his arms only a few hours before. . . .

The doll winked at him. It shifted in his palm, tossing back its raven hair. "Use them or lose them," it said, in a plummy, movie star voice.

Nelson dropped the head as if it had burned him, and he curled his arm around Clara, pulled her squirming onto his lap. He lay his burning finger gently along her small hand, on top of the pennywhistle.

"Think you can play something nice, sweetheart?" His voice trembled. "Think you can do that?"

175

Clara blinked and shuddered. Her lips worked soundlessly, the pennywhistle rattled in her loose grip. Nelson, horrified, shifted his daughter aside and jumped to his feet. Abigail swooped to the floor and came up with the head of Barbie, hoisting it aloft by the hair like MacDuff displaying the last of the Thane of Cawdor. Nelson turned and stumbled across the littered floor to the kitchen, where he drew a glass of water and held it to his lips with both hands to keep from spilling any. As he stood at the sink, Bridget wrapped her arms around him from behind.

"You're so good with the girls," she murmured, her cheek pressed between his shoulder blades.

Nelson forced a mouthful of water down his tight throat. He heard Abigail stomping through crumpled giftwrap, but he could not bring himself to look. Then he heard an astonishing thing, a lovely progression of notes, sweet, melodic, and pure. As Bridget shifted away from him, glowing with sudden pride, Nelson turned and saw his daughter Clara on the couch as she paused, glassy-eyed, to take a breath. Then she lifted the pennywhistle again to her pale lips and began to play a flawless rendition of "Greensleeves."

For a week after Christmas, Nelson was the lord of Harbour Hall. Nearly everyone else in the department had gone to Toronto for the annual MLA conference of English professors. With his new three-year lectureship, Nelson could afford not to be parading in an uncomfortable suit from hotel to hotel, shoulders hunched against the bitter wind off Lake Ontario. For the time being, until everyone came back at the beginning of winter semester, he could wear a pair of jeans and an old Sooey sweatshirt and walk the corridors of Harbour Hall as if he ran the place. The heat was on to keep the pipes from freezing, but the building was mostly dark; even the secretaries and the janitors had the week off. Every afternoon, to escape the racket at home, Nelson sat in his office or prowled the darkened halls like a retainer left behind until the king should return.

At the end of the week, on the afternoon of New Year's Eve, he emptied his leatherette briefcase in his office and carried it across the Quad to the Annex. At the check-out desk he got the tower key from a bored Korean work-study student who'd had nowhere to go for the holidays, and let himself into the Poole Collection. He had plucked up his courage at last to rescue all of James Hogg's works from their purgatory, smuggling them in several trips in his briefcase down the tower, across the Quad, and into his office. If the university didn't want them anymore, Nelson saw no harm in taking them home for his private collection. Coming breathlessly up the stairs to the top floors of the tower, he chuckled to think that he might end up with the most comprehensive collection of Hogg outside of Glasgow or Edinburgh.

The mesh of the cage door was freezing to the touch, surprising Nelson. The sclerotic old boiler in the basement of Thornfield Library usually gasped out enough heat to keep the tower at least in the mid-fifties, but this afternoon Nelson could see his breath as he stepped inside the enclosure. I should have worn my coat, he thought, shutting the gate behind him on its shrieking hinges. As he started up the clanging metal staircase, he encountered a steady draft, a brisk flow of freezing air pouring down the stair from the floor above. Nelson pulled down the sleeves of his sweater and hugged his elbows, his briefcase wedged under his arm. Maybe it's the ghost, he thought, giving himself a pleasant shudder that had nothing to do with the cold. Maybe he, she, or it is protective of the books up here, or worse—jealous of any of them returning to the world of the living. Maybe I'll have to wrestle with the dead to save James Hogg.

Nelson chuckled, his eyes on his feet coming up the stairs. Wrestling with the dead—didn't that just about sum up the nature of literary scholarship? He was plotting in his head the outline of a little humorous article on the subject that he might submit to *The Chronicle of Higher Education* when he came to the top of the stairs, lifted his eyes, and saw a pale figure standing at a window in the aisle before him.

The freezing air caught in his throat. The window was open, and the figure, in a milky haze of midwinter light, stood on tiptoe with its forearms on the sill, its head out the window. Cold air poured down the aisle, a frigid wind that tightened Nelson's cheeks and made his eyes water. The figure lifted slightly on its toes, raising its backside, pushing its head farther out the window. Another inch or two, a little pressure from its hands, and the figure could propel itself right out the window and headfirst onto the snowy Quad below. But that simple motion on its toes made Nelson's fear of the macabre shift into terror of another sort.

"Vita!" Nelson gasped.

Without standing up or even stepping back from the window, Vita looked over her shoulder at Nelson, her face half-obscured by her colorless hair. "Hey," she said, and she turned back to peer down the side of the tower.

Nelson forced himself to draw a breath of the freezing air. Seeing Vita leaning out an open window would be alarming under any circumstances, but especially considering that there was no other reason for her to be in the tower. Apart from Oscar Wilde and a handful of other transgressive authors, Vita wasn't much interested in canonical literature, let alone those dead white men whose books had been condemned to oblivion. The only books that interested her were those stiff-backed paperback volumes of theory from Routledge, Nebraska, and Duke, all of which resided deep in the bright, clean, climate-controlled vault of the Annex, which was directly below Vita's window. Nelson had a terrifying image of himself standing on one of the sharp-edged balconies of the Annex, looking up through the skylight into the gray sky and watching a body falling from the tower, a pinpoint at first, then a wriggling insect, then a blunt shape crazing the glass and crashing through in a dissonant shower of shards, its limbs broken and flailing, falling straight toward him. . . .

Nelson edged forward against the icy breeze, clutching his briefcase before him. "You're letting all that cold air in, Vita." He attempted a smile, but Vita wasn't looking. As he watched, she pushed herself up a little higher on the toes of her sensible, flat-heeled shoes. Nelson caught his breath again.

"How far down do you think this is?" he heard her say.

Nelson's finger was aflame almost instantly. But he was unsure whether to flee down the stairs or leap the distance between himself and Vita and haul her back in the window by the waistband of her trousers.

"It's even further," Vita said, "if you count the floors of the Annex."

Nelson's finger burned at the image of himself holding Vita by the ankles as she dangled from the tower, screaming, "Let me go!"

"Um, I thought you were at the MLA, Vita." He edged along the wall, the old floorboards creaking much too loud. "I thought you were giving your paper on . . ."

He hesitated to say "Dorian Gray and the lesbian phallus," for fear that reminding her of the Seminar Luncheon would send her over the edge, headfirst into the Annex skylight.

"Been there," sighed Vita. "Done that."

"I'm sorry?" Nelson came up to the next window along from Vita's, the briefcase trembling between his hands. He glanced through the grimy glass and saw, to his abrupt relief, the rusty iron bars that had been bolted years ago to the outside of every window in the tower. He relaxed a bit. Even if Vita had been able to pry up the sash, there were still the bars between her and the ground.

178

Vita lowered her heels to the floor. The cold wind brushed her bangs. "I did give my paper at Toronto," she said. "Two days ago. Nobody came."

"Gosh, Vita . . ."

Vita propped herself up on her forearms, gazing out across the Quad at the tops of bare trees and snow-covered roofs. A pewter-gray overcast rested like a lid over the campus.

"Miranda DeLaTour presented a paper at the same time as mine," Vita said matter-of-factly. " 'Uncompounded Essence, Cumbrous Flesh: On Oscar Wilde as Salome.' Everybody went to see her instead of me."

It took Nelson only an instant to understand that Miranda had appropriated Vita's subject at the conference, with a wittier title as well.

"I'm sure her, um, paper, I'm sure it . . . ," Nelson stammered.

"Her paper doesn't matter," said Vita. "What matters is that she knows how to construct herself as a 'real' woman." Vita hooked the air with her fingers. "And I don't."

Vita stood and turned to Nelson. The freezing air lifted her bangs away from her forehead and ruddied her skin. She smiled, and Nelson, astonished, thought he detected in her smile a trace of irony.

"She wore a black leather miniskirt with snaps up the side," said Vita. "I wore . . . this." She spread her hands to indicate her slacks and shapeless sweater. "Who would you rather watch for forty-five minutes?"

Before Nelson could answer, she was leaning on tiptoe out the window again, even farther than she had before. Nelson looked for a place to set his briefcase, and his breath seized up again: Leaning against the cold brick wall next to a stack of books were two rusted iron bars, their ends twisted and jagged where someone had snapped them free from the window and set them aside. He turned abruptly to Vita, and saw her leaning through the gap where the bars had been, her head and shoulders well over the windowsill.

"You know," she was saying, her voice whipped away by the wind, "I could bury myself headfirst in a drift from here and no one would even notice I was gone. Until spring, anyway."

Nelson couldn't breathe. His finger burned. Who had torn the bars off the window? Not Vita. She didn't have the strength. Did she?

The wind parted Vita's hair down to the scalp. She rocked on her toes, rising and falling. She smiled back at Nelson over her shoulder.

"Unless *you* told them," she said.

Another half inch and she'd be out the window. With a trembling hand, Nelson set the briefcase on top of the stack of books. His finger seared him, and the thought popped into Nelson's head that Vita was just a moment away from freeing up another budget line, that by the time she plunged through the glass of the skylight below, every member of the department under her would lurch up one place in the rankings, like pachinko balls popping into place. No one knew he was here with her; another quarter inch on the tips of her toes, and he was one place closer to the tenure track. . . .

Nelson lunged. Vita, startled, flinched away from him and started to lose her balance on the windowsill. Nelson clutched her with one arm around her waist the way he'd grab one of his daughters, and he hauled her back away from the window. Under the weight of her he lost his balance, and the two of them toppled backward over the stack of books, sending old volumes cascading to the floor and spinning toward the stairs. The iron bars danced end to end, clanging, against the floorboards.

Nelson and Vita were splayed together across the sliding tip of books, and to Nelson's alarm the pressure of Vita's wriggling backside in his lap aroused him. But in an instant she had heaved herself away and pressed herself against the shelves across the aisle from him. Nelson felt the leatherette of his briefcase under his hand, and he snatched it over his lap. He kicked back through the books until he was sitting with his back against the wall. His heart hammered, sweat beaded on his forehead. Vita grasped the top of her head with both hands, as if to keep her hair from flying off, and she gaped at him wide-eyed, her bosom heaving.

"Vita," Nelson said hoarsely, "I'm on the hiring committee . . ."

Vita dug her fingers into the tightly packed books behind her, as if she might scramble backward up the shelves.

". . . for the poetry position," Nelson went on. His hands trembled on the briefcase in his lap; his finger still throbbed. "Only they're not going to hire another poet."

He paused to catch his breath. The freezing air pouring from the window was shrinking the stiffness in his trousers.

"There's a possibility, Vita, just a possibility, that they might use the position to tenure someone who's already in the department."

Nelson swallowed and set aside the briefcase. The rough brick of the wall caught at the weave of his sweater, and he pulled away, rising to his knees.

"In fact," he said, "your name was mentioned."

As he watched, Vita underwent a dreadful transformation. A moment ago, balanced in the window eight stories up, contemplating the slow strangulation of her career, she had seemed relaxed, at ease, even giddy. Perhaps it had just been the winter wind, but there had been color in her cheeks, a light in her eye. Now the color drained from her face, her grip loosened on the books behind her, the gleam in her eyes was extinguished. She slid to the floor and tucked her legs under her; she clutched her arms across her stomach. She was pale and gaunt again, a hunted animal. Hope had returned to Vita Deonne.

"How do you know this?" Vita whispered, gazing up at him with haggard eyes. "Who have you been talking to? *What did they tell you?*"

Still breathing hard, Nelson stood. Without looking away from Vita he reached behind him and tugged on the window, once, twice, until it slid noisily shut, its ancient sash weights ringing. He fumbled with the stiff old lock until it clicked into place; then he sighed and sagged back against the windowsill. His finger still troubled him, but his pulse was slowing. His breath came easier. "You have nothing to worry about, Vita," he said.

Nelson stooped over Vita, resting his hands on his knees.

"I'm going to get you tenure," he said.

It wasn't until much later in the day—late that evening, in fact, when he was already in bed—that it occurred to Nelson to wonder how Vita had gotten in the tower. If there was only one key to the Poole Collection, and he had it, then how had she gotten inside the cage? But this question occurred to Nelson only as he was already drifting toward sleep, and by the morning, he had forgotten it.

11

Discipline and Punish

The winter semester began. On the first day of class, professors tenured and tenure-track, graduate students and undergrads, lecturers and adjuncts, secretaries and custodians, slackers and homeless men all returned hopefully to their places on Midwest's campus like an opera chorus filtering on stage, already singing, at the opening of the second act. The stage set of the university was dressed with mounds of snow, a shifting scrim of falling flakes, and a low ceiling of luminous gray cloud. The sidewalks leading to the four corners of the Quad had been indifferently plowed, and by midafternoon they were packed and polished to glassy ice by long files of booted feet feeding the slow-turning, clockwise maelstrom of class change. The surface of the Quad itself was scraped more or less clean by the tread of boots and the friction of salt and sand. Above the rotating wheel of parkas and scarves and woolen hats hung a frosty haze of human breath, like spray.

At the last class change of the day, as the astringent January light turned dusky, Nelson cut across the shuffling wheel, head and shoulders above the press of students. His classes were already going well; on this first day of class, he had given his students an assignment to summarize great works of literature as bumper stickers: *Moby Dick* as "Man vs. Nature: The Final Conflict" or *The Sun Also Rises* as "Isn't It Pretty to Think So?" or the collected works of the Brontë sisters as "Love Hurts." He was bareheaded and red-cheeked, feeling loose from a long run at the gym, and he walked with long strides, his finger humming pleasantly with heat like a filament. He even seemed brighter than the pale students around him, bundled in their bulky parkas; it was as if he walked in his own private little patch of sunshine.

He was on his way to the first formal meeting of the hiring committee, which was to start at four o'clock in Anthony Pescecane's spacious office on the eighth floor of Harbour Hall. Despite his frustration at the work he'd wasted reading poetry dossiers, Nelson marched across the Quad now with a new sense of purpose, one that fell happily outside of his own professional survival. Like Siegfried passing through the fire to rescue Brunnhilde, like Sir Francis Drake sailing into battle in the name of his virgin queen, like John Wayne crossing Monument Valley in search of Natalie Wood, Nelson strode manfully toward Harbour Hall, on his way to redeem Vita Deonne's career.

After her bout of spooky serenity at the window of Thornfield Library's clock tower a few days before, Vita had lapsed into twitchy watchfulness again. She had always been wary with Nelson on principle—as a heterosexual, as a patriarch, as a man she had caught in their office with his pants down—but there was a different quality to her wariness now, even in the few days since the winter term had started. The first time he had seen her after the term break, he had walked into their office to find her twisting the top of her head with both hands. As he came in, she snatched her hands away and caught her breath. After glancing down to see if his fly was open, he asked her if anything was the matter, and she turned as red as a plum, shook her head without speaking, and turned away. Once or twice he caught her looking at him when she thought he wouldn't notice, glancing quickly away when he turned.

These were spikes out of the usual white noise of Vita's paranoia, and Nelson concluded that she didn't trust his motives for offering to help her. That he *could* get her tenure was never in doubt: Vita took it for granted that even a *powerless* white male knew the password and the secret handshake. And even Vita—especially Vita—had to have noticed that the hate mail had dried up after Nelson had said he would make it stop; that he had suddenly gotten another three-year appointment from the department; that the Coogan had vanished from the face of the earth. In Vita's Manichaean universe, where goodness was the same as powerlessness, Nelson was untrustworthy in direct proportion to his newly restored ability to help her. His offer to help her get tenure had to be some new trick, some new kink in Vita's slow torture by the academic world, some new betrayal. It could only mean one thing: that he was acting on behalf of some larger, darker, sinister force devoted to her destruction—that, in other words, he was acting on behalf of Anthony Pescecane.

Which he had been, of course. Sort of. In his easy, privately sunny progress across the Quad, Nelson stumbled a step. His finger seared him. He stopped, momentarily flushed, at the railing above the long, shallow trench of the Annex skylight. The sloping sides of the glass were warmed from the heat rising from six stories below; steam from melting snow glowed in the skylight's fluorescent light, as if from a bluish crack in the earth. Indeed, a watery light wavered on the red brick of the old library above the Annex. Lifting his eyes nervously, Nelson was relieved to see no dancing figures behind the battlements of the tower, no pale faces in the upper windows, no wriggling figures plunging to earth. In the gathering dusk, it was impossible to see the gap where the two iron bars had been prized loose from one of the windows; there was only the wide, white, eyeless gaze of the clock face against the darkening sky. Then Nelson's finger cooled, and he started across the Quad again.

Inside Harbour Hall he found the elevator open for him like an invitation, and he stepped in. The door slid shut, and the car began to rise even before he had pushed the button. Someone on the eighth floor had summoned the car already, but Nelson allowed himself to pretend that the elevator had been waiting just for him. The truth is, Nelson thought, rising, whatever I did, whatever I'm doing now, whatever I'm about to do, it's all on behalf of other people. Of my girls, of Bridget, of Vita, of the department. Nothing I do is purely at the whim of Anthony Pescecane or even necessarily in his interest.

The elevator shot to the eighth floor and deposited Nelson with a little bounce onto the deep pile carpeting, as if encouraging him to approach his new responsibilities with a spring in his step. And why not? he thought. I have nothing to be ashamed of. If I benefit from my efforts on behalf of others, then my reward is commensurate with my service to the department, no more, no less. I live to serve.

No one was waiting for the elevator, so Nelson shrugged and crossed the carpet and took hold of the handle of the door to the chair's outer office. The door was a weighty panel of frosted glass, a classic piece of 1950s Madison Avenue moderne liberated by Pescecane from a renovation at BBD&O. But even before he had a firm grip, the handle was wrenched out of his grasp, and the door swung away from him. Suddenly Nelson was face to face with Lionel Grossmaul. The two men pulled up short in the doorway, equally alarmed. Lionel's eyes bugged out even more than usual. He was trying to put on a leather jacket, and the jacket was winning, pinching him by one wrist and jerking his other elbow painfully up behind his head. Lionel looked as if he was being attacked from behind by a monkey.

"What?" he grunted at Nelson.

Nelson stepped aside and held the door so that Lionel could pass. "I'm here for the meeting," he said.

"What meeting?" Lionel wrestled with himself inside the coat. The body of it was clearly too big for him, but the sleeves were too short and too tight, and he couldn't get his hands through the cuffs. It looked like a hand-me-down, probably from Pescecane.

"Um, the hiring committee meeting?" Nelson's arm began to ache from holding back the weighty door.

"Unh." Lionel's face turned red. He bit his lip. "Cah, cah, *canceled,*" he burst out, and his pale, stubby fingers squeezed out of the jacket's cuffs like sausages.

"Canceled?" Nelson's arm was beginning to tremble.

"Didn't you get the memo?" Lionel said in his strangled voice. He shot his wrists through the cuffs and switched off the lights. He glared at Nelson, and Nelson stepped back. The door swung shut and thrummed like a bass tuning fork. Lionel pulled a fat ring of keys out of his pocket.

"What memo?" Nelson's finger began to burn.

"The one that says, 'the meeting is canceled.' " Lionel jammed the key in the lock and turned it. He shouldered past Nelson toward the elevator.

"Canceled?" said Nelson again.

"Is there an echo in here?" asked Lionel. He flattened the elevator button with his broad thumb, and the door opened instantly. He stepped in, turned, and hit the button for the lobby, fixing Nelson with his glare to keep him back. As the doors began to shut, Nelson saw a campus mail envelope, folded lengthwise, sticking out of the pocket of Lionel's new jacket. Lionel noted where Nelson was looking and jerked his arm over the envelope.

Nelson's finger scalded him. He leaped forward. Lionel lunged for the control panel, hammering the buttons with the heel of his hand. But Nelson wedged his fingers between the doors at the last moment and pried them apart by main force. He stepped in, tall and broad-shouldered, his heart pounding.

Lionel cringed into the corner of the car as the doors shut behind Nelson. The elevator dropped.

"What's in the envelope, Lionel?" Nelson was breathing hard and sweating from the heat of his finger. He was aware of towering over Lionel, and he enjoyed it. "Where are you going?"

"None of your business," whispered Lionel, swallowing his words and bugging his eyes.

185

Nelson clutched Lionel by the wrist, his finger cooling instantly against Lionel's clammy skin.

"Guess again," said Nelson.

The hiring committee meeting had been moved, it turned out, to Pandemonium. Lionel Grossmaul trotted as fast as he could along the slick sidewalk on his short legs, slipping and sliding and trying to keep ahead of the longer-legged Nelson. Rather than let his hairless wrists protrude out of the short sleeves, Lionel hunched into the leather jacket and drew up his arms, glancing back fearfully every few steps. Nelson stayed off the icy pavement and strode through the growing dark alongside the sidewalk, rhythmically punching holes in the snow with his rubbers.

The campus mail envelope, Lionel had admitted as Nelson had grasped his wrist in the sinking elevator, carried the chair's handwritten notes on the three candidates he was considering for the open position, culled from phone conversations with cronies and former students all over the academic world. Anthony Pescecane had a more comprehensive network of confidential informants than J. Edgar Hoover: Every scrap of gossip, innuendo, and bad behavior he could find on each candidate was in the envelope—and these were the candidates he favored. He preferred to work from these notes rather than the candidates' CVs and letters of recommendation.

"Please don't tell him," Lionel pleaded over his shoulder, as he and Nelson came under the bright glow of a street lamp at the edge of campus. "Don't tell him I told you anything."

Nelson stamped his rubbers on a patch of clear sidewalk to shake loose the snow, and he hooked Lionel under his leathern elbow and nearly lifted him off the curb into the street. He led the trembling little man across the wet asphalt, pulling him up short as a campus bus hissed by. On the opposite curb Nelson lifted him up again onto the sidewalk.

"Let me go in ahead of you," begged Lionel, dancing on his toes. "Or after you. Just don't let him see us come in together!"

But Nelson did not let go. He maneuvered Lionel among the students passing through the dusk along the sidewalk, their breath wisping after them, and he hauled Lionel up short in front of the steamy window of Pandemonium. Nelson swung him through the door and guided him through the bright heat and wet wool of students crowded around the little tables and against the counter.

186

Anthony Pescecane and the hiring committee were meeting in a room at the rear of the café that was set aside for private gatherings or study groups. A wide picture window gave on to the main room, and beyond the noisy mob of students the hiring committee was brightly framed by the window around a large, round table, like the syndics of a Rembrandt merchant guild. Where Pescecane sat was clearly twelve o'clock, with Victoria Victorinix and Miranda DeLaTour to his left and right at two and ten, respectively. Round the table, at four and eight, sat Stephen Michael Stephens, asleep, and Marko Kraljević and Lorraine Alsace. As a potential candidate, Lorraine should not even have been in the room. But who would tell Kraljević he couldn't bring her?

The Canadian Lady Novelist sat at six o'clock with her back to the window. She was gesturing and reading from something on the table before her.

Nelson frog-marched Grossmaul on a zigzag course through the crowded tables, and without knocking he forcefully ushered Lionel through the blank door of the private room. The Canadian Lady Novelist froze in midsentence and midgesture, and all eyes around the table turned to see the sweating Lionel. Behind him Nelson pulled shut the door, dulling the racket from the café.

"You're late," Pescecane said. He sat with one powerful hand resting on its knuckles next to a tiny, gold-rimmed cup of espresso, while he held the other up to the light so that he could inspect his manicure with a practiced eye.

"I was . . . ," began Lionel.

"We were . . . ," said Nelson.

Pescecane silenced them with a gesture, and with a nod directed the Canadian Lady Novelist to continue.

"Thank you," she said, and she began to read aloud again from a glowing letter of recommendation; a fan of dossiers spread across the table before her. As she read, she was careful to fix her bright glance on the chairperson; there was something in the scene of the missionary reading Scripture to a savage chieftain.

All the chairs were taken, so Nelson edged against the wall, his parka rustling, while Lionel stood awkwardly alone. Morton Weissmann, who was technically on the committee as a vice chair, was not present. Around the table Miranda had not touched her bottle of Evian, and Victoria Victorinix sat with one half of a blood orange and the shredded skin of the other half on a plate before her. To her left Stephen Michael Stephens slept sitting up in spite of the triple cappuccino someone had placed before him; his shoulders rose and fell under a beautiful

187

sweater, knit in the colors of the African National Congress. Just in front of Nelson sat Kraljević and Lorraine Alsace. Professor Alsace wore her usual uniform—long skirt, baggy sweater—but Kraljević was dressed in full *Happy Days* regalia, from top to bottom—varsity jacket (number 13), button-down checked shirt, stiff jeans with rolled cuffs, a pair of Keds in mint condition. Marko and Lorraine sat with their foreheads touching, rhythmically sipping through two straws out of a single tall glass of Italian soda, mooning at each other like Mickey Rooney and Judy Garland over a malted. For once their hands were not in each other's laps, but twined together on the tabletop, over a dog-eared paperback copy of Foucault's *Discipline and Punish*.

With a wild glance over his shoulder, Lionel shifted another few inches away from Nelson. Meanwhile Nelson's eye was caught by Miranda, who tossed back her hair and narrowed her eyes slightly. Victorinix looked slowly up at Nelson from behind the dark disks of her glasses, her thin lips in a line.

The Canadian Lady Novelist read the letter with a rolling intonation, as if she were declaiming poetry, building to a crescendo.

"Whoa," said Pescecane, halting her with a lifted hand. "Wait a second. Where'd you say this guy teaches?"

"Alabama," said the novelist brightly. "He's the leading poet on the faculty there."

"Alabama?" The chair pursed his carmine lips to keep from smiling. "You're killing me."

"Oh, come on, Anthony, the writing program there has a national reputation." A maternal tone came into the novelist's voice. She wore a look of stern bemusement.

"You ever been to Tuscaloosa?" said Pescecane. "I gave a talk there once. It's like purgatory with a Wal-Mart. Who else you got?"

"You said you'd give me a fair hearing, Anthony." The stress of maintaining collegiality sounded in her voice. Nelson had read the same file, and had put the Alabama poet on his shortlist. Evidently no one had told the Canadian Lady Novelist that they weren't hiring a poet.

"Yeah, and so far you've given me Cincinnati, Ohio, and Tuscafuckingloosa," said Pescecane. "I said, pick your best three poets, and this is the best you can do? You got one left."

Kraljević and Lorraine had reached the end of their soda and were sucking air noisily up their straws. They batted their eyes at each other and twined their fingers more tightly over the Foucault volume. Stephen Michael Stephens shifted in his seat and murmured, "Aqaba. From the land."

"I tell you what, Anthony," said the Canadian Lady Novelist, sorting through the folders before her, "why don't I read the next candidate's letters *first*, and *then* tell you where she's from. . . ."

"Where *is* she from?" said Pescecane, instantly wary.

The novelist lifted a letter from another dossier, holding up a finger for silence. " 'Dear colleague,' " she read, " 'I am honored to be able to write to you today on behalf of . . .' "

"Where's she from?" Pescecane glowered across the table.

" 'Her erudition, her passion for excellence,' " the novelist went on, " 'her capacity for joy . . .' "

Anthony Pescecane snapped his fingers.

The novelist caught her breath. Pescecane lifted his chin. "Where? Is? She? From?"

The Canadian Lady Novelist swallowed.

"Northwestern Michigan University."

Pescecane rounded his eyes in disbelief.

"Northwestern *what?*" he gasped. "Where the fuck is that?"

"Traverse City, I believe."

"Traverse City." Pescecane looked away in disgust. "That's it. Put your files away, Professor. No more fucking poets."

"*Anthony* . . ." The novelist bore down on the word with every p/si of maternal authority at her disposal, but it was too late. Pescecane had already lifted his gaze to Lionel, who had edged around the table, watching Nelson sidelong, clutching the campus mail envelope before him like a talisman.

"The fuck you been?" Pescecane rolled his eyes at the Canadian Lady Novelist as if to say to Lionel, look what I have to put up with because of you. He took the envelope and did not bother to unwind the little string around the clasp, but tore off the top with his blunt fingers. Lionel edged into the narrow space between the chairman and the wall, watching Nelson with red-rimmed eyes.

Meanwhile the Canadian Lady Novelist fussily shuffled her stack of dossiers and pushed back her chair with Olympian dignity. She rose stiff-backed, as if aware that she was on display through the window behind her, though the

189

group around the table drew only an occasional glance from the students in the café. There were drapes along either side of the window, but they had not been drawn. Clearly Pescecane wanted to be seen in conference with his *capos,* even if he didn't want to be overheard.

"You know I have the greatest respect for you, dear," Pescecane said absently, unfolding the sheets from the envelope. "You let us worry about this mundane shit." He lifted his dazzling smile to her. "You just worry about winning the department a Nobel Prize."

The novelist lifted her coat off the back of the chair. "Would it really make any difference if I did?" she said.

But Pescecane was already engrossed with the papers in his hand, and meeting no one's eye, the Canadian Lady Novelist edged past Nelson and out of the room, closing the door silently behind her. A moment later she could be seen sailing through the crowd of students in the café like a silver-haired Athena.

From his position behind Pescecane, Lionel eyed the empty chair, licking his lips and shooting a glance at Nelson. Nelson edged along the window and lay his hand on the back of the chair, and Lionel flinched as if Nelson had struck him.

"Sit," Pescecane murmured, without looking up from the sheets of yellow notepaper in his hand. He lifted his eyes, surprised to see Nelson standing across the table where the novelist had been. Nelson hesitated, and Pescecane followed his glance and turned to see Lionel hovering tensely behind him. Pescecane smiled.

Someone rapped loudly on the glass of the window, and Nelson jumped. The collective gaze of the table swiveled to Morton Weissmann in his overcoat and tweed hat smiling from the other side of the glass.

"Am I late?" he said loudly.

A moment later he came through the door, swinging one of the café's bentwood chairs from two fingers. He placed the chair at the table between Lorraine Alsace and Nelson.

"I apologize for my late arrival," he said breathlessly, unbuttoning his coat and filling the room with his sharp-eyed bonhomie. "In the midden of paperwork on my desk, no doubt I misplaced the memo announcing the committee's change of venue."

He placed his hat on the table, fixing Lionel with his glance.

"It's my own fault, I'm certain of it." He draped his overcoat over the back of his chair and sat, crossing his legs at the knee. "One must be a veritable Schliemann of Troy to find anything on one's desk."

"Can we get you something, Mort?" asked Pescecane. "A little late afternoon pick-me-up? A cuppa Joe?"

"My needs are simple," said Weissmann, shooting his cuffs and crossing his arms. "I merely require to be brought up to speed. Perhaps someone could fill me in on our deliberations so far. Nelson?"

Nelson tightened his grip on the back of the chair before him.

"I hear you've been doing yeoman work on behalf of our department, Nelson." Weissmann gripped Nelson's wrist with his large, liver-spotted hand.

"Um, I," Nelson said.

"Be careful, Anthony," said Weissmann, squeezing Nelson's wrist. " 'Who does in the wars more than his captain can become his captain's captain.' "

Nelson felt his face get hot. Pescecane's eyes darkened. He glanced up at Nelson.

"Sit," he said. Then he spoke over his shoulder to Lionel, without looking at him. "Don't hover like a dog, for fuck's sake. Go find a chair somewhere."

Lionel edged slowly around the table, looking daggers at Nelson. Nelson pulled his chair back with a scrape and sat, crumpling his parka under him. Lionel slammed the door as he left.

Anthony and Cleopatra, Pescecane murmured, scanning his notes. He glanced up at Weissmann. Nelson saw Weissmann forcing a smile.

"You thought I wouldn't know," said Pescecane, pleased. He pressed the notepad sheets against the tabletop with his splayed hand and spun them toward Nelson.

"Nelson," he said loudly. "Just the guy I wanted to see. Take a look at these."

Nelson half rose, his parka hissing, and drew the sheets toward him. His hands were shaking, so he pressed them flat against the papers. For a terrifying moment the sheets read like gibberish, and he was afraid that he wouldn't be able to make out the chairperson's scrawl. But with all eyes on him he turned the pages right side up and found he could easily read the aggressive hand.

There were three pages, each headed with a name. On top was jennifer manly, who had broadened the mandate of queer theory to subjects outside of gay and lesbian studies. She was, Nelson guessed, Victorinix's first choice. Pescecane's notes about her consisted of a list of her known lovers—"Comprehensive?" he'd queried himself in the margin—and the notation that she was African American as well, a fact that Pescecane had underscored with three bold strokes of his Mont Blanc pen.

"Queer and black," he'd written at the bottom of the page. "A twofer."

With each succeeding page, Nelson's heart sank a little lower on Vita's behalf. The next candidate was David Branwell, a Yorkshireman of cruel good looks who was one of the leading theorists of Celebrity Studies. The compromise candidate was Lester Antilles, the postcolonialist Nelson had heard Miranda and Penelope discussing just before Christmas. Even though Vita's work fell squarely into the mainstream of Cultural Studies and could hold its own with the work of any of these—especially Lester Antilles—it was also a good deal more earnest and even, God forbid, more heartfelt. In cutting-edge scholarship, as in trendy cuisine, presentation was everything, and each of these candidates had branded him or herself, constructing a clearly defined, entertaining, and easily recognizable persona. They were smart, flamboyant, and playful. All Vita was, was smart. The stolid bricklaying of her prose didn't draw the eye like the baroque fretwork of jennifer manly or David Branwell.

But still, thought Nelson, Vita's already here at Midwest, and these three—he traced his warming finger along the edge of each sheet—these three have to get past *me*.

"So, Nelson."

Pescecane's voice made Nelson glance up.

"You got a problem with picking up any of these guys?" Anthony said.

Everyone who was awake around the table was looking at Nelson. Beyond the window Lionel hunched angrily in his hand-me-down jacket and turned in a slow circle in the middle of the crowded café, looking for an empty chair.

"Well," said Nelson, a little too loudly. "Any one of these would be a terrific addition to the department. Really."

Weissmann noisily cleared his throat behind his hand.

" 'Here come a trio of very strange beasts,' " he declaimed, " 'which in all tongues are called fools.' " A pause. *As You Like It,* Anthony. Though of course you already knew that."

"The line is 'a *pair* of very strange beasts,' Mort." Pescecane smiled ferociously.

"One adapts the play to the context of performance," said Weissmann.

Pescecane and Weissmann locked gazes. Nelson lowered his head. His finger ached.

"But it seems to me," Nelson said, breaking the silence, "we already have someone of this caliber in the department. Maybe she's not as . . . as well-known as these three, but that's only a matter of time. . . ."

Kraljević sighed heavily and began to flip through the pages of *Discipline and Punish* like a bored teenager. At the far end of the café, Lionel Grossmaul was in a tug of war over a chair with a dreadlocked young woman.

"I mean, I know we're busy," Nelson added quickly. "As a committee I mean. But I really think that if we took a close look at Vita Deonne's work, we'd find . . ."

Lorraine Alsace erupted in a fit of coughing. Kraljević grunted and rolled his eyes and shoved the paperback Foucault away from him. The book slid across the table and came to rest before Pescecane. Victorinix sighed and leaned back in her chair. Stephen Michael Stephens was snoring gently.

Suddenly the door banged open, and Lionel came in, breathing hard and sweating, a bentwood chair clutched in both hands before him. He banged the door shut and edged around the table, bumping the wall with the chair.

"You want to give an open budget line," asked Miranda, ducking slightly as Lionel passed behind her, "to someone who's already in the department?"

Grossmaul planted the chair against the wall, just behind Pescecane. He sat, his chest still heaving, and tried to cross his thick legs.

Pescecane regarded his manicure. "You misunderstood my question, Nelson," he said. "These three candidates are already scheduled for campus visits. What I'm asking you is, do you have a problem with picking them up at the airport?"

Nelson blinked across the table. His finger seared him. The rest of the committee relaxed, exchanging quick smiles. Lionel gasped. He uncrossed his legs and lurched to the edge of his little chair, trying to lean into Pescecane's peripheral vision.

"I'm doing that," he blurted, in his strangled voice. *"I'm* picking them up."

Pescecane ignored him, fingering the copy of *Discipline and Punish* on the table before him. "Think you can handle that, Nelson?" he asked. "Are you up to it?"

The heat of Nelson's finger made his forehead break out in droplets of sweat.

" 'Be bloody, bold, and resolute,' Nelson," intoned Weissmann.

"The fuck's up with you, Mort?" snapped Pescecane, glaring at Weissmann. "Working up your one-man show? 'The Bard and the Pedant: An Evening of Shakespeare with Morton Weissmann.' "

Weissmann smiled.

"I'm pleased, Anthony, truly. I'd no doubt that you knew a fair bit of Milton, but I'm pleased to see that Shakespeare meets your minimum standard of street cred."

"What's your point, Mort? You got something to say?" Pescecane smiled viciously. " 'To expostulate what majesty should be, what duty is, what day is day, night night, and time is time, were nothing but to waste night, day and time.' "

"Well, *Hamlet,*" said Weissmann condescendingly. "Every schoolboy knows *Hamlet,* Anthony."

"Then what's the next fucking line, Mort?"

Weissmann's smile froze.

" 'Brevity is . . .' " began Nelson, but Pescecane lifted his hand abruptly, silencing him.

" 'Give me leave to speak my mind,' Anthony," said Weissmann coldly, turning in his seat, " 'and I will through and through cleanse the foul body of the infected world.' "

Pescecane blinked, his mouth slightly open. Everyone at the table save Stephen Michael Stephens shifted his or her gaze back and forth between the two men like the crowd at Wimbledon.

"*As You Like It,*" Pescecane blurted. " 'Shall quips and sentences and these paper bullets of the brain awe a man from the career of his humor?' "

"*Much Ado!*" cried Weissmann. He uncrossed his arms and folded his hands on his knees.

Pescecane bent back a corner of the cover of *Discipline and Punish.*

" 'Rude I am in my speech.' " Weissmann said, his eyes shining now. His hands twitched, plucking at the weave of his trousers. " 'And little blessed with the soft phrase of *peace.*' "

"*O-thell-o,*" said Pescecane triumphantly, working over every syllable. "Act one, scene three." He smiled, showing his incisors. " 'Men of few words are the *best* men.' "

Weissmann caught his breath, and Pescecane started to laugh. Victorinix and

Miranda exchanged glances. Kraljević's eyes were aflame, and Lorraine played with his thumb with her long, pale fingers.

"Heh, heh, Henry . . ." began Weissmann.

"*Which* Henry?" snapped Pescecane. He looked as if he might come across the table.

"The fifth!" Weissmann leaped to his feet. His chair rattled, his overcoat slid to the floor. "Act three, scene two!"

"Hah!" Pescecane cried. "Scene *three!*"

Nelson coughed significantly into his fist. The two men turned to him.

"Well, actually, Mort's right," Nelson said meekly. "It's scene two."

"Hah!" cried Weissmann. He beamed wildly at Nelson.

"A hit," said Victorinix drily, "a palpable hit."

Pescecane slapped the table with the paperback Foucault, and the sound rang around the room. He leaped to his feet, his chair shrieking against the tile. Beyond the window, students at the closer tables turned to watch.

" 'I scorn you, scurvy companion,' " Pescecane snarled. His face was a deep, frightening red. " 'You poor, base, rascally, cheating, lack-linen mate! Away, you mouldy rogue, away!' "

Weissmann stood quivering, his pale, sagging face coming out in violently red blotches. " 'Knave, rascal, eater of broken meats.' " Spittle flew from Weissmann's mouth. " 'Base, proud, shallow, beggarly, three-suited, hundred-pound, filthy worsted stocking knave; lily-livered, action-taking, whoreson, glass-gazing, superserviceable, finical rogue . . .' "

Swaying on his feet, Weissmann paused to draw a wheezing breath. But Pescecane, dancing on his toes at the far side of the table, beat him to it.

" 'One-trunk-inheriting slave!' " he cried hoarsely. " 'One that wouldst be a bawd in way of good service, and art nothing but the composition of a knave, beggar, coward, pander, and the son and heir of a mongrel bitch; one whom I will beat into clamorous whining if thou deny'st *the least syllable of thy addition!*' "

Pescecane stopped, his chest heaving. Both men were hunched over now, their heads low, their shoulders up. Their breath hissed through their nostrils.

"Prating mountebank," spat Weissmann.

"Clod of wayward marl," growled Pescecane.

"Hedge-pig." Weissmann. Spit flew.

"Malt-worm." Pescecane, gutturally.

"Coxcomb."

"Sot."

"Jerk."

"Asshole."

"Greaseball!"

"Sheeny!"

"Goombah!"

"Yid!"

"WOP!"

"KIKE!"

The room rang with silence. Weissmann trembled, his face blotched with red, his lips drained white, his fists clenching and unclenching. Pescecane's chest strained against the buttons of his tailored shirt and his Armani suit coat. Above the tight knot of his silk tie his face was crimson. During the exchange he had snatched up the copy of *Discipline and Punish* and twisted it between his white-knuckled hands as if he might tear it in half. Miranda watched him in awe; Kraljević and Lorraine clutched each other, cheek to cheek. Stephens still slept, but restlessly. Victoria Victorinix had shrunk in her chair, her face as pale as a cadaver's. Beyond the wide window the café was silent, all the pale ovals of undergraduate faces watching wide-eyed and slack-jawed.

"Anthony?"

Just behind Pescecane Lionel Grossmaul leaned forward, his backside lifted an inch off his seat. He plucked at the sleeve of Pescecane's coat.

"Anthony?" he said again. "Picking up the candidates at the airport? That's *my* job."

Pescecane scarcely seemed to hear him. He wrenched at the book in his hands, his murderous gaze fixed on Weissmann. Nelson, clutching the edge of the table, his finger roasting, heard the angry hiss of Weissmann's breath. Somewhere in the silent café beyond the window a dropped spoon rang against the floor.

"What?" said Pescecane hoarsely.

"It's, it's, it's *my* job," said Lionel, speaking and swallowing all at once. "Picking up the candidates at the airport. Not, not . . . Nelson's."

Pescecane's chest swelled again, and he let out his breath slowly in a long hiss. Without taking his gaze from Weissmann, Anthony Pescecane lifted the copy of *Discipline and Punish* in his right hand as high as his left shoulder, then swung it down and away in a vicious backhand. A crack, a cry, and a clatter. Lionel Grossmaul went backward over his chair.

From the café the crowd let out a sound, half groan of sympathy, half moan of appreciation, like a football crowd admiring a spectacular sack. At the table in the meeting room Miranda flinched away from Pescecane, and Victoria Victorinix pushed herself back from the table with the tips of her fingers. Stephen Michael Stephens jolted awake.

"Yes, *effendi!*" he whispered urgently.

Nelson scuttled back, knocking over his own chair and pressing himself against the window. Marko Kraljević leaped to his feet. He rolled his shoulders under the varsity jacket like the young Marlon Brando itching for a fight. He gazed down at the groaning Lionel hungrily, eager to get his licks in. "Fuck-ing A," he said in a slow, breathy murmur.

"Meeting adjourned," said Victorinix, rising from her seat.

The crowd on the other side of the window began to murmur excitedly, a sound that rose quickly to a roar. Miranda snatched up her coat and dashed from the room. Lorraine clutched Kraljević by the wrist and pulled him out the door. Stephens rose, looking puzzled; he glanced at Victorinix, who merely shook her head and motioned him out the door. As Stephens edged past Nelson, Victorinix started to follow him, saw Nelson standing openmouthed against the window, and went the other way around the table, stepping lightly over Lionel, slipping behind Pescecane.

Pescecane stood pale and spent, his eyes dull. He sniffed and tugged at his cuffs, then lifted his overcoat off the back of his chair and stepped over the legs of his assistant, who was curled on the floor next to the wall under his overturned chair, groping at nothing like an animal in pain. Pescecane paused at the door to shrug into his coat. "Nelson," he said, without looking back.

Nelson cleared his throat and said, "Yes?"

"That airport thing," he said. "Take care of it."

"Sure," Nelson said, swallowing against a dry throat, and then Pescecane was gone. Nelson turned to watch him through the window, muscling his way through the crowd, who fell back at his approach, the pale, excited undergraduate faces turning to follow him like sunflowers. Kraljević swaggered after him, bowling over students in his wake, while Lorraine skipped gaily after them both, clutching her hands before her.

Nelson felt a hand on his shoulder. Morton Weissmann stood close to Nelson, his eyes shining, his face flushed. He breathed heavily through his mouth. "This is the moment, my friend!" Weissmann said, his voice hoarse with excitement. "This is the turning point! They have the numbers, but we the heights!"

Weissmann turned Nelson toward him with a trembling hand on each shoulder, as if he were going to kiss him. His bright eyes searched Nelson's face. His sour breath washed over Nelson as he spoke. "I've been waiting for this moment for fifteen years! A crack in their defenses, a stalwart ally at my side!" He banged Nelson on the shoulders with both hands. "Together again, ay, my son? He today that sheds his blood with me shall be my brother! Be you never so vile, Nelson, this day shall gentle your condition!"

Nelson's fingered flamed. He was tempted to grasp the old man by the throat, but he simply stepped back. "It's dinnertime, Mort," he said. "My family's waiting."

"Of course, of course!" Weissmann stooped to lift his coat from the floor, and he glanced up eagerly. "But tomorrow, Professor, we have to talk, we have to consider our next move, we have to . . ."

Nelson made for the door, and Weissmann, his overcoat hanging crookedly from his shoulders, his hat askew, clutched him by the elbow and held him back. "I understand, Nelson," he whispered hoarsely, with his finger to his lips and a glance toward the window. "Anthony believes he has you in his pocket, and that's just what we want him to think. . . ."

"I have to go." Nelson pulled free and stepped into the corridor leading to the café. But as he walked away, he heard Weissmann hissing hoarsely after him.

"Gentlemen now abed in England shall think themselves accursed they were not here!" Weissmann wheezed. He raised his trembling fist. "We few, Nelson, we happy few! We band of brothers!"

On the street, in the freezing dark, Nelson hurried away from Pandemonium. His hands shook as he tried to pull on his gloves, and he dropped one on the pavement. He stooped for it, and someone spoke his name in a plummy voice that sent a shiver of pleasure down his spine.

"Nelson," said Miranda.

He stood, his breath misting in a great cloud. Miranda DeLaTour came out of a darkened doorway wrapped in her coat, the belt tight around her narrow waist. As Nelson stood speechless, she plucked at the sleeve of his parka, rubbing the bright orange polyester with the slender fingers of her leather glove. Her nose wrinkled as if against an awful smell.

"You're not wearing this to the airport, are you?" she asked. She lifted her bright hazel eyes to him, and he felt a charge run through him to the tip of his finger.

"Do you have *anything* presentable to wear?" she said.

"Um . . ." Nelson's interview suit, the one his wife had bought for him in graduate school, had been sold several years ago to pay for diapers. All he had left were the dress shoes that went with it.

"First impressions, Nelson," Miranda said. "We're wooing these candidates as much as they're wooing us. Do you have to be anywhere right now?"

In Nelson's head, the image of his wife and daughters seated around the dining room table, knives and forks in their hands, winked out as if a plug had been pulled. In the darkness a meatloaf sprouted wings and flew away.

"No," he said. "I don't have anywhere to be."

On their way across the Quad to her car, Miranda and Nelson passed Vita scurrying through the cold with her head down. For a moment Nelson thought he might escape notice, but Vita glanced up and nearly stumbled, her jaw hanging open at the sight of Nelson and Miranda together. Nelson's ears burned; he felt guiltier in front of Vita than he had felt lying about his dinner. He gave her a weak smile and kept going. Miranda glanced at him, her eyes unreadable in the dark between street lamps.

In her Miata on the way to the mall Miranda rested her trim, gloved hand on the gleaming knob of the gearshift and maneuvered through traffic like a Formula One driver. Pursing her lips, she dashed from traffic light to traffic light, working the shift with precise, vigorous strokes of her arm, racing the Miata under each light just as it turned red. Nelson's seat was pushed back as far as it would go. His long legs were stretched out in front of him, the engine thrumming just beyond his knees, the pavement rushing by inches below his backside. He glanced sidelong at Miranda, and she wrenched back on the stick and floored the accelerator. Nelson was pressed deliciously deeper into his leather seat. He felt a tingling in his loins.

"Do you really mean to champion Vita Deonne for tenure?" Miranda said over the finely tuned engine. The light of passing street lamps flashed over her face. "Or are you after something else?"

"I really think Vita deserves it," Nelson began. But he was distracted by the bright neon rush of fast-food joints, chain stores, and strip malls beyond his window, Wendy's and Home Depot and Vietnamese restaurants all blurring into one long, green-and-orange sign, fronted by the blurry reflections of one long, slushy parking lot.

"You're only a lecturer, Nelson," Miranda said. Nelson felt a foolish thrill at the sound of his name on her lips. "There's nothing you can do for Vita."

The mall loomed up on the left like a white fortress, and as the light at the main entrance trembled on the cusp of turning red, Miranda swerved across the headlights of two lanes of traffic and powered through a tight arc into the vast parking lot, throwing up a great bow wave of snow melt as she shifted down across the empty rows of parking spaces.

"You intrigue me, Nelson," she said, her lips forming a moue.

She kept silent all the way through the bright cathedral space of the mall. The dinnertime crowd was sparse, mostly gawky teenaged girls and a few overweight, middle-aged women in huge parkas. At last Nelson and Miranda came to the Minnesota outpost of a New York haberdashery, a plush, dark cave with deep carpeting and faux oak wainscoting and soft heaps of expensive woolen clothing. Just inside the doorway she leaned back on one sharp heel and shook her hair, and a broad-shouldered, carefully moussed Minnesota boy in suspenders and a tie snapped to attention, beaming at her like a bridegroom. He turned down the wattage of his milk-fed smile when he realized that Nelson was with her, but he devoted himself to them nevertheless, striding manfully up and down the aisles of the shop in search of shirts, jackets, socks, and ties.

Nelson stood like a big, dumb paper doll as the boy held shirts and sport coats up to his chest and Miranda rocked back on her heel with her hand at her chin, considering. She hardly spoke, merely shaking her head or, more rarely, gesturing to the clerk to put an item aside for another look. Nelson glimpsed the tag of one shirt before the boy could whisk it away and nearly gasped at the price; it cost more than a week's worth of groceries for his family. When the clerk was off replacing Miranda's rejects, Nelson dipped his head to her. "I can't afford this," he whispered.

"You don't have to," Miranda murmured, fingering a tie draped around his neck. "Anthony's paying."

Miranda turned out to be more ruthlessly efficient at selecting a look for Nelson than Bridget was at Sears or Target. Nelson made only one trip to the changing room before Miranda told the clerk to wrap up the clothes—a pair of wool trousers, a shirt of Egyptian cotton, a wool jacket, and a tie.

"Do you have a better pair of shoes?" she asked, wrinkling her nose at his loafers.

"Yes," gulped Nelson.

The transaction was done while Nelson was in the changing room getting back into his khakis and his polyester parka. As he shambled between tables stacked with hand-knit sweaters under the jealous, skeptical gaze of the clerk, Miranda was already waiting out in the unnatural brightness of the mall's main concourse, tying the belt of her coat around her waist. Nelson came squinting into the brighter light like a refugee from Plato's cave, and she handed him the garment bag to carry, as if his reward for freeing himself from the cave's shackles was the direct appreciation of reality and a really nice sport coat. Then she turned on her narrow heel without speaking and led the way toward the car.

In the Miata Nelson clutched his new clothes to his chest with both arms as Miranda raced back toward campus, weaving through the sluggish red lights of the cars ahead of them. In the glare of the oncoming headlights she seemed to be laughing silently to herself. She said nothing until she asked him where he lived, and Nelson caught his breath. He wasn't sure which he dreaded more: Bridget seeing him stepping out of a sports car with a beautiful woman behind the wheel, or Miranda seeing that he lived in married housing.

"Um, just drop me off on campus," he said.

Miranda glanced unreadably at him. "What kind of car do you drive?" she said, lifting her chin as she swerved around a bus.

"A Toyota," Nelson said, leaving out what year.

Miranda pursed her lips. The Miata surged into the lane ahead of the bus. "Maybe you'd like to drive my car to the airport."

"Really?" Nelson gasped.

"I'm only kidding, Nelson." Miranda parted her lips. She glanced at him again. "You didn't really think . . ."

Nelson blushed and looked away. "No," he said. "Of course not."

Miranda gave a lovely, musical laugh that set Nelson's pulse racing. He felt a touch on his arm, an electric tingle as Miranda squeezed him lightly with her gloved hand. "You're sweet," she said, laughing to herself.

On campus she downshifted and glided to the curb before Harbour Hall, beneath a streetlight. Clutching the garment bag, Nelson awkwardly pulled himself up out of the little car onto the crusted snow of the sidewalk. As he stooped to shut the door, Miranda leaned across the seat and pressed one slender, leathered hand on the passenger seat.

"I hate to see you waste your time, Nelson," she said.

Her hazel eyes were cool and bemused in the light falling through the windshield. Nelson could not help noticing the smooth skin of her throat, the line of her back as she stretched across the narrow car, the way one hand lightly gripped the wheel while the other pressed against the seat where he'd been sitting only moments before.

"The only way Vita will get this position is if all three of Anthony's candidates get hit by a truck. Do you understand?"

Nelson nodded. Miranda smiled. Nelson swung the Miata's door shut, and the car leaped away form the curb, sleek and purring. Holding up the garment bag, Nelson watched the car go, the brake lights flashing once as it rounded a corner.

"Yes," Nelson said. "I understand."

He left his new clothes up in his office so he wouldn't have to explain to Bridget where he got them, or who had picked them out and paid for them. At home he found his dinner on the kitchen counter, Saran Wrap pulled tight over the plate—a slab of meatloaf, green beans, cold mashed potatoes. His wife was colder, putting the girls to bed without a word to him, silently refusing his help. Later, though, in bed, he tried to make it up to her, stroking her with his finger as he persuaded her to make love. Then, at a crucial moment, he touched her again, and Bridget yanked a pillow over her face so she could cry out without waking the girls.

Nelson came a moment later. Driving deep, he closed his eyes and silently mouthed the name, "Miranda."

12

The Three Stooges

Nelson's new clothes hung from a single hanger on a hook behind his office door. When he was trying to write, or speaking to a student during office hours, he found his gaze straying often to the flattened man-shape splayed against the wall: the hand-stitched shirt inside the herringbone jacket. A pair of discreetly patterned socks tucked in the jacket's breast pocket like a handkerchief. The wool trousers suspended at full length from metal clips. The clothes looked to Nelson like a freeze-dried university professor—just add tenure.

A few days after the meeting at Pandemonium, Nelson drove to the airport to pick up Lester Antilles, the first of the job candidates to visit. Nelson roared down the freeway in a nearly new Crown Victoria from the university's motor pool, through Minnesota dairy land sleeping under a heavy quilt of snow. His own little Toyota couldn't even go this fast; over fifty miles per hour, it shook and rattled and pierced him with drafts of freezing air through the loose seals around the windows. Its windshield wipers whined, its heater stank of exhaust. But the Crown Vic sailed over the wet pavement, throwing up twin fantails of water that corkscrewed together in the rearview mirror. When Nelson came up behind a convoy of trailer trucks, lumbering nose-to-tail like a line of elephants, a mere tap on the accelerator sent the sedan surging past them. Even at full throttle the Crown Vic was quieter than his living room, the wipers silent, the heater purring, the air smelling of Windex and air freshener.

Nelson's new suit of clothes was comfortable, but coming up the airport concourse, he tugged at the collar and pulled at his cuffs. He felt like some scrubbed, fidgety teenager dressed by his mom, sent to fetch an imperious uncle and told to behave himself. Waiting at the gate, he forced himself to concentrate on what he had to do.

In the dead of a Minnesota winter, Lester Antilles came off the plane in a white linen suit, an open-necked shirt, and canvas shoes. He was broad-chested and bullet headed, with a flat, impassive face and heavy-lidded eyes. His hair was cropped to within a quarter inch of his blunt skull. He wore thick-lensed glasses with clear plastic rims, a Saint Christopher's medal around his thick neck, and a big gold ring. He looked every inch the globe-trotting, guerilla intellectual—either that or a Colombian drug lord. Nelson couldn't make up his mind.

In a discipline where scholarly heft was defined by being more postcolonial than thou, Lester Antilles was the heftiest of the lot. As a graduate student at an Ivy League school he had announced to his dissertation committee that doctoral theses at major Western universities were a primary locus of the objectifying colonialist gaze on native subjects, and he refused on principle to participate in the marginalization of indigenous voices or to become complicit with the hegemonic discourse of Western postcolonial cultural imperialism. In practice, this meant that for six years he refused to take classes, attend seminars, or write a dissertation. As a result of this ideologically engaged nonparticipation, he was offered tenured positions even before he had his Ph.D., but by refusing to write a book or any articles on his topic—publishing with major university presses being even more complicit with imperialism than writing dissertations—he provoked a fierce bidding war. Columbia won by offering him an endowed chair and a full professorship, and on Morningside Heights he courageously continued his principled refusal to teach any classes, hold any office hours, publish any books, serve on any committees, or supervise any dissertations. For this demanding and theoretically sophisticated subaltern intervention in the dominant discourse, Antilles made well into the six figures, more money than the president of the United States.

His finger twitching, Nelson stepped in front of Antilles and spoke his name. Antilles stepped back, and his heavy eyelids rose a fraction. For a moment Nelson wondered if the man were deaf as well as professionally mute. But then the candidate lifted his hands to his ears and plucked out two tiny earphones, which were connected by a thin wire that plunged into the breast pocket of his shirt. Then he surprised Nelson by speaking in a whispery voice.

"You are from Midwest?" he asked without emotion.

Down the concourse and through baggage claim, Antilles made bored, monosyllabic replies to Nelson's queries about the flight. For the first time Nelson felt uncomfortable in his new clothes; he might as well have been wearing a pair of farmer's overalls for all the impression his new suit made on the candidate. In the car Antilles gingerly replaced the earphones and pulled a small cassette player out of his breast pocket. He flipped the tape, turned up the volume, and put the player back in his shirt pocket. He closed his eyes, and Nelson drove back to Hamilton Groves in the humming silence of the Crown Victoria, listening only to the thin, unidentifiable whine of Antilles's music. His finger burned uncomfortably on the steering wheel.

What to do? wondered Nelson. How to sabotage a man who left you no opening? For the rest of the day, Nelson missed all of the events at which Antilles did not speak. Nelson missed the meeting with the graduate student leaders of every ethnicity and sexual preference on campus, where Antilles did not answer their questions and the students went away in awe of Antilles's stunning critique of their own complicity with the dominant culture of the university. Nelson missed the lunch with the hiring committee at Peregrine, where Antilles actually spoke twice, once to order the mesquite grilled chicken and again to ask for the Grey Poupon. Nelson missed the private meeting with the faculty of the English Department, where Kraljević, Lorraine Alsace, and Penelope O hung on every word Antilles didn't say, and Morton Weissmann—unable to get a word in where no words were spoken—seethed in frustration.

Nelson did not catch up with Antilles, in fact, until the end of the day, when Nelson waited, finger smoldering, in the lobby of Antilles's hotel. The candidate came in near midnight after a presumably uneventful dinner at Pescecane's house, his earphones in place, his eyes dulled by the drone of the music. Nelson leaped up and met him in the middle of the lobby. Antilles's eyelids lifted in mild alarm, and he took a step back. Nelson took him by the wrist.

"I have a suggestion for your job talk tomorrow," Nelson said. Antilles blinked rapidly, and Nelson plucked the cassette player out of Antilles's pocket, took out the tape—Kenny G, of all things—and replaced it with a tape Nelson had made that afternoon. Rooting around in a box of old LPs in his basement, he'd found— stuck in between his Badfinger records—an old comedy album he'd loved when he was a kid, a record by a Vegas insult comic called *Hey Stupid: Frankie Carson LIVE! at the Sands*. Gripping Antilles's wrist with his right hand, Nelson used his left to press the play button on the cassette player.

"Knock 'em dead tomorrow, slugger." Nelson's finger turned to ice as he squeezed Antilles's wrist. "Break a leg."

After his third class the following afternoon, Nelson made his way to Lester Antilles's job talk. He stopped at the Student Union on his way and bought a big red apple, which he admired as he walked across the Quad.

He took his first bite as he came out of the cold into the lobby of Harbour Hall. The talk should have started fifteen minutes ago; no doubt an eager crowd was already hanging on every word that Lester Antilles wasn't saying. But over the crunch of apple in his ears, Nelson heard an agitated murmur and an arrhythmic clacking. Coming round the corner he found himself moving upstream against a steady flow of graduate students pouring out of Lecture Hall A. They were muttering angrily and shaking their heads, grumbling to each other. The clacking sound came from the doors of the lecture hall swinging shut on each knot of departing students. Nelson caught the door just before it clacked shut again and let himself in.

The room rustled with coats being pulled on and book bags being lifted out of seats. The angry murmur was nearly loud enough here to drown out the shrill voice of the candidate on the stage, who was gesturing stiffly at the backs of the departing audience.

"Yeah, g'wan, get outta here," Lester Antilles was saying in a sharp, Catskills whine. "I'm saving the good material for last, schmuckos. Who needs ya, ya buncha losers?"

Instead of his loose linen suit and canvas shoes, this afternoon Antilles was wearing large black oxfords, a pair of polyester slacks, and a broad-shouldered, double-breasted blazer. He paced back and forth in his big shoes, flop sweat soaking through his armpits. He mopped his glistening brow with a wadded handkerchief, his eyes small and sharp without his glasses.

"Tough room," said Antilles. "Who knew? Wassamatta, you don't like jokes? I knew I shoulda worked with a broad. Izzat it? Not enough tits on stage for ya?"

At that a whole row of young women of every hue got up in unison and filed up the aisle like an angry Benetton ad, their faces contorted with rage.

"Women, ladies and gentlemen, I tell ya"—Antilles threw an arm out at the retreating line—"can't live with 'em, can't leave 'em at the curb when you're done. God bless 'em. God bless you, ladies! I'll be here all week!" he shouted, as the line trooped out the door at the back of the hall. The last one out flashed him the finger. "Yeah, fuck you too, sweetheart!" he barked. "You wish. Like I'd let some angry dyke ride my love pony."

He swiveled on the brilliantly polished toe of his shoe. There were maybe fifteen people left in the audience, and half of them were pulling on their coats. Weissmann was not present, but near the back the Lost Boys sat biting their lips and clutching each other's knees, desperately trying not to laugh. The hiring committee sat along the front row. Pescecane glowered; Miranda furiously regarded her nails; Marko Kraljević (in a postal worker's uniform) and Lorraine Alsace watched as raptly as a pair of honeymooners at the Tropicana. Lionel Grossmaul leaned forward on the edge of his seat, as if at the end of his leash. Victorinix sat rigidly, and for once the back of her neck was visibly burning. Antilles fixed her with his gaze and came to the front of the stage.

"Victoria, honey, sweetie, baby! I kid!" He made a narrow, smirking little grin. "I jest! You know how I love the ladies! Not like *you* love the ladies, but hey, who does?"

Suddenly Antilles stiffened and rocked back on his heels. He rolled his eyes back in his head and waggled his tongue out of his mouth. "Please, Professor, is it a B-plus yet?" More waggling, more white of the eye. "Is it an A-minus?"

Victorinix shot to her feet and marched past the front of the stage. She turned with parade-ground precision and started up the aisle.

"These are the jokes, lady!" cried Antilles. "You were expecting maybe Gloria Steinem?"

The Lost Boys were doubled over, red faced and breathless. Halfway up the aisle Victorinix caught sight of Nelson, who was eating his apple with his long legs draped over the seat in front of him. She slowed and, astonishingly, snapped off her dark glasses, narrowing her icy eyes at Nelson as if she were about to speak. Nelson shrugged and took another bite of his apple. She swung her gaze away and glided up the aisle to the door.

"What an exit!" Antilles called out as the door clacked shut behind her. "Loved ya in *A Doll's House,* babe!"

He theatrically blew out a sigh and mopped his brow with the hankie. "That's okay, ladies and gentlemen, I *prefer* a more intimate crowd," he said, surveying the handful of people left in the hall. "It's more peaceful this way, ya know what I mean?"

He came again to the edge of the stage and fixed his narrow gaze at Stephen Michael Stephens fast asleep in the front row. Antilles lifted his eyes to his nearly nonexistent audience and put a finger to his lips. "Shh," he whispered. "My homey's asleep." He shook his head. "Look at him, ladies and gentlemen, a credit to his race. What's this boy doing all night that he needs to sleep all day?"

Antilles put one hand behind his neck and burlesqued a couple of slow pelvic thrusts. "Look out, Momma, here come da *night* train!" A pause for laughter, which didn't come.

"WAKE UP, STUD!" screamed Antilles, and Stephen Michael Stephens started violently.

"Somebody get my brutha man some chitlins," said Antilles. "Dude needs to keep his strength up."

As Stephens rose slowly, blinking, Miranda DeLaTour stood alongside him and took his arm, and together they started up the aisle. Only Kraljević and Lorraine remained in their seats, staring openmouthed. Pescecane was climbing the steps to the stage, Grossmaul right behind him.

Antilles spread his arms wide and grinned broadly at the rest of the audience, which consisted now of the Lost Boys and Nelson.

"Anthony Pescecane, ladies and gentlemen, the chairman of the board!" he cried. "It's Anthony's world, people; we just live in it."

Antilles swallowed hard as Pescecane came across the stage toward him. "Wassamatta, Tony, ya don't like the act?" His voice was beginning to tremble.

Lionel circled behind Antilles, his eyes bulging in rage. Antilles swiveled awkwardly, trying to keep them both in sight.

"I *kid*, Anthony, I jest!" He mopped his forehead. "What I say, I say with *respect*...."

Pescecane took Antilles's elbow and whispered something in his ear.

"Thank you, ladies and gentlemen!" Antilles threw his free arm high. "You've been a terrific audience! I mean that sincerely!"

As Antilles was hustled toward the steps between Pescecane and Grossmaul, Kraljević and Lorraine leaped to their feet, applauding madly. There were tears of joy streaming down Kraljević's face, and he whipped off his post office cap and flung it into the air. Grossmaul and Pescecane frog-marched Antilles up the empty aisle, and Kraljević and Lorraine fell in behind, still clapping. Watching them come, the Lost Boys clambered over each other up the aisle and out of the hall, the door clacking after them.

"What I say," cried Lester Antilles, trotting on his toes as they pushed him through the door, "I say outta love! You've been a beautiful audience! God bless! Drive safely!"

Kraljević and Lorraine followed, chattering happily. For a long, silent, breathless moment, the door swung. Then the clack of the latch reverberated down the empty hall. Nelson finished his apple, regarded the core from every angle, then lazily flung it. It bounced across the stage.

"One down," Nelson said aloud. He laced his fingers behind his head and stretched his legs. "Two to go."

Nelson received several phone calls that night. The first one was brief, from Pescecane himself. "That bum, Lester Antilles?" he said without any salutation, then, before Nelson could answer, "Let him find his own way back to the airport, the fuck."

The second call was from Morton Weissmann. "Nelson? Mort," he said. "We had a bit of luck today, my spies tell me. Professor Antilles deconstructed, if I might be permitted an intransitive use of the word. In point of fact, Nelson, we dodged a bullet, but 'tis more than we deserve or I expect. We need to be better prepared, Nelson. The next candidate may not be as, ah, manifestly unstable as today's turned out to be. You have a unique opportunity to probe his defenses, my good friend, on the ride back from the airport, and I'm counting on you to keep me . . ."

"I have to go now, Mort," Nelson said. "I hear one of the girls." This was untrue: With a touch and a word—"sleep"—the girls had never been easier to put down in the evening. Bridget was astounded.

"Of course, of course, Nelson," Weissmann said urgently, "but when you get a moment, we need to . . ."

Nelson hung up. Much later, near midnight, Miranda called. "Anthony's in a state, Nelson," she said in a hushed voice, as if she didn't want to be overheard. "Did Lester say anything to you in the car yesterday about what he intended by his job talk?"

"He scarcely spoke to me at all," said Nelson.

"Anthony's in a *state,*" she said again, and something about her conspiratorial hush, the lower register of her voice, made Nelson's pulse race.

"I was just the chauffeur," Nelson said. "I showed up in the clothes you bought me, and he didn't say a word to me."

"Well, he wouldn't, would he?" she said, with a hint of a laugh.

"Miranda . . ." Nelson said, shifting restlessly in his chair.

"I have to go, Nelson," she said breathlessly. "We'll talk again soon."

Late that same night Nelson sat in the blue glow of the furnace in his basement office, his hands poised over his computer keyboard as he contemplated the spreading stain on his literary map of England. Sussex was consumed, Cornwall was nearly gone. The stain spread as far west as Mount Snowden, as far north as Grasmere. Nelson lowered his eyes to an e-mail from Vita.

"What have you done?" it read.

In a brief clatter of keys, Nelson posted a reply.

"Nothing," it said.

A few days later Nelson took the Crown Victoria to the airport again to pick up the next candidate. David Branwell had burst onto the scene at a redbrick university in Britain as the author of *It's Not Unusual: The Tom Jones Way of Knowledge*, and since then he had worked his way to academic stardom through indispensable works on Wayne Newton, Englebert Humperdinck, and Siegfried and Roy. Indeed, it was not unusual for the dais to be littered with panties and boxer shorts after one of Branwell's talks at the MLA. The one question about him, though, the ugly, manhood-doubting whisper that echoed throughout the cultural studies trade, Pescecane had summed up in his bold hand, in his hand-written notes: *"Why not Elvis???"* The answer, evidently, which Branwell had given to half a dozen close confidantes, was that he *was* working on Elvis, but the world was not yet ready for what he had to say. When it was, he assured them, he would revolutionize the field of Presley studies. Fingering his stubbled jaw, the story went, he gave his cruel smile and said, "I have broken the code on *Roustabout*. Once and for all."

Branwell came out of the plane in tailored tweeds and handmade shoes, a tall, broad-shouldered Yorkshireman with dark eyes and thick, dark hair—a dark-skinned gypsy in aspect, in dress and manners a gentleman. He carried one small bag lightly and a garment bag over one shoulder. Even in his new clothes, Nelson felt like the gum-chewing CIA contact sent to meet James Bond. His finger thrummed.

But they did not shake hands. Bleary-eyed, his jaw blued with stubble, Branwell smelled of whiskey. "Are you my ride?" he asked in his north of England accent, rolling his consonants and swallowing his vowels.

"Yes," Nelson said, and Branwell handed him the suitcase and the garment bag.

"Christ, I need a quick one," Branwell said, striding away down the concourse.

The candidate stopped for two quick ones, in fact, between the gate and the parking lot—a shot of Glenlivet at one airport bar, a glass of beer at another, which he downed in one greedy gulp. Nelson trod at his heels, and he watched Branwell turn the heads of women and a few men. In the car Branwell tilted his seat back as far as it would go and closed his eyes before Nelson had even turned on the ignition. By the time they reached the highway the candidate was snoring in a slow, steady rhythm. Watching the road with one eye, Nelson lay his right hand across Branwell's hairy knuckles. The Yorkshireman's breath stuttered, but he did not stir.

"You're a very thirsty fellow," Nelson said.

But Nelson hadn't reckoned on the Englishman's native ability to hold his liquor. At every event Branwell spoke brilliantly, walked steadily, and drank prolifically. At every break in the schedule he made a beeline for the nearest men's room, where he would stand at the urinal blowing out sighs like a draft horse and pee for three minutes straight. Nelson knew, because he followed Branwell every time. Then Branwell would dash some water on his face, pull down the skin beneath his eyes one after the other, and examine his eyeballs in the mirror. Then it was back on stage, Nelson trotting after him.

Branwell's musky charm had its effect. He and Pescecane sized each other up—*Mean Streets* meets *This Sporting Life*—and they both seemed to like what they saw. Victorinix was even more emotionless than usual behind her dark lenses, but the other women of the department were unnerved by Branwell to varying degrees. Lorraine Alsace stared openly at him while Kraljević, in a beret and jodhpurs, glowered behind her back. Penelope O, who wasn't even on the committee, showed up at every event affecting a kind of Cockney mateyness as if to let Branwell know she had his number, while wearing red-patterned leggings that showed off her aerobicized calves and a sweater that threatened to slide off both shoulders. Even Miranda was affected. Her self-possession was a tad more self-conscious, Scarlett O'Hara studiously ignoring Rhett Butler. Pescecane either didn't notice or didn't mind, but it made Nelson's finger throb.

In the end, just before Branwell's job talk, Nelson stationed himself outside the men's room in the lobby as professors and grad students poured into Lecture Hall A across the hall. As he'd hoped, the hiring committee arrived late from a long, drinking lunch at Peregrine, David Branwell flushed and cruelly handsome

211

in their midst, Heathcliff with a buzz on. As the committee approached the lecture hall, Branwell extricated himself and glad-handed his way through the stream of people, his big-knuckled grip squeezing shoulders and forearms on his way toward a urinal.

But Nelson blocked him, taking the candidate's hand and squeezing back manfully, his finger sparking in Branwell's beefy palm. The Yorkshireman's musk, a blend of tweed, Guinness, and sweat, enveloped Nelson; and the candidate's dark, watchful eyes, only the tiniest bit bloodshot, flashed across Nelson's face.

"The men's room's locked," Nelson said, his finger cooling. "You'll have to hold it."

Branwell blinked and swayed. Nelson let go of his hand, and the candidate grunted something and turned away.

"Elvis. Aron. Presley," said David Branwell, very distinctly. The crowd caught its breath.

The candidate gripped the lectern firmly between both hands, as if he were about to fling it into the hall. There was a slight sheen to his forehead, but that might only have been the heat in the lecture room. Indeed, throughout Pesce-cane's fulsome and gruffly respectful introduction, the standing-room-only crowd had restlessly peeled off coats and sweaters and flannel shirts. Nelson stood in his shirtsleeves against the back wall, under the projection booth, his hands coolly folded over his loins.

"That's the name you've all come to hear me utter, innit?" Branwell's dark eyes flashed from under his glowering brow, and the crowd released its breath as laughter.

"Let me start from bedrock," he said. "I take it we're all agreed that for a number of years—perhaps still—Elvis was the chief modality by which the dominant popular culture absorbed and appropriated the Other. As a white truck driver from Memphis, he was himself a liminal figure, but implicated enough in the larger structures of feeling of the industrial West, in Williams's sense, to stand in even for a Yorkshire lad watching scratchy sixteen-millimeter prints of his films in the workingman's clubs of Grimethorpe. Thus fixed, both in the mineshafts of Northern England as well as in the *Gemeinschaft* of late monopoly capitalism, Elvis could appropriate the rhythms and tropes of black culture, literally deracinating them for white consumers of hegemonic cultural production."

Branwell paused to draw a breath. The audience was quiet, respectful, but so far he'd told them nothing they didn't already know.

"Now," said Branwell, smiling faintly, "I want to ask you something: What's the one Elvis picture you've never heard of?"

The audience murmured as if it might actually propose an answer.

"I'll tell you," said Branwell. "It's a little known film, never released, impossible to find on video, made sometime between *Love Me Tender* and *A Change of Habit,* an unusual, one might even say incredible collaboration between filmmakers of different styles, genres, and worldviews. Directed by Howard Hawks. Screenplay by Marguerite Duras and Frank Tashlin. Original songs by Brian Wilson and Kurt Weill."

The crowd's murmuring swelled. Some people were hauling out notebooks and pens.

"I am referring, of course," said David Branwell, "to Elvis's lost masterpiece, *Viva Vietnam!*"

A gasp rippled across the crowd. There was laughter and a smattering of applause.

"In this picture, for those of you who haven't seen it, and I doubt anyone here has, Elvis is Rick Dubonnet, a half-Cajun, half-Cherokee shrimper working the waters off the Mekong Delta in his boat the *Queen Creole,* with his crusty old sidekick "Sparks" MacGillicuddy (Edgar Buchanan) and his pet monkey Boney Joe (J. Fred Muggs). Right away you'll notice how Elvis reifies in his own corpus America's Orientalist fantasy of mixed blood, nicely judged between two marginalized ethnicities—straight-shooting white working class and the spiritually pure Native American."

The crowd leaned forward in their seats, rapt. Many were taking notes.

"Imagine," Branwell said, shifting his weight from one foot to the other, flexing his grip on the lectern, "imagine the opening sequence of this motion picture, a magnificent set piece of colonialist fantasy. Behind the opening credits, in brilliant Technicolor, the return to port of the *Queen Creole* is the occasion for an extravagant production number. Elvis, aka Rick, in his chinos and open-necked shirt, stands grinning with one deck shoe up on the gunwale while Sparks pilots the boat up the river. The villagers dance their traditional native dances along the shore in their conical hats and colorful pajamas. As they carry the baskets of glistening pink shrimp along the dock, Elvis, the happy, mixed-race American boy, friend to natives everywhere, curls his lip in a grin, pushes back his well-worn captain's cap, and lip-syncs to the song 'Mekong Gumbo.' ' "

Branwell swayed a bit behind the podium and gave an Elvis sneer. There were a few not entirely ironic squeals from the crowd. The sheen had brightened on Branwell's forehead, and he shifted from foot to foot a bit more restlessly.

"Situated between two ethnicities," Branwell continued, "Rick naturally has two lovers, one Asian, one white. But with the Asian woman he is not simply exercising his colonialist's prerogative among the dark women; the clear implication is that he is Other himself, at least in part. To retrofit Conrad's phrase, he is One of Them. His Vietnamese lover is Lo Phat, a sloe-eyed 'Oriental' beauty (Nancy Kwan), the daughter of the local chieftain Dam Yan Ky (Sam Jaffe). After the festival that opens the film, Rick and Lo Phat walk along the perimeter of the local American firebase and sing a love duet, 'The Moonlight, the Minefield, and You.' Comic relief is provided by Lo Phat's pesky kid brother, Arvin, and Boney Joe, who walk hand-in-hand along the beach behind the lovers, just behind the, um, ri, rising tide."

There was more warm laughter. Elvis, reflected Nelson, makes even intellectuals happy. He noted a slight twitch to the Englishman's cheek, an extra tension in the way his fingers squeezed and released the lectern. Nelson settled back against the wall.

"His other sweetheart," said the candidate, "is Cissy Westmoreland (Shelley Fabares), the pert daughter of the local American colonel (Brian Keith). At the annual base talent show, Cissy's shimmying beach number 'Bikini B-52' ties for first place with Rick's steel drum extravaganza 'Dien Bien Phooey,' and they find themselves in the winner's circle together under the watchful eye of Cissy's mother (Eve Arden). All of this—the erotic chemistry between Elvis and Cissy, between Elvis and Cissy's mother, and even between Elvis and Colonel Westmoreland—is witnessed by Arvin and Boney Joe from the bamboo rafters of the officers' club, and they race back to tell the jealous Lo Phat of Rick's flirtation with a round-eye."

Branwell paused, and a wince passed over his face; he was looking a little pale himself. His knuckles whitened as he squeezed the lectern and released it.

"Meanwhile," he went on, licking his lips, "Rick is taken aside by the base's CIA operative (Paul Lynde), the only one who knows that Rick was once an assassin in the army's secret Phoenix Program, sneaking into Vietcong villages at night to slit the throats of suspected VC officers. Now the CIA wants Rick to do one more mission up, up"—Branwell swallowed—"upriver, to liquidate a French rubber plantation owner (Ezio Pinza) who is offering safe puh, passage to the VC."

The murmuring swelled again; this was revelatory stuff, an insight into a transgressive side of Elvis. Leave it to this brilliant Englishman to show to an American audience a facet of American popular culture they didn't even know existed. Those who were taking notes were writing furiously to keep up. The murmuring was especially intense off to Nelson's right, where Morton Weissmann sat with his chin lifted and his lips pursed. Ever since Nelson had come into the lecture hall, Weissmann had been trying to give him the high sign. Weissmann had nodded at Nelson, he'd tugged his earlobe, he had put his finger along the side of his nose. Nelson ignored him. Meanwhile, the Lost Boys, who flanked Weissmann, were whispering urgently among each other and shooting glances at Branwell.

"Rick resists," continued the candidate, sweating and fidgeting, "but the CIA fellow has leverage: He knows that Rick's crusty sidekick, Sparks, was once a member of the Communist Party on the wa, wa, waterfront of San Francisco in the thirties. Rick has no choice but to go. As the shrimp boat ch, churns slowly up the Mekong with Sparks at the wheel smoking his corncob pipe, Rick stands at the stern waving farewell to the villagers carrying torches along the wa, wa, water, serenading them with a lovely slack-key guitar number, 'You Broke My Heart of Darkness.'"

Branwell shifted from foot to foot. He squeezed and released the lectern. He glanced toward the wings as if gauging the distance. He licked his lips, and Pescecane, seated at the table next to him, lifted the plastic carafe and offered to pour Branwell a glass of water. Branwell turned even paler and shook his head vehemently. He swallowed and went on.

One of the Lost Boys whispered urgently in Weissmann's ear. A few people near Weissmann hissed at the Lost Boys to keep quiet. This drew the attention of Pescecane, whose face darkened when he saw who was causing the commotion. His eyes fell upon Nelson standing at the back, and he jerked his head toward Weissmann. Nelson pointed at himself and raised his eyebrows and mouthed the word, "Me?" Pescecane nodded angrily and jerked his head again toward Weissmann. Nelson began to make his way, very slowly, through the crowd at the back of the hall.

"Unbeknownst to Rick, of course," Branwell was saying, his voice trembling, "Lo Phat is actually a colonel in the Vietcong. As she and Rick dodge each other in the hand-to-hand fighting during an assault on the American Embassy, they sing an edgy duet, 'Tet-à-Tet.' Meanwhile, Arvin attempts to frag Sparks, sending

215

Boney Joe aboard the *Queen Creole* with a hand grenade. But little does Arvin know that Sparks has been a Soviet agent ever since the Spanish Civil War, and . . ."

"I'm sorry," called out Morton Weissmann, standing, "but I can't let this go on."

Much of the audience turned to see who was interrupting, and from his seat on the stage Pescecane looked murderously at Weissmann. He shot another glance at Nelson. The Lost Boys slouched in their seats and pulled their heads down between their shoulders like turtles. Nelson, meanwhile, edged as slowly as he could toward the aisle.

Branwell breathed heavily into the microphone and sweated. He licked his lips and rhythmically gripped the sides of the lectern—squeeze and release, squeeze and release. He covered the microphone with his big hand and said, in a sotto voce loud enough for the whole room to hear, "Perhaps we should take a break, Anthony?"

"Hang on, David," said Pescecane. "This'll just take a second."

Branwell bit his lip.

"Loathe as I am to admit it in this august company," declared Weissmann from the audience, "I must confess I am not familiar with the Presley canon. But I have it on reliable authority"—here he gestured curtly at the Lost Boys, and they cringed further into their shells—"that the film you are interpreting for us does not exist."

Pescecane, whose mouth was open to speak, closed it again.

"I'm told," Weissmann went on, lifting his voice about the rising susurrus of the crowd, "with a rather high degree of certainty, that Elvis Presley never appeared in a film set in Vietnam."

Every head in the room swiveled away from Weissmann and toward the lectern. Nelson paused in his progress toward Weissmann to listen for the answer. Pescecane turned to Branwell, who gasped and wiped his dripping forehead with the sleeve of his coat.

"Well, if by 'exist,' " said Branwell in a tight voice, "you mean, were the scenes I am evoking ever committed to celluloid during Elvis's lifetime, the answer is no. They were not."

A collective indrawn breath from the crowd.

"But in a vastly more significant and *resonant* sense," continued the candidate, his knuckles white on the lectern, "*Viva Vietnam!* is an absolutely essential text, one that plays nightly in the multiplex of the American consciousness."

The crowd let out its breath in unison. Heads turned toward Weissmann, who stood smiling to himself. "But where can I *see* this film?" he asked.

Branwell twisted his hips behind the lectern, but even in his distress—perhaps because of it—he was getting angry. "Just close your eyes, Professor," he snapped, "and open your mind to the zeitgeist."

"But you cannot interpret a work that *does not exist!*" gasped Weissmann.

"Whether the text 'exists,'" said David Branwell, hooking his index fingers to make inverted commas, "in the extremely narrow sense you mean, does not in any way affect my reading of it."

An appreciative murmur swelled through the room. Even Pescecane relaxed, settling back in his chair and leveling a look of satisfaction over the heads of the crowd at Weissmann, who stood openmouthed and speechless.

"Perhaps you prefer a canonical authority," Branwell said, sweating. At the word "canonical," the crowd gave a derisive laugh.

"How about Oscar Wilde? 'To give an accurate description of what has never occurred is not merely the proper occupation of the historian, but the inalienable privilege of any man of arts and culture.'"

At the very mention of Oscar Wilde, Weissmann began to turn red in the face.

"Look, let me make it easy for you," said Branwell, coming out from behind the lectern. He was practically jigging from foot to foot like an anxious boy. "The technology already exists to create this film retroactively. It's only a matter of time before the entire *oeuvres* of Hawks and Elvis are digitized, enabling them to be reassembled in an infinite number of variations. Perhaps by another 'artist,' whatever that might mean in a digital context, perhaps by an artificial intelligence. Perhaps the various elements will simply assemble themselves fractally in the cyberverse, reproducing anti-entropically like crystals with no 'conscious' agency—which is as good a metaphor as one could propose for 'authorship,' for the way the dominant culture reproduces itself."

Branwell's accent became thicker as he became excited; he spoke with a half-civilized ferocity, his eyes full of black fire. Still, the relentless pressure of his bladder made him dance on the stage; he rocked heel to toe, clenching and unclenching his fists.

"Infinite variations of this film—Claudette Colbert instead of Shelley Fabares, Spencer Tracy instead of Edgar Buchanan, Errol Flynn instead of Elvis—will combine and recombine like mutant DNA. Once the film 'exists,' it will be as if *it had always existed.* The 'real' Elvis Presley films, in your reductive sense of the word, will exist only in the same sense that *Mona Lisa* is constructed out of the pixels of a billion postcards and T-shirts!"

A gust of applause swept the hall. The crowd were on the edge of their seats; a few around the margins of the room and in the crowded aisles were half-standing to get a better view. Weissmann stammered "I-I-I" in a vain attempt to break into Branwell's torrent. Pescecane was beaming.

"To say," cried Branwell, "that the corporeal Elvis is no longer accessible to us by any medium is the same as saying that *there never was a 'real' Elvis.*"

Branwell ground his molars and squeezed his eyes shut, and the crowd tilted forward, taking his agony for testimonial passion.

"Tell it!" someone shouted, and the crowd groaned happily in assent.

"The privileging of Elvis's materiality," said Branwell through gritted teeth, "is essentialist in the extreme. Elvis is not his body. Elvis is a bricolage, an infinitely mutable assemblage of signifiers. He is a template, the disintegrating negative from which his image may be struck *in all its infinite diversity!*"

"Amen!" cried someone. Half the room was on its feet in a revivalist fervor. Weissmann had dropped into his seat. Pescecane was laughing and clapping his hands. Branwell stood rooted to the stage, trembling all over as if a current were being passed through him. He dug his fingers into his palms; he squeezed his eyes shut.

"Elvis is a dream of the West, perhaps of the world," he said in a guttural moan, as if he were possessed. "For what is not connected with him to us? And what does not recall him? I cannot look down to the floor, but his features are shaped on the boards! In every cloud, in every tree—filling the air at night, and caught by glimpses in every object, by day I am surrounded by his image! The most ordinary faces of men and women—my own features—mock me with a resemblance!"

Nelson, even though he was taller than nearly everyone in the room, lifted himself on his toes.

"Elvis is the sea in which we swim!" Branwell cried, his eyes squeezed shut. "Elvis is the pounding rain! Elvis is the swelling tide!"

He swayed on his heels; he clenched his fists until his hands were entirely white.

"Elvis . . . is . . . a river!"

With an almost orgasmic groan, Branwell shuddered upright, and a dark stain spread copiously from his groin and down the length of his tweed trousers. His whole body swayed, and he rocked back on his heels, his face tipped back toward the ceiling, his mouth hanging slack. The crowd rocked back away from him in a wave that spread from the stage; it sharply drew in its collective breath. In a moment the room was silent except for the creak of seats, the rustle of bodies, and, if you listened closely enough, a heavy trickling as his epic micturation spread below Branwell's knee, filled his trouser cuff, and pattered over his shoe to the stage.

The candidate's shoulders loosened. His fists uncurled, and his hands dangled at his sides. He sighed heavily in the silence. Then his head flopped forward, and he slowly opened his eyes. For a moment he blinked at the crowd as if he had no idea who they were or where he was. Then the crowd, without speaking, began to settle, rustling and creaking, into their seats again. They averted their eyes.

Branwell's eyes widened. He glanced down at his trousers, then sharply up at the crowd again. His cheeks and forehead burned bright red, and he cringed, dropping his shoulders and pushing his knees together. He tried to cover himself with his trembling hands; he plucked at the soaking tweed against his leg. His mouth worked soundlessly. He glanced at Pescecane, his eyes watering, but the chairperson had already left the stage and was walking stiff backed and stone-faced up the aisle, the crowd parting for him silently.

Branwell backed across the stage, nearly doubled over, his eyes darting everywhere until they came to rest on Nelson at the back of the hall. He sobbed, his eyes brimming over. "I'm sorry, sir!" he whimpered. "I really tried, sir, truly I did, sir!"

But Nelson was already on his way out the door.

It wasn't until late at night, at his computer in the basement, under the spreading blot across his map of literary England, that Nelson realized he hadn't seen Vita at any of the events of the day. Still, as the furnace whooshed to life behind him, he tapped out a message to her anyway.

"Nelson, two," he typed. "Candidates, zip."

Striding up the airport concourse again several days later, Nelson knew he looked good. He didn't turn to see, but he was pretty certain people were glancing at him, wondering who he was, that tall, confident fellow in the casually elegant clothes. Vita would never understand, he thought, how nice it is to be the object of the objectifying gaze now and then. A more stylish haircut, a little makeup, some snappier clothes, and Vita wouldn't look half-bad. No Miranda DeLaTour, of course, but who was? It wouldn't kill Vita to perform her gender role a little more aggressively.

She could have learned a thing or two about gender as performance, in fact, from jennifer manly. At the gate Nelson picked the candidate right away out of the stream of disembarking passengers, even though he'd never seen her before. She was a short, trim African American; and she walked with measured steps and a clear gaze, treading the carpet proudly, carrying her head high. She wore a tight silk head scarf, gold and ivory, tied at the nape of her neck, a pair of earrings that glittered and dangled at every step, and two-thirds of a masculine pinstripe suit: trousers and a vest of gold-and-ivory brocade, both perfectly tailored to nip in at her waist. Her white shirt was open at the collar, her Doc Martens polished to a mirror sheen.

jennifer manly was the queer theorist of the moment. Her book on O. J. Simpson had provoked a bidding war between Routledge and Duke University Press and ended up as a bestseller for a subsidiary of Time Warner. In a stunning bricolage of Judith Butler, Frantz Fanon, and *Court TV,* she proved that Mark Fuhrman had planted the Bloody Glove as an act of repressed longing for O. J.; she implied something more than brotherhood between O. J. and Al Cowlings— "Whose 'gun' did O. J. hold to his 'head' in the Slow Speed Chase? Was it a 'naked gun'?"—and in a brilliant display of theoretical pyrotechnics, she showed how O. J.'s rage at constrictive and heterosexist constructions of gender had led him to a profoundly transgressive metaphorical act, murdering a "man" and a "woman" nearly simultaneously, thus placing the reductive dualism of "gender" itself *sous rature.*

manly's eyes widened expectantly at the sight of Nelson, and Nelson's finger seared him. He could end this campus visit right here, right now; he could take Ms. manly confidently by the hand and tell her to turn around and get back on the plane. He could see already that Vita had no hope in hell of competing with this stylish, confident woman, and he bit his lip against the heat in his finger. As manly gracefully sorted herself out of the crowd, Nelson nearly groaned against the pain, stunned at the vehemence of his visceral reaction, a pure, incarnate rage that shot straight up out of his subconscious like a shark, the undiluted voice of his medulla oblongata: She is not One of Us, his lizard brain said; she's black, she's queer, she hates your gender and your race. She's striding out of the airplane like a warrior princess—savage and superb, wild-eyed and magnificent—a fierce, bare-breasted African Amazon in a leopard skin and scarified flesh, out to avenge her race for the sixty million dead on the Middle Passage, to avenge her sexual preference for witchcraft trials and mass rape. She wants to take your job and seduce your wife, she wants to turn your daughters into lesbians, and she wants to make you—yes, you, Nelson Humboldt—pay personally for the sins of Western Europe, all three thousand years of it: slavery, patriarchy, capitalism, heterosexuality. She wants to pitchfork you and your kind up and over onto the dust heap of history; she wants your head on the end of her spear. Destroy her, said his brainstem. Do it now.

Nelson, overwhelmed, staggered back a step. He wrung his hands, afraid to speak, afraid to touch her. But before he could decide what to do or say, jennifer manly astonished him, not once, but twice, in a matter of seconds. She confounded all his expectations by being . . . charming. And left-handed.

"Professor Humboldt?" She tilted her head and gave him a radiant smile. Nelson found himself shaking her left hand, while his own right hand hung throbbing at his side.

"jennifer manly," she said, in a warm Southern accent with a tropical lilt to it.

"Nuh, Nelson." Her hand was warm and smooth, her grasp firm. "But call me . . . Nelson." He thrust his right hand into his pocket.

"Wonderful!" She beamed at him. "I'm so glad to meet you!"

All the way through the airport and out to the car, Nelson's finger was inflamed. Settling behind the wheel and turning the ignition, he could scarcely feel the key. He gripped the wheel tightly, sweating and nearly blinded with pain, and at the cashier's booth on the way out of the parking lot, he handed the large black woman in the booth his ticket and a couple of dollars and inadvertently brushed her hand with his burning finger. The pain vanished instantly.

"Sweet Jesus!" gasped the cashier, reeling back from the window and clutching her bosom.

manly, meanwhile, turned to Nelson. "Tell me about your work, Nelson," she said, as if she really meant it. "What sort of things are you doing?"

"Um, James Hogg?" Nelson accelerated away from the booth without waiting for his change. In the rearview mirror he saw the cashier in the booth drop out of sight in a dead faint.

"The Ettrick Shepherd!" cried Professor manly happily, as if she and Nelson had a friend in common. "Fantastic!"

All the way back to Hamilton Groves, Nelson talked about himself and his work under the enthusiastic provocation of jennifer manly. Everything he told her sent her into further ecstasies of admiration. Ph.D. from SUIE—a marvelous school, sadly underrated! Four comp classes a semester—essential, essential work; I'm ashamed I don't do more of it! Teaching undergrads exclusively—that's where the *real* battle's being fought, isn't it? Two daughters—how adorable! You must let me meet them!

"Technically, I'm not a professor," he told her, flattered into modesty. "I only have a three-year contract as a, as a . . . lecturer."

"Ah, but I've no doubt you'll prove your worth, Nelson." She dropped her silky voice an octave, thrillingly. "Let's keep our fingers crossed, shall we?"

Indeed, by the time Nelson had escorted jennifer manly up to the eighth floor of Harbour Hall, he not only wanted her as a colleague, he wanted her to share an office with him, he wanted to take her home for dinner, he wanted her to charm Bridget and dazzle his little girls. Lionel Grossmaul tried to block Nelson from accompanying manly into Pescecane's inner office, but Nelson shook his finger at him, and Lionel stumbled back into his chair. In the chairperson's office, Pescecane, in his shirtsleeves, rose from behind his massive oaken desk and threw his arms wide, embracing jennifer as she squealed in delight.

"Anthony Pescecane!" she cried, clutching his massive biceps. "At last we meet!"

"Love your work, jen," Pescecane said. "Big fan."

Miranda and Victorinix were waiting as well. jennifer and Miranda exchanged air kisses like a pair of divas. Victorinix's cheeks actually colored beneath the dark disks of her glasses, and she shook manly's hand and gave the candidate a narrow smile.

Nelson, meanwhile, hung back and rubbernecked. He had never been in the chair's office before; he had dropped Antilles and Branwell at the hotel. Pescecane's idea of decor combined the postmodern and the baronial: The suspended ceiling had been removed, exposing the steel beams and ducts overhead, and the cinder block walls had been sandblasted of every trace of paint. But the desk was an antique, vast and Gothic, squatting on its four clawed legs as if ready to spring off the dark red carpet at any moment. Around the walls were austerely framed film posters—*The Public Enemy, Little Caesar, Goodfellas*—culminating in a signed poster for *The Godfather* behind Pescecane's desk: "Tony—make me an offer I can't refuse—XOXO, Marlon."

"Dinner?" Pescecane asked, and Nelson, turning, nearly said yes. But a glance told him he wasn't invited. Pescecane was thrusting his arms through his suit coat, and Victorinix was arm in arm with a sparkling jennifer manly, escorting her out of the office. Nelson's heart sank as jennifer passed out the door without even a glance in his direction.

Miranda paused at the door. She glanced after the retreating party and took a step toward Nelson. "You know, Nelson, after the last two candidates, all jennifer has to do is show up sober and she's got the job." With a sly smile she started to turn away. "Tough luck for Vita, I'm afraid."

Nelson said nothing, but his finger burned.

Miranda paused a moment longer at the door, and looked him up and down. "You look good," she said.

At dinner, at home, Nelson pushed macaroni and cheese around his plate with his fork, glowering over the heads of his daughters, sighing at odd intervals that had nothing to do with Clara's tedious account of a party at school. Bridget kept up the conversation on her own, shooting glances at her husband.

"Look, Mommy," cried Abigail, holding aloft a cheesy noodle on the tip of her finger, "a booger!"

"Mom!" cried Clara. "Ewwww!"

"Girls," warned Bridget, then, to Nelson, "What kind of car do they give you when you go to the airport? Some old junker, I bet." She watched him expectantly, chewing a mouthful of macaroni and cheese.

"A Crown Victoria," he said.

Bridget blinked and swallowed. Clara pushed her plate away and crossed her arms.

"Finish your dinner, dear," said Bridget, watching Nelson sidelong.

"I'm not hungry anymore," said Clara.

"Boogers!" shouted Abigail. She had a noodle on each fingertip now. "Boogers and cheese!"

"Abby, stop," said Bridget. "Clara, eat your dinner."

"*He's* not eating." Clara glowered at her father, whose forkful of cooling macaroni had stalled halfway to his lips.

"He *loves* it," said Bridget, nudging him under the table.

Nelson looked at his fork. Somewhere across town the candidate and the other members of the hiring committee were running up several hundred dollars at the university's expense on nouvelle cuisine at Théorie Vert, Hamilton Groves' French restaurant. Meanwhile, on Nelson's fork were clots of limp pasta and congealing cheese food out of a box. He turned his fork over and let the macaroni plop onto his plate.

"See?" said Clara coldly.

"Boogers!" cried Abigail triumphantly.

"I'm *not* eating boogers," said Clara.

Bridget stared tight-lipped at Nelson. "You didn't wear *that,* did you?" She lifted her chin at him. "To the airport? In your Crown Victoria?"

Nelson was wearing the discount store jeans and threadbare pullover he had changed out of, and back into, in his office.

"Sure I did," he snapped. "The hell's wrong with it?"

The following day, Nelson's class schedule kept him from attending most of the activities of jennifer manly's campus visit: her audience with the Women's Studies faculty at their offices in Radclyffe Hall, her lunch at Peregrine with the hiring committee, her attendance at a rehearsal of an all-woman production of *12 Angry Men.* But as soon as his three o'clock class ended, Nelson dodged between students across the Quad in a light snow, hoping to get to Lecture Hall A on the ground floor of Harbour Hall before the candidate's job talk was over.

Halfway across the Quad, he nearly collided with Vita, who was running the other way.

"Vita!" he exclaimed. It was the first time he had seen her in days. "Have you come from manly's job talk? How was it?"

Vita wore a knit cap with a little pom-pom on top, and she ran with both her hands tugging it down over her ears. Her face was deathly pale, her eyes were wide. She looked right at Nelson without seeing him, then bolted like a rabbit in the direction of the old library in a long stride that surprised Nelson to see.

Inside the auditorium Nelson found that the talk was over, but at least a quarter of the crowd was still down by the proscenium in an eager huddle around jennifer manly, who sat posed at the edge of the stage like a pinup girl, legs crossed fetchingly, her hands crossed lightly over her knee. She bathed her admirers in a smile measurable in megawatts and said something brightly that Nelson could not hear. The little crowd of young women roared with laughter.

On the stage behind her, the hiring committee, or most of it, conferred in a little huddle of their own. Anthony Pescecane smiled and gesticulated, and the others were smiling back and vigorously nodding their heads. Stephen Michael Stephens was wide-awake, laughing. Victoria Victorinix was talking so animatedly that she looked lifelike. Only Marko Kraljević, in a priest's collar and cassock, and Lorraine Alsace looked angry and glum, as they watched Lorraine's chance at a job evaporate in the heat of jennifer manly's smile.

As Nelson came down the aisle, Miranda came toward him with her coat draped over her linked hands. As she approached Nelson, she tossed back her hair and lifted her chin at him.

"Wha, what happened?" Nelson whispered. "I couldn't make it."

Miranda pursed her lips and glanced back at the burbling crowd before the stage. "I think we have a winner," she said, and started up the aisle toward the door.

"But doesn't the committee need to meet?" Nelson trotted after her. "Don't we need to discuss this?"

Miranda stopped and turned slowly on her sharp heel. "There's the dinner tonight at Anthony's house," she said. "You know about that, of course."

"Of course." It was the first Nelson had heard of it.

"Good." She turned again. "You can tell me how it goes."

"Aren't you going to be there?"

Miranda's shoulders stiffened slightly.

"I don't think Anthony's wife would be comfortable with that," she said.

"Anthony's *married?*" Nelson caught himself. But Miranda was already out the door, the rapid click of her heels echoing back from the lobby.

"Am I invited?" Bridget said when Nelson called her from his office to say he was going to Anthony Pescecane's for dinner.

"It's a department thing, hon," he said. "It's not really a social event."

"Why didn't you tell me about it before?"

Nelson glanced around the office. Vita's desk was in disarray—papers loose, a jumble of pens, a collapsed pile of books. "I have to go, sweetie," he said.

"Aren't you coming home to change? You're *not* going to the chair of the department's house in what you wore to work today, are you?"

Nelson held his breath. He was standing in his dress shoes and the clothes Miranda DeLaTour had bought for him.

"I'll try to be home before eleven," he said.

He did sneak back to married housing long enough to snatch his car out of the parking lot; the bus did not run to Anthony Pescecane's neighborhood. He left the straighter, wider, cheaper streets of Hamilton Groves close to campus and ventured into the narrow, winding, wooded lanes in the hills overlooking the lake where the houses were large and hidden behind trees and privacy walls. His old Toyota rattled and farted, and he was afraid he might be pulled over by some private security officer wanting to know what he was doing in such a car among all these large, expensive houses. For all Nelson knew, it was some sort of misdemeanor to bring a ten-year-old Toyota, stinking of exhaust and dappled with Rust-Oleum, into this preserve of Mercedes, BMWs, and Jaguars.

He parked the car around a sharp bend from Pescecane's house, then trudged up the hill. It was snowing, and through the tumbling flakes he saw the house, a Frank Lloyd Wright original that cantilevered out from the side of the hill, a wide wedge of warm candlelight overlooking the frozen lake, and the lights of the town twinkling beyond. For an instant Nelson considered turning back, but his finger burned him, and he started up the steep, slippery driveway in his dress shoes, two steps forward, one back.

"Nelson!" hissed a voice out of the dark, and Nelson nearly lost his balance. As he scrambled for footing on the slick pavement, a hand clutched him by the elbow and hauled him behind a bush into a shallow snowdrift. Nelson's finger flared, but before he could do anything he was nose to nose with Morton Weissmann.

"Mort, what the . . . !"

"You're just in time!" Weissmann whispered hoarsely, a liquid gleam in his eye, his breath a mist of Canadian Club and Glenlivet. "I can't find a vantage point!"

He glanced up the slope at the warm light of the dining room window. His fingers kneaded Nelson's parka. A black pair of birding binoculars hung on a strap around his neck.

"There's no way to see in without being seen, though of course I haven't made my way around the side. . . ." His voice trailed off as he turned away. Nelson pulled free of Weissmann's weak grasp, and he glanced nervously about. Then he turned Weissmann firmly by the shoulders and grabbed the older man's hands. Weissmann wasn't wearing gloves, and his hands were cold to the touch. Nelson's finger hummed with heat.

"Mort, where are your gloves?"

"But you!" whispered Weissmann, his eyes brightening. "You can go inside! You can pass for one of them! You can penetrate the . . . the belly of the beast! I can't, of course. I'm not invited." He swallowed. " 'There lives not three good men unhanged in England, and one of them is fat, and grows old . . .' " Tears formed in Weissmann's eyes, and he began to sway on his feet. With a glance back at the house, Nelson slung Weissmann's arm over his shoulders.

"Where's your car, Mort?" Nelson said. "Where are you parked?"

But the elder professor had come by cab, it turned out, so Nelson led Weissmann, slipping and sliding, down the driveway and around the bend to his own car. He planted Weissmann in the passenger seat of the Toyota, fished the older man's gloves out of his coat pocket, and pulled them on as he would for his daughters.

"Nelson, you're our last chance," Weissmann said hoarsely, his eyes pleading. "The fate of literature in our department, at Midwest . . . my God, Nelson, perhaps in all of North America, depends on you! The barbarians are no longer at the gates, Nelson, they're in the banquet hall, feasting on our patrimony! Throwing the bones on the floor! Eating with their fingers!"

Nelson, wincing at Weissmann's breath, pulled off his own gloves and grasped Weissmann by the wrist. His finger sparked against the older man's papery skin. "Go to sleep, Mort," he said.

Back at the top of the driveway Nelson took a moment to draw a deep breath and stamp the snow off his shoes. Then he rang the bell. The door was answered by some sort of servant, a gray-faced, narrow-chested woman in a plain blue dress.

"Hi!" Nelson blurted. His finger burned in his pocket; it hadn't occurred to him that he might have to talk his way past a stranger. But the woman stepped aside without a word and let him in. By the time Nelson had taken off his parka, she was gone, and he found a closet himself and stuffed the coat inside.

He moved cautiously down a hallway lined with Asian art toward the glow of candlelight and the lilt of jennifer manly's voice. He hesitated in the doorway at the sight of the candidate and the hiring committee at a long table in Pescecane's dining room. Three bright candle flames were reflected in the dark, floor-length window on the far side of the table. In a hushed voice jennifer manly reached the climax of the story she was telling, and the entire table erupted into laughter.

Nelson's finger flamed, and he edged toward the dark hall. But as the table's hilarity subsided, manly, seated with her back to him, caught the movement of his reflection in the window and turned to him, smiling.

"Nelson!" she cried in her musical voice. "How delightful!"

The others turned, still smiling, and Nelson was trapped in their collective gaze like a fighter plane in searchlights. He stepped into the dining room, fidgeting with his cuffs. Pescecane's dining room table was laid with a tablecloth and matching napkins in little linen pyramids. The three tall candles stood down the middle of the table, and candlelight gleamed in the wineglasses and deep in the bottle of wine itself; it glittered off the sterling flatware and the silver saltcellar. For once Stephen Michael Stephens was awake, albeit yawning. Lorraine Alsace, in a long, black dress that bared her bony shoulders, and Marko Kraljević in some sort of après ski outfit—boots, ski pants, a bulky Charlie Brown sweater—sat across from each other, apparently enjoying themselves in spite of manly's success. In the warm glow Victoria Victorinix sat without her dark glasses, her sharp eyes shining. She even looked pretty, Nelson thought, in a pearl necklace and a silk blouse that caught the shine of the candlelight. The chairperson himself sat at the head of his table in a collarless white shirt and a leather vest—Pescecane Unplugged. He glanced at Nelson, then looked with genuine disappointment at manly.

"The fuck?" he said. "It's not time for you to go, is it?"

There were no empty seats at the table. Grossmaul was not present, and neither, apparently, was Mrs. Pescecane. Nelson noted her absence for later, so that he might smooth Bridget's ruffled feelings by pointing out that Pescecane hadn't even invited his own wife to the dinner.

"Of course not!" declared jennifer. "Nelson is simply late for dinner! Aren't you, sweetie?"

Pescecane leveled a dull gaze at Nelson, and Nelson endured it for a breathless moment. Then the chairperson spread his hands, inviting him in, and Nelson breathed again.

"Come sit by me!" jennifer held out a hand toward Nelson. She sat at Pescecane's right hand, so Nelson swung a chair—another Frank Lloyd Wright original—away from the wall and squeezed in between manly and Kraljević. As if on cue, the gray-faced housekeeper who had let him in appeared with a napkin, a wineglass, a cup and saucer, and silverware. Pescecane himself poured Nelson's wine—something from his cellar, the name of which Nelson couldn't read in the dusky light—and Nelson received the glass with his finger humming.

"jennifer," said Pescecane, handing the wine bottle over his shoulder to the gray woman without looking at her, "you were saying."

jennifer resumed her storytelling as the gray woman brought the soup—stracchiatella sprinkled with parsley—and went around the table ladling it out to appreciative murmurs. Pescecane had met his match as a raconteur in this candidate. manly began a story about one of the premier names in feminist theory, retailing it with wit, a talent for suspense, and a stand-up's sense of timing. Nelson felt like a gangly teenager invited to the grown-ups' table for the first time, and he knew to keep his mouth shut. But he was not so dazzled that he failed to recognize a transaction taking place: jennifer manly was laying the story at the feet of Anthony Pescecane like a gold bar. She already had the job, and this was her dowry, her bride price, the deal clincher. In return for providing Pescecane a direct line to the private life of a leading theorist, jennifer manly was guaranteed lifetime job security and a yearly income just shy of six figures.

"And what did Fwancesca *say?*" asked Lorraine Alsace, as rapt and bright-eyed as a girl, charmed by her rival.

"Nothing!" breathed jennifer manly. "She *blushed,* can you believe it?"

"Weader, I mawwied her," said Lorraine Alsace, and the entire table erupted in laughter again.

Pescecane's laugh was self-consciously hearty, but Victoria Victorinix lit up like a paper lantern, demurely pressing her napkin to her mouth. Nelson's finger flared slightly; Alsace's joke tugged at Nelson's memory, but not enough to free anything concrete. He sipped at his wine.

Each new anecdote topped the one before, and they were timed to climax just before the arrival of each new course, allowing the gray housekeeper to move freely around the table in the glow of each punch line.

"Is that a Russian hickey or a Japanese hickey?" asked jennifer manly, and the pasta came, a big bowl of fettucini with a tomato and porcini mushroom sauce, which Anthony made a show of serving, with a big wooden spoon and fork.

"And when they pulled back the sheet, it wasn't Tania! It was *Michaela!*" jennifer said, and the woman brought veal picatta, with rosemary potatoes.

"A true story! My hand to God!" and the gray woman brought a lettuce and radicchio salad, dressed with olive oil and red wine vinegar.

Nelson laughed and ate, ate and laughed. After the pasta he felt comfortable enough to take off his jacket. Indeed, there was only one unsettling note in the whole situation. In the diminishing uproar after each story, as the diners sighed and patted their lips with napkins and sipped their wine, Nelson noted how jennifer manly's gaze followed the gray woman around the dining room. manly was seated next to Nelson, but he could watch her eyes in the deep reflection in the wide window across the room, behind Victoria and Lorraine. There was something passionate and sympathetic in jennifer's look, and Nelson's first guess—straight from his lizard brain—was that in the heat of winning the love of the hiring committee, under the influence of the wine, in the warmth of the candlelight, the candidate was suddenly besotted with Pescecane's housekeeper.

But Nelson couldn't make sense of that—the woman was dull-eyed and middle-aged, her wrists were bony, her dull hair pulled back in a tight bun. She had crow's feet and a single black eyebrow. Even Victorinix, whose eyes shone like a prom date's, was looking better than this unlovely woman. And at any rate, despite jennifer's best efforts to catch the woman's eye—leaning forward, canting her head, lifting her eyebrows hopefully—the gray woman kept her eyes on her work, lifting away plates, fetching another bottle of wine, bringing Stephen Michael Stephens a glass of water, all with a sullen efficiency.

"Coffee, please, Maria," said Pescecane expansively, giving her a name toward the end of the meal. Then, to his guests, "Tiramisu next." He kissed the tips of his fingers. "You'll fucking die."

Maria left the room silently, with an armful of salad plates. Nelson rose to empty his bladder before the dessert came.

"Excuse me," he mumbled, but no one noticed; manly had embarked on another story.

He wandered up the dark hall toward a brightly lit doorway and came into the kitchen by mistake. The woman—Maria—was slinging the salad plates with surprising force into a sink already full of dishes. As Nelson tried to sneak back out, she turned.

"I'm, um, looking for the, uh . . ." He trailed off; she probably didn't even speak English.

But she made a sound deep in her throat and hooked her finger toward the left. Nelson nodded and stepped around to a little half-bath next to the pantry. He was tipsy, and he wobbled on his feet as he stood at the toilet.

Coming out again, he stepped into the light from the kitchen. The woman was seated at the kitchen table, her skin even grayer in the harsh overhead light. She was looking right at him and lighting a cigarette. Or rather, she was gazing blankly at the doorway as Nelson stepped into it. Beyond her, as she slouched in her chair, Pescecane's giant DeLonghi's espresso machine was gurgling and hissing. jennifer manly was speaking brightly in the other room, though Nelson could not make out what she was saying.

"I found it," he said, and the woman lifted her eyebrows and blew out a stream of smoke.

"Um, *habla Ingles?*" Nelson ventured. He could hear the pace of jennifer's voice quicken, and he did not want to walk in on her punch line.

The woman was drawing on the cigarette at the moment, so she just nodded.

"Wonderful meal," he said, still uncertain how much English the woman might know.

"Thanks," she said. Nelson wasn't sure if he detected an accent or not. He lay his hand on the side of the door. He couldn't think of anything else to say, but jennifer manly still had not reached the end of her story.

"Will, um, will Mrs. Pescecane be joining us later?" he asked.

The woman had just inhaled, and before she spoke, she widened her eyes and held up a finger for Nelson's patience. Then she gasped out a huge cloud of smoke, the same color as her skin.

"I *am* Mrs. Pescecane," she said.

Laughter erupted beyond the dining room door. Someone rapped lightly on the table, making the silver clink.

Nelson was blinded by embarrassment. He gripped the side of the doorway, blinking and soundlessly working his lips. By the time he could see again, the laughter had faded to a happy murmur, and Pescecane's wife was on her feet, stubbing out her smoke in a little tin ashtray. She turned out to have an accent after all, pure, undiluted Hoboken.

"You have to excuse me," she said in a husky voice like the aging Frank Sinatra's. "I gotta roast the nuts."

Back in the dining room Nelson's finger flamed so painfully it nearly brought him to his knees. He managed to make it back to the table, pull back his chair, and collapse next to jennifer manly. But as he turned to her, Mrs. Pescecane came in from the kitchen carrying a gleaming metal pot in one hand and a tray in the other, bearing little crystal dishes of tiramisu. The table chattered around them, and Nelson watched in the window as jennifer's urgent gaze followed the progress of their hostess. Mrs. Pescecane still did not return the gaze, but now Nelson saw that there was effort involved, that she knew she was being watched and chose not to look back. Nelson turned to look directly at jennifer and realized that the light in her eyes was not passion, but a carefully banked, sisterly anger, a tightly controlled urge to communicate to Mrs. Pescecane, if only through her eyes, that I, too, have waited on tables.

But jennifer didn't dare say anything, not if she wanted the job. Nelson's finger seared him. As Mrs. Pescecane circled the table distributing tiramisu and pouring espresso, Nelson was certain that if he stuck his finger in his glass, the wine would boil away to vapor. He was the only one at this table who hadn't known who this woman was, and jennifer manly was the only person to pay her any notice. Or who even tried to: Mrs. Pescecane wasn't having it. She leaned over Victorinix, who held up her small cup without looking, and Maria Pescecane filled the cup with espresso.

Nelson caught jennifer's gaze in the window. Like lovers at first sight across a crowded room, they slowly turned to look directly into each other's eyes. Nelson restrained a smile, and jennifer's nostrils flared ever so slightly, her eyes widened with a hint of alarm. Don't speak, she was begging him. Nelson leaned to her and took her wrist in his hand, his burning finger pressed against her pulse.

"Speak your mind," he murmured into her ear. "Say what you really think."

jennifer drew her breath in sharply. She blinked. Nelson's finger cooled, and he closed his eyes for an instant. But no one else noticed. Stephens was asleep at last, just in time for the coffee, his cheek scrunched against his shoulder. Kraljević and Lorraine were tucking into their tiramisu and eyeing Stephens's untouched dish. Anthony and Victoria were leaning together over the corner of the table and smiling, Anthony with his hands folded under his chin, two old adversaries genuinely enjoying their brief alliance. Maria Pescecane was making a final circuit of the table, collecting wineglasses between her bony knuckles.

"Anthony!" burst out jennifer manly, "I have an extraordinary idea!"

Her tone was as bright as before, her lilt as charming. But there was a catch in her voice now, her eyes a bit wild. Everyone looked up, expectant of more hilarity. Only Nelson looked down, regretfully contemplating the dish of creamy, glistening tiramisu that he knew he would never have a chance to taste.

"Why don't we all chip in," said jennifer, "and give your wife a hand cleaning up?"

Pescecane, still smiling, blinked at jennifer as if she was speaking in a foreign language. jennifer swallowed, her smile broadening desperately.

"I'm serious!" she said, laughing nervously. "I'm sure if we all roll up our sleeves, we'll have the dishes done in no time!"

No one else spoke. Nelson could almost hear the snow hissing outside the window. He thought briefly of Mort Weissmann, snoring in the Toyota.

"I mean, why not?" said manly. "We're all able-bodied. After this marvelous meal, I'm sure she could use the help . . ."

Victoria Victorinix's face faded to a pale mask again. The light in her eyes shrank to pinpoints, coldly watching, as if from the shadows, the idiot behavior of the warm-blooded. Lorraine and Kraljević gasped openly, their mouths hanging open to reveal a glistening pulp of tiramisu. Stephen Michael Stephens blinked awake suddenly. jennifer manly beamed her desperate smile around the table.

"Per, perhaps," she stammered, "Maria might even like to join us for coffee . . ."

Anthony Pescecane's smile died. He leaned slowly back in his chair, one bluntly knuckled hand resting on the tablecloth. His gaze dulled in jennifer's direction, and he lifted his eyes to his wife, who stood clutching two wineglasses in each hand. She met his look and shrugged, then shot a glance of pure disdain at jennifer manly. Then she left the room. The kitchen door swung back and forth, *thump thump thump,* a metronome for the silence.

"Well," said Pescecane. He picked up his napkin, dabbed at his lips, and began to crease the napkin slowly into quarters between his thick fingers.

"It's late," he said. "Perhaps, Nelson, you could give our candidate a lift back to her hotel."

Nelson lifted his gaze from the dish before him. "Sure," he said. "No problem."

Pescecane stood, and in a nervous shuffle everyone else stood too. jennifer manly was the last to rise, trembling and speechless. Her skin was as gray as Maria's.

With his fingertips brushing the tablecloth, Pescecane gazed at the center of the table and said, "Thank you all for coming." He turned and passed silently through the door into the kitchen. Victorinix glided around the table and out the door, without a glance at manly. Lorraine and Kraljević tiptoed out arm in arm, hissing at each other. Stephen Michael Stephens followed, rubbing his eyes. "No prisoners," he murmured.

Nelson turned to see jennifer manly hunched away from him in her chair, watching him with a look of pure terror.

"It's alright," he said. "I'll call you a cab."

He stood and paused a moment, fascinated by the three bright points of candle flame reflected in the window. He lifted his hand and pinched out each flame, feeling nothing. Then he swiped up a dab of tiramisu and licked it off his dead finger as he left the room.

13

L'arrêt de Mort

A few days later, just after dinner, Morton Weissmann arrived on the doorstep of Nelson's town house, bearing gifts. Bridget answered the door, and he bowled past her trailing cold air, beaming like some well-meaning but unreliable uncle out of Dickens, his arms full of three identical Lisa Simpson dolls from Toys "R" Us. Nelson, ascending from his basement office, found his former mentor seated on the sagging couch, trying to distribute a doll each to Clara and Abigail. Clara wouldn't come near him, but Abigail had already taken one of the boxes and was trying to pull another out of his grasp as Bridget stood to one side with a wary smile.

"Now, now, there's one for each of you," Weissmann was saying, theatrically avuncular, tugging at one end of the box as Abigail pulled grimly at the other, the first Lisa Simpson already cast aside.

"Professor Weissmann's here!" Bridget said brightly, as Nelson came in.

"What a charming little cottage!" boomed Weissmann when he saw Nelson. "I had no idea these town houses could be so snug!"

He tried to stand, and in the process let go of the box, and Abigail fell on her rear end with the doll across her lap. After a breathless moment she began to howl.

"And what adorable children!" Weissmann cried, awkwardly heaving himself up off the low couch. Bridget swooped up the bawling Abigail and spirited her upstairs. Clara bolted after her, hissing loudly, "Mom, why did that man bring *three* dolls?"

"What can I do for you, Mort?" said Nelson. His finger was cold.

"Ah, I think the question is, what can *I* do for *you?*" Weissmann dropped his voice conspiratorially.

"I'm not sure I follow, Mort."

"My good friend." Weissmann dropped his voice further, coming around the cluttered coffee table and grasping Nelson firmly by the biceps. "Is there someplace we can talk?"

After Pescecane's dinner party the other night, Nelson had driven the sleeping Weissmann home, then woken him and helped him through his front door. The last Nelson had seen of him, Weissmann had been treading heavily up the stairs of his handsome old Tudor-style home, muttering, "A plague of all cowards! Give me a cup of sack, rogue!" Now Nelson surveyed his own living room of painted cinder block and plasterboard and second-hand furniture, in its permanent state of chaos—wooden blocks and scattered Legos and splayed kids' books underfoot, clothing in heaps, stained sofa cushions awry—considered the dank gloom of the basement, and at last gestured to the dining table. The smeared and crusted dishes from dinner—franks and beans and creamed corn—were still waiting to be carried away to the sink, and Weissmann gave a wince of a smile as he gingerly pulled out a chair, not bothering to disguise his inspection of the seat before he gathered his overcoat about him and sat. Nelson sat across from him, pushing an empty milk carton out of the way.

"I don't need to tell you, Nelson," Weissmann said, making as if to rest his forearms on the table and then thinking better of it, "that things in the department are somewhat in a state of flux at the moment. Things are not going Anthony's way, I'm happy to say. As you're well aware, at least two of his hand-picked candidates 'deconstructed' themselves, as it were, and as for the third, the estimable Professor Branwell . . . well, modesty forbids me to recount the cause of his intellectual, ah, incontinence. . . ."

Weissmann looked away as if he expected Nelson to say something, but Nelson only folded his hands on the sticky tabletop. It wasn't clear if Weissmann really thought he was the cause of Branwell's disaster, or if he simply wanted Nelson to think so. Nelson wondered if Weissmann could tell the difference anymore.

"The point is, Nelson," Weissmann went on, "there's a tenure-track position still to be filled, and unless our estimable chairperson decides to beat the bushes further for more of these, these 'scholars,' the chances are very good—very good *indeed*—that the committee may be looking very seriously at an internal candidate. . . ."

Down the stairs swelled three voices, one adult's and two children's, all talking at once. Only Abigail's was intelligible, shrieking, *"Mine! Mine! Mine!"*

236

". . . now hear me out, Nelson," Weissmann was saying, though Nelson had not opened his mouth. "I appreciate your loyalty to your office mate—as fundamentally misguided as it may be—but let's be honest, my friend, Vita Deonne is scarcely tenurable. I mean, my Lord, you've struggled through her prose. You've tracked the labyrinthine windings of her, her 'argument'—if you can even *call* it an argument, which I sincerely doubt. . . ."

"What's your point, Mort?" Nelson sat back and crossed his arms. Up until now, his finger had remained cool and without feeling; Weissmann was scarcely worth the bother any longer. But now it was beginning to ache with the desire to simply see this foolish old man out of his house, out of his life, out of the way.

"Well, the *point,* Nelson, the *point,* as you say, is that we—that is to say, you and I—are in a position to propose another candidate. Someone much better suited to our purposes." Weissmann's eyes filled with a pale, desperate glow. Old trouper that he was, Weissmann was pausing for effect, but the need in his eyes was making him almost laughable.

Nelson was puzzled. Surely Weissmann didn't mean to put up one of the Lost Boys. None of them had finished his dissertation yet as far as Nelson knew. And Weissmann himself, during their luncheon last semester at Peregrine, had called them the intellectually halt and lame. But who else could he have in mind? He surely didn't mean Lorraine Alsace, the other possible internal candidate. And what did he mean by "our purposes"? Just who did he mean by "we"? Nelson's finger throbbed.

"Is this one mine?"

Nelson turned to see his eldest daughter, Clara, holding out at arm's length, with both hands, a box in which a plush, flesh-colored Lisa Simpson was encased behind cellophane. Across the side Nelson could clearly see a sticker that read FINAL MARKDOWN! $2.98, and he wondered just how long the doll had been gathering dust in a sale bin before Weissmann grabbed three of them.

"Of course it is, my dear," said Weissmann. Winking at Nelson, he added, "I brought one for each of your lovely daughters, Nelson. I know how siblings quarrel."

"Can I keep it?" said Clara, pulling the doll a little closer.

"Sure," said Nelson. "Say thank you to Professor Weissmann."

"Call me Uncle Mort," said Weissmann, beckoning Clara with a creepy smile that was half Mr. Micawber and half Uriah Heep.

Clara dropped the doll and ran screaming up the stairs again. "Mommy, Mommy!" she cried. "Is that man my *uncle?*"

"How charming!" muttered Weissmann.

"Who did you have in mind for the job?" said Nelson.

Weissmann peered at Nelson across the table, the avid light in his eyes narrowing to something cannier and more calculating. He slowly smiled.

"Why, you, of course," he said. "Surely it's occurred to you."

Nelson's finger flared. A taste, both sweet and bilious, rose to the back of his throat. For a moment he was blinded, and he saw behind his eyeballs a view of the Quad from the highest floor of Harbour Hall, a springtime view with the trees in full leaf and the lilac bushes in bloom. From an office window—*his* office window—high above the ground, he saw fit young people sunbathing, tossing Frisbees, playing guitars. Through the glass skylight of the library Annex he saw the long tables lined with the little round heads of earnest young scholars deep in their studies, and he saw, towering just a little higher than his window, the shining clock face of the bell tower on Thornfield Library, its hands proudly pointing to the high noon of Nelson's career.

". . . of course, we're not talking about tenure *right away,*" Weissmann was saying. "To be honest, Nelson, your publication record isn't really the stuff of tenure. Not that you haven't already done some significant work, my boy, but you'll need some *major* publications; and on the tenure track, you'd have seven years to rectify that deficiency—a couple of important articles a year, a book or two, under my tutelage, of course . . ."

And, as if Harbour Hall was made of glass, Nelson saw from his height, ranged below him in the crystal boxes of their offices, the entire department, democratically arranged, each according to her abilities, each according to his needs, a shining little city where scholarship and pedagogy, theory and praxis, were equally balanced, where the women of the Composition Department—ruddier and better fed, in nicer clothing—had offices side by side with the young queer theorists and the old New Critics, where undergraduates were as enthusiastically welcomed as graduate students, where Vita Deonne lay down with Morton Weissmann, where Nelson the Philosopher King stood high astride a happy, enlightened republic of learning, literature, and love. . . .

". . . but the fact that you're not immediately tenurable," Weissmann went on, "or even really tenure-track material for the moment—and let me stress that, my good friend, *for the moment*—why, we can turn that to our advantage, Nelson; it means the department won't have to pay a tenured salary, as it were. You know I only have your best interests at heart, Nelson, but if the department can get you at a *discount,* so to speak, if hiring you saves the department *money,* it makes you a more attractive prospect, don't you see. . . ."

Something smashed upstairs, and Bridget gave a bark like a top sergeant. Nelson's crystal palace shattered before his eyes into razor-edged shards; a freezing Minnesota wind blasted the naked trees around the Quad; the hands of the clock on the tower pointed at blackest midnight; whilst a pale, indistinct figure jigged and kicked behind the battlements. Before him now he saw Weissmann across the table with shining eyes and a sheen of sweat on his upper lip. Nelson stood, blinking. His finger was throbbing again.

". . . and I'm not saying it won't be difficult, Nelson, especially at first, just the two of us taking on the forces of ignorance and ideology; but together, my boy, shoulder to shoulder once again, we can be the thin end of the wedge, the first men over the wall to retake the plundered citadel of our cultural patrimony. . . ."

"How many children do you think I have, Mort?" Nelson said.

Weissmann, interrupted, looked at Nelson with his mouth slack. "I beg your pardon?"

"How many children do I have?"

Weissmann made a noise deep in his throat. "Why, I . . ." He looked at his hands as if he might count Nelson's children on his fingers.

"Thanks for coming, Mort." Nelson offered his hand; and when Weissmann took it, Nelson hauled the older man out of his chair.

"Let's keep this between the two of us, Mort," he said, his finger sparking in Weissmann's loose, fleshy grip. Weissmann blinked rapidly and swayed on his feet. "I'll give it some serious consideration and get back to you, okay? We don't want anybody to catch on to what we're up to."

Still clutching Weissmann's hand, Nelson steered him into the hall, opened the door, and swung him out into the cold, onto the front steps. Weissmann's eyelids fluttered, his mouth worked soundlessly.

"Gloves, Mort," said Nelson, as he shut the door. "It's cold out, buddy."

A sharp knock brought Nelson back to the door. Weissmann stood on the doorstep, bouncing on the balls of his feet, twisting his gloves in his hands. "Did I mention that our friend is back?" he said.

"What friend, Mort?" Nelson kept his hand on the door, ready to shut it in Weissmann's face.

Weissmann dropped his voice. "Our anonymous letter writer. I've received a new, how shall I put it? A new communication, let us say. And I don't believe I'm the only one."

Nelson's stomach twisted. "That's not possible," he said. The Coogan, he was certain, was pub-crawling in Chicago, living the life of the flamboyant Irish poet.

"The Coogan . . ." Nelson began. "He can't be . . ."

"Oh, it's not our Celtic friend." Weissmann glanced from side to side. "Just as before, these missives are hand-delivered directly into departmental mailboxes. It has to be someone on campus." He smiled wickedly. "It appears, my boy, that you and Anthony tried and convicted the wrong man."

"It's a copycat," Nelson blurted. He started to close the door. His finger troubled him.

"I don't think so!" sang Weissmann. "Not if I'm any judge of the English language. It's the same fellow!"

"Thanks for the heads up, Mort."

Nelson slammed the door. His finger seared him. He felt queasy. What if Anthony had got it wrong? What if Nelson had helped to end the career of an innocent man?

Another rap on the door. Nelson wrenched the door open. *"What?"* he barked.

"Valentine's Day!" cried Weissmann, edging forward as if he meant to come in again. "I neglected to remind you of my annual soiree, to which you and . . . you and . . . your lovely wife are . . ."

"Yeah, we know." Nelson pushed the door toward Weissmann. "Every year, Mort. The whole department."

"It's the highlight of the academic year, Nelson! Everyone's invited, regardless of . . ."

Nelson grabbed Weissmann's wrist through the crack in the door. His finger sparked. "Go *home,* Mort."

Weissmann blinked, stumbled backward, and fell, landing on his rump at the bottom of the steps. Nelson shut the door.

Inside Bridget had brought the girls downstairs, and Abigail was aggressively ripping open the third box while Clara rattled her Lisa Simpson between both hands and held her ear to the doll's chest.

"She's supposed to talk," Clara said.

"What did Weissmann want?" said Bridget.

"The usual," said Nelson. "A spear carrier. A Sancho Panza to his Don Quixote. A fool to his Lear."

Bridget, whose literary tastes ran to *Gone With the Wind* and *The Little House on the Prairie,* waved Nelson's allusions away. "Can he help us?" she asked.

Nelson scarcely heard her. He watched as Clara rattled her doll more vigorously, and as Abigail pulled hers by the nose through a ragged tear in the side of the box. He turned away, toward the basement.

"I'm not saying you should trust him," Bridget called after him, "but maybe it wouldn't hurt to be nice to him."

Halfway down the steps into the dank gloom, Nelson laughed.

"Nice," he said. "That's rich."

Late that night, in his basement, Nelson fretted over his evening out with Timothy Coogan the previous semester, and soon had himself convinced that even if Coogan turned out not to be the author of the poison pen letters, he had been a dangerous influence anyway. All that talk about sleeping with his students, all that self-pity. And he had, after all, ranted at some length about how the Jew Weissmann and the lesbian Victorinix were out to get him. Surely Nelson had done nothing wrong.

Fortunately, he was interrupted from his fretting by a frantic e-mail from Vita, and they volleyed back and forth for a while. As he waited for each of Vita's responses, he sat back in his creaking chair with his fingers laced behind his head and looked at literary England rotting above his desk. The features of the map at the center of the stain were obliterated now, leaving only an oily sheen in the blue glare of the furnace. It almost looked as if some other, more sinister image were soaking through the paper.

To: Nelson Humboldt <nhumboldt@umidwest.edu>
From: Vita Deonne <vdeonne@umidwest.edu>
Anthony's sent me a letter, saying I'm up for early tenure review. He wants me to present a paper to the whole department NEXT WEEK!!!! OH MY GOD!!!! What should I DO?

To: Vita Deonne <vdeonne@umidwest.edu>
From: Nelson Humboldt <nhumboldt@umidwest.edu>
Geez, Vita, I dunno. Maybe you should . . . GIVE THE FUCKING PA-
PER! Ya think?

To: Nelson Humboldt <nhumboldt@umidwest.edu>
From: Vita Deonne <vdeonne@umidwest.edu>
But WHICH PAPER??? Does he want me to present "The Lesbian
Phallus of Dorian Gray" AGAIN? Or would that look like I don't have
anything else on hand? And what if he didn't like it the last time? Or
what if he did and Victoria didn't? How bad would it look to present
THE SAME PAPER TWICE IN SIX MONTHS???

P.S. Please don't YELL AT ME!!!

To: Vita Deonne <vdeonne@umidwest.edu>
From: Nelson Humboldt <nhumboldt@umidwest.edu>
Calm down, Vita. I'm not the one who's YELLING. Think about it:
You never actually got around to presenting the Dorian Gray paper
the last time, okay? So polish up the ol' lesbian phallus (ha ha); it'll
be fine. I promise you that Weissmann will keep his mouth shut this
time.

To: Nelson Humboldt <nhumboldt@umidwest.edu>
From: Vita Deonne <vdeonne@umidwest.edu>
But Miranda just did a Wilde paper at the MLA!!! How can I possibly
compete with MIRANDA???

To: Vita Deonne <vdeonne@umidwest.edu>
From: Nelson Humboldt <nhumboldt@umidwest.edu>
Vita, read my lips: Miranda . . . already . . . has . . . tenure. You're not
in competition with her. The only other internal candidate is that freak
Lorraine Alsace, and you can wipe the floor with her.

To: Nelson Humboldt <nhumboldt@umidwest.edu>
From: Vita Deonne <vdeonne@umidwest.edu>

242

But I AM in competition with MIRANDA!!! She's Anthony's MODEL for a woman academic! How can I COMPETE WITH THAT???

At this point Nelson was nearly ready to sign off, drive over to Vita's house in spite of the late hour, and have this conversation with her face to face. With Vita within reach, he could perhaps instill her with confidence. But he clicked on REPLY and continued.

To: Vita Deonne <vdeonne@umidwest.edu>
From: Nelson Humboldt <nhumboldt@umidwest.edu>
You have the same basic equipment as Miranda. You just refuse to use it. Would it kill you—just this once?—to put on a skirt? You're the one who's always telling me gender is performative—so PERFORM, goddammit. Doll yourself up. Wear your hair back. Flash a little leg, Vita. You study OSCAR WILDE, for chrissakes. Take a hint from him, and BE YOURSELF, only MORE SO.

There was a long silence after this. And then:

To: Nelson Humboldt <nhumboldt@umidwest.edu>
From: Vita Deonne <vdeonne@umidwest.edu>
Nelson, you've completely misunderstood what is meant by performativity. There's no point in continuing this exchange until you've reviewed essential texts by Hegel, Nietzsche, Althusser, Foucault, Mackinnon, Austin, Butler, and Lacan. Check the bib of my paper for the citations.

Nelson was furiously typing a reply—"Jesus H. Christ, Vita, will you give it a rest for once?"—when another message from Vita interrupted him.

To: Nelson Humboldt <nhumboldt@umidwest.edu>
From: Vita Deonne <vdeonne@umidwest.edu>
To say I have the "same basic equipment" as Miranda is a nakedly essentialist statement. Passing over the issues of identity raised by your use of "same," and the frankly heterosexist use of the word "equipment" when referring to the materiality of two women, I DO NOT have the same equipment as Miranda. Not even CLOSE.

243

Nelson tapped his fingers lightly on his keyboard. Then he typed one more message.

To: Vita Deonne <vdeonne@umidwest.edu>
From: Nelson Humboldt <nhumboldt@umidwest.edu>
I think I know why you're so upset. You got another poison pen letter, didn't you?

He sent it, waited ten minutes, then sent it again. When he still hadn't heard from her after another ten minutes, he switched off the computer.

"The thanks I get," he muttered, climbing the creaking stairs.

The next day Nelson canceled his office hours in the afternoon and went to the gym for a run. Since Thanksgiving, he had been frequenting the field house once a week, and since Miranda had taken him shopping, he had started going nearly every day. What was the use of a new suit of clothes (which still hung behind his office door) if he was the same flabby, breathless fellow underneath? As tremulous freshmen gingerly rapped at his office door, Nelson was jogging with increasing ease around the indoor track, edging past trim young men and women nearly half his age. He was surprised at how quickly he got his wind back. Now and then some young stud would hog the inner lane, and once or twice, when no one was watching, Nelson came up behind close enough to brush the runner on the small of his back with his finger, staggering the boy with a cramp or the sudden onset of shin splints. Lately, though, Nelson simply edged past on his own power, with long, confident strides.

This afternoon, Nelson, feeling pleasantly drained, bounced lightly down the stairs from the running track, exchanging nods with the ropy-muscled young men who passed him going up, and smiling at the taut young women in sports bras taking the stairs two at a time. Walking down the corridor toward the locker room, he heard a steady, arrhythmic *thud, thud, thud,* as if someone was pounding a bag, and it turned out someone was: Through a door Nelson saw a squat, thick-chested man hammering a leather punching bag, which was held from behind by someone who was only visible as a pair of pale legs. Nelson kept walking, and the thudding stopped. It was replaced by the flaccid slap of sneakers and a gasp, more slapping and another gasp, and finally the high-pitched squeaking of his own name. "Neh, neh, Nelson!"

244

With his hand on the locker room door, Nelson turned to see a panting Lionel Grossmaul propped by one hand against the wall; he was dressed in a ragged pair of cutoffs, a yellowed T-shirt that was loose around his shoulders and tight around his belly, and a pair of old-fashioned, no-brand sneakers. His hair was matted; his thick were glasses misted with perspiration.

"He . . . he wants . . . he wants to . . ." gasped Grossmaul, gesturing limply over his shoulder back toward the room with the punching bag.

"Who?" Nelson said, though he already knew.

". . . to see . . . to see you," said Lionel, but Nelson had already passed Lionel on his way back up the corridor. He came through the door to see a bare-chested Anthony Pescecane mopping his face with a towel. The chairperson wore a silky pair of boxing trunks, shimmering red, with a new pair of lace-up boots. His massive shoulders and broad chest and meaty thighs were thick with hair, and he had biceps and pecs like a professional. Breathing hard, he lowered the towel and narrowed his eyes at Nelson.

"Humboldt," he said, panting. "The very fucking guy I wanna see."

He flung the towel past Nelson and turned the punching bag slowly with both hands. Lionel passed Nelson, peeling the towel off his face. Lionel draped the towel over Pescecane's expensive gym bag with trembling hands, then stepped behind the punching bag, clutched a pair of canvas handles, and set his feet against the floor. He pressed his face against the bag, skewing his glasses, and he squeezed his eyes shut and tensed his entire body. Pescecane tightened the leather straps over his knuckles and glanced at Nelson.

"You're letting me down, Humboldt," said the chair. "You fucked up."

He hit the bag with his right fist. Grossmaul grimaced and clenched his toes.

"Really," said Nelson. "How's that?"

"That thing you said you'd take care of? You didn't."

Pescecane hit the bag again with his left, dancing on the balls of his feet and swaying his head, as if looking for an opening. Grossmaul steadied the bag, grimacing.

"That thing?" Nelson said. His finger began to smolder.

"Don't fuck with me, Humboldt. You know what I'm talking about." Ducking his head and weaving from side to side, Pescecane hit the bag more quickly. His calves tightened as he lunged; the flesh along his flanks shuddered. Grossmaul clung to the bag for dear life, wincing with every blow. His pale, plump, hairless legs trembled.

"That thing with the letter?" Nelson said finally.

Pescecane mimicked Nelson in a mincing voice. *"That thing with the letter?"* He whacked the bag. "In case you haven't heard, the fucking letters have started up again. You got the wrong guy, asshole."

Pescecane's heavy breathing was punctuated by the *thud, thud* of his fists against the bag. The air began to smell of his powerful sweat.

"Hey, *you* told me it was the Coogan."

"I told you *nothing.*" Pescecane planted his feet and jabbed viciously and repeatedly at the bag with his right where an opponent's head would be, striking with his left suddenly at the bag's midriff. "We had a *conversation.* You drew your own *conclusion,* and you got . . . the . . . wrong . . . guy."

Nelson said nothing. He crossed his arms, thrusting his burning finger into his damp armpit.

Pescecane's pounding looked less like pugilism to Nelson and more like a wise guy hammering somebody in a rage. On the far side of the bag Grossmaul hung on desperately, sweat pouring off him, his glasses askew, his legs quaking. His mouth was slack, and he moaned a little with each blow.

"Hold the fucking bag still!" shouted Pescecane, pounding the bag savagely. Grossmaul's arms trembled; he was losing his grip on the handles. Pescecane stopped suddenly and stepped back, his massive chest heaving, sweat running in rivulets through his body hair. He pointed a fist at Nelson. Grossmaul cracked an eye open and ever so slightly relaxed his grip on the bag.

"And where were you during Branwell's talk the other day, huh?" Pescecane said. "You blind, Nelson? You fucking deaf? The fuck was up with you?"

"I was right there, Anthony."

Pescecane drew a breath and swung at the bag, a roundhouse punch that made the whole bag shudder and rocked the unprepared Lionel back onto his heels and nearly onto his backside.

"It's a simple thing I was asking," gasped Pescecane, rubbing the knuckles of his right hand. "That fucking Weissmann makes a fool of my candidate, in public, and you stand there in the back of the hall like, who, me?"

Nelson said nothing. Lionel swung back and forth with the bag and then let it go. He staggered away, straightening his glasses.

"What'd that cocksucker Weissmann ever do for you?" Pescecane said.

"Not much." Nelson's finger was making him sweat.

Pescecane started to run in place and shake his hands at the ends of his arms. "You ever see *Conan the Barbarian*, Nelson?"

Nelson shrugged.

"You remember what Conan said the meaning of life was?" Still jogging, Pescecane grinned at Nelson's puzzlement. Lionel was bent over, gasping, with his hands on his knees.

"To crush your enemies, Humboldt," said Pescecane, his voice wavering as he jogged in place, "and hear the lamentation of their women." He looked at Nelson sidelong again. "Do you want to be my enemy, Nelson?"

Nelson hesitated a moment. "No," he said at last.

"I can't do a thing for your friend Vita unless you back me with Weissmann." Anthony stopped jogging and stood panting in place. "You know what Mort can do for you, Nelson? Zip. Nada. Squat. But me? The only way Vita's going to be tenured is if I say so, *capiche?* It pays to be my friend."

Nelson lifted his chin, pursed his lips, and recrossed his arms. He couldn't decide whether he should just walk away or take Anthony by the wrist and bring him to his knees.

"I'll give her one week to get her ducks in a row." Pescecane tightened the leather straps on his hands. "Then I'll give her a job talk and an interview with the committee. After that, no promises."

"What about the letters?" Nelson said.

"What about the letters?" Pescecane shrugged. "Fuck the letters. I don't give a rat's ass about the letters. For all I know you're writing them yourself; and you know what, Nelson? I don't give a shit."

Pescecane brushed his nose with one fist, then with the other. "Now get the fuck outta here. You're a real disappointment to me."

Nelson opened his mouth, but closed it again without speaking. Red-faced with anger, his finger burning, he turned toward the door. Pescecane hunched into a fighter's stance again, then lifted his chin and barked, "Lionel! Hold the bag!"

But Grossmaul was in a little world of his own, wiping his glasses on the tail of his T-shirt, his bug eyes red-rimmed and weary. With both hands Pescecane heaved the bag in Lionel's direction. Lionel replaced his glasses on his nose. He saw the bag coming and cringed out of the way, throwing his hands over his face. The punching bag breezed by him, missing him by inches, and Lionel peered up from behind his hands.

"Just tell your friend Vita she's got one chance," Pescecane said. "Tell her not to fuck it up."

Nelson hesitated in the doorway. Pescecane practiced his footwork. The bag swung in a wide, slow circle, creaking at the end of its chain. Lionel slowly straightened, a slow look of relief passing over his face as he contemplated this rare instance of good luck. Then the punching bag clobbered him from behind, lifting him off his feet and sending him sailing into the air. Nelson turned away, and from the room behind him he heard a thump, a cry, and a crack. One half of Lionel's glasses came skittering out the door into the hall, and Nelson stepped over it.

"You hear me, Humboldt?" cried Anthony Pescecane.

After he showered and dressed, Nelson sulked across campus toward his office. Usually he enjoyed the walk, as the heat of his run radiated into the Minnesota cold; but today he reviewed his encounter with Pescecane as he crossed the Quad, improving his own performance each time. As he waited for the elevator in Harbour Hall, he forced Pescecane to his knees in his mind. The doors opened and a couple of pale, underfed composition teachers got out; they flinched at the sight of Nelson glowering, but he scarcely noticed them. He stepped into the elevator and jammed the button for the eighth floor. He had no business up there, but he wanted to walk up and down on Anthony Pescecane's plush carpet just to show that he could. As the doors began to slide shut, he unzipped his blood-stained parka with a single, forceful tug.

"Hold the elevator, please!" someone cried. Nelson looked up angrily, prepared to ignore whoever it was. Then he saw Miranda striding toward him on the high heels of her boots, the skirts of her unbuttoned overcoat skirling, her hair flying. Nelson thrust himself between the closing doors and wrenched them apart with both hands.

"Nelson!" Miranda glided into the car, fetchingly breathless. "The very man I want!"

"Hold, please!" cried someone else from the lobby.

Nelson's thumb hovered over the button that closed the door. A snowman was coming toward the elevator, an immense quilted parka with a round, white face on top. It was Linda Proserpina, waddling as fast as she could. Nelson closed the doors, and as it clattered shut, Linda's mouth formed a perfect O.

Nelson turned to Miranda. Regarding herself in the blurred reflection of the elevator doors, she sighed and rocked back on one sharp heel, running the fingers of her black gloves through her hair, lifting it out of the collar of her coat. Her face was flushed; the heat of her perfume filled the car. Nelson's own heart hammered as if he had been running himself. He felt the motion of the car in his knees. Had she just said that she wanted him?

Miranda looked at Nelson sidelong, then she leaned past him, their coats brushing, her hair passing within inches of his lips. She ran the tip of her slender gloved finger down the control panel and flicked the elevator's power switch. In a whining diminuendo, the elevator slowed. Somewhere, distantly, a bell began to ring.

"This is the only safe place for us to talk," she said, peeling her leather gloves off one long finger at a time. "I can't really be seen with you, Nelson. For the moment anyway."

The elevator stopped with a little bounce that nearly staggered Nelson off his feet. He touched the wall to steady himself. Under her overcoat Miranda wore a cashmere sweater and a pair of wool slacks, each nipped in to show off her waist. Pearls glistened at the shallow juncture of her throat and collarbone. She leaned her shoulders against the wall across from him, pushing her hips forward through her parted coat. She smiled slyly. "What are you up to, Nelson?"

Nelson felt the slightest twinge of heat in his finger. "What makes you think I'm up to anything?" He was pleased at how steady his voice was.

Miranda caught her breath. "Tell me this, then," she said. "How did you do it?"

"How did I do what?" He was aware of the bell, ringing and ringing, somewhere up or down the elevator shaft.

"Come on, Nelson, you can tell me." She cocked her wrist, the black gloves in her fist draped over her fingers. "I didn't expect you to be coy about it."

"Who's being coy?" Nelson's finger hummed with a steady heat.

Miranda sighed and looked away. A lock of her black hair brushed against the sharp line of her cheek, and she brushed it back, swinging her gaze up at Nelson again.

"How did you sabotage all three candidates?" She thrust her shoulders forward, her hands clasped over her lap. She gave him a knowing smile.

"I'm just a lecturer, Miranda." He managed a narrow smile. "I'm just the guy who picked them up at the airport."

Miranda settled her shoulders back against the wall; she lifted her knee, her sharp heel propped against the wall. She looked him up and down. "You look good, Nelson. Are you working out?"

Nelson said nothing, but he tingled all over. The ringing of the bell seemed to be coming from the inside of his head. He turned to switch the elevator on again. In a moment Miranda had crossed the car and stopped him with a hand on his wrist.

"Why Vita, Nelson? Tell me that at least. You're not seriously interested in helping her career, are you? What do you get out of it?"

She was very close to him now, her eyes shining, searching his face. He could smell her skin beneath her perfume; he could feel the heat coming off her face.

"Has someone promised you something?" She was nearly whispering, her warm fingers curled around Nelson's wrist. "Is that it? Who is it, Nelson? Tell me."

He felt her breath on his cheek. His finger flamed. All it takes is a touch, he thought, and she's mine, right here, right now. Just a touch.

"It's not *Mort,* is it?" There was just a hint of mockery in her voice, but it did not deflate Nelson. Quite the opposite.

"Of course not," she murmured, dropping her eyelids. "Why would Mort be pushing Vita?" She lifted her eyes to him again. "Is it Victoria?"

Nelson shifted, afraid she might notice his growing discomfort. She did not release him.

"It's *not,* is it?" Miranda's eyes widened with pleasure. "It's not *anybody,* is it? It's *you.* You're doing this for *yourself,* aren't you, Nelson?"

"Unh," said Nelson, deep in his throat, meaning nothing by it. He wished he could discreetly adjust himself.

"And you were behind the letters, weren't you? You set up the Coogan to make an opening for yourself, isn't that it?"

Nelson swallowed. What if I kissed her right now? he thought. What if I did?

"But what I don't understand is why you started them again. Who are you after this time?" breathed Miranda, her eyes gleaming with moisture. Her grip tightened around his wrist. Her nails pricked his skin. "What you need is an ally, Nelson. You need someone you can trust."

Her face was very close to his now, her chin lowered, her eyes hooded. "You need me," she whispered.

Nelson squeezed his eyes shut and saw a throbbing red. His hands trembled. The bell rang. Miranda seemed to press herself against him, to reach around him. "Screw your courage to the sticking-place," she murmured.

250

There was a click and the rising whine of the elevator coming to life. The bell stopped, the elevator lurched, and Nelson, reaching for Miranda to steady himself, found that she had stepped back across the car. She was pulling on her gloves and gazing steadily at her blurred reflection in the elevator door. She lifted a gloved hand to brush back her hair.

Nelson steadied himself against the wall, staring openly at Miranda with wild eyes. She glanced once at him, and then away, as if she didn't know him.

The elevator jerked to a stop, the doors opened. Miranda pursed her lips and glanced at Nelson. He swiveled his gaze to the open door and saw Vita standing in the deep carpet of the eighth floor, clutching her mail to her chest with one hand. In her other hand she held an open letter; a plain white envelope, empty, lay at her feet. She was wearing her cold weather outfit, a vast shapeless poncho like an old blanket and a hand-knit wool cap with a fuzzy ball on top. She lifted her wide-eyed gaze from the letter to Miranda and then to Nelson. Miranda's shoulders began to shake with laughter.

"Another victim, Nelson?" she laughed.

Vita spun and hurled herself against the door to the stairwell, banging it open and charging down the stairs. The letter drifted through the air in her wake, settling silently like a fallen leaf on the carpet.

"Vita!" Nelson lurched out of the elevator, toward the stairwell door.

"Nelson!"

The sound of Miranda's voice stopped him in the doorway, and he whirled. Miranda stood just back from the open doors of the elevator, lacing her leather fingers over her lap.

"What?" gasped Nelson.

She lowered her head and peered up at him. A glossy strand of hair brushed her cheek. She gave him a heartbreaking smile.

"Anthony is *terrified* of you," she said, as the doors slid shut.

Nelson hustled halfway down the stairs after Vita, then remembered the letter on the carpet, and ran back up. He snatched it off the floor without looking at it and stuck it inside his coat. Still breathless, he stopped into the department office and checked his own mailbox: The only item was a plain white envelope.

Five stories down, he burst into their office, thinking he might find Vita there. The little room smelled of her strong soap, but her desk was undisturbed, her pens were in place, her blotter was squared. Sweating in his parka, Nelson collapsed in his creaking chair and rolled slowly across the linoleum. He pulled Vita's letter and the unopened envelope out of his parka. The letter was a pastiche, as the one last semester had been. The opening was from *The Merchant of Venice,* slightly adapted:

("I stand for judgement. Answer: Shall I have it?")

Hath not a Christian *eyes?*
If you prick him, does *he* not *bleed?*
If you poison him, does *he* not *die?*
And if you wrong him, shall *he* not
REVENGE?

What followed was a long, lacerating paragraph titled "The Fine Print" that Nelson recognized as an adaptation of an excerpt from an obscure essay by T. S. Eliot, in which civilisation with an *s*—Western, Christian, heterosexual—was defended against the relativism of "free-thinking Jews." Buzzword was set against buzzword in a pure distillation of the Culture Wars: Homogeneity and stability were Good; tolerance, inoffensiveness, and diversity were Bad. Eliot's fear of Jews had been expanded by the anonymous author to include lesbians and gays. Despite Semitic and homosexual influence, Western culture, said the updated essay, was "the highest culture the world has ever known."

Nelson opened the envelope that had been waiting in his box and found that his letter was identical to Vita's. He laid them side by side on the desk before him and leaned over them, trying to concentrate. Was Weissmann right? Did they come from the same hand as the first letter? Was it even possible to tell? And who was writing the things anyway? Did he owe Timothy Coogan an apology?

But as hard as he tried, Nelson was distracted by a perverse, swelling sense of pride in having received one of the letters himself. The provenance of the letter dwindled in importance; his guilt over what Anthony had asked him to do to the Coogan faded. Whoever wrote these letters, Nelson thought, for whatever reason, thinks I'm important enough to threaten anonymously.

Nelson pushed himself away from the desk and stood in the glare of the overhead light. He felt restless, annoyed, and frustrated, all at once. He read the titles of the books lined up across the back of Vita's desk, in descending order of size—*I Got Your Phallus Right Here: The End(s) of Gender. Bring Me the Head of Alfred Douglas: Oscar Wilde, Sam Peckinpah, and the Narrative of Decapitation. This Too, Too Solid Flesh: Shakespeare as Phallus.* Nelson groaned. If Vita could combine her theoretical rigor with just a tenth of what Miranda had just marshaled in the elevator, she could be president of the fucking university.

What about *my* theoretical rigor? he thought. However important the anonymous letter writer thought he was, Weissmann was right: Nelson would never be tenured with his publications so far. He could bend James Hogg into an infinite number of shapes like a balloon animal, and Hogg would never be anything more than a clammy Calvinist. Gazing across the office at Vita's books, he recalled her admission that she'd never actually read *The Importance of Being Earnest* because it had no theoretical significance for her. Primary texts are problematic, Vita had once told him; they have no theoretical rigor. They cannot be *contained.* And that, Nelson concluded, was the problem with his own work: It wasn't that he hadn't found the right theoretical template for Hogg, it was that he had not problematized the primary text enough. There was too much Hogg and not enough theory.

Nelson glanced at his watch; he had an hour and a half before Bridget expected him for dinner. He folded up the letters and stuck them in his desk; he switched off the light. His new suit of clothes swung from its hanger as he slammed the door. It was time to visit the Annex.

Even though it housed the university's main collection—only the rejects remained in the Thornfield Library above, caged like deposed royalty in the clock tower—the new library was still known only as the Annex. As if to reify this hierarchy, the architects, an Argentine collective known as Orbis Tertius, had placed the main entrance deep in the fundament of the old library, where Nelson wrenched open one of the wide, glassy doors and trotted down a wide stair of shallow steps into processed air and a diffuse, shadowless, fluorescent glow. He hurried past the smooth blond curve of the circulation desk and crossed the noiseless pastel carpet to the wide V of the atrium. At the point of the V was a fountain, a shallow, brass-lined hyperbolic depression in the concrete, with a gently plashing stump of water burbling from the focal point. The water trickled from the basin over a groove in the wide end of the V and fell through the windless space of the atrium to another basin on the lowest floor.

Nelson paused to double over the railing, where he saw, on the five cantilevered balconies below, the bent heads and splayed elbows of young people at tables along the edge of each balcony, a nimbus of books and notebooks and loose papers on the tabletops around each of them. Every other one seemed to twirl an uncapped Hi-Liter—yellow, pink, or green—between his or her fingers. A low, rumbling, starship hum filled the atrium, which seemed to Nelson to come from the stacks themselves, receding out of sight away from the edge balcony, deeper into the Annex under Nelson. He pushed away from the railing and glanced up through the skeins of windblown snow on the skylight at a cold, featureless sky. The old Gothic clock tower leaned into the north wind, its clock face a pale, foreshortened oval.

Riding the glassed-in elevator to the lowest floor, Nelson felt more energized already. Unlike the old library, with its nooks and grottoes, its levels and half-levels, its vibrating iron staircases, and its ringing metal floors, its low ceilings and hissing pipes wrapped in asbestos, the Annex had all the cool angularity of a Cubist painting. The passage of the monumental edge of each floor just beyond the glass of the car made Nelson feel that he was part of something monumental himself. He began to see why the withdrawn books had been exiled to the tower of the old library—who needed all those old volumes anyway? What on earth had he been doing feeding for so many years, like a carrion beetle, on the abandoned carcasses of the university's rejects? Why were so many of them now rotting in his basement, stuffed into milk crates?

On the sixth floor Nelson headed into the stacks, where, at the deepest, most fundamental level of the Annex, the university's collection of literary criticism was shelved. His finger hummed like a filament as he passed down the brightly lit aisle between volumes of theory and cultural studies, letting his eyes glide over the spines of the books. For the last several years he had been afraid of running into his colleagues here, where someone who hadn't spoken to him in months would be forced, face to face, to acknowledge his presence. Nelson would feel obliged to make excuses, like a footman caught in the master's study, while the other, smiling desperately as if at a panhandler, would wonder silently why a man who taught four sections of composition needed to be in the research library at all. Now Nelson knew that he should have come here years before; the only distinguishing characteristic of a literature professor at the millennium was that he or she wrote about other people's writing. Apart from that, the writing he wrote about didn't even need to be literature, or writing about literature, or even writing about writing about literature. He needed theory.

He stopped near the halfway point of the long, fluorescent-lit aisle, books towering on either side, shelves receding seemingly to the vanishing point in either direction. Most of the books were new, with velvety, embossed spines, or slick, laminated paper covers, each volume tagged with its little white catalog designation. These weren't the sort of books Morton Weissmann had in mind for Nelson to write—Weissmann had once said that the "R" for Routledge on the spine of a book was like the Mark of the Beast—but that only made them more thrilling to Nelson. In the glare of the long bulbs overhead, he could not make out names or titles, but he ran his hand along the shelves, caressing the spines as if he could soak up the text of each one through the tip of his burning finger.

In the unflickering glare, at the center of a severe perspective, Nelson suddenly felt the visceral truth of the world as text; he apperceived the fundamentally linguistic nature of reality. Everything was text, at every level of existence, all the way up from quarks to queer theory. Words arranged in lines; lines arrayed on pages; pages pressed together, bound, and trimmed in books; books arranged cover to cover along a shelf like the words in a line of text; shelves stacked one atop the other like lines of text on a page; rows of shelves pressed together, with just the barest passage for a reader, like the pages of a book. And here he was, a mote of consciousness at the center of this rectilinear grid of information, this circuit board of signifiers, his little lump of appreciation accreted like a pearl out of all this text. The theorists were right; Vita was right. None of these volumes was the product of individual consciousness: It was the other way around. He, Nelson Humboldt, was the distillation of textuality, a bit of condensation, a by-product, a speck. . . .

Nelson's finger hummed with pleasure. While this way of looking at text made it difficult to distinguish one volume from another, let alone decide on one that might help him jump-start his career, it also implied that it didn't matter which one he chose, not really. Nelson, his breath coming quickly, looked both ways, up and down the aisle, then put his finger in his mouth and licked it slowly. He thought he could feel the heat of it on his lips and tongue. Then, glancing to either side again, he lifted his finger toward the glossy spine of a large paperback, anticipating with beating heart the slick squeak as he ran his wet finger down the lamination. . . .

"Professor Humboldt," said Marko Kraljević, "I am the gaze incarnate."

Nelson jerked his finger away from the book, startled to breathlessness. Kraljević stood several yards away, striking a pose on the carpet in the bright light. Today he was dressed as a nineteenth-century professor, his fireplug body wedged into a tight waistcoat, a morning coat, and a high-waisted pair of trousers whose cuffs broke just so over his polished black boots. The high, starched collar of his shirt stuck right up under his chin, his extravagant cravat bristled on either side of his brutally scraped jaw. A golden watch chain was slung across his stomach. A pince-nez perched on his broad nose, its silk ribbon looped into a vest pocket.

Nelson's finger flared; he tried to draw himself up. Kraljević carried a silver-headed walking stick, and he twisted the sharp end of it into the carpet, shifting all his weight onto one leg. He plucked off the pince-nez and brandished it at Nelson, revealing two pink dents on either side of his nose.

"I am the Panopticon," he declared in his thick accent. "I observe you—yes, *you*—from every angle. *Le Panopticon, c'est moi.*"

Working the cane into the carpet with his wrist, he took a step forward. Nelson resisted the urge to step back. His finger burned.

"But!" Still clutching the pince-nez, Kraljević lifted a thick finger, his hand nearly swallowed up by his wide, starched cuffs. "I am *not* the Panopticon of the center, looking out. No, no, *no!*"

He stepped to one side, and Nelson made a judicious lateral move, refusing to yield any advantage.

"I am the Panopticon of the *periphery,* the Panopticon of the *margin,* the Panopticon of the *subaltern.* I look *in* at the imperial center to *fix* it in my gaze and *exclude* it."

He thrust his finger forward, still moving in a wide arc.

"*You,* Nelson Humboldt, are the *subject* of the gaze. I center you in my marginal gaze in order to *exclude* you, to make you the *accursed share. You,* Nelson Humboldt, are the Other, not I. No, no, not *I.*"

Nelson was backed up against the shelves behind him; he felt the books shifting behind his shoulders and elbows. He wanted to grasp Kraljević by the wrist, or even by the throat, press his burning finger into the man's thick flesh, and force him to his knees.

"Something I can do for you, Professor?" Nelson asked through a tightening throat.

Suddenly Kraljević thrust himself to within a foot of Nelson, forcing Nelson back on his tiptoes against the books behind him.

"*I!*" cried Kraljević. "*I?* What can *you* know about yourself? Can you once see yourself complete? I think *not*. Only I—I!—can see you complete, as if in a glass case. I see the thrumming of your nerves, the pulse of your blood, the churnings of your intestines!"

Nelson ground his teeth. One inch closer, and he'd flatten this little bastard. Kraljević rocked back on his heels.

"As for my own intestines . . . *hunh*." Kraljević shrugged, he replaced his pince-nez upon his nose, he dabbed at his forehead with a silk handkerchief plucked out of the breast pocket of his morning coat. "I am an intellectual scatologist. *You* . . . "—he gestured at Nelson with his walking stick—". . . are unassimilable. You require *excretion*."

Kraljević whirled, swinging his stick into the air. With his back to Nelson, he parted the skirts of his morning coat and lifted his leg as if he were about to break wind, and Nelson flinched away, pitching half a shelf of books onto the carpet. Kraljević whirled again and thrust his face at Nelson.

"*HAH!*" he laughed, baring his teeth. "*HAH!*"

A gust of garlic and peppers blew over Nelson. He moved suddenly past Kraljević into the center of the aisle, making the little man jump back to the far side of the heap of books on the carpet. Nelson tugged his disheveled parka into place; he flexed his fists. The fire in his finger was making him sweat.

Kraljević stooped and snatched up a book from the little heap on the carpet, turning it this way and that in a three-fingered grip.

"Something there is in all men," he said, pursing his lips, "that profoundly rejoices in seeing books burn."

"The fuck do you want?" said Nelson.

"Tenure," said Kraljević, letting the book drop from his fingers. It landed, sliding, on the heap of books on the floor.

"You *have* tenure," said Nelson, narrowing his eyes. Another moment, and he'd reduce this little fraud to cinders.

"For *her!*" cried Kraljević, and he lunged forward like a fencer, thrusting the point of his walking stick past Nelson, within an inch or two of Nelson's face. Nelson flattened himself against the shelves, knocking more books onto the heap on the floor. He looked past the quivering tip of the stick. Lorraine Alsace stood demurely a few yards up the aisle, within a haze of fluorescent light like a goddess risen from the sea. Her shoulders drooped, she clasped her hands before her, she twisted the toe of one black slipper into the carpet. She hung her head and glanced coyly up at Nelson under her heavy brows. She batted her eyes at him.

Kraljević lay the walking stick firmly against Nelson's chest.

"I hold you captive," said Kraljević, "in the prison house of my discourse. You must do as I desire. And what I desire is *tenure for Lorraine Alsace!*"

With a grunt, Nelson wrenched the walking stick away from Kraljević. But not all of it—there was click and a hiss, and Nelson found himself holding a mere wooden sheath. Kraljević jumped back a step, still holding the silvery handle and brandishing a long, thin blade, the point of which circled in the air a foot or so from Nelson's chest. Nelson's finger seared him, and he wanted to lunge for Kraljević, sword or no sword.

"I will place you *sous rature,* Professor Humboldt," said Kraljević, his face flushed, his eyes dark behind the pince-nez trembling on the bridge of his nose. "If my beloved Lorraine Alsace, my sweet contested territory, does not receive tenure by the end of the term; if it goes instead to the egregious Vuh, Vuh, *Vee-ta*"—he bared his teeth in a vicious smile—"or to *you . . .*"—he jabbed slightly at Nelson, who tried not to flinch—"I shall erase you, and you will vanish forever, like a face drawn in sand at the edge of the sea."

Kraljević traced an intricate figure in the air with the point of his blade, then drew a long, slantwise slash through it. He held the blade to his nose as if saluting his opponent. Then he lunged forward, and Nelson parried him with the wooden sheath of the walking stick. The two men found themselves chest to chest in a clinch—Nelson wide-eyed and glaring down at the shorter man, Kraljević narrow-eyed and teeth bared. They sprang apart, Kraljević thrust with his blade, Nelson parried with the sheath, and they inched up and down the narrow aisle, thrust and parry, under the fluorescent light. Over the clacking of blade and sheath, Kraljević snarled, "Nelson! What is this 'Nelson'?"

"You'll find out!" growled Nelson, sweating under his parka.

Kraljević barked, a high-pitched squeak, and as the fight ebbed and flowed, Nelson was barely aware of Lorraine Alsace declaiming somewhere nearby, sometimes from behind him, sometimes from the aisle to the right, sometimes from the aisle to the left.

258

"But who's talking about Nelson?" said Kraljević, breathlessly. "In other words *on* Nelson? Shall I discourse *on* Nelson, that is to say (i.e. [*id est* {that is}], that is) inscribe my text {*texte*} on his living flesh, eye ee, textualize his corpus (corpse? One can only hope!), so . . ."

Kraljević lunged with his blade, Nelson parried with the blunt sheath.

". . . or shall I discourse {*discours* [*discursus* (*discurrere*)]} on the subject {*sujet*} of Nelson's corpus, or shall I sub/ject the corpus of Nelson to my dis/course?"

A slash, a tear in Nelson's parka. Nelson swerved, stepped back, swung wildly with the stick.

"What is the upper edge {*bord*} of Nelson? What, indeed, is the lower edge of him? With the edge {*tranchant*} of my blade/discourse, shall I trenchantly fold his upper edge into his lower edge, subject him to a process of invagination, fold him into himself in a layer of loose folds, suitable for the penetration {*pénétration*} of my point . . . of . . . *view* . . . ?"

Kraljević jabbed at Nelson, but Nelson, heart pounding, drove him back with a flurry of blows. He could stop this in a moment, of course, with a mere touch upon Kraljević's flesh, but he was afraid of that blade, of its keen edge catching his finger against the wood of the sheath, slashing, drawing blood, sinking to the bone or worse. . . .

"OR," cried Kraljević, wild-eyed, his blade quivering metronomically from side to side, parrying, "shall I release you from the politico-institutional frame of narrative, shall I release your text from its margins, what I call your text, your corpus, shall I cause your corpus to overflow its margins {*débordement, debordement*} by the release of your corp/uscles, your core/pus, shall I cause a leakage {*coulage,* or should I slash a little lower, *fuite*} of tissue, a releasing of the dam of your damned textuality {*maudit texualité*}, so that you are henceforth no longer a corpus/text/cortex, but a differential network, a web of *différance* and *différence,* a fabric of traces referring endlessly forever and ever amen to everything but yourself, flowing over, running over, bleeding . . . pustulent . . . decaying. . . ."

Kraljević ducked and came up under Nelson's sheath, straight for Nelson's

---

Lorraine Alsace said, "Nelson. Nel. Son. Nil son. No son of mine. (Nilsson? [brother bought a coconut, he bought it for a dime]) Nil sun. Dark, darkness. Blindness, with no insight. In Latin, son is 'guilty,' Nelson is the guilty son, or perhaps the son without guilt {*sans culpibilité*}, a guiltless parricide? *Au français,* son is 'sound,' Nil/son is no sound, a silent killer, conniver, a back-stabber, throat, and Nelson, terrified for his finger, was forced back onto the pile of books in the aisle, which slid and shifted under his feet. He waved the sheath wildly, desperate to keep his footing.

"AHA!" shouted Kraljević. "Nelson experiences polysemia, the shifting of the text under his feet—Foucault and Derrida, quaquaquaquaqua—as in a moment he him/self shall be polysemous, his boundaries {bord} overrun, the text of his corpus, the corpus of his text shifting, uncertain, dissolute, leaking, *spurting.* . . ."

In the last moment before he fell, Nelson clutched Kraljević by his lapels and pulled the little Serbian over on top of him. They tumbled onto the pile of books, rolling and grappling. Nelson pressed the wooden sheath against Kraljević's windpipe; Kraljević held Nelson by the throat with one hand and clutched his blade like a dagger with the other, aiming the point of it into Nelson's eye. Nelson's finger was smoking, but clutching the sheath, fending Kraljević off, there was no way to shift hands. Instead, with his left hand he snatched up a volume from the pile—*Blindness and Insight,* read the spine—and held it up just as Kraljević thrust. The blade drove straight through the book, its point stopping an inch from Nelson's face.

"Nicely done!" cried Kraljević. "You de Man, Nelson!"

But Nelson only growled in Kraljević's face. With a supreme effort he pressed Kraljević with the sheath and heaved up with his legs, flipping Kraljević over his head and onto the carpet. The sheath and the sword-in-the-book went flying, bounding against the carpet. Nelson dived for the blade, but Lorraine Alsace stepped up and yanked it out of his reach. Kraljević, meanwhile, crawled rapidly up the aisle, clutching the sheath, his bulky backside working under the flaps of his morning coat.

Nelson jumped to his feet, sweating under his parka, his heart hammering. He stood panting while Lorraine, with a bony hand under his elbow, helped Kraljević up, murmuring in his ear. Kraljević's collar was awry, his cravat twisted, his coat rucked up around his shoulders. His pince-nez swung from its ribbon, one of its lenses cracked. The two men glared at each other across the flattened

---

an arriviste, a Jew. A herder of sheep, a rootless person, he fawns like a spaniel, he grins when he bites. And so a verdict, unambiguous, final: the triumph of life {triomphe de la vie}—to wit, *my* life {ma vie}, specifically, my professional life {ma vie professionnel}—over the lackey of the Jew Weissmann, whom we seek to arrest {arrêter}: L'arrêt de Mort!"

pile of books, their chests heaving. Nelson adjusted his parka, which was leaking little white pellets of stuffing where Kraljević had slashed it. Kraljević straightened his tie and righted his collar; with shaking fingers he stuffed his cracked pince-nez into a pocket. Then he shrugged away the trembling hands of Lorraine Alsace, drew himself as tall as he could, and stuck his hand inside his waistcoat.

"I trust I've made myself clear," he said, panting.

Nelson blinked at him, speechless with rage. His finger throbbed. Kraljević wheeled away, thrusting the empty sheath of his walking stick under his arm like a swagger stick. Lorraine followed, grimly trying to pull the blade out of the book as she walked. She managed it just as they passed out of sight at the end of the aisle, dropping the book to the carpet with a barely audible plop.

Outside, Nelson stalked across the Quad in the thickening dusk, panting, heart pounding, sweat freezing on his forehead. He pressed his hand to the slash in his parka, trying to keep the little pellets from spilling out. A gentle snow dusted over the cleared patches on the Quad and the steps of Thornfield Library, and the bright lamps around the Quad popped on all at once as he passed. His breath misted in the bright light. He glanced back; the snow falling through the warm light of the Annex skylight was like the flakes in a snow globe. The glowing white clock face on the tower read five-thirty against the darkening sky. Dinnertime. Still breathless, Nelson directed his steps toward the bus stop.

He was afraid of being seen in this state, flushed, with his parka sliced open, so he took a short cut, a little alley between a university parking structure and a row of shops along Michigan Avenue. The alley alternated between harsh light from above and gritty reaches of shadow littered with crushed cans, broken bottles, and crumpled food wrappers. Even in the cold, the alley smelled of beer and piss.

Nelson's breath was coming easier now, and he stopped under a floodlight over the rear door of a shop and took his hand away from his parka carefully. A little cascade of pellets trickled down the polyester. A few pellets stuck to his hand, and he shook them off. The wind blew up the alley, smelling rank, swelling his open coat. Nelson fumbled for the zipper with his stiffening hands. His finger was cold; he could scarcely move it.

"Care to help the homeless, sir?" asked a voice, reverberating off the walls on either side.

Nelson froze, the zipper of his parka halfway up. He glanced back and saw no one, only the slanting shadows across the long slit of alley, the snow filtering through cones of harsh light. He turned forward and saw Fu Manchu standing in the rear doorway of a restaurant up ahead, his back to the battered metal door, his massive arms crossed over his chest. His head was wrapped in the flag bandanna; he had pulled a frayed plaid blanket tight around his shoulders. The light above the door buzzed and flickered, fitfully illuminating Fu Manchu like a menacing figure in a fun house.

Nelson thought about turning back the way he'd come, but instead he lowered his head and hurried past the doorway.

"Thanks a lot, bitch," said Fu Manchu after him.

Nelson stopped again and turned. The unsteady light lit the homeless man's pale forehead and left his eyes and mouth in shadow. Then the light went out, leaving only his knuckles and the tip of his nose visible in the doorway.

"What did you say?" Nelson said.

"You heard me, bitch." The light flickered on, and Nelson could see the snow falling between him and the doorway. Fu Manchu lifted his chin and pulled the blanket tighter, squeezing it through his bare fingers. "Keep walking. I don't want your fucking money."

Nelson stared at the man. Then he started walking toward him. Fu Manchu cocked his head to one side and then the other. He worked his fingers in the folds of the blanket. "You don't want to fuck with me, asshole," he said. "I'll fucking kill you."

The light crackled and hissed and flickered off, and Fu Manchu stepped into the alley, a hulking silhouette against the backdoor light of a shop behind him.

"Really," said Nelson. He walked up to within arm's reach of Fu Manchu. Nelson's finger burned distantly, as if it belonged to someone else.

"Walk away, man, I'm warning you." Fu Manchu shook his head in the dark. "I'm giving you this chance, asshole."

"I just want you to do one thing," Nelson said, flexing the fingers of both hands.

The light above him came on with a pop, and Fu Manchu shrugged off the blanket. All he wore underneath was a T-shirt and a denim vest; his arms were bare. He stepped up to Nelson in the narrow alleyway, his chest thrust forward, his fists at his sides, clenching and unclenching.

"What's that?" he said. "Suck your faggot cock?"

Nelson started to laugh. The light buzzed again and began to flicker rapidly on and off and on. Fu Manchu swung at Nelson, his meaty fist approaching in slow motion in the strobing light. Nelson caught the fist in his right hand and squeezed, his finger sparking painfully.

"No," said Nelson, gritting his teeth. "I want you to die."

In the flashing light it took all of Nelson's strength to hold Fu Manchu's fist back. Then all the tension went out of the homeless man's arm, as if his strength had been switched off. The light came full on again, and the homeless man's features blurred in the bleaching light.

"Goodness!" said Fu Manchu.

His eyes rolled back in his head; he made a choking sound. Nelson jerked his hand away, and the man corkscrewed slowly to the pavement, sprawled on his side amid the grit and broken glass on the stained concrete.

Nelson stood over him, panting, feeling nothing. The falling snow caught on his eyebrows. At his feet Fu Manchu lay with his knees up, his eyes staring up into the dark beyond the lamplight. His mouth was still working, but all that came out was a hollow gulping, like a drain. He stiffened suddenly in a spasm, he flopped onto his back, he kicked one leg out flat. His breath hissed out of him, feathering the hairs of his moustache.

Before he knew it, Nelson was on his knees next to Fu Manchu. Perhaps it was the cold, but he was shuddering all over, his hands trembling over the man's chest. Nelson touched him gingerly, then yanked his hand away. Slowly he lowered his shaking hand and touched the base of the man's throat with the tips of his fingers. Fu Manchu's skin was turning cold already.

"Don't," Nelson whispered, hoarsely. He could barely hear himself. "Don't."

The snow fell endlessly through the floodlight. Nelson was about to clamber to his feet and run when Fu Manchu arched his back and cried out, his voice ringing off the close walls. Then he sagged to the pavement again, his limbs awry, his mouth twisted, gulping air in ragged wheezes. The light flickered out.

Nelson scuttled back through the snow, crouched on his toes and fingertips in the dark like a runner at the block, his parka bulked up around his ears. Then he scuttled forward again, feeling for the blanket with both hands. He found it, rough and greasy to the touch, and tossed it lightly away from him, hopefully over the man on the pavement.

"Ohhhhh," sighed Fu Manchu in the dark, and Nelson sprang to his feet and ran, pelting up the narrow alley between grimy walls, the snow pattering against his face, the freezing air rasping in his throat. He charged out into the street at the other end, and he didn't slow until he reached the bus stop.

14

Victoria's Secret

Nelson burst into the town house in a blast of cold air, huffing and puffing and stamping the snow off his boots, just as Bridget was setting a tuna casserole on the table. From upstairs came squeals and a frightful thumping. He stripped off his rubbers and pitched them onto the midden of boots and mittens and scarves at the bottom of the closet; he hauled off his parka, squeezing pellets out of the gash and onto the floor amid the dirty, melting snow.

"What happened to your coat?" Bridget wiped her hands with a dishtowel.

"Nothing," he said breathlessly. "Ripped it."

He couldn't find a hanger, so he just stuffed the leaking parka into the closet and wedged the door shut. The house was full of the sickening smell of cooked tuna and noodles, and with a glance past his wife at the mismatched dishes on the dinner table, he plunged down the basement stairs in his stocking feet.

"Are you alright?" Bridget peered into the dark from the top of the stairs, twisting the towel between her hands.

"Fine," he called back. "Shut the door, please."

"Dinner's ready."

"I'm not hungry. Shut the door, will you?"

On this cold evening, the furnace ran constantly, filling the basement with a dry heat. Blue light gleamed in the rotting poster over his desk; a line of blue flame quivered in the screen of his computer. Nelson heard the hammer of the little feet on the floor above; shrill, indecipherable shouts; the weary bark of his wife.

He started up his computer and shifted the mouse restlessly on its pad—a gift from his daughters that Bridget had picked out, illustrated with a caricature of Charles Dickens—while he waited for the browser to load a byte at a time through the sclerotic old chip in his computer. Now that he was making more money, he ought to allow himself a new machine, something with gigabytes of memory and stereo speakers and a joystick; he could easily persuade a salesman to give him a huge discount.

He reached a search engine at last, typed in the name "Marko Kraljević," and waited again for the information to trickle through the pinhole of his ancient modem. There was little chance of getting near Kraljević again; the theorist was too canny, too unpredictable. Not to mention the danger for Nelson—he couldn't risk injuring his finger. But some of the things Kraljević and Alsace had said in the library set off alarms in Nelson's head. Could it be that Kraljević was the author of the anonymous letters? Or had he merely been quoting from them, trying to rattle Nelson? Presumably the man had a CV on file with the department, and someone in authority had reviewed it and checked his references. All Nelson knew of Kraljević's history was that his reputation worldwide depended entirely on a series of papers he had delivered on the conference circuit in Europe. What he had done before that was veiled by his own silence and by his colleagues' lack of interest.

Nelson was still waiting for the search engine page to load when he heard the rising intonation of a small voice.

"Daddy?" Clara stood on the bottom step of the basement stairs and clutched the railing, her skin blued by the light from the furnace, her hair limned by the bright light from the top of the stairs. He hadn't heard her come down. She shifted her weight from one foot to the other, ready to bolt.

"What?"

"Mom wants to know, do you want her to save you any food?"

"Uh-uh."

He stared at the screen, wishing his daughter would go away. She watched him in the blue glare for a moment, then dashed up the steps.

"Mommy! Mommy! Daddy says *uh-uh!*" she shouted as she reached the top. She disappeared into the glare at the top of the stairs.

"Shut the goddamn door!" bellowed Nelson.

He barely noticed the return of the blue gloom around him. Several pages of citations for Kraljević had loaded finally, and Nelson paged down through them, his finger poised over the clicker of his mouse. Most of them were European or American university web pages from conferences going back five years, listing Kraljević as a presenter, a discussant, or even the topic. Nelson glided by these without interest. Then, at the bottom of the fourth page of references, Nelson found a web address that didn't look altogether European. He clicked on it, and after another ten-minute wait he found himself at an old web page of the National University of Belgrade, dated several years ago, that listed the faculty for Social Sciences. The page offered him a choice between Serbian and English, and he clicked to a page written in a freestyle English—"Welcome on this page! While study includes social, informatical, statistic, and management sciences, it is inter-disciplinaire"—that listed the entire faculty in alphabetical order and the courses they taught. Each entry was accompanied by a postage stamp of a mug shot, so that a row of tiny, blunt Serbian faces ran down the left margin of the web page. Nelson clicked down to "Kraljević, M.," where he saw a little photo of someone he didn't recognize, a gray-haired, squinty-eyed man who must have been at least sixty. His courses were listed as Informatics for Kulturologists and Physical Education.

"What the . . . ," murmured Nelson, and then he noticed that the photo beside the next entry showed the man he knew as Marko Kraljević, a little thinner, perhaps, with long black hair combed over the blunt dome of his head. His dark eyes drilled out of the screen at Nelson.

"Jamisovich, S.," read the entry. "Fenomenology of Spirit I and II. Modern Weapons Systems."

" 'Modern Weapons Systems'?" murmured Nelson in the blue dark.

"Nelson!" His wife's voice came down the stairs. He ignored her.

"They must have switched the photos by accident," he whispered to himself. But already a doubt was gathering at the back of his brain.

"Nelson!" Bridget used her top sergeant voice at half throttle.

Nelson turned away from the screen. "What?" he barked back.

"You have a phone call."

He expected to hear her say, "It's the police." His finger vibrated with heat. He jerked his hand off the mouse and looked away from the computer screen. "Uh, who is it?" he asked.

He couldn't see the top of the stairs from where he sat, only the long shadow of his wife down the steps. What if somebody had seen him come out of the alley? What if that same someone had come across the body of a homeless man cooling under a thickening blanket of snow? Assuming there was a body to come across, that is—the last Nelson had seen of Fu Manchu, he was gasping and flopping like a beached fish.

"It's someone named Gillian."

r flared. His old office chair creaked as he turned slowly away
Did you say Gillian?" he said.

ng." Bridget's shadow slithered up the steps as she stepped away
t.

rned to his computer and palmed his mouse, intending to bookmark
ciences faculty page. But it was gone, replaced by a little white box
i a "fatal error" in his computer.

n," Nelson said, and he pushed away from the screen and dashed up-
here he found the phone dangling against the wall. Bridget was carrying
ty plates away from the dinner table, and she glanced at him with a look
aid, "Who's Gillian?" Abby and Clara hissed in each other's ears, giggling
stealing looks at their father. Nelson picked up the phone and stepped
und the corner into the vestibule, pulling the cord tight.

"Victoria wants to see you." Gillian's voice was hard, as if they were standing
oe-to-toe outside a contested classroom. He could almost hear her glaring at
him down the phone line.

"What for?" said Nelson. The letters, he thought. She wants to talk to me
about the letters.

"Come and find out," said Gillian.

"When?" he said.

"Tonight. Now."

"Where?"

"Her house. I'll come get you."

Nelson had no idea where Victorinix lived; she'd never had a departmental
function at her home, as far as he knew. He flashed on an image of himself in
the faded plush of a large, vintage limousine, with Gillian wrapped up in a great-
coat in the front seat, a fur hat pulled down to her eyebrows, a scarf pulled over
her nose and mouth; she would drive him in the silent, padded old car through
a wood full of shifting shadows and mysterious blue lights, to a Gothic mansion—
turrets, gables, deep embrasures—and deposit him in a gray courtyard where
dry, dead leaves scraped across the flagstones, and he would mount a stair toward
a massive wooden door that seemed to creak open by itself; wolves would howl
in the woods, and he would whirl to find that the limousine was already gone,
without a sound. . . .

"No," Nelson said. "Someplace else."

There was silence on the other end of the line. Nelson could not even hear Gillian breathing. "Where?" she said at last.

Nelson certainly couldn't invite Victoria here, and though he was no longer quite as afraid of the undergraduate chair as he had been, he certainly didn't want to be alone with her in her office again.

"Pandemonium," he said. The coffeehouse was bright, public, crowded.

Gillian made a harsh sound, as if she were clearing her throat. After a moment Nelson realized that she was laughing.

"This is a very private meeting, Nelson." She spoke as if to an idiot. "Victoria has no intention of being seen with you."

Nelson's mind raced. He had no intention of meeting Victorinix in an enclosed space.

"The Quad," he heard himself say.

Gillian gave another humorless laugh. "Do you want to meet with her or not, Nelson?"

"The Quad," Nelson said more firmly. "At midnight."

Gillian said nothing. Nelson peeked around the corner at his family. The girls had vanished, and Bridget was furiously wiping down the table, pretending not to look in his direction.

"You want privacy, right?" Nelson kept his voice low. "Think of it as no-man's-land."

"How can I?" said Gillian. "You'll be there."

Nelson said nothing. The Quad was brightly lit, with clear sight lines through the trees in every direction. His finger thrummed with a steady heat.

"The Quad or nowhere," Nelson said. "You check with Victoria and let me know."

As he turned to replace the phone in its cradle, he heard Gillian sigh. He lifted the phone to his ear.

"Alright," she said.

Nelson drove to campus after Bridget had gone to bed, creeping along the snowy roads in his buzzing, drafty little car. He parked on the far side of Harbour Hall—his was the only car on the street—and he let himself into the darkened building with his key. His rubbers squeaked in the dim hallways. In his chilly office he turned on only the desk lamp, and in the wedge of light he shucked off his parka and his rubbers and replaced his discount khakis and sweater with the trousers, shirt, and sport coat hanging behind his office door. He sat on the edge of the desk and pulled on his big, black dress shoes; lacing them up, he paused to part the plastic blades of the blinds and peer down into the Quad. Several inches of snow had fallen since dusk, but he decided not to put his parka back on. Tonight he was constructing himself as a colleague of Victoria's, not as her shambling, awkward, tongue-tied minion. He'd brought one of the poison pen letters he'd read that afternoon, and he slipped it inside his jacket. He left the light on, locked the door, and went down to the lobby.

A few falling snowflakes still sparkled in the lamplight around the Quad. The bitter air stung Nelson's nose, and he felt the cold in his windpipe and his sinuses. Even so, he did not button his jacket or put his hands in his pockets. As he followed the unplowed sidewalk through the bare trees, his were the first pair of footprints in the heavy powder. The snow crunched and squeaked underfoot. The clock atop Thornfield Library struck midnight, the hard ringing of the bell muffled by the snow. Each black lamppost cradled a white globe lit from within by a single, brilliant streak of light, illuminating the Quad like a stage. The bare elms cast their shadows upward, their branches limned by snow, their bony fingers silhouetted against an eerily glowing gray sky. Through the trees he saw the wide, foursquare buildings around the Quad, with their turn-of-the-last-century cornices and patterned red brick. BIOLOGY declared one of them through the trees, in floodlit stone letters. CHEMISTRY, announced another. As the last, dull note of the bell faded, he could hear the distant roar of their heating vents. His finger throbbed.

Nelson stopped a few paces out onto the virgin snow of the Quad. The upward glow of the Annex was dimmed by a translucent layer of snow on the skylight. He glanced through the trees in all directions, then, as casually as he could, up at the top of the clock tower. The clock face hung like a moon, its just-parted hands silhouetted against the white glow. Above the clock the crenelations of the tower were etched against the sky. No one looked back at him.

"Nelson!" said a voice behind him, and he whirled so quickly he nearly fell over. Gillian approached, only a few paces away; her tracks led across the snowy lawn from behind a leafless elm. She looked huge in a black overcoat, a pair of fluffy, white earmuffs over her pierced ears. His finger flared, and before he even thought about what he was doing, Nelson swung his bare right hand and clapped it over her mouth.

"Don't move," he hissed, his finger sparking. "Don't say a word."

Gillian's eyes widened more in startlement than alarm. He'd caught her in midstride, and when he pulled his hand away, she wobbled for a moment, all her weight on one unsteady leg. Then she keeled over sideways in the snow. She lay there on her shoulder like a toppled statue, gasping hoarsely. Her eyes blazed at him. Nelson reached for her again.

A long, distant howl interrupted him. He jerked his hand back and cringed, glancing up at the library tower. No one was there, but the howl rose to a shriek, and Nelson spun to look behind him. Victoria Victorinix seemed to glide toward him out of the dusk between the Annex and the old library. Her long, white coat fell to her ankles, giving the impression that she floated above the snow, leaving no tracks behind her.

"Listen to them," she said, her voice cold and aristocratic. The shrieking rose higher in the distance. "Children of the night."

Nelson's heart hammered, his finger blazed. Then, as the shriek died away, Nelson at last recognized the sound: On this snowy night, some boy stewed in beer and testosterone had found a patch of bare pavement and was laying rubber. Nelson sighed. He stood and lifted his palm to Victorinix. "That's close enough," he said, barely keeping his voice steady.

Victoria stopped instantly, poised in the snow with her hands in her coat pockets, a tall cone of coat with her bare, cropped head atop it. She lifted her narrow chin toward Gillian.

"Let her up, Nelson." Victoria's voice was as clear and cold as the air itself. "She'll freeze."

Victoria's face was unusually white and gleaming, as if she were made of ice, and she was not wearing her little, round, tinted glasses. Her gray eyes glinted like a wolf's in the lamplight, not angrily, but curiously, as if she had just come upon something in the middle of the forest that might be good to eat.

Nelson glanced back at Gillian. The grad student was shuddering in the snow, grunting, her mouth working.

"Stay where you are," he said to Victorinix, and stepped back to Gillian. He stooped over her and insinuated his fingers between her glove and the cuff of her sweater, pressing her wrist. He was surprised to find that her skin was warm. "Get up." His finger sparked.

Gillian rose surprisingly lightly, as if he were raising her by her wrist. When she was standing, her eyes fixed furiously on him, he pointed across the Quad and said, "Go stand over there and don't move. Say nothing. Hear nothing."

He released her, and she turned slowly away, reluctant to release him from her angry gaze. She shambled through the snow to a spot near the center of the Quad where she could keep both Nelson and Victorinix in her sight.

Nelson straightened his sport coat. He didn't feel the cold.

"I suppose you wanted to see me about this." He pulled the letter out of his jacket.

Victorinix stood perfectly still twenty paces away, as if hovering an inch above the snow. Her breath hissed at the sight of the letter. With a chill, Nelson realized that she was laughing.

"I couldn't care less about the letters, Nelson," she said. "They've served their purpose. Put it away."

Puzzled, Nelson slid the letter back inside his jacket. What did she mean, *They've served their purpose?* He glanced at Gillian. Together the three of them made a perfect equilateral triangle on the white Quad. "Then why did you want to see me?" he said.

"I want to know what you want, Nelson," said Victorinix. She seemed bemused by him, her lips pursed as if at the unexpected precocity of a dull child she did not particularly like.

"What does Nelson want?" he said. "That's a new one, huh?"

Victorinix smiled. Her long canines glittered. "It would never have occurred to me before to ask," she said. "I suppose it's to your credit that I finally have."

"Gosh," Nelson said. "Imagine my relief."

"I don't mean to underestimate you." Her smile vanished, but her eyes glittered at him. "I promise you, Nelson, I'll never make that mistake again."

"You have no reason to hate me, Victoria."

"I don't hate you, Nelson. Until recently, I never even gave you much thought."

Nelson winced at the heat in his finger. "You *fired* me," he said, a little more angrily than he'd intended.

"The department fired you, Nelson. I was only the instrument."

"But you enjoyed it."

Nelson detested the rising whine in his voice, but his finger was making him sweat.

"What I enjoy," said Victoria Victorinix evenly, "is beyond your comprehension."

Nelson looked away. Gillian glowered at him across the glittering snow of the Quad; she shot a pleading glance at Victorinix, as if to say, *Release me.* Her breath hissed out of her in white gusts.

"I don't mean this personally, Nelson, but you don't belong at Midwest." Victorinix paused. "I let you go because you're a mediocrity. A good teacher? Perhaps. But your scholarship is unoriginal and uninspired."

Nelson wondered what would happen if he lunged for her right now. He wondered if he could take her. Victorinix seemed to sense what he was thinking, and she slid her hands—pale, long-fingered—out of her pockets.

"Maybe you should show me a little respect, Victoria," he said. He flexed his fingers in the cold, all of them numb but one.

They held each other's gaze for a long moment. Nelson's finger nearly tormented him into action, and he thought he detected a tension in Victorinix's jaw, a coiling of her fingers. But neither of them moved, and at last Victoria slid her hands back into her pockets, as if sheathing a weapon. "You still haven't answered my question, Nelson," she said.

"You asked to see *me,"* he said. "What do you think I want?"

"Tenure for Vita Deonne?" Victorinix sighed, almost sadly. "What do you hope to gain by that?"

"What do you have against her?"

"I don't have anything 'against' her. I simply don't think she's tenurable."

"Oh, come on," Nelson said. "Her work is . . ."

How to characterize Vita's work? Transgressive? Subaltern? Counterhegemonic? Or merely disturbing?

"Squarely in the theoretical mainstream," he said.

Victorinix laughed, a muted, icy bell. "I think I'm a better judge than you of what's in the theoretical mainstream."

"Whatever." Nelson sighed. "Vita's terrified of you."

"Vita's terrified of everyone, Nelson."

"But especially you, Victoria. And for the life of me, I don't understand why. I'd have thought that you and Vita were in the same . . . camp, if it's not too mediocre of me to point it out. Theoretically speaking, you're sisters."

"I never thought you'd take such a keen interest in feminist theory," Victorinix said in an icy monotone.

"I never thought I'd be fired by a lesbian." Nelson shrugged. "Live and learn."

To Nelson's surprise, Victoria looked as if he'd slapped her.

"Hey, I'm sorry if I've struck a nerve," Nelson said, pleased. "I'm only—what's the expression?—speaking truth to power?"

"You think I'm powerful, Nelson?" Victoria's gaze narrowed.

"Please," he said.

Victoria slid a few steps forward. Nelson's finger flared, and he tensed himself. She stopped a dozen paces away, her face a taut, bony mask.

"Let me tell you about power, Nelson." Her voice was almost a growl. "Fifteen miles from where we're standing, in every direction, are thousands of decent, warm-blooded citizens, just like you, who do their jobs and love their children and pay their taxes and wouldn't hurt a dog—and nearly every one of them would just as soon burn me at the stake, cut out my heart, and bury my headless corpse at a crossroads. They will never accept me as *human,* Nelson, let alone as 'normal.' "

She glanced through the trees at the looming classroom buildings, at the bare, lamplit trees, at the Quad under its quilt of snow. "This little world of the university is supposed to be my Coventry. It's where people like you put people like me, where you can keep us all in one place and watch us carefully. It's where you pretend to treat us like equals, and where I'm supposed to pretend that I can be myself without fearing for my life."

She leveled her ancient and unforgiving gaze at him again. "You can leave Hamilton Groves and go anywhere you want without looking over your shoulder every minute of every day. I cannot. Now, you tell me, Nelson, which one of us is more powerful?"

"Spare me." Nelson's finger scalded him. "I don't need to hear about frustration from the woman who nearly ended my career. From where I sit, lady, you give as good as you get, maybe even better."

Victorinix started to speak, but Nelson abruptly lifted his burning finger at her.

"No!" he barked. "All this ideological tit for tat, all the faction fighting, the whole culture war, you could end it, Victoria! You could end it tomorrow if you wanted to, if it weren't to your advantage to keep it going!" He paused. "You could be the peacemaker if you really wanted to."

"Nothing like a guilty white man to sentimentalize the Other, is there, Nel-

274

son?" Victoria bared her long teeth in a vicious smile. "Even in the depths of your fear and hatred of me, you think I ought to be better than you are. Purer, more noble, more compassionate. It's up to me to make a consensus, work things out, send everybody home happy and well fed. It's up to me to be Mother."

"Why not?" cried Nelson. "Why not be better than ... than ..." Who? he wondered, instantly embarrassed. Than heterosexuals? Than men? Than me?

"Who do you think taught me the game?" Victoria glided a fraction closer. "Who do you think taught me the rules by trying to destroy me? Decent men like you, Nelson."

The two of them trembled with anger, half a dozen paces apart. Gillian shuddered some distance away, her eyes twitching from one to the other.

"Whatever has happened to you, Victoria," Nelson said, his voice shaking, "*I didn't do it.* Did it ever occur to you that I'm not the enemy, that I don't mean you any harm, that I might even be on your side?"

Victoria closed her eyes and shook her head. "I especially don't trust your goodwill, Nelson. I and my kind have suffered some of the worst atrocities at the hands of the well-meaning."

"That's not fair," Nelson began, but she cut him off with a gesture.

"Has it ever occurred to you that I am essential to your identity, Nelson?" Victorinix said. "You define yourself by what you are not. You define yourself by excluding the Other from your idea of 'normal' and 'moral' and 'decent.' And out of all the Others there are, I'm the most 'Other' of them all. Because all the power to define identity is in the hands of well-meaning men like you, I have no choice but to define myself by my Otherness. So I embrace it, I celebrate it, because I have no dignified alternative. I have no dream of inclusion in your world because your world cannot exist without excluding me. This is not 'theory,' Nelson. This is experience talking."

Victorinix stood absolutely still, like a speaking statue. "What I do crave," she went on, "is your heedlessness. I crave the same blissful unself-consciousness that is your birthright. I crave the ability to walk in the daylight without the constant, pointed reminders of just how 'Other' I am. I crave your literally thoughtless sense of identity, Nelson, your ability to be yourself, safely, without having to think about it."

Nelson held himself very still. He heard the snow filtering through the trees.

"Vita, on the other hand," Victoria continued, "wants to destroy your blissful,

275

heterosexual unself-consciousness. She wants to make you as quiveringly self-aware of your own uncertain identity as she is."

She glanced at Gillian—the graduate student's eyes brightened like a dog's at the attention—then turned her gaze on Nelson again.

"Vita is not merely attacking gender, Nelson. Vita wants to take apart the whole idea of identity, brick by brick. And that's the problem. She wants to reveal not only the void at the center of your identity, but the void at the center of *mine*. She wants us all to think about what we are, all the time, as she does. She wants all of us in free fall forever, falling and falling and never coming to rest."

A sudden squall of wind blew under the trees and through the Quad, filling the lamplight with glittering flakes of snow. Nelson turned away from the brief stinging against his cheek. Victorinix merely closed her eyes. When the oceanic hiss of the snow subsided, she opened them again.

"But you *hired* Vita." Nelson said.

"I did more than that, Nelson," said Victorinix. "I offered her sisterhood. I offered her a chance to become like me."

"I've never been clear about that," Nelson said, curious now, "but I thought she already was."

"Vita has no idea what she is, or what she isn't." Victoria's eyes blazed. "I, on the other hand, know exactly what I am. I've never had the slightest doubt. Gender, sexuality—they're not crossroads; you don't just pick a path and see where it goes."

She pulled her white, long-fingered hand from her pocket and held it before her face as if considering something separate from herself, turning it this way and that.

"All things proceed from Nature, don't they? All things in heaven, in the earth, and under the earth, act and live as Nature ordains." Victorinix smiled as if at a private joke, and she replaced her hand in her pocket. "We're just poor, forked creatures like you, Nelson, only with one less tine. We're ambitious, lustful, greedy, vain, duplicitous, self-serving, arrogant, jealous, and hateful. When we're cornered, we fight with claws and teeth. We take no prisoners; we have no pity for the weak." She smiled, exposing her long teeth. "We jig, we amble, and we lisp. Patriarchy has given us one face, and we've made ourselves another."

"Is that how you offered sisterhood to Vita?" Nelson pursed his lips. "You need to work on your salesmanship."

Victorinix threw her head back and laughed, exposing a long reach of smooth, white throat. Nelson's finger flared, and he felt a trickle of fear.

"You have no idea how funny that is." Suddenly Victoria was in motion, gliding over the snow toward Nelson. His fear flooded him, and he started violently, stumbling backward. The snow dragged at his feet. Victorinix seemed to loom over Nelson, her face as white as the clock face in the tower above.

"Stop!" Nelson's cry was swallowed up by the snow. He crouched, one arm up, ready to fend Victorinix off with his right hand.

"I offered Vita *paradise*, Nelson!" Victorinix cried. "I offered her a community of passionate friends, of intimate companionship! A community where there are no fathers and husbands, where every woman is mother, daughter, sister all at once, where maternity comes from mutual penetration, mutual touch, where all we exchange is blood and trust and love!"

She cast her eyes to the dark sky and cried wordlessly. Nelson cringed.

"Not *romantic* love," she snarled, swinging her blazing eyes to him, "but a material and sensual love with no dominance or hate in it, a love in which we do not bear children, but create *companions,* in which at the moment of rebirth you are my sister, my lover, my equal, in which the seducer grants all her powers to the seduced at the moment of seduction. . . ."

Victorinix's voice cracked in a sob, and she turned away from Nelson, her long-fingered hands clasped to her slim, white throat. She seemed to diminish in front of Nelson, her back to him, her head bowed, her shoulders heaving. Only the sharp plane of her cheek was visible to him as he straightened from his crouch. His heart still pounding, he glanced at Gillian. Even though she could not hear a word that passed between him and Victorinix, the graduate student was weeping, her cheeks streaming in the cold, her mouth open as if to cry aloud.

"What happened?" he asked.

Victorinix inclined her head toward him, but still he could not see her eyes. "I seduced Vita, Nelson. Or I tried to."

"So?" Nelson shrugged.

"I revealed myself to her."

"And?"

"I put my hand up her skirt."

Nelson rolled his eyes. *"And?"*

Victorinix turned slowly, rotating on her own axis, her hands folded before her, her face gaunt with age and disappointment.

"Vita is a man, Nelson."

The winter wind gusted through the trees again. A little whirlwind of driven snow, swirling and scintillating, danced through the spaces between Nelson and Victorinix and Gillian. Gillian, her tears freezing on her cheeks, looked desolate. Victorinix stood perfectly still. Nelson blinked, his mouth hanging open.

"I'm sorry?" he said at last. The whirlwind stretched itself like a waterspout and rose into the air, a white stream vanishing in the dark above the lamps, toward the top of the library tower.

Memories of Vita flashed before Nelson's inner eye like a slide show: Vita in their office with her legs crossed tightly at the knee. Vita in his home, playing catch with his daughters and throwing like a girl. Vita the wallflower huddled like a child in her chair at the Seminar Luncheon. Vita in her plush bathrobe with her knees together, clutching the lapels shut at her throat with both hands.

"It's the worst kind of male arrogance," Victorinix said. "Vita thinks she can do anything better than a woman, even *be* a woman better than a woman can. Whatever her intentions, Vita's—how should I put this?—her philosophical position is just a disguise for a kind of patriarchal universalism. By claiming gender is performance, she gets to be anything she wants to be." She made a gesture of exasperation. "Only a man would conceive of such freedom and act on it. Vita can see materiality as a trap if she wants to; she can play house inside a skirt and a pair of panties, but it will never do away with the brute fact of what's between her legs."

Nelson's mind was racing. Nelson could remember nothing alluring about Vita, for all her girlish shyness. He recalled no firm curve of hip, no flash of well-turned calf, no swelling of breast, no sweet hollow of lower back—only Vita in her shapeless dresses, her baggy sweaters, her loose trousers, her helmet of bangs. But neither was there anything epicene about her—no deep voice, no hint of a hairy upper lip, no Adam's apple. If such a thing was possible, Vita seemed to be without gender.

"I don't play at what I am, Nelson," Victoria was saying, "and I don't appreciate someone like Vita coming in and claiming solidarity with me on the basis of what? Theory?" She laughed icily. "She wants to turn her own epistemological dilemma into ontology. She's pulled in one direction by rootlessness and in the other by intellectual vanity. She values her own intellect above all else, and yet she cannot understand who she is, let alone make the world conform to what she wants it to be. So rather than admit that maybe she's not up to the task—or that there's more to the world than even intelligent people are capable of grasping—she tries to make the slipperiness of signifier and signified into a fundamental principle. She has reified her own uncertainty and decided to prove that the world itself is a product of panic."

Nelson scarcely heard her. Maybe Vita's lack of allure proved that Victorinix was wrong—or lying. Wouldn't a man posing as a woman make the most of it? Didn't drag queens flaunt thighs and breasts and taut, creamy skin? Didn't cross-dressers sashay and pout and swing their hips? Another icy gust blew stinging snow against his cheek. He remembered Vita clutching the top of her head as if her hair might fly off. He blinked, and Victorinix came into focus before him, regarding him silently.

"Vita's a *man?*" he said.

Victorinix sighed in exasperation.

"I saw a picture once of her brother," Nelson said. "That wasn't her brother, was it?"

"Vita doesn't have a brother."

"So Vita used to be . . ."

"Yes, yes," said Victorinix impatiently, "Vita was Robin Bravetype."

"So you're absolutely sure? I mean, you felt her . . . his . . . I mean you . . ."

"Well, I don't have a lot of experience, Professor, but it stiffened when I touched it."

"Jesus," breathed Nelson. "So much for sisterhood, huh?"

"She has a penis, Nelson. That's where I draw the line."

Even though Gillian couldn't hear him, Nelson lowered his voice. "Jesus, Victoria, what were you thinking?" he said.

Victoria blinked, which was as close as she came to showing embarrassment. "I'm a lonely and—in my extremely circumscribed way—powerful woman," she said, "surrounded by attractive, passionate, intelligent young women looking for firm guidance. If you rise any further in this profession, you will face the same temptations."

"For God's sake, Victoria, you sound just like Mort Weissmann."

Victoria shrugged.

"I'm only human," she said.

"But Vita could destroy your career!" In his head, Nelson heard Vita at her most hectoring and insistent, delivering one of her set pieces on the maze run by every woman in academia, where leering sexual predators with twitching fingers waited around every turn. The university's code of professional ethics applied to Victoria as well as to anybody else; the conservative members of the faculty, not to mention members of the state legislature, would leap at the chance to pillory a prominent lesbian for sexual harassment.

"Think, Nelson." Victorinix had reconstructed her icy hauteur. "I could destroy *her* career as well, simply by exposing her. The Weissmanns at this university would rise up in outrage, while the Cultural Studies folk would revile her for keeping it a secret. There are other transgendered people on campus, but Vita, for reasons I don't understand, is trying to pass." Victorinix sighed derisively. "Gender as subversively parodic performance doesn't work if you don't tell anybody about it. But as it stands, I don't tell her secret, and she doesn't dare tell mine."

"Who else knows?" he said.

"No one. Until now."

Nelson's finger had begun to burn again.

"I'm offering you a chance to better yourself beyond your talents, Nelson." Victoria moved a little closer to him, lowering her voice. "You could expose me, perhaps even ruin me, but what do you get if you do? You still have Vita between you and what you want."

The two of them were tête-à-tête now, within arm's reach in the glare of the snowlight.

"And what *do* I want?" His finger pained him so much, Nelson could scarcely breathe.

"Tenure, you foolish man." Victorinix gave him an almost coquettish look. "You want the position you think you're trying to get for Vita."

Nelson's heart hammered.

"I don't know how you sabotaged all the other candidates," she said, "but you have my grudging admiration. There's only Vita now between you and tenure."

"And Lorraine Alsace."

"Lorraine has no claim on her own," said Victorinix. "She'll receive tenure only to keep Kraljević happy. And I can help you with him."

"How?" Nelson murmured. Again he was aware of the letter in his inside pocket.

Victorinix shook her head. "That's my bargaining chip, Nelson. If you help me with my Vita problem, I will help you with your Kraljević problem."

"What about Anthony?"

"Anthony believes in nothing," said Victorinix, "except himself. He can talk the talk, he can play the role of the engaged academic, but ideology, social justice—they mean nothing to him." She smiled bitterly. "He feels no obligation to be right, only an obligation to be interesting. What his subordinates do below him, who comes out on top, doesn't matter to him, as long as he gets to be Il Padrone. This is his greatest flaw, but it is also what makes him dangerous. A man who believes in nothing is capable of anything."

Nelson turned abruptly away from Victorinix. He drew a deep breath of the cold, midnight air. He looked about him in a slow spiral, through the trees at the darkened buildings looming all around, at the bare branches underlit by the lamplight, at the top of the tower etched against the glowing sky. His gaze lingered there a moment. Did he detect a movement atop the tower? No, he decided, it was only blowing snow. He turned back to Victorinix.

"You want to be chair of the department, don't you?"

"You're full of surprises, Nelson. Perhaps I misjudged you."

"And you want me to get rid of Vita for you."

"I'll never be chair as long as Vita has my career in her hands."

"And you have her secret in yours."

"So to speak." She smiled. "Sometimes a phallus is only a phallus."

"Tenure her."

Victorinix only laughed. Her teeth shone in the lamplight.

"Why me?" Nelson said. "Why do you need *me* to do your dirty work?"

"You dispatched Timothy Coogan very efficiently."

Nelson repressed a cringe. The letter dragged at his jacket like a lead weight.

"You stopped Lester Antilles, David Branwell, and jennifer manly cold," Victoria continued. Her eyes glittered with something like collegial admiration. "You seem to be the man for the job."

"And in return?"

Victoria's gaze was cool again, gray eyes with no hint of human feeling in them. "I will tenure you," she said.

"Anthony may not see things your way," he said.

"I can deal with Anthony," she said.

"Sure you can," Nelson said, smiling. "Perhaps you want me to get rid of him too."

He watched with pleasure as a shadow crossed Victoria's face. He knew that she was calculating the risk, plotting ahead like a worried chess player confronted with a move she hadn't foreseen. If Nelson could take on Anthony himself, she was thinking (thought Nelson), then he could take on *me*. When the shadow passed and she spoke again, she was gratifyingly uncertain.

"I will take care of Anthony, Nelson. You needn't trouble yourself."

Nelson held her gaze a moment longer, then he stepped away from Victorinix and crossed through the snow to Gillian. Her eyes widened at his approach, a mixture of rage and fear. Nelson lifted her wrist and slipped his finger inside her sleeve, against her skin.

"Go home," he said. "Sleep. Remember nothing of tonight."

Gillian's lashes flickered, her jaw trembled. With a final glance at Victorinix she turned and shuffled away through the snow, leaving a wide track as she passed into the trees.

Nelson turned back to Victoria, but she was no longer on the Quad. She stood perfectly still halfway up the snowy steps of Thornfield Library. Perhaps the glare from the lamplight obscured them, but Nelson could see no footprints in the snow leading to the steps.

"Where do we stand, Nelson?" Victoria's voice was clear, but distant.

"I've got a lot to think about," he said.

"Don't think too long, Nelson," said another voice.

"Who said that?" cried Nelson. His eyes darted through the trees of the Quad, seeing no one. Even Gillian was gone. Then he heard a savage hiss, something sibilant and guttural, and he turned to the library steps to see Victoria Victorinix crouched and twisted in her coat, her hands free, her long fingers brandished like claws. Teeth bared, her eyes wild, her face was turned to the sky, and Nelson lifted his gaze slowly to the top of the tower.

"What are you two up to?" asked the voice.

Nelson was suddenly frozen through, but not by the cold. Watching them from behind the battlements at the top of the clock tower was a pale, oval, featureless face lit by the dim lamplight from below. It had no eyes, no mouth, but something white streamed away from the face into the night, perhaps only driven snow, perhaps long, white hair.

Nelson's finger went stone cold, his skin prickled all over. The hissing stopped, and he heard a sound like the flapping of a blanket. He looked down, and the library steps were empty. Victorinix was gone.

"Run, Nelson," said the voice.

Nelson dashed all the way around Harbour Hall to his car, skidding and sliding in the snow. His trembling hands fumbled with the keys as he glanced over the roof of the little Toyota back toward the Quad. Behind the wheel, he ground the key and pumped the gas so hard the car stalled, and he started it again more slowly, his heart beating in his throat, his mouth dry. Nothing moved beyond the windshield except gusts of snow, and for no particular reason he started the windshield wipers. The clacking rhythm was his only comfort as he careened and slid all the way home.

His heart was still pounding as he came up to the steps of his town house. He opened the door as quietly as he could. The only light came from the little fluorescent bulb over the sink in the kitchen, casting a pale glow halfway across the littered living room. He glanced up at the ceiling as if he could see through it to his sleeping family, then he plucked at his tweed coat. His regular clothes were still in his office. Bridget hadn't seen these new clothes, so he opened the basement door slowly and started tiptoeing down.

After a few steps he stopped. The blue screen of his computer gleamed, throwing the long shadow of someone across the cement floor. Nelson gripped the wooden railing. He heard the creak of his office chair, and the shadow moved slowly. He glanced back up the stairs, contemplating a dash back out into the snow.

"Come down, Nelson," said his wife.

Nelson released the railing. He tottered down the steps on watery knees to find Bridget rotating slowly in his chair, her arms crossed, her long legs twined together. She had not dressed for bed; she was still in her jeans and sweatshirt. Nelson glanced past her at the glowing screen.

"What are you doing at my computer?" he said.

Bridget tightened her arms and fixed him with her gaze. "Nelson," she said, "are you having an affair?"

Nelson stopped. "What?"

"Who's Gillian?" She tapped her fingers on her elbow.

Nelson groaned and turned back toward the stairs. "I don't have time for this, Bridget," he said. "It's one o'clock in the morning."

Suddenly his wife was right behind him, dragging him around by his wrist. The empty office chair squealed backward across the floor.

"Why aren't you wearing your own clothes?" She was struggling to keep her voice down.

"These *are* my clothes." He yanked his arm free.

"Oh, *please,*" snapped Bridget. "You wouldn't know clothes like these from, from . . ." Her face worked itself into knots.

"Only a woman would buy you clothes like these." Her eyes blazed at him out of the dark. "Was it Gillian?"

He turned on his wife and pushed his face into hers. *"Gillian?* Gillian's a fucking *dyke,* alright?" he shouted. "Gillian is Victoria Victorinix's killer lesbian bodyguard, okay? Gillian wouldn't know what to *do* with a man!"

He shouldered past her, and Bridget turned with him. Her chest was heaving.

"It's Vita, isn't it?"

Nelson stopped. He turned, his eyes wide.

"Oh, my God, it is, isn't it?" She clapped her hand over her mouth. "All those e-mails . . . oh, my God, Nelson, you don't *write* to anyone else. . . ."

Nelson blinked at Bridget. His mouth hung open.

"You son of a *bitch,* Nelson!" She balled her fists and leaned toward him, shouting. "You brought that woman into our *house!* You let her play with our *children!*"

Bridget quivered inches away from him. She was only seconds from striking him, Nelson knew, and he started to laugh. The laughter started in his belly and worked its way up into his chest; it welled up in his throat and came out in little, staccato grunts. His shoulders began to shake with merriment; it spilled out of his nostrils, hissing rhythmically.

Bridget's eyes widened; her mouth hung open. She was breathing as hoarsely as a marathon runner.

"Stop that," she gasped.

Nelson tipped back on his heels and laughed out loud. He pinched his eyes shut, squeezing tears down his cheeks. He pressed his palms over his eyes.

"Stop that!" Bridget shouted.

Nelson sobbed with laughter. He doubled over and stamped his foot.

"You don't understand, Bridget," he gasped. "Vita's a . . . Vita's a . . ."

Nelson swayed unsteadily, wheezing with hilarity and snorting up mucus. Bridget drew a deep breath as if she were about to plunge into cold water.

"You *asshole!*" she roared, and she reached back and slapped Nelson as hard as she could. The blow knocked him back against his desk. She drew another breath and came at him again, and Nelson caught her by the wrists, squeezing hard, holding her off.

"Listen to me!" He was crying and laughing all at once. His cheek stung with heat. *"Listen to me!"*

Bridget struggled, her eyes wild. Suddenly he rattled her, and she froze, her chest heaving. To his own disgust, the fear in her eyes gratified him. He panted in her face, his cheeks wet with tears, stray gusts of laughter shaking his shoulders. He jerked her up against him, still gripping her wrists.

"Everything I do," he whispered wetly in her ear, *"everything I do,* I do for you and the children! Do you understand? It doesn't matter how low, how underhanded, how *mean* it is, *I do it for you!"*

He barely recognized his own voice, hoarse with snot and nearly incoherent. He and Bridget stood nose to nose. She was wild-eyed with fright, breathing hard. Her wrists twisted slightly in his grip. He was scarcely aware of his burning finger, pressed against her flesh.

"Why can't I make you *happy,* Bridget?" His voice broke, and he started to cry. "Just be happy, Bridget, okay, please? Just let me make you *happy. . . ."*

His finger sparked, taking him by surprise. Bridget shuddered in his grasp. She gave a little cry and blinked at him. Even in the dim blue light from the computer screen, Nelson could see her face relax, see the rage evaporate.

He released her and stepped back, his hands trembling. "Oh, God," he whimpered. "Oh, God, no. Wait a second. Hold on now. Sweetie, don't listen to me. . . ."

Bridget swayed from side to side. She rolled her shoulders, and tilted her head to one side. Her eyes shined moistly in the dark. She smiled at him. To his dying day, Nelson would remember the look of pure joy crossing his wife's face as the worst thing he ever saw.

"Oh, *Nelson!*" she crooned. "Oh, my darling man!" Before he could stop her, she threw her arms about him, her cheek pressed to his, murmuring in his ear.

"Oh, sweetheart, you don't have to say a thing! Whatever you're doing, I know it's for the best."

Nelson tried to peel her away with his left hand, but he kept his right hand in the air over his head, afraid to touch her again. "Don't," he whispered.

She pulled back from him, her fingers linked behind his neck. Her eyes glistened; her skin glowed. She looked ten years younger.

"Make love to me," she murmured.

Nelson's heart twisted, and he felt himself shrivel. He knew he could stop her with a touch, but what would he say to her? Don't be happy?

"I . . . I can't," he whispered.

"No?" She pursed her lips and canted her head.

"It's late," he managed to say.

"Oh, my poor baby," she cooed. He'd heard her say this before, but never so unironically. It chilled him to his spine. "Let's get you to bed," she said, threading her hand through his elbow and leading him toward the stairs. He half-turned to his desk, meaning to turn off his computer, but she tugged him on.

"I'll take care of it," she said. "You work much too hard, my darling."

Numbed, he let her lead him up the stairs. Halfway up, she stopped and threw her arms about him again. Nelson held her stiffly, his right hand hovering in space, away from his wife.

"I'm the luckiest woman on the planet, Nelson," she whispered. "You make me so *proud*."

15

Curriculum Vita

When Nelson awoke at six the next morning for his eight o'clock class, Bridget was already out of bed. He followed a rich aroma of gourmet coffee downstairs to find his beaming wife bustling about the table in a skirt, a blouse, and makeup, while his daughters sullenly tugged at the collars of pinafores they wore only when they saw their grandparents. Brought up short in the middle of his suddenly tidy living room, his cheeks still stinging from aftershave, Nelson saw the good plates on the table instead of plastic ones, matching juice glasses instead of Pokémon cups from Burger King, a creamy tablecloth, a bowl of fruit, and a toast rack he didn't even know they had.

For a moment he thought he was still asleep. On those occasions when he didn't bolt out the door with a cold Pop Tart, breakfast at the Humboldts was usually screamingly entropic—Nelson in sweat pants and T-shirt, smelling of his underarms and grinding ancient Froot Loops to dust in the carpet; the girls in their nightshirts or half-naked twisting in their seats and splashing milk everywhere; Bridget in her threadbare bathrobe, hair disheveled, bags under her eyes, leaning on one elbow and chewing half a slice of dry white toast.

"Girls! Say good morning to your father!" Bridget, radiant this morning in eyeliner and blusher, posed in the kitchen doorway with colorful oven mitts on her hands.

"Good morning, Father," mumbled Abigail and Clara.

"I know you're pressed for time in the morning," Bridget said, coming grandly around the table like Jane Wyatt, "so I kept breakfast simple." She ushered Nelson into his chair and hovered over him with a tropical oven mitt lightly on his shoulder. "We have Belgian waffles with strawberries and cream, or, if you prefer, we have baked eggs Gruyère and whole wheat toast."

Nelson numbly surveyed the table, avoiding the eyes of his daughters. They were glaring at him.

"Or would you prefer a bagel?" said Bridget, her eyes shining with solicitousness. "We have plain, egg, garlic, onion, onion and garlic, cinnamon raisin, sun-dried tomato . . ."

"Say *something,* Daddy," muttered Clara. "We can't eat until you do."

"Bagel," Nelson said hoarsely.

"Plain, egg, garlic, onion . . . ?"

"Plain," said Nelson, and Bridget swung around the table and into the kitchen, humming.

Clara fixed her father with an accusing stare. "Isn't the living room *clean,* Daddy?" she said, through gritted teeth. "Mommy got us up at *four* this morning, and we picked *everything up.* Isn't it *nice?*"

"Clean!" shouted Abigail, yanking angrily at her stiff little collar. "Clean! Clean! Clean! Clean! Clean!"

"Nelson, darling?" sang Bridget from the kitchen. "Do you want butter on your bagel? Salted or unsalted? Or lox? Or cream cheese? We have plain, garlic, herbed, herbed garlic. . . ."

Nelson jumped up from the table, his finger troubling him, and went into the kitchen. He did not touch his wife, but only snatched a bagel from the immaculate cutting board in front of her. She blinked at him, startled, and for a terrifying instant Nelson saw something like fear in her eyes.

"I gotta go," he said, averting his gaze. "Um, don't do anything complicated for dinner, okay?"

Her eyes softened.

"Of course not, darling!" she cooed, and Nelson fled.

On campus, Nelson tried all day to get in touch with Vita. He sent her e-mails; he called her machine at home and left a message; he left the largest, yellowest Post-it he could find in the center of her desk blotter. He even went out to a pay phone and left a voice mail message on their office phone, returning to the office to find the red light blinking steadily. He hurried back after every class to catch her at her desk, but either she wasn't coming in at all or she was avoiding him.

He still wasn't sure what he was going to do about, or with, or to, or for Vita. What Victorinix had proposed the night before throbbed at the back of his head like a bruise; no matter what else he tried to think about, it was always there. But he also remembered that brief moment of fear and uncertainty he'd seen in Victoria's eyes, and that memory eclipsed the pain somewhat. What if he took Victoria on directly? She was plainly afraid that he would, which told him that he had a chance of succeeding. But even if he did, he and Vita would remain untenured. What if Victorinix were right, that the only way to tenure for him was through Vita?

At the end of the day, returning to the office after his last class, he paused inside the door, keys in one hand, student papers in the other, and smelled Vita's strong soap. A glance told him she wasn't there—the blinds were shut, her chair was pushed in—but the big yellow Post-it was gone from the center of her blotter. Nelson dropped his papers on his desk and opened the semester schedule booklet, tracing the listing of graduate English classes with his smoldering finger. He found Vita's graduate seminar—on Wilde and gender—and noted the room number. It was ending just about now, as the sun was going down.

The lobby between Harbour Hall and the adjoining classroom building was empty this late in the afternoon, the fluorescent lights gleaming, the floor slick with tracked-in snow. Nelson took his time. When he saw Vita, when he was able to lay his finger along the inside of her wrist, what would he say to her? He could end her career on the spot; he could dispatch her the way he had dispatched the Coogan. He could tell her to leave and save the department the trouble of firing her, to save herself the embarrassment, to make way for him. . . .

He took the stairs to the third floor of the classroom building. The hallway lights were just flickering on in the interior dusk, and Nelson walked alternately in glare and darkness up an empty hallway of scuffed yellow tile, accompanied only by the reverberation of his own squeaking footsteps. Perhaps he could touch Vita and make her comfortable with her own . . . what? Femininity? Masculinity? (Even now, he couldn't bring himself to think of her as "he.") Perhaps he ought to tell her, as he took her by the hand, simply to be comfortable in her own skin.

At the moment, though, he was mainly curious. Who was Vita? *What* was she? And what did she *think* she was? In the door well of her classroom he peered through the half-open door. Her students were gone. The shades were drawn within, making the room even dimmer than the hallway; the classroom's little tables were fitted into a hexagon, surrounded by a jumble of mismatched chairs.

He saw Vita's satchel, a legal pad, and a well-thumbed Penguin of *De Profundis* on one side of the hexagon. Holding his breath, he heard the swoosh of an eraser against a chalkboard.

Nelson had often wondered about Vita as a teacher. He had never sat in on one of her classes, but he'd heard she had a reputation for severity. As querulous as she was with her institutional betters, she was evidently rigorously doctrinaire with her students. He had seen one of her syllabi once, in which she had provided her students, on their first day in class, with a list of words they were forbidden to use; anyone who used *truth, beauty, universal, book, story, author,* or *literary* would be flunked immediately.

I wonder if anybody ever tried? Nelson had wondered. Today he concluded that he'd never know, and he stepped into the classroom and pulled the door shut quietly. To the right of the door, Vita was methodically wiping the blackboard with parallel strokes of a small eraser. She stiffened slightly under his gaze, but she kept cleaning the chalkboard, pretending she didn't know he was there. She stood on tiptoe to reach the top of the board, and Nelson's glance slid automatically in a long *S* curve down the inside of her arm and along her chest, across her waist, around her backside, and down her extended thigh and calf. She wore her usual baggy sweater and loose trousers, and Nelson detected no sign of her gender, one way or the other.

He locked the door. At the click Vita mimed startlement, not very convincingly.

"Nelson!" she gasped. She clutched the eraser with both hands.

"Vita." Nelson leaned against the door, his hands curled around the knob behind him.

"You frightened me." She stepped back, pressing the eraser to her sweater.

"Did I?" he said.

Nelson didn't move, but Vita kept backing away. "I got your note," she said. "What did you want to see me about?"

She glanced at the eraser in her hands, then quickly set it on the ledge under the blackboard. There was a pale rectangle of chalk dust on her sweater, centered neatly over her sternum. Between where her breasts ought to be, thought Nelson.

"Who are you, Vita?" Nelson pushed away from the door.

In the twilight of the classroom Vita looked gray in her shapeless clothes. He could make out her round face, her bangs cut straight across, her eyes fixed on him from behind her glasses.

"Anthony's scheduled a job talk for me. Next week. On a Friday." She backed around the hexagonal table. "Why do you think he scheduled it on a Friday, Nelson? Why give me all week to worry about it?"

"You didn't answer my question." Nelson continued slowly toward her.

"Why not have the job talk on a Monday?" Vita insisted. "Or some evening earlier in the week? Why does he want me to wait so long?"

She backed into a stray chair, making it screech against the linoleum. She yelped and jumped away from it.

"Who are you, Vita?" Nelson said.

She narrowed her eyes at Nelson. "Who told you to ask me that?" She was nearly whispering.

"I've been reading your work, Vita." Nelson lifted the stray chair silently out of his way with both hands. "You've got me thinking about the nature of identity."

He stopped and laid his hand with its burning finger against the cool blackboard.

"So who are you, Vita? *What* are you? That picture on your desk of your 'brother' "—Nelson mimed quotation marks—"that was you, wasn't it?"

Vita came to her place at the table. Without taking her eyes from Nelson, she stuffed the notepad roughly into the satchel so that a corner of it stuck out; then she shoved the book in after it; then she tried to pick up a pen from the tabletop. She fumbled at it three times before she got her fingernails under it, and then she dropped it. The pen skittered under the table, and she bent to pick it up, glancing away from Nelson for an instant.

Nelson pushed away from the blackboard and came around the hexagon. At the scrape of his shoes Vita glanced wide-eyed over the edge of the table and shot to her feet, snatching up her satchel before her like a shield.

"Are you sure," she said with a quaver in her voice, "that you are intellectually prepared to unpack the complexities of identity, Nelson? Especially mine?"

"You're a professional teacher, Vita." Nelson's finger burned hotter. "Teach me."

They stood across the hexagon from each other. Clutching her satchel with both hands, Vita glanced at the door, then at Nelson. She twitched toward the door, and Nelson lurched sideways in the same direction, startling a chair. She lunged the other way, and Nelson countered, his finger flaring.

"Come on, Vita," he said. "Knock it off."

Vita trembled on the far side of the table. "Are, are, are you going to Mort Weissmann's party?" she asked. "Do you think I should go? If I don't, it might hurt my chances of tenure, but if I do . . ."

"Answer the goddamn question!" Nelson shouted. His finger scalded him. I should just vault the table, he thought, and put an end to this.

Vita's eyes shot all over the room, looking for a way out.

"Isn't it the case," she said, her voice quavering, "that to name what I am is to diminish me, to acknowledge the authority of hegemonic culture over me? Could we not say that to name me is to reduce me to a subject of power, to subject me?"

"I'll ask the questions, Vita." Nelson clenched and unclenched his fists. "Is this one of those deals where you've always known you were a woman? Are you one of those 'woman trapped in a man's body' kind of guys?"

Vita twisted her satchel between her hands.

"Could I not just as easily say that I'm a man trapped in a woman's body?"

"But you have a man's body!" Nelson exploded. He pounded the tabletop before him.

Or does she? Nelson wondered, even in his rage. Maybe Victorinix had lied; maybe she told Nelson that Vita was a man as a way to drive a wedge between them.

"Vita," Nelson said, his finger searing him, "I need you to take off your clothes. . . ."

Vita yelped and jumped six inches straight up in the air.

"I knew it!" she cried. "You want to rape me!"

Nelson staggered back as if she'd punched him in the stomach.

"No!" he gasped. "I'd never . . . I wouldn't . . ." He unclenched his fists and held up his palms. "Vita, I just need to know if you have a penis, and if you don't, then we don't have a problem."

"If I do have a penis," Vita said, tightening her grip on the satchel and narrowing her eyes, "would that necessarily make me a man?"

"Yes!" shouted Nelson.

"Could we not say that such a claim on the basis of mere materiality is essentialist in the extreme?"

"Okay, so you're a woman!" Nelson threw up his hands. "Why not just get the operation, for God's sake? Why *pretend?*"

"But doesn't the culture of the 'operation' presuppose that sex is gender?"

Vita's knuckles were turning white as she gripped the satchel. "Why should I have myself cut and mutilated to determine who I am?"

"Drop your pants, Vita!" Nelson jabbed his burning finger at Vita. "Let's get this over with!"

"Could it not be the case that the 'body' is not coterminous with identity?"

"Drop your pants," Nelson cried, shaking his finger violently at her, "or I'll do it for you!"

"Isn't it the case that identity, gender, and, indeed, body are radically polysemic, that their spurious unity is only a product of hegemony as a modality of social control . . . ?"

Bellowing, Nelson heaved the tables apart with a tremendous clatter and waded across the center of the hexagon. Vita flung her satchel at him two-handed as if she were passing a basketball, straight at his head. He caught the case with both hands, staggered under the surprising force of it, and flung it back at her. But Vita had already dodged around the side of the hexagon nearest the door. Nelson sprang for the nearest table, vaulted it one-handed, and landed on the other side, his feet scrabbling on the linoleum. Vita rattled the knob, then fumbled frantically at the lock, glancing back at him, her hair flying. Nelson slammed the door shut just as she got it open, pressing it with all his weight in the palm of his hand. Vita tried to duck around him the other way, but he blocked her with his other hand against the blackboard, barricading her in the corner.

The slam of the door reverberated down the empty hall. They breathed hard in each other's faces. The pale rectangle of chalk dust on Vita's sweater heaved up and down in the dark.

"What have you got that I haven't got?" Nelson glared down at Vita. "Why are you tenure track while I'm dragging my family through the *shit* just to keep a crummy fucking lectureship?"

Vita pressed her hands to the walls on either side, as wild-eyed as Lillian Gish on an ice floe.

"I'll tell you what you haven't got," Nelson said, "and that's a goddamn vagina!"

He thrust his burning finger within an inch of Vita's nose. "Just what do you think you're doing, Vita?" he said. "Help me understand. Are you *passing?* Is that it?"

Vita grabbed Nelson's wrist so fast that Nelson was shocked into silence. In a breathless instant Vita had twisted Nelson's right arm behind his back and forced him up against the wall. Nelson's cheek was mashed against the cool blackboard. Behind him his finger flared, searing him all the way up his arm.

"Ow!" he cried.

"You're a self-pitying fool," Vita breathed, "if you think the way to get ahead in academia is by posing as a woman."

"Let me go!" Nelson said, but Vita held him tightly by the wrist, slowly twisting his hand. He struggled to yank it free, but Vita only pushed his wrist higher, up between his shoulder blades.

"Once upon a time," she said through gritted teeth, "my name was Robin. I lived as a man, I thought as a man, I loved as a man. But this disgusted me. It made me ashamed. I loved women and hated them; I felt their pain and inflicted it, all at once. Was I passing then, Nelson? Can you *pass* when you have no choice?"

"God*dammit,* Vita . . ." He could barely speak for the discomfort; his eye was squeezed shut against the blackboard. The smell of chalk was overwhelming.

"Because all the *rights* and *privileges* I had as a man," Vita continued, twisting Nelson's arm for emphasis, "were normative and prescriptive, imposed on me by the voice of an authority that names me, and is therefore inherently dictatorial and oppressive."

Nelson groaned, his breath misting the blackboard. He lowered his shoulder as she pushed his arm back, the pain in his arm socket as sharp as the pain in his finger. He slapped the blackboard uselessly with his other hand. Fucking *bitch*, he thought.

"Power is all there is, Nelson." Vita's breath warmed his ear. "Power is everywhere, power subsumes everything, there is nothing to oppose power. Everything presupposes power, everything is derived from power. Only from power can you derive the ability to subvert it, to transgress it, and so I used my power to be what I loved."

Tears squeezed out of the corners of Nelson's eyes. He was damned if he would cry uncle.

"So let me get this straight," he managed to say with his cheek flattened against the blackboard. "You decided to be a woman because *you feel sorry for them?*"

Vita twisted Nelson's wrist tighter still, and he gasped. His knees trembled. His finger scalded him, burning hotter than it ever had before. Out of the corner of his eye Nelson saw Vita's face just beyond his twisted shoulder. Her gaze was unnaturally bright in the dusk of the classroom.

"When I was a man, Nelson, I thought like a man, I reasoned like a man. But when I became a woman, I put away masculine things. Now you see me as in a glass, darkly, but soon we will meet face to face. Now you know me in part; soon you will see me as I see myself. Race, class, and gender abide, these three: but the greatest of these is gender."

Vita released Nelson. A backwash of heat from his finger seared him all the way up to his shoulder, and with a cry he sank to his knees and collapsed against the wall. He squeezed his eyes shut against the pain, supporting his right wrist with his left hand. The blackness behind his eyelids swam with stars, his heart pounded in his chest. He heard Vita's footsteps, the brief screech of a chair being moved, the scrape of her shoe as she bent to pick up her satchel.

He cracked his eyelids, and out of the swimming motes of light, he saw Vita standing over him. Her hair was awry, her face flushed. Her eyes were full of a crazy light.

"What do you think I should wear to Weissmann's party Saturday?" she asked, and she stripped off her sweater.

Nelson's finger was suddenly as numb as a stone, but his wrist burned where Vita had twisted it, and his shoulder throbbed.

"Oh, my God, Nelson, I suppose Miranda will be dressed to kill."

Under her sweater, Vita had the flat chest and broad shoulders of a man.

"Should I even try to compete? Or would I just look foolish?"

She kicked off her shoes, and they flapped against the wall on either side of Nelson. "But what if I don't dress up?" Her hands worked at the waistband of her slacks.

"Oh, God, will the tenure committee be offended if I don't? Will Anthony expect me to wear a cocktail dress? Would it hurt me or help me to show off my legs?"

Vita dropped her trousers and kicked them away. Through red waves of pain Nelson saw, just above his eye level, a pair of firm thighs, a flat belly, and a purplish penis dangling from a nest of dark, wiry curls.

"Or will everybody only laugh at me if I do . . . ?"

Vita pressed her palm to her cheek and canted her head. Above Nelson stood a trim, not overly muscular young man with shoulder-length hair cut in bangs. All Vita wore was a pair of glasses.

"I don't like being laughed at," Vita murmured, as if to herself. "I don't look good in black."

Nelson lunged, crying out from the pain in his arm as he tried to grab Vita with his right hand, to relieve the heat in his burning finger against Vita's flesh. But he grasped only air, landing painfully on his shoulder. Looking up from the floor he saw the classroom door swinging open. From the hall he heard the slap of bare feet.

Nelson, groaning, pushed himself to his feet, kicking away Vita's sweater and slacks. He staggered into the door well. His heart hammering, motes still swimming before his eyes, he peered down the hall.

The lights in the hall were still flickering, but in an odd way: Each fixture came on as Vita passed below it, only to flicker off again as she passed beyond it. She capered down the hallway as if under a stuttering spotlight, kicking her heels, swinging the satchel by its handle. Her hair flew, her penis flopped. Nelson pressed his hand against the wall, afraid he'd fall over, and he heard something that evaporated the heat in his finger and chilled him all the way to his spine. He couldn't be certain, but it seemed to him that Vita Deonne was laughing.

For dinner that night Bridget had prepared beef wellington, Dauphine potatoes, and steamed baby peas with a mirepoix. Abigail and Clara stared at their plates in sullen incredulity.

"You told me to keep it simple, darling!" protested Bridget cheerfully.

After dinner, in his basement office, he checked his e-mail. Above his computer screen, in the bluish light of the furnace, the map of England was one large, glistening, sodden blot, with only the tip of Cornwall, Guernsey, and the Shetland Islands visible at the margins.

He found a message from Victoria Victorinix, which read simply, "Well?"

Nelson drummed his fingers on the desk top. His arm was still sore from this afternoon. Dealing with Vita was going to be harder than he thought. I can't risk talking to her in private again, he decided. It'll have to be somewhere public, someplace with lots of people around.

He lifted his hands to the keyboard, but he didn't touch the keys. He smiled to himself and lowered his hands. The keys clattered under his touch.

"I'll see you Saturday night," he wrote to Victorinix, "at Weissmann's party."

16

The St. Valentine's Day Massacre

Morton Weissmann lived in a comfortable old neighborhood of long streets and huge old trees. Most of his neighbors were likewise tenured professors, many of the same generation as Weissmann: late middle-aged or even elderly men with much younger wives and large, well-appointed houses—massive bookcases, a lavishly stocked liquor cabinet, two or three surprisingly young children—where they lived a Cheeveresque life of the mind circumscribed by the *New York Times,* the *New York Review of Books,* and National Public Radio. Tonight, as Nelson and Bridget arrived in their rattling old subcompact, Weissmann's street looked like a Christmas card, with the old maples on either side forming a dark web of bare branches against a brilliantly starry sky, each snow-covered yard lit by the warm glow of porch lights and living room windows. Here and there a snowman stood on a snowy lawn, the creation of some professor's second family by a former graduate student.

"Oh, Nelson!" Bridget clutched her husband's wrist, her eyes gleaming in the drafty dark inside the car. "Wouldn't it be *wonderful* to live on a street like this?"

Nelson smiled. The smell of Bridget's perfume in the small car was arousing him a little. When Nelson had told her that he was taking her to the department's annual Valentine's Day party, Bridget had thrown her arms around his neck. The fact that they had not gone for the previous three years—a fact that used to stand for their humiliation like a coat of arms—didn't seem to matter anymore. Now, under her coat, Bridget wore a striking little black dress that showed off her shoulders and lifted her bosom and drew attention to her still-handsome dancer's thighs. When he had first seen her in the dress that evening, striding toward him on high heels, head canted and hands lifted to fit an earring, he concluded that his accidental touching of her the week before may not have been such a bad thing after all.

Weissmann's mock-Tudor house was charmingly lit by discreet little spotlights in the bushes; a line of cars gleamed in the porch lights along each side of the street. Nelson parked, and then came around the car to hold the tips of Bridget's fingers as she tiptoed through the snow to the sidewalk. Coming up the walk to Weissmann's front door, she took his arm and switched on her party smile. Nelson heaved open the heavy oaken door without knocking, but he held Bridget back in the vestibule so that he could check the lay of the land. Directly ahead were the stairs to the second floor, while to the right, junior professors and lecturers clustered across the deep carpet of Weissmann's parlor, murmuring to each other amid the dim lamps and overstuffed furniture—sizing each other up, silently surveying their own prospects, trashing the reputations of those whose backs were turned. Threading her way through the clustered professors, Miranda DeLaTour was walking away from Nelson in a shimmering red dress with her hair up, revealing a long reach of bare back. Everyone in the room, men and women, was either sneaking glances or openly staring as she passed.

Nelson shifted his gaze left of the stairs to the wainscoted dining room where Weissmann's long dining table was lined with tall red candles and crowded with plates of candies, cakes, crudités, and cocktail weenies. At the far end stood a little skyline of bottles—bourbon, vodka, tonic water. In the warm candlelight the department's graduate students were crowded two deep at the table, pretending to graze but gorging on the free food, meanwhile watching as nervously as gazelles for larger, more powerful animals. Somewhere farther back in the house Ella Fitzgerald was singing "Bewitched, Bothered, and Bewildered."

"Nelson!" cried Mort Weissmann, listing out of the parlor, his big hands spread wide. "And your lovely wife, ah, um . . ."

"Bridget!" She canted her head and beamed at the professor. "Thank you *so much* for inviting us!"

Weissmann grasped her by the shoulders and peered through her open coat straight down the front of her dress.

"Charming!" he muttered hoarsely, his liquid eyes fixed on Bridget's breasts. "Splendid!"

For years Weissmann's annual Valentine's Day party had run in cycles, alternating between his married years and his bachelor years. During his marriages, each party had been an elaborate affair, with decorations and games and seasonal delicacies and one beaming wife or another to do all the work. Weissmann himself had presided in a red cardigan and tie. In between marriages, during his cycles of predation, Weissmann had not bothered with decorations or games or special foods; everything was catered, the lights were dimmer, the music louder. During these years Weissmann wore an open-necked shirt and tight trousers and Italian loafers. But it had been years since he had lured a graduate student into marriage or since he had looked presentable in tight clothing or an open-necked anything. Tonight he wore a smoking jacket and a red cravat; and though it was hard to tell in the dim party light, he seemed to have dyed the gray out of his hair. He wrapped his arms around Bridget and planted a wet kiss near her ear, burying his cheek in her hair and closing his eyes. Bridget shone her party smile at the ceiling and rolled her eyes at Nelson, who put his smoldering finger on the back of Weissmann's hand.

"Help her with her coat, Mort," he said.

Weissmann lurched back, blinking, and Bridget allowed herself to be turned out of her coat. Nelson steered her away by the elbow while Weissmann ran his eyes down her back.

"Where is everybody, Mort?" Nelson said.

Weissmann, still watching Bridget, kneaded the collar of her coat in both hands. His eyes flickered toward Nelson. "Everybody important," he said in a wet, ninety-proof whisper, "is in the back, in the study."

Nelson started after his wife into the dining room, but Weissmann caught his sleeve.

"Nelson!" He attempted a hoarse sotto voce, but succeeded in drawing glances from the crowd at the dining room table. Nelson did not turn, so Weissmann hurried after him, clutching Bridget's coat like an obsequious maitre d'.

"When you have a moment, Nelson," he said, his eyes desperately alight, "we need to speak somewhere in private. We need to . . ."

Nelson lay his hand on the spotted, papery skin of Weissmann's knuckles. "Careful with the coat, Mort," he said. "Put it somewhere safe."

Weissmann blinked and swayed and turned slowly toward the stairs to deposit Bridget's coat in an upstairs bedroom. Nelson steered his wife past the hunted eyes of the graduate students at the dining room table, noting the absence of the Lost Boys as he guided Bridget into the kitchen.

The music was louder now, Frank Sinatra singing "The Lady Is a Tramp." Nelson saw Miranda again ahead of him; she had circled the other way through the house to pose in the far doorway of the kitchen, her hip canted under the sheen of her dress, her long, red nails curled around a drink. She lifted the glass to her lips and met Nelson's eye over the rim. Nelson felt his face get hot, and Miranda smiled as if she might burst out laughing. Bridget followed Nelson's gaze over the heads of the crowd in the kitchen, and Nelson looked away and pretended to adjust his jacket collar. He was wearing the clothes Miranda had bought for him. Bridget wheeled in front of Nelson and ran her fingers under his lapels. "And who is that?" Bridget gave Nelson a narrow look.

"A-a-a colleague," said Nelson. "I forget her name."

A peal of giddy laughter caught both Nelson's and Bridget's attention; and as Bridget turned to look, Nelson saw Miranda turn and sway into the study. Meanwhile a giggling Penelope O was leaning against the kitchen counter in a red lace-up bustier and a leather miniskirt slit to her hip, at the center of a rapt semicircle of undergraduate boys and a pair of avid girls. She'd bent one knee to show more thigh, her spike heel denting the enamel of Weissmann's dishwasher. With the light over the sink limning her shoulders and teased hair, she was sloshing her martini glass so that the semicircle of admirers, mindful of their shoes, stepped back with each sweep of the glass and then contracted again like a single organism, keeping close to her.

"When I was on a hiring committee at the University of Washington," she was saying, "we didn't even *read* the CVs of white men. I mean, *really . . . !*"

She swung the glass again and tossed her head, and the young men licked their lips and swayed back and forward.

". . . the last thing that department needed was *more white men!*" Penelope laughed and swung the glass to her lips, and her admirers nodded earnestly and murmured agreement, their eyes fixed on Penelope's cinched breasts, her shapely waist, her firm calves. Nelson squeezed Bridget's shoulders and then sidled through the crescent of boys and girls to Penelope, ignoring the sharp glances and muttered imprecations.

"You're looking lovely tonight, Penelope." Nelson lay his hand on her bare shoulder.

Her eyes had the same wobbly, liquid gleam as Weissmann's as she surveyed Nelson from head to toe. She gave him a slow, lubricious smile. "You're not looking too bad yourself, Norton," she said, with a matey inflection.

"It's Nelson," said Nelson, pressing his finger into her shoulder blade and leaning forward.

"Say, listen," he whispered, "have you ever noticed what a *really good-looking guy* Mort Weissmann is? For an older man, he's pretty damn hot." He leaned closer, brushing her ear with his lips. "I hear he fucks like a savage."

Nelson stood away as Penelope blinked rapidly. She wobbled frighteningly on her one spike heel. The other heel gouged a little arc in the face of the dishwasher. Nelson waded back through the knot of boys to his wife.

"Another colleague?" Bridget said, but he only folded her hand through his arm and led her toward the back of the house.

At the end of a short hall leading from the kitchen, Weissmann's study was the largest room in the house, a long, high-ceilinged hall like an English gentleman's library, with tall bookcases and long windows and dark, exposed beams. Discreet but expensive speakers at the room's corners poured more Ella Fitzgerald over the crowd. Nelson paused with Bridget in the archway. At one end of the room, on a stiff, six-legged couch before a blazing fire, Victoria Victorinix looked up sharply from the cluster of female graduate students at her feet, silencing with a gesture one who was gesticulating earnestly. Behind the sofa Gillian came out of the shadows into the flickering firelight, biting her lip at Nelson like a fearful child regarding a large and dangerous dog. At the other end of the study, behind Weissmann's massive old wooden desk, Anthony Pescecane stopped his restless swiveling in Weissmann's desk chair to glare at Nelson over the letter opener propped between his index fingers. Miranda was leaning against the desk with her smooth back to Nelson again, and she only half-turned to see what Pescecane was looking at, a screen of hair before her eyes. Lionel Grossmaul hunched in the shadows between two bookcases behind Pescecane, and at the sight of Nelson he nearly choked on a mouthful of beer.

"Gang's all here," Nelson murmured, leading Bridget into the study. Ella started to sing "Something's Gotta Give."

Nelson steered Bridget through the crowd into the middle of the room, where the Canadian Lady Novelist was improbably in conversation with Marko Kraljević and Lorraine Alsace. Tonight Kraljević was dressed as a Cub Scout, complete with blue shorts, gold neckerchief, and a little blue cap over his close-cropped hair. He had his back to Nelson, but as Nelson approached, Lorraine Alsace clutched Kraljević by the shoulder and hissed something in his ear. Kraljević whirled and instantly swung Alsace in front of him, placing her between himself and Nelson. The Canadian Lady Novelist, meanwhile, shined her Olympian smile on Nelson and Bridget.

"Happy Valentine's Day, Professor!" she said with a nod.

"And to you," said Nelson, smirking past Bridget at the little blue cap bobbing behind Lorraine Alsace's shoulder. "I'd like you to meet my wife, Bridget," he added, and Bridget offered her hand, first to the Novelist, who gave her a three-fingered shake like a British royal, then to Alsace, who gripped it limply.

"So nice to meet you!" Bridget said, and she twisted her shoulders to offer her hand around Alsace to Kraljević, who refused to take it, glancing fearfully past his partner.

Nelson, taller than everyone present, lifted his eyes toward Victorinix across the room. She turned, the pale dome of her skull unwarmed by the firelight, and reached behind the couch to clutch Gillian, who stooped as Victorinix whispered urgently in her ear. Gillian cast about for a place to set her drink and came from behind the couch.

Nelson glanced over his shoulder at Pescecane, who was gesturing in Nelson's direction to Grossmaul. The wad of white tape holding the bridge of Lionel's glasses together bobbed up and down.

"Nelson!" Bridget touched his shoulder to get his attention. "Someone's talking to you, darling!" He turned to see the Canadian Lady Novelist smiling at him.

"I was saying that you're making quite a splash in the department these days." The Novelist rolled a glass between her large hands. "I'm hearing all sorts of interesting things about you from my spies."

Behind her, Kraljević was creeping in a wide circle, with Alsace propped in front of him as a human shield.

"Darling, isn't that *wonderful?*" Bridget blinked happily. "You're the man of the hour!"

Before Nelson could reply, he was touched on both elbows simultaneously.

"Victoria wants to speak to you," said Gillian on one side, while on the other Lionel gulped, "Anthony wants you."

Nelson held up his hands. His finger burned him. "Don't fight over me, girls!" he laughed.

Behind his broken glasses—one lens was cracked all the way across—Lionel Grossmaul's eyes popped open as if he'd been slapped. Gillian kept a pace or two back.

"I'm sorry." Nelson smiled at the Novelist and his wife. "Duty calls."

He turned to Gillian. Over her shoulder he saw Victorinix cutting through the crowd. "Let's go," he said, watching Victorinix pass through the short hallway and disappear into the kitchen.

As Gillian backed out of Nelson's reach, Lionel tugged violently at his sleeve. "Anthony wants to see you," he said, and Nelson whirled and caught him by the wrist. Lionel tried to pull free, but Nelson tightened and twisted his grip. The Novelist blinked nervously, while Bridget's smile stiffened.

"Tell Anthony . . ." Nelson paused. "Tell him whatever you want."

His finger sparked. Lionel sucked his breath in sharply and blinked behind his cracked glasses. Nelson released him. Lionel's face turned red; his eyes bulged. He pivoted away on his heel.

"Anthony!" Lionel shouted loud enough to stop conversation around the room. "I want to talk to you!"

"Will you ladies excuse me?" Nelson said to the Canadian Lady Novelist and his wife.

Gillian backed through the crowd, never taking her eyes off Nelson. Kraljević cowered in a corner of the room under a speaker, with Alsace propped in front of him. Behind him, Nelson heard his wife apologizing on his behalf to the Novelist, who was following Nelson's departure with a look of maternal concern.

"Now you know what my life's like these days," Bridget was saying with mock frustration. "I hardly *ever* see him anymore. . . ."

Gillian led Nelson through the kitchen, where the young men who had been hovering around Penelope O were milling aimlessly without her. Through the archway into the dining room, Nelson saw Weissmann at the far end of the table, trying to interest the obliviously grazing crowd in his annual cutting of a heart-shaped cake, usually an occasion for Mort to make a semicoherent encomium to love, crammed with half-remembered quotes and jokes of his own. But tonight Penelope O had backed him with her swelling bosom into a corner of the wainscoting, where he stood on tiptoe with the cake cradled in one arm and the knife brandished defensively across his chest. Fixing him with her shining gaze, Penelope swiped the cake with her index finger and licked the frosting off her finger with long, slow strokes of her tongue.

"Here," said Gillian. She stood in a little nook under the stairs, behind an open door, keeping it between her and Nelson. A paneled, carpeted stairway led into Weissmann's basement, dimly lit by an overhead fixture.

"She waits," said Gillian.

"After you," said Nelson.

Gillian shook her head and stepped back from the door, letting it swing free. Nelson shrugged and started down the stairs. He heard Gillian's heavy tread behind him on the top step. The party faded: the susurrus of chatter; Lionel Grossmaul calling for Anthony Pescecane to *"Listen to me,* goddammit!"; Sinatra singing "I Got It Bad and That Ain't Good."

Nelson descended a couple of steps, listening for Gillian behind him. As soon as he heard the tap of the door closing, he turned and lunged, grasping Gillian by the throat. She reared back wide-eyed, flattening herself against the door. Nelson tightened his grip. His finger sparked again.

"She doesn't love you," Nelson said. "She never will."

He let go of Gillian, and she sagged slowly down the door to the top of the steps. She stared straight ahead for a moment with her mouth slack and her sunken eyes filling with tears. Then she dropped her face into her hands and began to weep. Her shoulders heaved, tears dripped through her fingers to the carpet. Nelson turned and went down the stairs.

At the bottom he rounded a corner into a narrow hallway paneled with cheap plywood and lit by a single, yellow bulb. The stiff indoor-outdoor carpeting smelled of mold. There were two open doorways, one on either side. Out of the door on the right came the flat voices and flickering blue glare of a television. Nelson peered in. Silhouetted against the TV light, the Lost Boys leaned forward on the edge of an old leather sofa. On the screen of the large television, whooping Zulu warriors charged through yellow grass under a flawlessly blue sky, toward a rampart of mealie bags manned by red-coated British soldiers. A volley cracked and rattled, smoke gushed across the screen, and dozens of Zulus clutched their naked chests and rolled their eyes and fell. The Lost Boys pumped their fists, bit their lips, stamped their feet.

"Get 'em!" cried Vic.

"Kill 'em all!" cried Dan.

"Fuck them *up!*" cried Bob.

"Story of our lives," said Vic, leaning back into the couch.

"I dunno," said Bob. "It's different somehow."

"What?" said Vic.

"How?" said Dan.

"The white guys win." Bob shrugged. All three of the Lost Boys sighed.

"Nelson," said a voice behind Nelson, and he crossed the hall and stood to one side of the opposite doorway. He narrowed his eyes. The feeble light from the hall and the glare from the TV did not penetrate the dark within the room. Through the door he could smell laundry detergent and the stink of a drain.

"Come into my parlor," said Victoria Victorinix out of the dark.

Nelson shook his head.

"I don't think so." He slid his hand along the rough wall inside the door and found the light switch. He flicked it with his burning finger, and nothing happened.

"Home field advantage." Victoria's voice had the flat reverberation of cinder block, impossible to place within the room.

Behind him Nelson heard an officer on the TV shouting orders.

"What have you done about Vita?" Victorinix said out of the darkness.

"What have you done about Kraljević?" Nelson kept just outside the door.

"You misunderstand your position, Nelson," said the voice. "You need me more than I need you."

"Shh." Nelson lifted his finger. "Listen."

The battle noise from across the hall had subsided, and in the relative quiet Gillian could be heard at the top of the basement stairs, sobbing. Nelson listened for Victorinix, but for a moment he heard nothing. "What did you do to her?" asked Victorinix at last. She sounded a little less sure of herself. Nelson was pleased.

"I told her the truth," said Nelson. "Now all I have to do is go back upstairs and tell Anthony to give me tenure, and I won't need you at all."

He started to turn away.

"Nelson!" hissed the voice in the laundry room.

He paused.

"Lorraine Alsace wrote the letters," said Victorinix. "Not the Coogan."

Nelson's finger stung him. He fought back a memory of the Coogan's empty office, a haunted place.

"And Anthony knew it all along, didn't he?" he said.

"Anthony wanted to use the letters as leverage," Victorinix said out of the dark, "to open up a budget line so that he could hire Alsace, if that's what it took to keep Kraljević."

"They served their purpose," said Nelson. "That's what you said."

He saw the poet kneeling in the snow. *Murderer,* gasped the Coogan.

"Anthony had to pin the letters on someone so there wouldn't be an uproar," Victorinix went on. "But apart from protecting Alsace, he didn't really care who left, as long as somebody did. The Coogan was the most vulnerable."

Thank God for that, said Penelope O. *The last thing the literature department needs is a poet.*

"So why did he bother with the other candidates?" Nelson said through a tight throat. "Why waste everyone's time?"

"Because he didn't want to give Kraljević that kind of clout," Victorinix said out of the dark. "He wasn't even sure he wanted to keep him. Kraljević didn't write the letters, but he has his own problems."

Nelson glanced back through the door behind him at the television. The Zulus had retreated; a sweaty, young Michael Caine was shouting orders. The phrase "Modern Weapons Systems" popped into Nelson's head.

"He not an anti-Milosevic Serb, is he?" Nelson said.

"He's not even Marko Kraljević," said Victorinix. "He was a member of the nationalist intellectual elite, the youngest member of the Praxis group, a professor at the National University who also led a paramilitary group in the recent troubles."

"So his reputation as a theorist . . ." Nelson began.

"Is legitimate, Nelson. There's no law that says you can't be a postmodernist *and* a war criminal." Victorinix laughed. "In some quarters, in fact, a reputation for atrocity actually adds to your cachet."

"But why did he flee Serbia then? Wouldn't he have been safer in Belgrade?"

"A number of paramilitary leaders, especially those who might know about Milosevic's involvement in ethnic cleansing, have been assassinated. It's easier to hide from Interpol than it is from your own former comrades."

"But why would Anthony allow him into the department?"

Victorinix's low laugh rang off the invisible cinder blocks. "You're such a child, Nelson," she said. "Don't you know that Anthony's developing a *brand* here? And that Kraljević is the major component of our brand identity? Anthony wants every book and article and graduate student we produce to come out as *ruthless* as Kraljević. Anthony doesn't care what else Kraljević does. Or has done."

"What exactly *has* Kraljević done?" Nelson managed to say.

A light switched on, a small fluorescent bulb over the laundry room sink. Nelson squinted against the sudden glare; he glimpsed a lime green washer and dryer, a sink, some metal shelves filled with boxes. A pair of patterned wool socks were draped forlornly over a wooden drying rack. As Nelson watched, Victorinix lowered her hand from the light fixture and picked up a small black object from the top of Weissmann's washing machine. Nelson backed away from the doorway. But Victorinix was holding a cordless phone. She tapped in a number.

"Who are you calling?" he said, but she ignored him.

"Is this the FBI?" she said into the phone. "I'd like to report a sighting of an international war criminal."

"What the . . . ?" Nelson said. What was the name beside Kraljević's picture on the Belgrade web page? It starts with a *J,* he thought.

"Jamisovich," she said, enunciating each syllable clearly into the phone, and then spelling it. "Slobodan Jamisovich. Also known as 'Commander Dragan.' " A pause. "No, don't talk, just listen. If you check with The Hague and Interpol, you'll find he's wanted for war crimes in Croatia and Bosnia, dating back ten years. I believe his nickname was 'the Butcher of Srebenica.' "

With the light coming from behind her, Nelson could scarcely make out Victorinix's face.

"It doesn't matter who I am," she said into the phone. "He's posing as a professor at the University of the Midwest in Hamilton Groves, Minnesota, under the name of Marko Kraljević." Once again she spelled the name. "This evening you'll find him at a Valentine's Day party at . . ."

She lowered the phone and covered the mouthpiece with her palm. "What's Weissmann's address, Nelson?" she asked.

Nelson backed away from the door. He glanced back up the narrow hall, gauging the distance to the stairs. Gillian had subsided to a whimper. There was almost no sound from the TV room behind him.

"Well, I don't know the address," Victorinix said into the phone, "but it's the home of Morton Weissmann, another professor in the same department. Literature." A pause. "Go ahead and trace the call if you like. This isn't my phone."

Victorinix pressed the disconnect button and lay the phone on the washing machine. Nelson tensed his knees; he shifted his weight to the balls of his feet.

"There, Nelson." Victoria's eyes glittered. "I've done my bit. Now, what have you done for me?"

Nelson bolted for the stairs. The light in the laundry room went out, as well as the light in the hallway. There was a rush of clammy air out of the laundry room door, and then a presence at his ear, very close. In the dark Nelson flattened himself against the paneling. An icy breath brushed his cheek.

"Better hurry, Nelson," whispered Victorinix. "I'm not entirely sure I need *you.*"

Nelson cringed away from her and staggered back through the door of the TV room. He heard Victorinix's chilly laugh move up the stairs. The light in the hall flickered on again, and he heard the murmur of voices, the waxing and waning of music from the top of the stairs. He could no longer hear Gillian.

He pressed himself against the wall just inside the TV room, his heart hammering, his finger burning him. On the television the Zulus had risen to their feet again, and they were chanting and rhythmically thumping their spears against their cowhide shields. Each of the Lost Boys was pitched forward on the sofa, on the edge of his seat. A Welsh soldier behind the British rampart began to sing in a handsome baritone, and one by one, all the other redcoats joined in.

"Men of Harlech, stop your dreaming," sang the soldier, *"can't you see their spear points gleaming?"*

The camera tracked along the rampart until all the redcoats were singing, while the Zulus chanted and stamped and hammered their shields. It was an imperial Battle of the Bands.

But someone else was singing along, not quite in tune—someone in the room. Nelson stirred from the wall and looked about him in the dark. The singer wasn't any of the Lost Boys. They had noticed the singing too, and they sat straight up on the couch and looked around like frightened prairie dogs.

"Are you . . . ?"

"Not me . . ."

"Then who . . . ?"

The whole regiment of white soldiers on screen sang lustily, but whoever was singing in the dark behind the couch was nearly as loud. One of the Boys muted the television. The song continued from out of the dark, in a warbling, unsteady tenor: *"Men of Harlech, come to glory, this will ever be your story. . . ."*

In the corner of the room, barely lit by the glow of the television, Stephen Michael Stephens slept in an old, overstuffed easy chair. His head bobbed and his mouth worked as he sang.

"Keep these burning words before ye," he sang slowly, with deep feeling, building to a finish, *"Welshmen do not yield!"*

308

Stephens's chin fell to his chest. The Lost Boys stared wide-eyed at the black man asleep in the dark. Behind them, on the TV screen, three ranks of British soldiers silently fired one after the other into a mass of undifferentiated black bodies.

"How long has *he* been there" said Bob.

"Do you think he heard us?" said Dan.

"Uh-oh," said Vic.

Nelson crossed through the dark at the back of the room toward Stephens, and the sudden movement startled the Lost Boys. They leaped to their feet with a single intake of breath. Nelson bent over Stephens without touching him.

"WAKE UP!" shouted Nelson.

Stephen Michael Stephens struggled to sit up in the overstuffed chair, and he blinked at the bright screen across the room. The sound was still off, and the camera was tracking slowly across a grotesquely writhing heap of glistening black bodies. Gut-shot Zulus struggled and failed to rise off their bellies. The camera came to rest upon three ranks of sweaty, dirty, wide-eyed white soldiers, their guns still smoking.

"Jesus wept," intoned Stephen Michael Stephens. "Jesus wept."

He pushed himself up from the chair and narrowed his eyes at the screen. Then he noticed the Lost Boys in a trembling knot to one side of the television set.

"It's just a movie," said Dan.

"Doesn't make me a racist," said Bob.

"I was rooting for the Zulus," said Vic.

"Me too!" said Bob.

"So was I!" said Dan.

"What on earth is wrong with you people?" shouted Stephen Michael Stephens, and he pushed past Nelson out of the room. A moment later Nelson heard the voice of Peggy Lee—"I'm Beginning to See the Light"—and then the slam of the basement door.

The Lost Boys rushed out of the dark next to the television and tried to dash past Nelson. But he caught two of them and rammed their heads together with both hands. The third one blocked the light from the hallway as he ran out the door.

"You know how it is," said one.

"You understand," said the other.

"Heh heh," said the first one.

Nelson's prairie liberalism swelled in his breast, and he squeezed their heads together until the two Lost Boys yelped.

"You guys belong in law school," he said through gritted teeth. His finger sparked so strongly he felt it, through both heads, in his left hand. "You don't belong in a literature department."

Nelson released them and they staggered out the door and up the hall.

"Tell Dan, too!" Nelson called after them.

"That was Vic!" one of them called back, from the stairs.

"No, I'm Vic," said the other. "That was Bob."

"No, *I'm* Bob. . . ."

Nelson heard the basement door open and close. On the television a British officer picked up a Zulu shield and jammed it upright in the earth. Who am I rooting for? Nelson thought. And then: I'm rooting for myself.

Coming up out of the stairway, Nelson closed the door behind him. There was a tension to the party now, a hissing undercurrent to the murmuring. Oddly, there was no music. He was alone in the kitchen, so he peered around the corner of the nook and into the dining room. The head of the Composition Program, an immensely fat Linda Proserpina, had pulled a chair up to the table in front of a heated serving dish full of meatballs in red sauce; she was spearing one meatball at a time with a toothpick, straight out of the dish and into her mouth. Otherwise, the room was empty.

Nelson peered the other way, through the kitchen toward the study. From near the archway Bridget caught his eye. Lifting her drink high, she slipped sideways against the current of the crowd moving into the study and came into the kitchen.

"Nelson, Vita's here," she said in a low voice. "You'd better come."

The heat in Nelson's finger flared. "Did you say Vita's here?" he whispered.

"Hurry up, Nelson." She glanced back at the study, and dropped her voice even lower. "Nelson, she's wearing *my dress.*"

Bridget hurried into the hallway; through the arch Nelson could see that the crowd was all facing one way, aligning itself like iron filings under the influence of a magnet.

"Oh, boy," Nelson breathed, and someone laid a hand on his shoulder and pulled him around.

"May I talk to you for a moment, Professor?" The Canadian Lady Novelist squeezed Nelson's shoulder, looking at him like a severe but loving grandmother.

"Not now." He shrugged her off and started to turn away.

"I've been watching you these last few weeks, Nelson." She spoke more firmly, as if to a difficult child. "And I just want to offer some friendly advice."

"About what?" He hesitated.

"About rage, Nelson."

"Rage?" Wincing at the sudden pain in his finger, Nelson turned and looked at the Novelist.

"Most people think that rage is like steam, that you can let it out in bursts and relieve the pressure." The Canadian Lady Novelist replaced her large hand on his shoulder and looked deep into his eyes. "But rage is like a muscle, Nelson. The more you exercise it, the stronger it gets. Do you understand what I'm saying to you?"

Nelson started to laugh, and the Novelist, a little puzzled, smiled back at him.

"You bet," said Nelson, and, still laughing, he grabbed the Novelist by her large nose and twisted it. She gasped and went cross-eyed, clutching at his wrist. But Nelson, his finger burning, only twisted harder.

"The fuck have you ever done for me, huh?" he hissed. *"The fuck have you ever done for me?"*

He swung her by her nose into the nook under the stairs, up against the basement door. He let go of her, and she clutched the doorknob with both hands to keep from sliding to the floor. Nelson turned toward the study; through the hallway he saw members of the crowd standing on tiptoe and craning to see something at the desk end of the room. They were falling silent in a wave, from front to back. A bass burp issued from the speakers, then a long, crackling hiss. A piano began to play a slowly rollicking tune, in the tinny intonation of an old recording.

Then, wriggling out of the crowd like a wasp out of its nest, Marko Kraljević shouldered his way out of the study, through the hallway, and into the kitchen. Lorraine Alsace trotted at his heels, wringing her bony hands and whimpering. Kraljević—or Jamisovich, depending on your point of view—was red-faced and sweating; he crushed the Cub Scout cap in his thick fingers as if he were trying to tear it apart. He was muttering to himself, and he stopped short when he saw Nelson in his path.

311

"Ustasha!" he cried, spittle flying. "Croat! *Turk!*"

"Jew!" cried Lorraine Alsace. "Faggot!" She tried to hurl herself past Kraljević at Nelson, but Kraljević held her back.

Nelson beckoned them both. "I'm taking all comers tonight," he said. "You want some too?"

Kraljević recoiled, his eyes wide, his mouth working furiously. He grabbed Lorraine Alsace by her hair and dragged her in front of him. She gasped and squeezed her eyes shut, but she didn't scream or struggle. The piano music held the attention of the crowd in the study.

"I'm going to come back and kill you all!" growled Kraljević, backing out of the kitchen into the dining room, holding Alsace by the hair in front of him. "FBI or no FBI!"

He backed along the side of the table, while from the other side Linda Proserpina gaped at him, an impaled meatball halfway between the dish and her mouth. Kraljević flung Lorraine away from him into a corner and bolted out Weissmann's front door; Alsace clawed her way up the wainscoting and dashed after him, calling out tearfully, *"Schatz! Mon amour!"*

Nelson straightened his lapels and shot his cuffs; his finger hummed with a steady heat. Out of the corner of his eye he glimpsed the Canadian Lady Novelist trying to sneak by behind him, and he snapped his fingers under her nose. She yelped and jumped back, flinging open the basement door and disappearing down the steps.

Nelson walked into the dining room. Linda Proserpina watched him as if he might try to snatch away her dish of meatballs, but she didn't stop eating.

"Linda," Nelson said. "How you doing?"

"Nehsuh," said Linda Proserpina with her mouth full.

Cold air gushed through the open front door, and Nelson closed it. From the study he thought he heard someone singing along with the piano music. He circled into the parlor, where Lionel Grossmaul and Anthony Pescecane were nose to nose in the middle of the carpet, not quite shouting at each other.

"Calm the fuck down," Pescecane was saying. He had both palms up, and he was glancing past Lionel's shoulder into the study through the arch at the end of the parlor, trying to see what was going on.

"You should be riding *my* coattails, you fraud!" Lionel stood on tiptoe, trying his damnedest to loom over Pescecane. "I should have been the chair of this department!"

312

Nelson's finger flared, and he tiptoed past the two men toward the study. Pescecane reached out for him as he passed, digging his blunt fingers into the shoulder of Nelson's jacket.

Nelson let himself be turned around.

"I know what you're trying to do, you fuck," Pescecane said in a low growl. "Don't think you'll fucking get away with it."

"Anthony," said Lionel behind him.

"My foot soldiers will move up and down the halls of academe," Pescecane went on, "and you'll be dead."

"Anthony!" insisted Lionel, yanking at Pescecane's shoulder.

"Nobody will publish your articles," Pescecane said with a vicious smile, "nobody will review your books, nobody will invite you to conferences. You'll be lucky to teach at some podunk fucking community college. . . ."

"*Anthony!*" cried Grossmaul, and he grabbed Pescecane by the shoulders and twisted him around. Lionel's face was the color of a tomato; his eyes bulged behind his cracked glasses.

"I taught you everything you know about theory!" he shouted. "Goddamn you for learning my language!"

Nelson edged away, into the wide arch just behind Weissmann's desk, where he found himself facing the majority of the department—professors, associate professors, assistant professors, postdocs, adjuncts, composition teachers, grad students, and undergraduates—all wide-eyed and openmouthed at the sight of Vita Deonne, in a little black dress and spike heels, doing a slow hootchie-koo atop Mort Weissmann's ornate old desk. She canted her weight first on one sharp heel, and then the other as some long-dead blues piano player hammered out a monaural accompaniment.

"*If I should . . . take a notion,*" she was singing, in a nasal, smokey whine, "*to throw myself in . . . to the ocean, 'tain't nobody's bidness . . . if I do. . . .*"

Across the crowd Nelson saw his wife glaring at Vita; as near as Nelson could tell, Bridget and Vita were wearing the same dress. Stephen Michael Stephens, still furious from his rude awakening in Weissmann's basement, was shaking his head in disbelief at another white travesty of black culture. Even the unflappable Miranda was gaping in astonishment. Weissmann and Penelope O were nowhere to be seen. Of all the crowd, only Victorinix seemed unaffected by the spectacle of Vita; she looked on coolly from before the fire at the far end of the room, while a silently sobbing Gillian watched her from a shadowy niche between two bookcases.

"*If I call my . . . self a woman,*" Vita went on, grinding her hips, "*it don't make me . . . less than human . . .'tain't nobody's bidness . . . if I do.*"

Though he couldn't see her face, Nelson thought Vita looked good. She strutted confidently to the rhythm atop firm calves and thighs; she shimmied her shoulders like a showgirl. Her hair was pulled back for once; she wore some sort of jeweled choker and dangly earrings that caught the light. Perhaps from the front the low cut of the dress reveals a flat chest, perhaps the choker draws attention to an Adam's apple, but from where I'm standing, thought Nelson, Vita's a babe. For once, Nelson thought, she's performing her chosen gender identity to the hilt. So to speak.

From the parlor behind him Nelson was dimly aware of a voice rising—"*Are you listening to a single word I'm saying?*" bayed Lionel—but it wasn't loud enough to distract the astounded crowd from Vita's dance. She bumped on her heels up to the edge of the desk; she tossed her head in a wild circle. She swayed and lightly stroked the tops of her thighs with the tips of her fingers, toying with the hem of her dress.

"*If I should . . . flash my penis,*" she sang, and she lifted her skirt.

The crowd gasped and reared back from the desk in a single motion. All except Victorinix at the back, who did not even flinch.

"*. . . hope that won't . . . come between us,*" Vita sang, swishing her hem from side to side and shimmying back from the edge of the desk. "*'Tain't nobody's bidness if I do!*"

The breathless silence that followed was filled only by the piano coming round to another verse. Vita, still swaying, fingered the straps of her dress. Nelson's finger, which had cooled since his encounter with the Canadian Lady Novelist, began to burn again. But before he could step up to the desk from behind, before Vita could shuck her dress, before the astounded crowd could draw a breath, the voices exploded from the parlor.

"*The fuck do you think you're doing!*" cried Pescecane.

"*You son of a bitch!*" bellowed Lionel Grossmaul. "*You've stolen my life!*"

There was a bright flash and the sound of something shattering. The pale faces of the crowd swiveled toward the archway; Nelson whirled. Lionel Grossmaul was brandishing a smashed table lamp, which was still plugged in. The broken filament sizzled and spat sparks; the little shade was burning as it rolled away.

314

At Lionel's feet, Anthony Pescecane lay twitching on the carpet, his back arched, his arms and legs convulsing, blood oozing from a blackened gash along the side of his head.

Only Vita did not turn to look; she was dropping her right shoulder to slide off the spaghetti strap of her dress.

" *'T'ain't nobody's bidness...*" she was singing, but the rest was drowned out by the moan of the crowd as they rushed forward. Nelson was ahead of them, though, and he grasped Lionel by the wrist as Grossmaul raised the sparking lamp for the coup de grâce. Nelson yanked him off his feet, into the hands of several furious graduate students who had been waiting years for just this opportunity. As these young men and women hauled the raging Grossmaul to the carpet, Nelson jerked the cord out of the wall and tossed the lamp behind a sofa. He stamped on the burning lampshade until it was out, and then, as the crowd surged around him, he fell to his knees next to the shuddering Pescecane.

"Keep back!" Nelson shouted, waving his hands. "Give him room!"

Pescecane stared blindly at the ceiling; his back bowed up off the floor. His limbs quivered uncontrollably.

Nelson bent over Pescecane and pressed his burning finger along the side of the chair's throat. He doubled over and put his lips to Pescecane's ear.

"Don't die," Nelson whispered, "but don't wake up."

His finger sparked. Pescecane stiffened, then relaxed. Nelson pulled away, his hand still on Pescecane's chest. Anthony exhaled slowly, expelling all the air from his lungs. Nelson was dimly aware of the muffled shouts of Lionel somewhere near, the urgent whispers at the back of the crowd. Pescecane did not blink; he did not draw a breath. Nelson held his own breath; for a long moment all he heard was the tinkling of the blues piano, unaccompanied by Vita.

Then Pescecane sucked in his breath with a moan; his eyelids fluttered and closed; his back arched one more time. He clutched Nelson by the front of his jacket, dragging Nelson toward him with surprising force. His mouth worked silently. Nelson grabbed Pescecane's wrists, trying to pry his fingers loose.

"*It's ... not ... fair!*" gasped Anthony Pescecane. Then he let go of Nelson, his head rolled to the side, and he began to take in shallow, rasping breaths. Nelson sank back on his ankles. He lifted his eyes and saw pale faces circling him, eyes blinking, lips moving. Out of all that motion, he found only one fixed point—the icy, glittering gaze of Victoria Victorinix as she met his eyes and then turned away.

. . .

For the next hour Nelson was barely aware of what was going on. He allowed several hands to tug him to his feet and settle him in a chair; someone thrust a drink into his fingers. A moist-eyed Bridget appeared at his side, and he suffered her to clasp him around the neck and murmur wetly in his ear.

But all the while he watched as Victorinix—the new chair of the English Department, though who would dare say so out loud?—talked to the paramedics and steered the police away from Nelson for the time being. He watched as she stole glances at him past the shoulder of a detective, looking away again coolly when he met her gaze. He watched as Pescecane was carried out on a stretcher, an IV line plugged into his arm, an oxygen mask over his nose and mouth. He watched as a limp, black-and-blue Grossmaul was frog-marched out of the room by two burly policemen, his hands cuffed behind his back. He watched as the crowd was ushered out the front door by uniformed cops, gawking back at him as they struggled into their coats. He watched as Weissmann and Penelope O stumbled into the parlor from upstairs; Weissmann—his cravat missing, his smoking jacket unbelted, his shirt buttoned wrong—drew himself up and demanded to know why all his guests were leaving and what the police were doing in his house, while Penelope tucked herself back into her bustier and never took her eyes off Weissmann.

Nelson roused himself. With a touch, he gave Bridget the keys to the Toyota and sent her home—"The sitter will be frantic," he said—assuring her that someone would give him a ride. He retrieved her coat from upstairs and folded her into it; he allowed her to wrap her arms around him and whisper in his ear how proud she was of him, how much she loved him. After she left, he spoke to the police for a few moments, promising to provide a fuller statement in the morning.

Finally, Nelson stood alone in Weissmann's parlor—Penelope had dragged poor Mort back upstairs—looking down at the bloodstain and scorch marks on the carpet.

"Nice work, Nelson," someone said, and he followed the sound of the voice into the study. Victorinix was alone, wrapping herself in her cloak. Gillian was gone.

"I guess you're chair of the department now," Nelson said.

Victoria buttoned the top of her cape with her long, white fingers. She said nothing.

316

"What's that make me, I wonder?" asked Nelson.

"You've . . . what's the word?" She pulled on her gloves. "You've *neutralized* the search committee."

"You still need to fill the budget line, though, don't you?" Nelson smiled. "Guess it's up to you to tenure me."

With both hands, Victorinix fitted her little round glasses over her nose, obscuring her eyes.

"Come see me on Monday," she said. "In Anthony's . . . in the chairperson's office."

She turned. Nelson lifted his voice. "Where's Vita?"

Victoria kept walking. "What's left of her is on the desk."

Nelson glanced at the desktop. Vita's dress lay in a puddle of crepe de chine. Her earrings and choker lay atop the dress, as if arrayed on velvet in a jeweler's case. One of her high heels was toppled on its side, while the other stood upright, as if she'd just stepped out of it. Nelson stuck his hand into the upright shoe, wondering for some reason if it might still be warm from Vita's foot. But the lining was cool and dry.

"Like a cocoon," Nelson murmured, "left behind by a butterfly."

He heard a rustle and looked up. Victoria Victorinix was gone. Miranda DeLaTour walked toward him across the study, wearing her long overcoat over her red dress. She held her car keys in one hand, her gloves in the other.

"More like a skin," Miranda said, "left by a snake."

Nelson said nothing. He took his hand out of the shoe.

"May I offer you a ride, Professor?" said Miranda.

In her Miata, Miranda did not even ask Nelson where he lived, but drove them instead toward campus. In the narrow cockpit of the car, in the shifting lamplight, he watched her profile. She was smiling as if at some private joke. When she returned his glance, he did not look away.

She pulled to the curb on the street side of Harbour Hall and turned the engine off. The Miata was the only car on the street. She turned to him.

"I'd like to stop here for a moment," she said. "Do you mind?"

"Not at all," said Nelson.

In the elevator they leaned side by side against the rear wall, their shoulders brushing. In the dim light of the eighth floor, Miranda let them into the chair's suite of offices with her own key. They passed Grossmaul's rigorously ordered desk, and Miranda let them into Anthony's inner office. Nelson watched from the door as Miranda crossed to the windows overlooking the Quad, letting her overcoat slide to the floor. Nelson felt along the wall for the light switch, and without looking back, Miranda said, "Leave them off."

The blinds were open, and the room was filled with the pale glow of the lamps around the Quad, reflected off the snow eight stories below. In this cool and ethereal light Miranda's face and shoulders and bare back were the color of bone. Nelson crossed the room, stepping over the limp overcoat, and stood just behind her. He ran his smoldering finger along her arm, thinking of nothing in particular. Without turning round, Miranda lifted her hand and grabbed his wrist, pulling his arm around her shoulder from behind. As Nelson pressed up against Miranda's back, she lifted his finger between her perfect teeth and bit it, lightly, just above the tip. Nelson wrapped his other arm around her waist, cupping his palm over her hipbone against the warm sheen of her dress. Through the window he saw the tower of Thornfield Library lit from below by the light from the Annex. The tower looked as if it were only a few feet away, just beyond the window. Windblown snow trailed off the top of the tower into the dark. Nelson closed his eyes and pressed his face into Miranda's hair, and she lifted her chin and bared her throat for him.

"Sweet Nelson," she said, "make me immortal with a kiss."

Soon they were sprawled on the surface of Anthony's desk, their bodies gleaming like porcelain in the lamplight from the Quad. Nelson had spread the overcoat over the desktop, for comfort, but Miranda had pushed it off again. The heat was turned down for the weekend, and Nelson's buttocks were freezing against the cold varnish of the desk. Miranda swayed above him, grinding against him slowly. She parted her lips and tossed her hair; with her dark nails she raked her thighs, her belly, and her breasts. He knew it was a performance, that she was vamping for him, but at the moment, he didn't mind. She looked down at him through the screen of her hair. "Say something bad," she breathed.

"What?" gasped Nelson.

"Say something *really* bad." She twirled a lock of black hair around her finger. "Something *forbidden*."

Nelson couldn't help it; he started to laugh. "Like what?"

"Come on, Nelson." Miranda bit her lip and ground hard against him. "Say it."

Nelson groaned. Miranda fell forward, splaying her hands against the desk, propping herself over Nelson. Her nipples brushed his chest, her cool hair fanned across his face. Her breath was hot in his ear. "Something you've never said out loud," she whispered.

Nelson could hardly stand it.

"I think . . ." he gasped. "I think . . ."

He flashed on the Lost Boys watching TV in the basement. He saw a thousand angry Zulus charging straight toward him.

"I think affirmative action," he panted, "is a really bad idea."

"Yes!" cried Miranda. She reared up and threw her head back. Nelson, emboldened, clutched her by the hips.

"I think," he groaned, "I think . . ."

His chest swelled like a balloon, and suddenly he dug his fingers into Miranda and rolled her over, onto her back. Her shoulders thumped against the desk, and she squealed in surprise. Behind his eyes he saw the long, bright rows of shelving in the lowest level of the Annex.

"There is no exercise of the intellect," he rasped, plunging into her, "which is not, in the final analysis, *futile*."

"Oh, *yes!*" Miranda bucked against him. "Oh, *fuck!*"

"I think," said Nelson, and he pulled out of her and dragged her to the edge of the desk. He spun her over by her waist, pressing her face down over the edge.

"Oh, *God,* Nelson," groaned Miranda, pushing herself up on her toes.

"I think," he said, and he dug his toes into Anthony Pescecane's carpet and plunged into Miranda with a grunt. A line came to him out of nowhere—*he priketh harde and depe as he were mad*—and he thought, I'm *swiving* her. I'm *swiving* Anthony's woman. His finger burned inside her hip, and she shuddered and cried out.

"You want to know what I think?" Nelson gasped, thrusting harder. "I'll tell you what I think."

He looked up past Miranda's straining shoulders, through the window, and saw just what he expected to see, a little silvery figure atop the library tower, jigging in the windblown snow, dancing to the same rhythm as Nelson and Miranda.

"I think," said Nelson Humboldt, as stern as death, "that I'm the angriest man you ever met."

PART THREE

The Blazing World

... though I cannot be *Henry* the Fifth, or *Charles* the Second, yet I endeavour to be *Margaret* the *First;* and although I have neither power, time nor occasion to conquer the world as *Alexander* and *Caesar* did; yet rather than not to be mistress of one, since Fortune and the Fates would give me none, I have made a world of my own: for which no body, I hope, will blame me, since it is in every one's power to do the like.

—Margaret Cavendish, *The Blazing World*

17

To Reign in Hell

On the bright and blustery morning of Good Friday, Nelson Humboldt did not get up until ten o'clock. He was waked by a kiss from his wife, and served breakfast in bed by his two well-scrubbed daughters, who were home from school for the holiday. Clara carried the tray: poached eggs and whole wheat toast, a linen napkin, a daisy in a bud vase, a folded *New York Times*. Abigail carried in both hands, very carefully, a large glass of freshly squeezed orange juice.

"Good morning, Father," they said, in robotic unison. There was a dullness to Clara's eyes that still bothered Nelson a little, but Abigail was bright-eyed, playing along as if waiting on Daddy were a game. Then Bridget ushered them out of the room, so that Daddy could read his paper and have his breakfast at his leisure.

"Your father works *very hard* for us," Bridget whispered, just as she did every morning.

An hour and a half later she drove him to work—the girls rode quietly in the backseat—and dropped him off a block from campus; Nelson did not think the undergraduate chair of the department should be seen getting out of a ten-year-old Toyota. He had his heart set on a new SUV or a Volvo station wagon—a family vehicle, in other words, that also bespoke power and style—but even with his new salary and the moral authority of his handshake, Nelson wasn't sure he could talk a salesman down to a price he could afford.

"Say good-bye to Daddy!" Bridget said in a singsong as she pulled up to the curb and Nelson opened the door. The girls sang out in two-part disharmony, little Abigail nearly screaming, "Good-*bye,* Daddy!"

"Mind your coat," Bridget said, and Nelson swept the skirts of his new overcoat carefully around his legs as he got out of the car. He had refused the cashmere coat Miranda had wanted him to buy, settling instead for a dark wool

323

overcoat with long skirts and wide lapels, in which he could wrap himself like a moody existentialist, flipping the collar points up to his cheekbones like Sartre or Camus on his way to a café. His old parka, with the bloody palm print on the front, had been stuffed into a milk crate and kicked under the basement stairs.

Now, as he strode past the shops along Michigan Avenue, swinging his new leather briefcase and exchanging nods with students and colleagues, Nelson felt like anything but an existentialist. Coming round the kiosk onto campus, he had a brief tremor of alarm, accompanied by the unpleasant memory of Fu Manchu trembling in the snow that night in the alley. An instant later he had banished his old nemesis from his mind, reassuring himself that the homeless man had simply moved on to some other, greener pasture—Madison or Ann Arbor, or perhaps even sunny Austin.

Meanwhile the Minnesota sun was scaling a sky of deep, burnished blue. The sunlight slanted steeply through the bare branches of the elms around the Quad, picking out every brick and cornice of the clock tower atop Thornfield Library. March's snow was melted, except in the shadows under the lilacs beneath the lowest windows of the library. The bushes themselves were beginning to bud, but they were not yet in leaf. Now and then a sudden gust with a Canadian edge to it blew across the Quad, and students hurrying to their twelve o'clock classes still clutched mittens and draped scarves loosely around their necks. But this morning Nelson walked hatless, scarfless, and gloveless, with the hem of his coat flying in breezes from Winnipeg.

"Whan that Aprill with his shoures soote," he murmured, marching through the door of Harbour Hall. He pressed the button for the elevator and glanced at his watch; his eleven o'clock class was just ending. His teaching schedule had not changed since February—there were still four classes a day to teach, Monday, Wednesday, and Friday—but now they were conducted by his teaching assistant, Gillian. Ever since Nelson had assumed the duties of acting undergraduate chair, Gillian had conducted all his composition sections, assigned and graded the papers, held office hours, all on Nelson's behalf—and without daily supervision, so long as she did not stray from Nelson's syllabus. In consideration of this she made a surprisingly good salary for a doctoral candidate, for although he had been undergraduate chair for only six weeks, Nelson had managed to raise the salaries of all the composition teachers, but Gillian's especially. Meanwhile Nelson was free to pursue his research of James Hogg and attend to his administrative duties. It was a pleasant arrangement all the way around, though Nelson had noticed lately an increasing gauntness in Gillian's face whenever she came to report to him. But even that might be for the best; after all, it wasn't as if she didn't need to lose the weight.

Nelson rode the elevator alone to the eighth floor, cradling his new briefcase lightly in his fingers before him. He would just have time to check his mail and take care of some paperwork before meeting with Victoria Victorinix to discuss the graduate curriculum committee meeting next week. They had both agreed that the meeting would go more smoothly if they ironed out their differences in advance; Nelson naturally intended to stress an intimate familiarity with the canon of English literature, while Victorinix would no doubt insist upon mastery of the theoretical project from Heidegger on. Nelson hoped that, in the end, through the sort of negotiation with which he was becoming more adept, and through his own increasingly potent statesmanship, their differences could be narrowed to a few credit hours either way. Now, confidently riding the elevator to his new administrative office on the top floor of Harbour Hall, wearing his beautiful new coat, his dead finger lightly tapping his slim new leather briefcase, he had at last—dare he say it?—the moral authority to implement the sort of enlightened centrism he had advocated since his first days in the department. Perhaps, thought Nelson aphoristically, good intentions and the moral authority to implement them are one and the same thing. As soon as he got to his office, he decided, he would have to write that down.

With a cheerful *ding!* the elevator deposited him on the plush carpet of the eighth floor. He turned right, past the department offices and the copy room. Of course, he had to admit that enlightened centrism was a little easier to maintain when the department's chief ideological extremists were, for one reason or another, hors de combat. Slobodan Jamisovich, aka Marko Kraljević, was probably not even in the country any longer, but on the lam from the Justice Department, Interpol, and the International War Crimes Tribunal. Lorraine Alsace was gone as well, widely suspected to be playing Bonnie Parker to Kraljević's Clyde Barrow. Kraljević had been summarily sacked by the dean of Liberal Arts when his real name came to light, while Alsace was technically still a lecturer, but no longer receiving a salary. Which leaves *two* new budget lines to fill, thought Nelson, sensibly.

And at the other end of the spectrum, Morton Weissmann, who could usually be counted on to turn the graduate curriculum meeting into a call-and-response testimonial to the greatness of Shakespeare, Milton, and Eliot, was these days taxed to the limits of his physical and emotional endurance by the obsessive attentions of Penelope O. Living proof of the essentialist canard that no man would ever turn down sex, Weissmann trudged wearily across the Quad and up the halls of Harbour Hall like an Edwardian polar explorer manhauling a sledge toward his own certain death. Penelope O conducted her astonishingly popular classes as energetically as ever, but Weissmann looked as if he hadn't slept in weeks, yawning loudly during committee meetings, falling fast asleep in class. Though Nelson had never heard the racket himself, the rumor was that late every afternoon one could pass outside the pebbled glass of Professor O's office door on the seventh floor and hear the rhythmic creaking of office furniture and Penelope's cries of "Teach me! Oh, teach me! Oh, teach me!" followed very soon after by Morton Weissmann's climactic shout of "This . . . *this* . . . THIS . . . *ENGLAND!*"

Poor Mort! Nelson was thinking, when he was lunged at from the doorway of the faculty lounge.

"Professor Humboldt!" cried the Canadian Lady Novelist, thrusting a foil-wrapped parcel at him with both hands.

"Professor," sighed Nelson, pirouetting elegantly on the carpet. He glanced once over the Novelist's shoulder at the urns of coffee in the lounge. He had hoped to grab a quick cup, but he did not want to be trapped in the room with her yet another morning.

"I hope you like pecan rolls," she said, her eyes bright. With both hands she squeezed the parcel. "If you don't, I can bring you something else tomorrow."

"Oh, *gosh*, pecan rolls." Nelson backed slowly away, clutching his briefcase with both hands, hoping to avoid taking the package. Ever since his encounter with the Novelist at the Valentine's Day party, she had been trying to make up for Nelson's disappointment in her with a relentless, slow-motion avalanche of baked goods: bran muffins, sourdough biscuits, cinnamon rolls, dinner rolls, homemade pies with and without lattice crusts, layer cakes with and without fruit fillings, torts, tarts, pastries, pasties, cream puffs, potato bread, banana bread, carrot cake, coffee cake, fruit cake, and cookies of every variety, with every possible permutation of coconut, walnuts, chocolate chips, and raisins.

"These are different from the pecan rolls I brought on Tuesday," she insisted, digging her fingers into the foil. "I rather suspect that you didn't care for those because the pieces of pecan overwhelmed the roll. Now, those pecans were sliced *lengthwise,*" she said, cutting horizontally with the side of her hand, "while these are more sort of *chopped,* if you will. . . ."

Early on, weeks ago, Nelson had taken the Novelist by the hand as she had thrust a basket of braided bread at him, and he had told her, "Thank you, you've done enough." But evidently the vehemence of his declaration to the contrary at the party was not to be reversed except by his acceptance every day of her gift of bread.

"I'll give them a try," he said, taking the parcel. Her shoulders sagged, and she lumbered off, relieved of her burden for the day.

With the warm rolls wedged under his arm, Nelson let himself into his office. Now that Victorinix had moved into the chair's suite at the end of the hall, Nelson had taken over her former office. The blinds were lifted to let in the spring sunshine, and the severe shelves and desk were gone. For the time being Nelson was working with a standard-issue desk, chairs, and shelving from university stores, but he had a new wooden desk and a padded office chair on order, and over the summer he hoped to have the office painted something other than Sepulcher White.

He set down the briefcase and the rolls and poked through the mail on his desktop, delivered every morning by one of the secretaries from the main office. The phone was already blinking at him, so he picked it up before he took off his coat. Hoping that one of the messages would be from Miranda, he closed the office door as he punched in the code for his voice mail, and as he cycled through the menu, he peered through the glare in his window at the top of the clock tower. It had been weeks since he had seen anything odd there, and he was beginning to wonder if all he had ever seen or heard was some aerodynamic trick of the tower, some plume of snow blown off the tower into the dark, accompanied by some murmur of the wind through its crenelations. In the bright, spring sunlight, the top of the tower simply looked old and worn, not like the gloomy, Gothic habitation of ghosts.

The first several messages were from Weissmann, who was angling ever more obsequiously for an interview with Nelson, offering plans, advice, alliances. Nelson listened to only a few seconds of each one, until the last message, when Weissmann gasped in the middle of his pitch and, away from the phone, cried wearily, "Oh, sweetness, not *now* . . ." followed by the abrupt return of the dial tone.

The next message was from a Sergeant Garrison of the Hamilton Groves Police Department, to whom Nelson had reported Vita's disappearance a week after the Valentine's Day party. "Just checking in," the sergeant said, a master of the Joe Friday sentence fragment. "Nothing to report."

Nelson was distracted through the next few messages—a plea from a graduate student desperate for a composition section; a mumbled message from Linda Proserpina, speaking with her mouth full; a call from Gillian asking him to call her back—by his thoughts of Vita. Late on the Sunday afternoon after the Valentine's Day party, he had wound his way into the student ghetto again to Vita's second-floor apartment, where he had shivered in the cold on the porch and pressed her doorbell for five minutes with no result. He couldn't even hear it ringing within. Then, as he was about to give up and go away, he pounded on her door with her fist, and the door swung silently open into a clammy twilight.

"Vita?" he called up the stairs, only to hear the surprisingly harsh echo of his own voice.

As he climbed the stairs, he saw in the dusky light, just inside the living room doorway, what appeared to be a nude human body hanging by its heel, with pink, bloated limbs and wide, lifeless eyes. Nelson nearly pitched himself back down the stairs. But he crept forward and saw that it wasn't a body, but an inflatable sex doll—female—hanging from the ceiling. Something stuck out from between its legs, and as Nelson edged closer, he saw that it was a plastic model of a submarine, jammed into the doll's vagina. Nelson peered past the doll and saw that the room was an inverted thicket of dangling stuff, suspended by fishing wire from hooks screwed into the ceiling. Just beyond the doll was a mobile of the solar system made of birth control devices: a big erect condom full of plaster of paris for the sun, orbited by a rubber diaphragm, an IUD, a sponge, a plastic syringe, a pill dispenser, all fixed on hoops of wire. Farther in were a hockey stick and a baseball bat bound together into a sort of cross; a Cub Scout uniform and a Brownie uniform hung and arranged to look as if they were fucking; a bright orange hunting vest with license attached, impaled by a length of deer antler draped with purple ribbon. All of it hung motionlessly, though just his slight motion in the doorway set the inflatable doll to turning slowly. The little sexual solar system began to quiver.

Nelson checked the other rooms. Apart from the display in the living room, the apartment was stripped to the walls: The furniture was gone, the rugs pulled up, the curtains ripped down, the toilet paper snatched from the dispenser in the cold little bathroom. Nelson couldn't tell if the electricity still worked because all the bulbs had been removed from the ceiling fixtures. Strangely, there was a good deal of undisturbed dust on the floors, as well as cobwebs in the windows and the corners of the ceiling. Nelson knew from sharing an office with her that Vita was a fastidious housekeeper, but her empty apartment smelled only of dust and ancient varnish. It looked as if no one had lived here for months, if not years. Stranger still, nearly all of the internal doors were gone, lifted off their hinges and taken away someplace, giving the apartment an unsettling echo that magnified every tiny creak of the floorboards or rustle of Nelson's coat.

He went into the living room again, trying to avoid touching the stuff hanging from the ceiling. Even so he brushed something small and firm with his shoulder, which turned out to be a jockstrap filled with what looked like raw, pink hamburger. He left it swinging as he passed a pair of women's pumps with their four-inch heels sharpened to points and their narrow toes filled with concrete; a television remote wrapped in barbed wire; a fierce goalie's mask embroidered in pink needlepoint; an enormous brassiere turned into a plant hanger, each cup holding a small, thorny cactus.

"What is this place?" Nelson murmured, and answered himself silently: a cabinet of curiosities. A map of the contents of Vita's consciousness.

He made his way toward a photograph on the wall at the end of the room. The things around him were made to spin and sway by the slight breeze of his passage: a dark, shriveled human head, cut about with slashes and scars, as if someone had been practicing upon it with a sword. A Gumby with a bazooka barrel grafted between its legs. A nude G.I. Joe with a bushy vagina and a knife blade protruding from the slit. A nude Barbie crucified on two lengths of model railroad track, and around her head, instead of a crown of thorns, a twist tie printed with the old Wonder Bread slogan—Builds Strong Bodies Twelve Ways!

He came to the photograph, a small color snapshot behind glass in a simple wooden frame; it was affixed to the wall, but Nelson couldn't see how. The photo showed Vita *and* her brother, Robin Bravetype, standing with their arms around each other in front of a small suburban house. Nelson's finger stung him, but otherwise he felt a chill: Victoria had told him that Vita didn't have a brother, and he was certain Vita herself had admitted to him that she used to be Robin. Yet here was a photo of the two of them.

The slow sway of dangling stuff at the edges of his vision made him uneasy, but he reached for the photo. Before he could touch it, the frame slid suddenly down the wall to the floor at his feet. He jumped back, startled, starting a chain reaction across the roomful of dangling items. The glass shattered, but the frame remained upright, leaning against the baseboard. Now there was only one person in the photo, Robin Bravetype. Nelson backed quickly away, colliding with the Barbie, the shrunken head, the bazooka Gumby. The end of the baseball bat and the blade of the hockey stick spun at him on their axes as if they were aiming at him; the pink goalie's mask swung at him, screaming silently. Nelson threw his arms over his head and doubled over and ran from the room. The inflatable sex doll squeaked as he rubbed past it, and he burst into the vestibule breathing hard, his heart racing. He nearly dashed down the stairs, but there was still one door left in place, one of the three that had stood at the top of the stairs, the one that Vita had once thrown herself against to keep him from opening. Nelson glanced down the staircase in the thickening dusk to make sure the door below was wide open, then he tensed himself in the crepuscular light and slowly turned the rattling old knob.

The door swung open on its own. Vita hung in the bare closet from a hook, her head drooping over the chest of her plain brown sweater, her shoes dangling a foot off the floor. Nelson yelped and leaped back. His heart threatened to pound through his chest; his finger turned ice cold. Then, blinking in the dim light, he realized it wasn't Vita, but her clothes: The sweater hung from a hanger, the trousers were crudely stitched to the hem of the sweater, the shoes tied to the cuffs of the trousers. A brown wig hung from the wire hook of the hanger, its neatly trimmed bangs brushing the front of the sweater. It's Vita's husk, Nelson thought, the skin she's shed. It hung in the empty closet the way Nelson's new suit of clothes had hung behind their office door, a flat simulacrum of a college professor. Nelson stepped closer, nearly into the closet, and reached for the empty sleeve of the sweater. A chill little breeze came from behind him, from the room full of dancing, twitching stuff, and whisked round his ankles and into the closet, making the trousers and the sweater shimmy in a series of waves, making the bangs of the wig flip up as if Vita were raising her head. Nelson slammed the door and bolted down the stairs, heaving up against Vita's porch railing in the dark with his finger searing him. . . .

"Darling," breathed Miranda's voice in his ear, and Nelson caught his breath. Through the sunlight pouring through his office window he saw the clock tower and blue April sky. He closed his eyes and sighed and attended to the voice mail message in his ear, a warm current pulsing through his loins. Miranda could not call him at home, and she didn't trust e-mail except for professional messages. He turned away from the window and tucked his chin between the collars of his overcoat as he listened to the rest of her message.

"What have you done to Victoria Victorinix?" asked Miranda in a playfully insinuating voice. "I just got the most frantic phone call from Gillian, of all people. She seems to think that Victoria is missing, poor girl. So have you buried her under your basement floor out in married housing, you wicked boy?"

Nelson cringed at the sneering way Miranda said "married housing."

"I hope you drove a stake through her heart first," Miranda continued. "Wouldn't want her coming back to haunt us." Her voice dropped, and Nelson heard someone else in the background. "How soon can you get away this evening?" she whispered. "I'm looking forward to doing something bad on Good Friday."

Nelson was already tapping Miranda's number on his phone when someone knocked on his office door. Still cradling the phone, he reached across the office and cracked the door, lifting his eyebrows at the person in the hall.

"Professor Humboldt?" It was Mrs. Treadway, the doughy temporary secretary the department had hired to fill Lionel Grossmaul's position as the chairperson's administrative assistant. Grossmaul himself was on the run. Much to everyone's astonishment, an armed accomplice in combat fatigues and a ski mask had rescued Grossmaul at gunpoint during a pretrial hearing to establish Grossmaul's sanity. More astonishing to Nelson than the actual escape was the fact that Grossmaul had a friend. The last anyone had seen of Lionel, he was jumping into a car in front of the courthouse in his orange prisoner's jumpsuit.

"Yes?" said Nelson, hoping to indicate to Mrs. Treadway by his intonation that he was very, very busy. His meeting with Victorinix wasn't for fifteen minutes yet; he could hardly believe that she'd sent this nonentity to come fetch him.

"There's a gal in the chairman's office who'd like to speak to you," said Mrs. Treadway. No matter how many times she was corrected—and Nelson had corrected her himself on a number of occasions—Mrs. Treadway would insist on saying things like "gal" and "chairman."

"Professor Victorinix?" Nelson hesitated at the end of his phone cord; an automatic voice was telling him to please dial or hang up. Why would Mrs. Treadway call her boss, the chair of the department, "a gal in the chairman's office"?

"Well, no," said Mrs. Treadway, who resembled one of the Canadian Lady

Novelist's large, soft dinner rolls, encased in polyester, "Professor Victorinix ain't come in today. In fact, she ain't been in since, oh, Wednesday."

"I don't understand." Nelson blinked through the crack in the door. His finger was beginning to trouble him. "Who wants to talk to me?"

"Well, it's that teaching assistant of yours, I think. She says she wants to talk to you, so I tell her, his office is down the hall, but she says, 'no ma'am, I won't go down there. . . .'"

By now Nelson had hung up the phone and started down the hall, still in his coat, toward Victoria Victorinix's office. Mrs. Treadway followed at his heels, explaining all the way down the hall.

"She says to me, 'You go down there and tell him I want to talk to him *right here*.' 'Well, I'm sure I don't work for you, young lady,' I tell her, but she says, 'I'm not leaving this office till he comes down *here*. . . .'"

Nelson pulled open the massive door to the chair's suite of offices. Officially, Anthony Pescecane was only on extended leave. But if there was anything unseemly about Victorinix taking over Pescecane's office and his desk, no one objected. At Nelson's urging, Miranda had filed a sexual harassment complaint against Pescecane; no action was being taken on the complaint as long as Pescecane was still in a coma, but Nelson considered it insurance. He had been to see Pescecane only once in his room in the university medical center. Anthony was no longer breathing with a respirator, but he still lay unconscious in his bed, umbilically attached to an IV drip and several monitors. The one time Nelson had visited, Mrs. Pescecane had been seated next to her husband's bed in the gray twilight of the room, engrossed in a battered paperback copy of *The Last Don*. When Nelson asked her to leave him alone with her husband, she only shrugged and pushed herself up out of her chair, taking her book and a pack of cigarettes with her. Nelson had spent just a moment alone with Pescecane, long enough to grasp his clammy wrist, look in his vacant eyes, and say, "Take care of yourself, Anthony. We're doing just fine without you." He was pleased to see the green readout of Anthony's brain function take a little dip.

Nelson lifted his palm to silence Mrs. Treadway and keep her from following him into the inner office. He stopped just inside the door. Gillian stood across the office by the wide windows that overlooked the Quad; she was wearing her parka and clutching her knit cap in both hands. From where he stood, all Nelson could see beyond her through the window was the clock tower, looking pale in the steep noon sunlight. He ostentatiously looked at his watch.

"So, Gillian," he said, "who's teaching my twelve o'clock class?"

"What have you done with her?"

"What have I done with whom?"

"You *fucker.*" Gillian took a step away from the window, twisting her hat in her hands. "You fucking son of a bitch."

Nelson glanced back at Mrs. Treadway, who was standing on tiptoe, trying to see past his shoulder. He stepped into the office and shut the door behind him.

"Come on," Nelson said, "let's go down to my office." He gestured toward Anthony's private entrance, the one that led directly to the hall.

Gillian snorted derisively. "Yeah, right," she said. "You think I'm stupid enough to be alone with you in your office, you bastard?"

"You're alone with me right now in Victoria's," he said.

He did not step toward her, but she flinched from him anyway, glancing toward the door, edging along the side of Anthony's old desk. Victoria had replaced Pescecane's bookcases and film posters with her own austere prints and shelves, but she had kept the big, ornate desk. Nelson, his finger heating up, tried not to think of making love in here with Miranda.

"You can do whatever you want with me," Gillian said. "You already do."

Away from the glare of the window, Gillian's features were easier to make out. Her jaw trembled, her lips worked, she blinked as if she had just come out of darkness into a bright light. She had lost some weight, and she looked pale and weakened because of it.

"People have a way of coming to harm around you, or just . . . vanishing. . . ."

"Oh, come on, Gillian." Nelson sighed and crossed his arms. His finger was bothering him.

"No, you *listen to me!*" she shouted, from behind the desk. "You do whatever you want to me, I can't stop you, but if you hurt Victoria"—she choked up for a moment, then continued—"if you've hurt her *in any way,* I'll kill you. I don't know how, but I mean it. I'll kill you."

Nelson uncrossed his arms and spread his hands. "Gillian, I have no idea what you're talking about. I'm supposed to meet Victoria, well, now, to talk about the graduate curriculum requirements. . . ."

"You're a cold, heartless bastard." Gillian shook her head. "If I thought I could get to you, I'd kill you right now."

"What on earth are you talking about?"

"She's *missing!*" shouted Gillian. "Since Wednesday morning, maybe since

333

Tuesday night! God!" She looked away out the windows, wrenching the hat between her hands, biting her lip to keep from crying. "I can't find her anywhere. She hasn't been in her house, she hasn't been here, she hasn't been teaching her classes." She fixed her angry, red-rimmed glare at Nelson. "So don't stand there, you smug fucker, and tell me you don't know anything about it."

Nelson clasped his hands before him and rubbed his burning finger as covertly as he could. Some powerful but unrecognizable emotion was welling up in his chest. He blinked at Gillian, unable to speak for a moment. He had no idea where Victorinix was, had had no hand in her disappearance, if that's what it was, but a combination of rage, happiness, fear, relief—all at once—was filling his heart.

"I didn't," he managed to say. "I don't." He licked his lips. "That is to say, I didn't know Victoria . . . Professor Victorinix was missing. I don't know where she is. This is alarming news. Have you . . . have you called the police?"

This was *wonderful news,* was what Nelson wanted to say. He wanted to throw open a window and shout it down to the Quad—Victoria is gone! She's fled, scarpered, vanished! The Wicked Witch is dead! He wanted to call Bridget right away and tell her that, through no effort of his own, without lifting his finger, Victoria Victorinix had given up, thrown in the towel, yielded to his moral authority, and he was now acting chair of the department! *Acting chair!*

"The police don't care," Gillian was saying. "She's just another crazy dyke from the university, is what they think. They say she has to be gone for a week before they'll even look into it. A *week,* you son of a bitch!"

But Nelson was scarcely listening; he was basking in the delicious pain of his finger and imagining the departmental meeting where he was elected by acclamation to the chairmanship of the department. He was imagining the Solomonic justice he was going to dispense, the lifting up of the lowly composition teachers, the bringing of balm to the wounds of the culture wars, on both sides. Best of all, he was imagining himself behind Anthony's desk, with Miranda displayed at full length on the leather sofa across the room, imagining himself rising and coming around the desk, loosening his tie. . . .

Gillian punched him. She completely blindsided him while he was lost in fantasy; she came around the desk and hit him solidly, right across the jaw. He fell against the wall and slid down in a heap, more surprised than hurt or angry. As the light returned to his eyes and he looked up at her, rubbing the spot where she'd connected, she danced back on her toes like a prizefighter, keeping out of the reach of Nelson's burning finger. The name of a TV show popped into his head—*Touched by an Angel*—and he laughed: *Clocked by a Lesbian.*

"*It's not funny!*" she howled at him, cocking her fist to hit him again. "*Tell me what you've done with her!*"

With speed and power that surprised even him, Nelson propelled himself up off the floor and clamped his long fingers over Gillian's face. His dead finger sparked ecstatically.

"I haven't done anything to her," he said. "Calm down."

Gillian's whole body clenched under his grip, but just as suddenly she relaxed, and Nelson put his arm around her waist and half-carried, half-walked her over to the sofa, where they sagged together against the leather.

Nelson's mind was already racing. It may be a week before the police can act, he thought, but in the meantime steps will have to be taken. I'll have to call the dean this afternoon. . . .

He was aware of a pressure at his shoulder. Gillian was burying her face in his coat, kneading the wool with her fingers. She was weeping.

"Oh, God!" sobbed Gillian. "Oh, Victoria!"

"There there," said Nelson, patting the stiff bristles of her hair. "There, there."

Back in his office he made four phone calls, the first to Sergeant Garrison at the police department.

"Hadn't heard that," said the laconic detective, when Nelson told him about Professor Victorinix's disappearance. "Look into it for you. If you like."

"I'm sure it's nothing," Nelson said, hoping his glee did not echo down the phone line.

"That department of yours," said the lieutenant, in a rare complete sentence, "is some kind of black hole or something."

Next Nelson called his wife. Again he tried to sound appropriately concerned.

"What a terrible way for it to happen, darling," she said, "but would this mean that you . . . well, that you're going to be . . . ?"

"*Acting* chair, sweetie," Nelson said. "Actually, acting acting chair, since technically, Anthony's still in charge. It's just until we get this situation straightened out."

"Am I allowed to say," she whispered down the phone, "how *wonderful* this is for us? And how much you *deserve* this, darling? And how *proud* I am of you?"

Nelson finally cut her off, telling her he would probably have to come back to campus late this evening for an emergency meeting with the dean and the president of the university so that a temporary change of command could be arranged.

"Oh, of course!" cried Bridget. Then, dropping her voice again, "How lucky the university is, darling, to have someone as capable as you ready to step in at a moment's notice. . . ."

"Yes," Nelson said, "yes, they are."

Next he called the dean's office, and was put right through. In the background Nelson could hear the creak of the dean's chair as he sat up straight. Six weeks ago, when Victoria Victorinix, per their agreement, had submitted a tenure recommendation for Nelson, the dean had returned it the next day, with "Are you kidding?" scrawled across Nelson's CV. Nelson had picked up the phone immediately to arrange an appointment with the dean himself, then thought better of it. Instead, he had marched into the dean's office at lunchtime, silencing the dean's secretary with a touch, and caught the dean eating a tuna salad sandwich at his desk. He had taken the dean by the throat with his scalding finger and pushed him up against his fine oak paneling.

"I'm Nelson Humboldt," he had said as tuna salad tumbled out of the corners of the dean's mouth. "Remember that name."

Today Nelson explained the situation—Victoria Victorinix was not legally missing yet, but the business of the department needed to continue—and asked for a letter appointing him acting chair of the department.

There was a moment of hesitation at the other end of the line.

"Perhaps I should come over to discuss it," Nelson said. "Over lunch, say."

"I'll speak to the president," gulped the dean. "You'll have a letter by the close of business."

Finally he called Miranda.

"So," she said, purring down the phone like a well-satisfied cat, "what *did* you do with Victorinix?"

"Nothing!" cried Nelson happily, with a glance at the pebbled glass of his office door. He lowered his voice. "That's the beauty part! I didn't have to do a thing! Not a goddamn thing! She must have just looked at the lay of the land and taken off on her own!"

Miranda laughed down the phone, a sound that nearly made Nelson hard just to hear it. "I understand," she said. "You don't want to say over the phone. . . ."

"Honestly, Miranda," he said, dropping his voice, "I really don't know where she is."

"Well, you don't have to tell me now," she said, "but I guarantee, you will tell me later."

Nelson caught his breath at the thought.

"Have you given any thought to who your acting assistant chair will be?" The tone of Miranda's voice changed a fraction.

A little current began in Nelson's loins and ran up his spine. "Perhaps you'd like to submit your CV," he murmured.

"Would you like to see my letters of recommendation?"

"Well, yes, I suppose I'll have to see those as well. When are you available for an interview?"

"You're the *chair* now, darling. You tell me. I live to obey."

Right now, thought Nelson, as the current reached his eyes and he was blinded suddenly by the image of Miranda on her knees, on the carpet of his office. He spun in his office chair, away from the door, his face blazing, his finger throbbing. Through the window, in the clear, pale sunlight, he saw the clock tower, the hands of the clock inching toward one o'clock. All those useless, moldering old books caged in the Poole Collection, Nelson thought, and me caged up with them, just another Dead White Male. Nelson felt his finger warming. *That's* who was haunting the clock tower, he thought; *I* was the ghost of Thornfield Library. If ever a place needed exorcising . . .

"Tonight," he said. "At midnight."

"Midnight?" Miranda's voice lost a little of its heat.

"Yes, midnight." Nelson smiled to himself. "In Thornfield Library. In the clock tower."

She was silent for a moment, and then she said, "Nelson, are you crazy?"

This was the Miranda he didn't like, the one without the plummy Carol Lombard intonation.

"It's only *April*," she protested. "It'll be *freezing* up there. Why don't you come to my place?"

"Hey, lady," he said, "do you want the job or not?"

There was a silence down the phone line. Nelson watched the afternoon light glinting off the hands of the clock, off the bricks of the battlements atop the tower.

"That's not funny, Nelson," she said.

"Clock tower, Miranda. Midnight."

He hung up. He knew she'd be there.

Bridget didn't ask him why he shaved, showered, and changed his clothes at eleven o'clock that night. As he left, he kissed her and pressed his finger along the side of her neck and told her not to worry and not to wait up.

"I won't," she said, but she followed him to the door. As he stepped over the litter of toys in the married housing courtyard, she called to him. Nelson turned and saw his wife silhouetted in the bright doorway of his town house.

"I think it's *good*," he heard her say, in a tremulous voice, "that you're getting to know your colleagues better."

He parked the car on a side street near campus and walked the rest of the way. The shops along Michigan Avenue were all dark, but the empty street was brightly lit, and from a block away he heard the throb and crash of a live band from a student bar. He passed a few young couples, and a lonely young man or two, hurrying along with their hands in their pockets. Nelson walked with his coat buttoned to the top and the collars flipped up, holding the warmth of anticipation inside.

As he stepped under the street lamps on campus, he saw the tower of Thornfield Library rising above the budding branches of the trees. The white clock face glowed, while the lower floors of the old library were washed by the light from the skylight of the Annex below. The graduate library was open until two on a Friday night, and on the Quad Nelson passed a few late-night students coming and going.

The last time I was here this late, thought Nelson, I was on my way to confront Victoria Victorinix. He rolled his shoulders under his handsome coat. I wonder where she's gone, he thought. The last time he had seen her, she had been seated behind Anthony Pescecane's desk in what was by then her office—and which is now mine, thought Nelson—and she had regarded him with the same cool manner with which she had tried to fire him back in October. But this time Nelson had not been squirming in some hard seat, but sitting comfortably on the leather sofa across the room. Miranda had taught him how not to lean forward with his knees splayed like a big, dumb basketball player, but how to settle back as if he had no intention of leaving, one leg crossed over the other at the knee, his arm along the back of the couch. How to sit, in other words, as if he owned the place.

338

He couldn't remember now what they had been talking about—some departmental matter, no doubt, upon which Victoria felt the need for Nelson's advice—but he did remember how comfortable he had felt discussing it with her. He remembered how small and pale Victorinix looked behind the desk, and how easy it was for him to stand and cross the room on his long legs and tower over her at the massive desk as they both consulted a paper. In fact, he had almost said, "Don't you think we work well together, Victoria?" But he hadn't. He was afraid she might take it as a threat.

Miranda was waiting for him in the foyer of the Thornfield Library, huddled in a long coat. Nelson took her by the arm, and without saying a word he escorted her through the darkened, empty stacks of the old library, up narrow, clanging metal stairs, past rank after rank of old cast-iron shelves, rising through floors of stamped, whitewashed steel. On the last floor below the tower, in the dim light of a single bulb hanging over the stairs, she pulled him into the empty stacks and kissed him, digging her nails into the back of his neck. "What have you done with Victoria?" she murmured.

"The same thing I'm going to do with you," he said, and he pried her off him and stepped back, taking her hands and walking backward, tugging her toward the tower.

"Do we have to go up there, darling?"

"Yes," he said. "All the way to the top."

At the bottom of the tower stairs, Miranda stopped, clutching the banister.

"Nelson," she said, "it's cold up here. And damp. Why don't we go back to your office?"

"What are you afraid of?" Nelson's finger was warming as he took her hand. "Don't you want to see the ghost?"

They climbed the dark, empty tower, through room after empty room. The light of the lamps around the Quad below rose through the warped and dirty glass of the tall windows. Miranda clutched Nelson a little tighter as they came up to the gate in the fence of unpainted steel mesh; the smell of old books and dust seemed to pour through the stiff wire. Nelson dug in his pocket for the key, while Miranda clung to him with one hand and clutched the lapels of her coat with the other.

"Nelson," she said, "you didn't really bring Victoria up here, did you?"

Nelson fitted the key in the lock. He hadn't been here in weeks, and he expected the lock to be stiff with disuse, but the key turned easily.

"Oh, but I did," he said. "I lured her up here and flung her off the top of the tower. She turned into a bat and flew away."

Miranda tightened her grip on his arm. "You're scaring me," she said. "Is that what you want me to say?"

Nelson put his arm around her waist as he pocketed the key. "Actually, yes," he said.

He hauled the gate back on its shrieking hinges and pulled Miranda in after him. The gate clanged after them, and he pressed her up against the mesh of the door and kissed her hard. She wriggled and tried to laugh, but he could tell she was trembling.

"What are you afraid of?" he whispered in her ear. "Afraid Victoria's going to show up?"

He held himself back from her. Miranda's eyes searched his face. He bared his teeth and hissed and lunged at her throat. She shoved him back, and he laughed. "That's not *funny!*" she cried, and she pushed past him into the aisle.

"Quit playing games, Nelson." She clutched her lapels with both hands. "I'm on your side. Where's Victoria?"

He started toward her. "I have no idea."

She stepped back, stumbling over a book on the wooden floor. "Nelson, you know where she is, don't you?"

"I tell you what," he said. "Go up one more flight, and I'll tell you."

"Cut it out, Nelson." She glanced over her shoulder, at the tall wooden shelves crammed with malodorous old books looming over her in the darkness.

"One more flight, and I'll tell you everything."

She glared at him in the dim light. Then she marched up the aisle, around the banister, and up the next flight of stairs, her heels clanging on the steps. Nelson followed at his leisure, watching her legs as she went up the stairs. He came to the bottom of the next flight and looked up at her.

"Now take off your coat," he said.

"Nelson." Her intonation was half-plea, half-warning. Nelson said nothing. Glancing back into the dark behind her, Miranda began to unbutton her coat. Nelson started up the stairs slowly, one slow step at a time. He began to unbutton his own coat. As Miranda's coat fell open, he caught a glimpse of flesh and lingerie.

"Is she waiting up here somewhere?" Miranda's eyes darted all around her, searching the darkness. "Is this some kind of trick?"

Near the top of the steps Nelson shrugged off his own coat and draped it over the railing. He began to unbutton his jacket. "Drop the coat," he said.

"It's *cold.*" Miranda backed away from him.

Nelson shook his finger at her. "Drop it."

Miranda let the coat slither to her feet, and she stepped back into the shadowy aisle. Nelson saw white skin, a black strap, the glint of her hair as it swung.

"You're frightening me," Miranda said.

"I'm the ghost of Thornfield Library!" Nelson said in a quavering voice. He waggled his fingers at her. "Look on me, ye unbelievers, and beware!"

Miranda stepped backward into the pale light of one of the arched windows, wearing only a bustier, panties, and a garter belt and stockings. Her legs were together, the toes of her pumps pointed straight at him. She was clutching her shoulders, her arms crossed over her breasts. Nelson stopped and sighed at the sight of her. "So," he murmured, "are you scared yet?"

Miranda's eyes widened suddenly, and she gasped. She pulled one hand off her shoulder to point at something behind him.

"Oh, come on," Nelson said.

Miranda opened her mouth wide, but she was speechless. Her arm trembled.

"For crying out loud, Miranda." Rolling his eyes, Nelson turned.

A pale figure rushed at him out of the dark. Nelson yelled and threw up his arm. Miranda shrieked. Nelson fell against the cold wooden floor, and as he tried to rise, he was bowled over by Miranda leaping over him and down the stairs. A pair of hands grasped him by the shoulders, and he wriggled out of the jacket and plunged headfirst down the stairs, scrambling on his hands and knees, tumbling the last few steps. Scrabbling to his feet, he glanced back to see the pale figure rushing down the stairs at him, arms outstretched.

Nelson dashed around the banister and down the next flight of steps. Ahead he saw Miranda clawing at the mesh of the door, hauling it open on its screaming hinges.

"Hold the gate!" he shouted, but Miranda dashed through without looking back and let the gate slam behind her. She leaped shrieking down the stairs, the back of her thighs flashing in the dark. A glance back showed Nelson someone pale racing round the banister. His knees nearly gave out, but he staggered up the aisle toward the gate. He slipped and slid on the books under his feet, he was tugged at by the volumes crammed into the shelves. Halfway up the aisle he tripped over a volume, sending it spinning across the floor, and he fell headlong, catching himself in the mesh of the gate by his fingers just before he hit the floor. The pain in his dead finger was sudden and unbelievably sharp. He screamed and, in spite of the pain, tried to drag himself up by the mesh, hand over hand.

A pair of cold hands grabbed him by the ankles and pulled him right up off the floor, so that he hung by his fingers from the gate. He hauled on the mesh as hard as he could, trying to twist his ankles free, but the hands only pulled him harder.

"Help me!" he gasped through the wire, into the darkness down the stairs.

The hands tightened their icy grip, pulling harder. One by one, Nelson's fingers loosened from the mesh.

Nelson tried to cry out again, but he could only squeak in pain. He hung from the mesh now only by his right index finger. As the hands yanked him off the gate, his dead finger was wrenched free of his hand. Nelson howled as he fell, only to be abruptly silenced by the stunning impact of his head with the floor. The darkness spun, full of throbbing points of red. The cold closed in on him, and he looked up to see his severed finger dangling from the mesh above him. Pain shot up his arm and down his leg like electricity.

A pale face loomed over him out of the darkness, and Nelson saw a pair of bright, unblinking eyes looking down at him.

"Time to pay the piper, Professor," said Vita Deonne, and then everything went black.

18

La Vita Nuova

When Nelson awoke, he was in Hell. He was alone in a windowless room with walls of smoking brick and a floor of heaving, buckling wooden planks. A furious red glare stabbed through the cracks in the floorboards, and a stinging smoke poured through as well, tightening Nelson's windpipe and searing his eyes. A huge red clock numbered backward, with hands like blades, filled one wall, driven by the black gears and counterweights of a vast machine that hung from the rafters over his head. At the center of the clockworks a gleaming, coiled spring throbbed like a black heart, while a razor of a pendulum sliced the air beneath. In the flickering red gloom above the machine Nelson saw massive, blackened rafters, upon which crouched shadowy demons with angry red eyes, naked creatures the color of boiled lobster and the size of action figures, with bulging muscles and enormous penises and protruding eyes like Peter Lorre's.

Nelson was naked, too, and the burning floorboards singed his skin, making it impossible for him to find a position where he had a moment's respite from the pain. He skittered frantically across the floor like a droplet of water sizzling across a hot, greased pan. But as bad as that was, the pain in his right hand was worse, a deep, unreachable, scalding heat centered on his finger, a heat that made him want to grasp the nearest living creature—his wife, his lover, one of his innocent daughters—and press his glowing finger into her defenseless flesh and feel that cool release. But his finger was gone: All that remained was a bloody stump and the unassuagable pain. There was no possibility of relief.

He tried to weep, but his tears scalded him. He tried to scream, but his throat was too parched.

"I'm sorry!" he gasped, the smoke pouring down his throat with every breath. "I'd take it all back if I could! Please, let me breathe! I'll burn all my books!"

Then the demons leaped screaming from the rafters, sliding through the gears of the machine and swinging hideously from the counterweights. They capered around him on the heaving, flaming floorboards, slashing at him with their claws, sinking their needle-sharp teeth into his calves and thighs, dancing on his chest as they laughed and shrieked his name in painfully high-pitched voices. One of them plunged his teeth into Nelson's penis, worrying it viciously like a growling, hungry dog. Nelson's mutilated hand blazed with pain like a torch. He howled for mercy, his mouth full of burning smoke.

"No!" rang out another voice, as clear and strong as an enormous bell, and a pale, long-fingered hand reached over Nelson and swatted away the gibbering demons on his chest.

"No!" cried the bell-like voice again, tolling, "No!" another ten times, as the hand yanked the rest of the demons off of Nelson's legs and groin and flung them away into the smoking gloom.

Nelson felt his head lifted and laid in a lap. A pair of hands began to wrap his injured hand in long loops of cool fabric, binding up his wound. Against all expectation, in spite of Nelson's horrible, burning remorse, the pain in his hand began to ease. He looked up at the figure bending over him and saw a long, narrow face with no eyes, nose, or mouth, only a shining, elongated oval of silver.

"Am I dreaming?" whimpered Nelson, cool tears at last filling his eyes. "Please say I'm dreaming."

"We are such stuff as dreams are made on," said the voice, "and our little life is rounded with a sleep."

"What?" said Nelson.

The figure stroked its long fingers over Nelson's eyelids, closing them.

"Nothing human is alien to me," said the voice.

Nelson was aware of the red glare fading, of the crackling floorboards settling into place, of the air clearing and cooling around him. He could breathe now, and lie still. From overhead he heard the slow, rhythmic clanking of the enormous clock: The thick teeth of immense gears met and meshed, giant cylindrical counterweights rattled up and down at the ends of chains, and a massive pendulum slowly swung, *tock tock tock,* over Nelson Humboldt's uneasy head.

When he opened his eyes again, the first thing he saw was the pale, narrow face of Victoria Victorinix, looming above him.

"No!" cried Nelson, and he tried to throw his arm over his eyes. But something cold and hard encircling his wrist jerked his arm violently back.

"Knock it off, Nelson," Victoria said. "Open your eyes."

Nelson cracked an eyelid. Victoria's face hung over him, pale and drawn. She was not wearing her tinted glasses, and her usually icy eyes were red rimmed and tired. She lifted her left hand, and Nelson felt his arm lifted at the same time.

"See?" she said.

He opened his other eye. He and Victoria were linked together at the wrist by a pair of silvery handcuffs. His right hand was bandaged with a scarf or a large handkerchief, tightly looped around his wrist and his palm. The cloth was stained with blood where his right index finger used to be.

"Oh, God," Nelson breathed.

"Can you sit up?" asked Victoria, peering into his eyes.

Nelson lifted his head. He was stretched out full length on a cold wooden floor, and he saw to his relief that he was wearing his clothes and his shoes. Victoria had settled herself cross-legged next to him, her left hand beside his right hand on the floor, linked by the gleaming cuffs. She looked uncharacteristically disheveled, with her cropped hair bristling and bags under her eyes. She wore a pair of silk pajamas, buttoned all the way to her throat.

"I can try," he said.

Victorinix reached awkwardly around him, hauling at his shoulder with her right hand, and Nelson managed to sit up against the rough brick wall behind him. Weariness dragged at him like weights along the entire length of his body, especially in his legs. His injured hand throbbed. His throat was as dry and rough as sandpaper, and he felt very hungry. He struggled a little higher against the wall and glanced around him.

He and Victorinix were in a large, square, high-ceilinged room, with a rough wooden floor and dark, brick walls. A glowing white clock face filled one wall, its numbers in reverse; the hands seemed to have just passed twelve. The clock was lit by a circle of neon bulbs around the rim; the bulbs were cowled on the inside, however, so that the room was lit only by a pale, bluish light. A slow, rhythmic clanking came from the mechanism of the clock, a surprisingly compact assemblage of brass gears and flywheels suspended by beams and cables over the center of the room. There was no throbbing spring, no slicing pendulum. To one side of the clock, five bells—four smaller ones in ascending size, and one large bell—hung from a framework of thick beams.

"This is still Hell, isn't it?" Nelson whispered, his throat aching. "I'm not out of it yet."

"We're in the clock tower." Victoria sounded hoarse as well. "I've been here several days." She ran her free hand over her bristling hair. "You've been here almost twenty-four hours."

"I've been out for a whole *day?*" Nelson was appalled. Bridget must be frantic, he thought. Then, as events of the last few months came flooding back, he reconsidered. Would she miss me? he wondered. Would anyone miss me? Do I even *deserve* to be missed?

"You lost a lot of blood," Victorinix said. "I bound your hand as best I could."

"Then today is . . . ?"

"Saturday night, Nelson. Just before midnight. It will be Easter Sunday in less than five minutes."

Now he realized that he was seeing the clock from behind. It took some groggy effort to flip it in his mind, but the hands read 11:58. A low, whistling moan seemed to run round the room. It's the April wind, thought Nelson, howling around the corners of the tower.

"Where's Vita?" he said, lowering his voice.

"The last time I saw Vita," said Victorinix, "was in my bedroom. She was coming at me with a bottle of chloroform."

"You haven't seen her since?" Nelson glanced around the dim room.

"When I sleep, someone leaves me food and water. But I haven't seen a soul."

Victoria lifted her left wrist, tugging Nelson's hand off the floor like a dead thing. "How are you feeling?" she said. "Can you stand?"

"I'm not sure."

"Try."

Victoria got her bare feet under her and stood, pulling Nelson up with her. He clambered up unsteadily, swaying on his feet. The guilt flooding him tried to drag him under; he felt like a drowning man, sinking into black water.

"I think I need to sit back down," he whispered.

"Not yet," said Victorinix, dragging him forward by the cuffs.

He stumbled after her under the clock and into a corner of the room, toward a narrow, iron, spiral staircase that corkscrewed through the floor and up to the ceiling. A steel grating lay across the hole in the floor where the steps passed through, and the grating was padlocked to a ring in the floorboards. The room wobbled around Nelson on a shaky pivot. His knees were watery. He was about to pass out when Victoria knelt before the grating, and he sank gratefully to his knees next to her. Through the mesh he could see the tottering, overstuffed bookshelves of the Poole Collection in the room below, lit in a dramatic chiaroscuro by a single bright bulb. The moaning wind seemed to press against the ancient glass of the windows below.

Victorinix pushed the fingers of both hands through the mesh and rattled the grating. The heavy old Yale lock jerked against the ring in the floor, but did not yield. Victoria's features were crosshatched by the shadow of the mesh cast by the light below.

"It's loose." She fixed him with her red-rimmed eyes. "I'm hoping the two of us can pull it free. Can you manage?"

He saw little black stars floating before his eyes. His injured hand throbbed. He glanced at the clock face: 11:59. Somehow it seemed important to get the grating open before midnight. He nodded.

"Good," Victoria said. "On the count of three."

Nelson pushed the fingers of his good hand through the cold steel grating, as well as the pinky and third finger of his injured hand. He drew a breath and tightened his fingers.

"One," said Victoria, "two . . ."

A loud clang came from above, and Nelson felt the vibration of the metal staircase through the grating. Still clutching the mesh, he looked up through the spiral of the stairs. A steel trapdoor at the top led through the ceiling to the roof of the tower, and it was being swung away, revealing a black square of sky. The sound of the wind became louder. A foreshortened figure with a pale face stood over the square, looking down.

Nelson gasped and released the grating. For a moment Victorinix gazed up wide-eyed, then she released the grating as well and scuttled back from the spiral staircase on her knees, dragging Nelson after her by the handcuffs. The dark figure started down; footsteps rang down the stair. Victoria stood and hauled Nelson to his feet with surprising force, and he staggered after her as she pulled him under the clockworks again toward the far side of the room.

"My life," said the figure, conversationally, "has been shaped by what people call a peculiarity in me."

Vita came round and round the stairs—or rather, Robin Bravetype did, a compact, wiry young man with close-cropped hair and a goatee and moustache. He wore black slippers, a black T-shirt, and a pair of black jeans tight enough to make it clear, even in the pale light, that he wasn't wearing any underwear. Robin's sex, if not his gender, was clearly outlined in denim. He smiled all the way down the steps, fixing his eyes on the two retreating professors every time he came around the spiral.

"I have no fear of men, as such," Robin went on, "nor of their books. I have mixed with them—one or two of them particularly—almost as one of their own sex."

The room whirled before Nelson. He felt colder. Was the moaning wind twisting down the stairs? His knees trembled, and Victoria pressed him up against the rough brick wall.

At the bottom of the spiral stair Robin stepped lightly into the room. His features were hard to read against the glow behind him. At the top of the clock the minute hand squeezed out the last interval between itself and the hour hand, which was already pointing at twelve.

"So God created man in his own image," said Robin. "In the image of God created he him."

He tread as gracefully and as silently as a cat into the room, carefully placing one foot before the other as if he were walking a tightrope.

"Male and female," he said, indicating Nelson with one hand and Victoria with the other, "created he them."

"What's he doing?" Victoria muttered.

"I'm gonna faint." Nelson sagged against the wall.

Victoria yanked hard at his cuffed wrist. "Don't," she said.

Robin stopped at the center of the room, directly under the clockworks. Over his head the works began to whirr and tick faster. He pulled a corner of his T-shirt out of his jeans, showing a flash of white flesh, and he thrust his hand under the shirt.

"He took one of Adam's ribs and closed up the flesh thereof."

The T-shirt bulged and rippled as Robin worked his elbow up and down. He knitted his brow in concentration, he bit his lip; he looked like someone digging blindly in a sack. Meanwhile the clappers on the smaller bells began to play the little Big Ben melody, four notes down, four notes up, filling the room. The floor vibrated under Nelson's feet, and he began to tremble. Victoria threw her arm across his chest to keep him from falling over.

As the clock played the second half of the tune, the clapper of the huge bell ticked back, getting ready to strike the hour. Over the ringing of the bells, Nelson and Victoria heard a loud, sharp *crack!* Robin winced. He pulled his hand out from under his shirt. He held a curved white bone.

"This is now bone of my bones, and flesh of my flesh," he declaimed loudly over the final four notes of the bells, turning the bone over in his hands. "She shall be called Woman because she was taken out of Man."

"Did he just . . . ?" Nelson said.

"Not possible," snapped Victoria.

The clock played the final four notes, and as they faded, Nelson saw the clapper of the large bell reach its zenith. The clockworks whirred faster and faster. Victoria pressed her hands over her ears, dragging at Nelson's wrist, and Nelson hunched his shoulders.

The clapper fell, and Robin tossed the bone straight up into the air, into the clockworks over his head. The bone was swallowed instantly by the compact mass of gleaming brass, and with a loud *clank* the works began to shudder—gears lurched and ground against each other without turning, wheels jerked violently in place. Hissing sparks flew from the works; gray tendrils of smoke rose from the gears. Then, with an even louder *clank,* the works seized up, and the falling clapper stopped instantly an inch from the largest bell.

Just as abruptly, the last reverberations of the smaller bells stopped. The room was suddenly silent. After a moment Victoria cautiously lifted her hands off her ears. Nelson lowered his shoulders.

"What's going on?" whispered Nelson.

"*Sh,*" hissed Victorinix.

The clock hands pointed to midnight. Silhouetted against the clock face, Robin posed perfectly still, heel to toe, under the clockworks. His shoulders were thrust forward and his arms twisted behind his back. The room was absolutely silent. The frozen clock made no sound. Nelson could no longer hear the wind outside.

"This curious child," Robin said, breaking the silence, "was very fond of pretending to be two people."

He pulled one hand out from behind his back, empty, but with the other he pulled, as if from thin air, the figure of another person, handing her out into plain view as if doing a gavotte. It was Vita, wearing her plain brown shoes and one of her shapeless brown dresses, her colorless bangs hanging nearly in her eyes. She posed with surprising grace alongside Robin, their hands lifted together like those of a pair of acrobats.

"But it's no use, thought Alice," said Vita, her voice identical to Robin's, "to pretend to be two people."

"Wait a minute," muttered Victoria.

"Oh, boy," said Nelson.

"Why, there's hardly enough of me," declaimed Robin and Vita in unison, "to make *one* respectable person!"

Together they began to disrobe. Robin peeled off his T-shirt, as sinuously as a male stripper. Vita pried off her shoes, then she bent at the waist, clutched the hem of her dress, and hauled it over her head. In his grogginess, fear, and remorse, Nelson registered that Robin was wearing a tight sports bra, and that Vita was utterly flat-chested. What's more, Vita's panties had a suspicious bulge in them. Robin wriggled out of his bra, freeing a pair of small breasts, and then kicked off his slippers and slithered out of his jeans, revealing a neat triangle of brown hair and the thin, bloodless lips of a vagina between his legs. Something long and pink tumbled out of the crotch of his jeans to the floor, and Vita, who had just slipped out of her panties to reveal a swinging penis, stooped and snatched up the pink object.

"This is a queer thing, to be sure!" said Vita, turning the object this way and that. "However, everything is queer today."

"It's a severed finger," Victoria whispered.

"It's *my* severed finger!" Nelson gasped.

Vita tossed the digit over her shoulder. She and Robin stood naked under the stopped clockworks in the eerie silence, two small piles of clothing at their feet. Robin looked broader in the hips and narrower in the shoulders than he'd seemed before, while Vita seemed narrower in the hips and broader in the shoulder. And though they were naked, they were not yet finished with their mutual reconstructions. Vita lifted both hands to her head in a gesture Nelson had seen a hundred times before, but this time she plucked off her helmet of hair and handed it to Robin, and Robin peeled off his goatee and moustache and handed it to Vita.

Nelson groaned. He leaned on Victoria's shoulder for support. He wished he could lie down again.

"Very clever," Victoria called out, "point taken." She shifted under Nelson, trying to redistribute his weight.

But Vita and Robin ignored her, continuing with their tableau vivant.

"Of the men who came into the world," said Robin, twisting Vita's hair onto his head, "those who were cowards or led unrighteous lives were changed into women in the second generation."

As he spoke, Vita patted her new facial hair into place under her nose and over her chin. Now, to superficial appearances anyway, Robin had become Vita,

350

and Vita, Robin. Nelson wondered if he was delirious. Perhaps he had imagined the whole thing; perhaps they had merely switched places.

The new Robin began to yank at his penis as if it were a handle.

"To the girdle do the gods inherit," he muttered. "Beneath is all the fiend's."

He gave his penis an angry tug.

"There's hell! There's darkness! There is the sulphurous pit!" he cried, tugging it harder and harder the while. "Burning, scalding, stench, consumption! Fie, fie, *fie!*"

"Dear God," Nelson gasped, thinking of the pain.

With a sound like parting Velcro, Robin tore his penis and testicles away from between his legs.

Nelson's legs gave out, and he sagged to the floor, dragging Victorinix with him. Together they landed with their backs against the wall, their legs splayed in front of them.

Victoria clutched Nelson's hand.

"Is it *detachable?*" she whispered urgently.

"Not ordinarily," gulped Nelson.

"What a piece of work is a man!" declaimed Robin, holding the trembling cock and balls aloft in the cool light of the frozen clock. Nelson saw only a smooth patch of flesh between his legs.

At the same time, Vita was reaching between her legs with both hands and, with a rubbery *thwack!* pulled her vagina, uterus, and ovaries out of herself, like a big, complicated balloon. Vita and Robin then exchanged equipment: She took the penis ensemble from him, and he took the quivering uterus and its accouterments from her.

"How infinite in reason!" cried Vita, clapping the penis between her legs.

"How infinite in faculties!" Robin parted the smooth patch between his legs with the tips of his fingers and then, hand over hand, began to stuff the quivering organs inside himself.

"In form and moving how express and admirable!" Vita peeled the breasts off her chest and held them out to Robin, one in each palm like a pudding, with a cherry red nipple on top.

"In action how like an angel!" Robin placed them on his chest and adjusted them until the nipples were even.

"In apprehension," they cried together, exchanging their hair again, bangs from Vita to Robin, goatee from Robin to Vita, "how like ... a ... *god!*"

Suddenly, with the shriek of grinding metal, sparks cascaded from the clock-works, smoking little atoms that bounded off the floorboards and filled the room with the singeing stench of hot metal. Gears jerked, wheels lurched. The clapper of the big bell fell another half-inch without striking. Hot sparks skittered across the floor toward Nelson and Victoria, stinging them like needles; Victoria launched herself onto Nelson's lap, and Nelson clasped her to him. The clock-works shrieked as if in pain, a high, grinding whine. The beams that supported the mechanism shivered; the whole room vibrated. The clappers of the smaller bells began to strike dissonantly, but the big bell still did not strike. Nelson and Victoria clung to each other.

Then, in a spasm, the gears lurched, the wheels spun free, and the machine extruded a shining figure that fell straight toward the floor. The big bell struck the moment the figure hit the floor. It landed hard on its feet, knees bent to absorb the shock, and then sprang instantly erect, striking a pose, heel to toe, arms raised in an acrobat's gesture of *ta-da!* as the room rumbled to the rever-beration of the bell. The hot glare of the sparks faded, but even in the dimmer glow of the clock face, the figure seemed to change colors, from gold to silver to ebony, a steady, liquid shimmering. Its limbs were sleek and smooth, its shoul-ders and hips narrow. It seemed to have no gender at all. It had no face.

"Be not afeard," the sprite said, in a voice with the hollow resonance of a bell. "The isle is full of noises, sounds, and sweet airs, that give delight and hurt not."

Victoria's mouth worked wordlessly. Nelson clapped his free hand over his eyes. "Oh, God," he moaned, "I really am in Hell!"

Vita/Robin and Robin/Vita danced around the figure in the blue light, jigging with their knees up and elbows flying. Vita's breasts bobbed, Robin's penis flopped to the rhythm. The clapper of the big bell was ticking slowly back to strike again.

"For spirits, when they please," sang Vita, "can either sex assume, or both, so oft and uncompounded is their essence pure."

"Not tied or manacled with joint or limb," sang Robin, "nor founded on the brittle strength of bones, like cumbrous flesh."

Then, in unison: "But in what shape they choose," they sang, "dilated or condensed, bright or obscure, can execute their airy purposes!"

Between them, the sprite under the clock posed and preened like a ringmaster. The big bell struck a second time.

"While we are in the body," the sprite said, "we are absent from the Lord."

Then the sprite clapped its hands and stepped back, and Vita and Robin charged straight at each other, skipping into the air at the last moment. Just as the bell struck a third time, they collided under the clockworks. Instead of rebounding or collapsing in a heap, however, they seemed to enter into each other's flesh, struggling inside a single skin like two people fighting in a sack. The sheet of skin bulged and puckered and rippled for a long, horrible moment. Then their faces popped out on the opposite sides of a single head, and, like a balloon inflating, they filled out into a doughnut of flesh, joined at the shoulders and hips, their arms and legs and genitalia on the outside. It was an impossibly awkward construction, a badly engineered ouroboros. For the moment the creature stood unsteadily on Vita's legs, like a woman with a huge burden on her back.

"Tell me," said Vita's face, "when does the soul attain truth? In attempting to consider anything with the body, is she not deceived?" The bell struck *four*.

"Yes," said Robin's face. He waved his arms and legs uselessly in the air like an overturned beetle.

The sprite came up from behind and stuck its faceless face in the hole of the creature, as if it were peering at Nelson and Victoria cowering against the wall. It placed its long-fingered hands on the inside of the doughnut hole and rolled the twinned creature clockwise in the direction of Robin's face. Vita was rocked back on her heels; she clawed at the air with her hands.

"And is thought not best," she cried breathlessly, "when she takes leave of the body, when she has no bodily sense or desire, but is aspiring after true being?"

"True," grunted Robin, landing on his feet with a thump and staggering a few steps. The bell struck *five*.

"And in this," cried Vita, her legs madly pedaling the air, "the philosopher dishonors the body. His soul runs away from his body and desires to be alone and by herself?"

"What you say," groaned Robin, staggering under the weight of himself and Vita, "has a wonderful truth in it!"

The bell struck *six*, and the sprite suddenly jumped up into the hole and, crouched over, began to run in place like a hamster on an exercise wheel. With a mutual shout of dismay, the Vita/Robin doughnut began to roll ponderously around the room, thumping rhythmically against the floorboards.

"For the body is a source of endless trouble!" shouted one of the faces.

"It is liable to diseases which impede the search for true being!" cried the other.

They flailed their arms and legs, they scrunched their faces in pain each time their heads were rolled under, they yelped when their genitals and breasts were mashed against the floor.

"It fills us full of loves!"

"And lusts!"

"And fears!"

"And fancies!"

"And endless foolery!"

Meanwhile the sprite jogged faster inside the rolling wheel of flesh, and the wheel rolled faster and faster, in a wider and wider spiral around the room, leaning inward, rumbling like a mill wheel.

"Whence come wars?"

"And fightings?"

"And factions?"

"Whence but from the body!"

"And the lusts of the body!"

Now the wheel was merely a fleshy blur thundering around the outer perimeter of the room, the wind of its passage gusting over Victoria and Nelson with each circuit. The running sprite was a blur as well, a continuous, shimmering flash. The wheel rolled closer and closer to Victoria and Nelson. The bell struck *seven*.

"Stop it!" Victoria shouted. *"Stop it!"*

"Mommy!" cried Nelson, burying his face in Victoria's neck.

The wheel missed them by a hair.

"If we would have pure knowledge of anything," howled the wheel, its two voices indistinguishable now, *"we must be quit of the body!"*

As suddenly as it had sprung in, the sprite jumped easily out of the doughnut, and the wheel began to lose its momentum and spiral in upon the space under the clockworks in a drunken circle, until, just as the bell struck *eight,* it collapsed on its side with a tremendous, room-rattling thump and broke apart. The sprite stooped first to Vita, hauling her up by her elbow, and, as she staggered dizzily about before the clock face, it hauled Robin to his feet as well.

Victoria struggled off Nelson's lap and tried to step into the center of the room, but Nelson was unable to rise, so she leaned as far as the cuffs allowed her, shaking her free fist at the trio of figures under the clockworks.

"Who are you?" she cried, her voice trembling. *"Who are you?"*

"*What* are you?" whispered Nelson.

"I'm nobody," said Vita, blinking with dizziness. "Who are you?"

"Why, you are nothing then," said Robin, rubbing his eyes, "neither maid, widow, nor wife."

"I am all the daughters of my father's house," replied Vita, a little more steadily, "and all the brothers too."

"Thou art a fiend!" snarled Robin, finding his feet at last. "A woman's shape doth shield thee."

"In men the organ of generation becomes rebellious and masterful," snapped Vita, her hands on her hips, "like an animal disobedient to reason, maddened with the sting of lust, and seeks to gain *absolute sway. . . .*"

The sprite snapped its fingers as the bell struck *nine,* a ringing tone that reverberated around the room.

"Lord, what fools these mortals be," it said.

The three figures—Robin, Vita, and the sprite—now stood roughly equidistant from each other under the clockworks. Robin and Vita were sharply silhouetted against the glowing clock face, while there was something almost imperceptibly liquid about the outline of the sprite.

"Ah, but what *about* the body, Vita?" asked the sprite.

"Could we not say," Vita began, with something of the old, querulous tremor in her voice, "that the radical polysemia of the corpus, in its sedimented materiality . . . ?"

"Speak English!" protested Robin. "I don't know the meaning of half those long words, and, what's more, I don't believe you do either!"

The sprite clapped its hands like a schoolteacher at the same moment as the bell struck *ten,* silencing them both.

"What about the body, Vita?" it asked again, and it snatched off one of its feet.

"What about the feet, Skeet?" it said, tossing the foot at Vita.

At the same moment Vita pushed back her hair and tugged off her ear.

"What about the ear, dear?" she said, tossing it to Robin as she caught the foot.

"What about the dick, Nick?" said Robin, yanking off his penis and testicles and pitching them through the air at the sprite with one hand, as he caught Vita's ear with the other.

"What about the knee, Dee?" called the sprite.

"What about the toe, Joe?" said Vita.

"What about the butt, Tut?" said Robin.

In sheer astonishment, Victoria sank to her knees, allowing Nelson to relax his extended arm. Across the room, under the clockworks, silhouetted against the glowing, backward clock face, the triangle of figures was juggling body parts in three directions. To begin with Nelson could follow individual pieces—an elbow; a nose; a pink, quivering lung—but then they began to juggle faster, pulling themselves apart in the process, slowly diminishing until each figure began to resemble an anatomy chart. Vita was down to a single eyeball and the skein of her nervous system; Robin was mostly missing between his ankles and his collarbone, except for his intestinal tract and a kidney. Yet somehow three voices still issued from thin air.

"Gender!" cried Vita.

"Race!" shouted Robin.

"Class!" sang the sprite.

By now the sprite was only a pair of hands in midair, furiously juggling, while the air between what remained of the figures was a three-way blur of body parts. The bell struck *eleven.*

"Hetero!" Vita

"Homo!" Robin.

"Bi!" The sprite.

"Lesbian!"

"Gay!"

"Transgendered!"

"Father!"

"Son!"

"Holy ghost!"

The bell struck *twelve,* filling the room. Victoria clapped her hands over her ears. The bell was so loud Nelson could not hear himself screaming. Yet, still, as if from the middle of his head, he could hear the three voices from the triangular blur of feet and hands and viscera.

356

"Faith!" said Vita.

"Hope!" said Robin.

"Charity!" said the sprite.

"And the greatest of these is . . ."

"And the greatest of these is . . ."

"And the greatest of these is . . ."

The thunderous reverberation of the bell hurt Nelson's ears, and, with dread, he watched the clapper rise one more time. He tried to cover his own ears, starting a tug of war with Victoria over his cuffed hand.

The clapper swung toward the bell. All three of the voices under the whirring clock sang, in a kind of harmony, "And the greatest of these is . . ."

The bell struck *thirteen*. A heartbeat later the room shook violently, as if the tower was swaying from side to side. My God, thought Nelson, the tower *is* swaying. The smaller bells danced on their mounts, filling the room with a deafening, dissonant ringing. Across the room the wide, white clock face shivered, sagged, and shattered. The frosted glass cascaded shrieking into the room; great icy segments splintered into tiny, sparkling shards.

As the shattered glass sprayed across the floor, Nelson and Victoria hugged each other tightly, averting their faces. In the midst of the cacophony, Nelson was surprised to note that Victorinix had a living heart, and that it was pounding madly. The shrill crashing of the glass subsided; the mad ringing of the bells faded. Nelson felt Victorinix relax her grip on him, and he lifted his face from her shoulder and peeked.

The figures, either whole or in pieces, were gone; not so much as a fingertip or an earlobe lay on the floor, only glittering pieces of the shattered clock face. There was a huge, dark hole edged with jagged glass where the clock face had been; the hands of the clock, still attached to the axle that connected them to the clockworks, pointed straight up against a velvet sky. The wind was moaning again, pouring through the empty clock face, filling the room with cold air. A pulsing reddish glare came from below. Nelson heard men's voices, shouting.

The tower lurched once more; more falling glass tinkled against the floor. Nelson and Victoria exchanged a glance. The shouting from below was louder, and there were sharp, rapid reports, like someone hammering rhythmically on tin.

"Is it safe?" whispered Nelson.

"Come on," said Victoria.

She struggled to her feet, pulling Nelson up with her. She stopped at the edge of the broken glass—she was barefoot.

"You'll have to carry me," she said.

"I'm not sure I can." Now that he was standing, Nelson felt the loss of blood more acutely.

But before he could object further, she had clambered onto his back, tugging his cuffed hand across his chest. She was as light as one of his daughters, but Nelson still felt dizzy. He started across the room, glass crunching under the soles of his shoes. The rhythmic, metallic percussion outside grew steadier, and there was a speedy whine Nelson recognized from old westerns as a ricochet.

"That's gunfire," he said, and he stopped a few yards away from the edge of the hole. Victoria tightened her clasp around his neck. A steady breeze blew through the empty clock face, chilly but full of spring fragrance. Nelson tiptoed forward, and he and Victoria peered warily over the jagged edge of the ruined clock face, the wind blowing in their faces.

Far below, in the middle of the Quad, Marko Kraljević and Lionel Grossmaul were firing automatic weapons through the trees at the buildings all around. Grossmaul fired in one direction, Kraljević in the other. Kraljević was wearing combat fatigues, but Grossmaul still wore his orange coveralls from the county jail, which only emphasized his sloping shoulders and his wide behind. Between them Lorraine Alsace crouched over a canvas bag, and as Nelson and Victoria watched, Kraljević ceased firing, ejected a spent clip from his gun, and gestured to her. She tossed him a fresh clip, and Kraljević slammed it home. He fired on automatic, spraying bullets; the muzzle flashed in a steady, strobing rhythm, followed half a beat later by the sharp, metallic reports. In the direction of fire young leaves jerked and branches flew off trees, and Nelson could hear the dim crash of broken windows and the whine of ricochets. Grossmaul, however, aimed and fired a shot at a time, methodically shooting out the windows of Harbour Hall. Spent clips were littered at their feet; Kraljević crunched them under his black boots as he turned.

"What happened at Kosovo Polje?" shouted Kraljević. "Where did he die, the glorious Prince Lazar?"

"Tyrant! Sorcerer!" screamed Grossmaul, taking out another window. "You cheated me of my life!"

Nelson inched closer to the edge of the hole. Directly below the tower, through the bright, sunken V of the Annex's skylight, he saw the tiny, foreshortened figures of a pair of security guards—the only people in the Annex early on a Sunday morning—scurrying away from the cantilevered balconies toward the exits. A reddish glare flickered on the lawn around the skylight.

"Oh, God!" moaned Nelson. He saw specks before his eyes.

"Quiet!" hissed Victorinix, tugging at his throat.

As if he had heard, Kraljević, pausing to eject one clip and jam another into his weapon, looked up at the clock face.

"The Turk!" he cried. "I'll strike and slay them with their swords! I'll kill nine Turkish pashas!"

Grossmaul wheeled and looked up at the tower as well. "Kill them!" screamed Grossmaul, and he and Kraljević lifted their weapons toward the tower and fired.

Victorinix yanked on Nelson's neck and pulled him back from the edge. Bullets sprayed through the remaining glass and thudded into the walls with little puffs of red dust.

Victorinix tried to maneuver Nelson across the room with her knees, as if he were a horse, but he staggered against a wall. He could feel his knees weakening again, and his right hand throbbed with pain. His bandage was glistening; he was bleeding again. He smelled smoke.

"Put me down," Victorinix said, and Nelson sagged to his knees next to the wall. She immediately tugged him to his feet again, dragging him sweating and dizzy around the edges of the broken glass toward the spiral stair. A bullet rang off one of the bells. The tower rumbled again and shifted under their feet. Nelson's knees wobbled dangerously under him, but Victorinix tugged him on, toward the stair.

The wind through the gap in the wall carried streamers of gray smoke. It also carried the tinny hammering of the automatic weapons and a new sound, the irregular pop of pistol fire and the indecipherable blare of a bullhorn.

"The police are here," said Victorinix, dragging Nelson to a stop at the spiral stair.

No more bullets ricocheted around the clock room; Kraljević and Grossmaul were firing back at the police. They were still shouting, but Nelson could not make out what they were saying. He blinked down at the grating. Smoke wafted up through the mesh. Next to the grating, the padlock lay open in its ring.

"How the . . . ?"

"It doesn't matter, Nelson." Victorinix bent and yanked the grating back with one hand, sending it clanging to the floor. She started down the steps, tugging Nelson after her. Nelson's vision swam with black stars.

"I'm sorry, I can't." He sat heavily on a step. "Go on without me."

Victoria whirled and yanked violently on the handcuffs.

"I *can't* go on without you, Nelson! Those idiots outside have firebombed the tower! If we stay here, we'll both die!"

Nelson groaned and stood, and Victorinix descended the stairs, through the hole in the floor. Waist deep in the hole, Nelson stopped again and tugged on the cuffs. "Wait!" he cried. "There's Vita!"

Victorinix squeezed up into the hole with Nelson, sticking her head above the edge. Across the floor, amid a glittering litter of glass, someone lay curled in a corner of the room. The person was nude, head tucked down and knees to chest. All Nelson and Victoria could see were the bumps of its spine and seam of its buttocks. There was no way to tell if it was a man or a woman or anything in between. At this distance Nelson could not even tell if it was breathing.

He struggled to climb up out of the hole.

"She might be alive! We have to save her!"

Victoria furiously yanked his arm. She grabbed his lapels and dragged him round to face her. "There's nobody there." She fixed him with her gaze.

"But . . ." Nelson tried to turn his head to look at the curled figure across the room, but Victorinix dug her fingers into his jaw and wrenched his gaze back to hers.

"There's . . . no . . . one . . . there!" she said. "We woke up alone in the tower, Nelson. We saw no one; nothing happened."

"But Robin . . . ," protested Nelson. "That . . . sprite . . ."

"You lost a lot of blood, Nelson. You were delirious."

She let go of his jaw.

"But I saw it!"

Victorinix turned and descended the stair, dragging Nelson after her. "Nothing!" she shouted. "No one!"

Nelson's eyes sank below the floor. He caught a last glimpse of the pale figure.

"I'm sorry," he whispered.

Victorinix dragged Nelson through the roomful of books below, then down the stairs until they reached the lowest floor of the Poole Collection. The gunfire and shouting outside were muffled, though once a stray bullet clinked through a window and came to rest with a thud in some hapless volume. Coming down the last flight of stairs, Nelson's vision swarmed with black spots, his legs gave out, and he fell the rest of the way. Victoria clutched the banister for dear life and cursed under her breath as he nearly wrenched her arm out of her socket. Still, she struggled toward the gate, dragging him by the wrist, and Nelson crawled after her as best he could. Gray smoke drifted through the gate; through the mesh Nelson saw nothing but the dim, dusty steps and thickening billows of smoke.

Victoria grabbed the cold metal knob of the gate and pulled. Nothing happened, and she pulled harder, grunting. Nelson crouched at her feet like a three-legged dog. He pushed his fingers through the mesh and tried to help, but it was all he could do to hold himself up. Victoria pulled once more, angrily, with all her strength. She gave a long, inhuman hiss of rage.

"It's locked!" she snarled. "Where's the key, Nelson?"

"It's supposed to open from the inside without a key," he gasped. His eyes watered from the smoke. "It must be jammed."

Victoria threw back her head and roared. She rattled the door violently, but still it wouldn't open. She hung by the mesh for a moment, wild-eyed and breathing hard. Then she tugged Nelson across the floor down the aisle between the wall and the bookcases, toward one of the windows. Books cascaded from the stacks along the wall; whole towers of volumes tumbled over in Nelson's wake. Smoke was seeping now in threads through the cracks in the floorboards, and Nelson felt the heat of the fire through his palm and knees.

Victoria yanked hard on the handcuffs. "Can't you stand up?" she said.

Nelson dragged himself upright, pushing himself up on a stack of moldering old books, then pulling himself by the windowsill. Victoria heaved up the sash one-handed, and the chill, fresh wind blew back the smoke from Nelson's eyes and throat. The gunfire below rang off the brick all around.

There were no bars on this window. It can't be the one, thought Nelson, where Vita nearly jumped; that's on the other side of the tower. So who pulled these bars off?

Victoria thrust her head out the window. Nelson peered down too; they were on a side of the tower away from the Quad, where the ground rose in an embankment to meet the building. The windows lower down cast wide fans of flickering red light on the lawn below.

Victoria seemed to survey the wall under the window. Then she held up the handcuffs linking her to Nelson and looked at them in astonishment, as if at her own rotten luck. An image welled up out of Nelson's lizard brain, a snapshot of Victoria Victorinix crawling down the wall of the clock tower headfirst, her pajamas billowing in the wind, while he watched mournfully from the tower window, the flames rising behind him.

"We'll have to jump," she said. "It might only be three stories, perhaps four . . ."

They were propped shoulder to shoulder in the window.

"Perhaps . . ." Nelson said, gasping in the fresh air.

"Perhaps what?" said Victoria.

"We could break our fall," he said.

"How?" Her eyes narrowed.

Nelson turned and looked back at the room full of books behind them.

"We could make a pile under the window."

Victoria peered at him with her ancient, disinterested gaze. "Alright," she said.

Nelson and Victoria each grabbed a handful of books from the heap against the wall, and, struggling against the handcuffs, heaved the books out the window. The volumes disappeared in the dark, and a moment later Nelson heard a series of dim thumps against the grass below. His eyes met Victoria's.

"Alright," she said.

They worked awkwardly for the next two or three tries, one or the other overreaching against the constraint of the handcuffs, but silently they established a rhythm, and soon they were heaving whole stacks of books out the window. His injured hand tormented him, his eyes stung from the smoke filling the room, but Nelson managed to lift a few more books each time.

Soon they were pitching armsful of books out the window. Nelson glimpsed titles and authors as the books flew out into midnight darkness—names that had tumbled from the canon or had never quite made it in—Sir Walter Scott and Edmund Spenser and Rumer Godden and Thornton Wilder and Edna Ferber and John Galsworthy. Nelson saw books nobody read anymore or, at least, nobody studied: *The Anatomy of Melancholy* and *Spoon River Anthology* and *The Young Lions* and *You Can't Go Home Again* and *Butterfield 8* and *Kristen Lavransdatter* and even, to his surprise, a volume of James Hogg that he had missed in his earlier visits, *Tales of the Wars of Montrose*, volume III. The books flapped open as they fell, their spines cracking, their pages flailing in the air like the wings of wounded birds as they dropped through the dark. But Nelson and Victoria did not pause to look; they lunged for the nearest shelves first, pitching books in a stoker's rhythm into the maw of the night. Nelson caught a glimpse of the stack of books below, a roughly conical heap whose surface shifted and slid under the rain of volumes. It occurred to him that, at the very least, the books they were flinging out the window might survive the fire.

Meanwhile the rhythm of the gunfire picked up, like popcorn rattling in a pot. Under the irregular popping of the police handguns ran the steady hammering of the automatic weapons; the unamplified roaring of Kraljević and Grossmaul was nearly as loud as the hollow blare of the bullhorn, shouting at them to cease fire. From this window Nelson could not see the Quad, but he glimpsed police officers in Kevlar vests dashing from tree to tree between Harbour Hall and the library; he saw the bright sparks of their pistols firing.

Then, as one last load of minor authors—Somerset Maugham and Pearl Buck and James Gould Cozzens—went bouncing and tumbling down the side of the tower, Victoria stopped Nelson with a hand on his injured wrist. Nelson could barely stand for his watery knees, and his vision swam with a swirling galaxy of black stars.

"That's enough," said Victoria. She leaned out the window and surveyed the heap of books below. She put her hand under Nelson's wrist and nudged him up toward the windowsill.

"You first," he said, his knees about to buckle.

Victoria sprang lightly into the window, crouching on the sill in her bare feet. The moment she was no longer next to him, propping him up, Nelson sagged toward the floor.

"Come on!" she cried, hauling at the cuffs with both hands.

But Nelson sat gasping against the wall, his legs splayed uselessly. His bandage was soaked now; blood dripped down his sleeve.

"I . . . I'm sorry," he panted. His hand pounded with pain, his head sagged toward his chest. "I just *can't.*"

Smoke was gushing up the stairs through the gate; a pall of it hung among the bookshelves, sinking lower. Flames were licking through the cracks in the floor. Nelson felt the heat in the seat of his pants, but he couldn't move. The last thing I'll ever see before I go to Hell, he thought, is burning books. His vision began to turn black.

A pair of cool hands lifted his face. Fingers pried open his eyes. He saw Victoria's face before him, her pupils narrowed to vertical slits like a snake's. "I've never done this with a man," she murmured, as if to herself.

363

"Done what?" mumbled Nelson. His eyes stung, his nose and throat burned with smoke.

He was never certain afterward if what came next had ever really happened. In the garish light of the burning library, Victoria popped the top three buttons of her pajamas and bared her breast. Teary-eyed in the stinking smoke, Nelson thought she had the skin of a much younger woman. As he watched numbly, she drew a sharp fingernail across her skin, and dark, thick blood welled out. He felt her hand at the back of his neck, felt his head tipped forward, felt his nearly lifeless lips pressed to Victoria's warm, gushing breast. He'd wonder for the rest of his life, but it seemed as if he were swallowing her blood, which tasted of iron and something sweet; he felt it flowing warm and thick down his throat, spreading its heat through his chest and into his limbs. His vision began to clear; the swirling black dots faded before his eyes. He felt a hand lifting his chin. His eyelids popped wide, and his gaze met Victoria's. Her pupils were round and distant again, as they'd always been.

"Let's go," she said.

"You betcha!" cried Nelson, astonished at his own sudden vigor. He pulled his legs under him and shot straight to his feet, and he jumped with Victoria into the window, where they crouched side by side like a pair of gargoyles. Below them the night was more vivid than he had ever seen it before. The shadows were full of movement and detail; the trees hummed like tuning forks. Under the popping of gunfire and the roar of the flames, Nelson heard crickets chirping and owls hooting and even worms and grubs and moles burrowing through the dirt in the lawn below, in a hurry to get away from the burning building. Directly below the window the sprawling heap of books was painted red by flames pouring out of the lower windows.

Nelson's muscles tingled with new life; his legs tensed under him. It was all he could do to keep from springing off the windowsill.

"Hey, can we *fly?*" he cried happily.

"Don't be ridiculous," said Victoria, and she jumped. An instant later Nelson was yanked by his wrist into the night, and he fell screaming into the dark.

He didn't remember landing, nor did he remember crossing the lawn to Harbour Hall, nor the elevator ride to the top floor. The first thing he did remember, in fact, was starting awake on the sofa in Victorinix's office, his injured hand newly wrapped in a fresh bandage and placed carefully across his chest. He wore his half of the handcuffs; the little linking chain dangled. Firelight danced on the ceiling, and Nelson heard shouting and gunfire. He sat up, his head swimming, and saw Victorinix in her sooty, torn pajamas and a pair of running shoes, crouched at the window overlooking the Quad. She beckoned to him, the other half of the handcuffs still around her wrist. "Come watch, Nelson," she said, the pale dome of her head limned in the red glare of the burning library.

He rose to his feet, feeling light-headed but steady, and she gestured for him to keep low.

"Mind the glass," she said.

The windows of the chair's office had all been shot out; the carpet was covered with fragments. Nelson doubled over and crunched over the glass and knelt beside Victorinix at the window. Below him the Quad was spectacularly alight from the flames of Thornfield Library. The shadows of trees and lampposts streaked away across the lawn; clouds of hot sparks drifted into the black sky. A churning bolus of flame boiled out of each window of the old library, the flames lashing the brick above, turning it black. The clock tower was livid with billowing, rippling sheets of flame, as if the brick itself were on fire. Crimson smoke poured out of the round hole where the clock face had been; the melted minute and second hands drooped over the edge. The air was filled with an unholy, crackling roar.

"All those books!" gasped Nelson.

"Yes," murmured Victoria, the fire reflected in her eyes. "All those books."

"At least the Annex is safe," he said, but as he lowered his eyes to the Quad below, his heart sank. The tiny figures of police officers wearing vests and helmets crouched behind trees, firing past the library. Grossmaul lay on the Quad, his head at the center of a spreading tide of his own blood. Lorraine Alsace was sprawled a little farther on, but Kraljević/Jamisovich had retreated into the gully of the Annex skylight. He was still shooting, desperately trying to keep his footing on the steep, slippery glass, but he was firing at too steep an angle, into the trees above the heads of the police all around. Cracks were spreading all around him in the glass of the skylight, and as he staggered away from the breaking glass, the web of cracks only spread wider and faster. Even so, as he emptied one clip, he pulled another out of his belt and rammed it into the gun. Marko Kraljević, literary theorist, had reverted finally and irrevocably to Slobodan Jamisovich, Commander Dragan, the butcher of Srebenica.

"What's he shouting?" whispered Nelson.

Victoria only shook her head.

Then a deeper rumbling than that of the fire caught the attention of everyone—of Jamisovich on the splintering skylight; of the cops in the trees; of
Nelson and Victorinix in their window atop Harbour Hall. The tower of
Thornfield Library was shifting in place, sagging under its leading edge, tearing away from the rest of the library. Flames shot up from the widening
crack, and through the rumble of the crumbling foundation and the hoarse
roar of the fire Nelson thought he heard bells chiming from the sagging
tower, almost as if they were playing a tune. As his eyes followed the natural
flow of flames up the brick of the tower, he saw a bright figure on the parapet on top; it seemed to be dancing to the rhythm of the bells, jigging and
kicking and waving its arms.

"Oh, my God, it's Vita!" He clapped his hand over his mouth. "Or Robin
or . . . whatever . . ."

Victorinix lifted her eyes to the top of the tower. The shining figure was
surrounded by a swirling halo of incandescent smoke; the brilliant shower of
sparks cascading upward seemed to be reflected in its silvery skin. Far below,
the cop closest to the tower was running for the trees, waving his comrades
away from the library; the other cops were falling back toward the buildings
around the Quad. Jamisovich lifted his weapon and fired a steady stream of
bullets at the top of the slowly tilting tower; he seemed to be screaming wordlessly. Atop the parapet the shining figure stood ramrod straight amid the flames,
its arms at its side like those of a diver gathering concentration. Over the roar
of the fire and the chiming of the bells and the percussive rattle of Jamisovich's
gun, Nelson heard a ringing voice, declaiming poetry.

> *"Reason, in itself comfounded,"* it sang,
> *"Saw division grow together,*
> *To themselves yet either neither,*
> *Simple was so well compounded."*

The song seemed to come from the center of Nelson's head, but he turned to
Victoria. She was watching the top of the tower, her eyes wide.

> *"That it cried, 'How true a twain*
> *Seemeth this discordant one!*

366

Love hath reason, reason none,
If what parts can so remain.' "

"You hear that, don't you?" Nelson said. "I don't think I'm hallucinating."

"Hear what?" murmured Victoria, but her eyes were on the figure on the tower.

"So between them love did shine
That the turtle saw his right
Flaming in the phoenix sight:
Either was the other's mine."

The tower buckled and gave way, and the top of it fell forward. As the flaming parapet dropped from beneath its feet, the shining figure arched its back, jack-knifed, and executed a perfect dive, plunging in a perfect silvery streak toward the skylight of the Annex below. Just behind the diving figure the flaming mass of the tower plunged straight down, streaming roiling smoke and hissing sparks. The glass of the skylight splintered beneath Jamisovich, and he fell, still pumping the trigger of his empty gun. An instant later the roaring, sparking, crackling shaft of flaming tower penetrated the narrow skylight of the library Annex, pouring through the gash in the earth with an almighty rumble.

Nelson and Victoria cowered behind the windowsill, but after a moment Nelson peeked over the edge. A volcanic gusher of flame, smoke, and sparks issued from the ground, spouting higher than Harbour Hall, even higher than the clock tower had stood. A scalding heat washed over Nelson, and he recoiled from the window. The light of the flames filled the office with a hellish glare.

Nelson and Victoria huddled together and squeezed their eyes shut. The pillar of flame rising from the Quad seemed as if it would roar forever and split the earth apart, but in a moment it faded. The heat in the office receded; the light dimmed. Peering over the edge of the window again, Nelson and Victoria saw the shell of the old library silhouetted against the inferno within. One of the walls collapsed in an eruption of sparks and smoke. From the Annex, meanwhile, poured thick, churning smoke, stained red by the leaping flames below.

"It looks like the gate to Hell," said Nelson. He clutched the windowsill with his fingertips and peered over it like Kilroy. He felt a relief mixed with guilt, a feeling so overwhelming that it bordered on regret that he wasn't being burned alive at the bottom of the Annex. I ought to be buried under tons of smoking brick, he thought. I ought to be screaming in mortal agony as the flesh peels back from my bone, as my blood boils to vapor, as my eyes and brain . . .

Victoria sighed and rose from the window. She crunched over the broken glass to her desk, pitched the glass on her chair to the floor, and sat. Nelson turned away from the burning library and from his scalding remorse to watch her. Victoria's pajamas were ripped and sooty; the sharp planes of her face were etched in ash.

"You realize what this means, don't you, Nelson?" she asked.

Nelson tried to think, but he was tired and sore and guilty and astonished. "No," he said meekly.

"For all intents and purposes, you're chair of the English Department."

Nelson blinked at her. He cradled his throbbing hand close to his chest.

"I'm sorry?" he said.

"Look out the window, Nelson." Victorinix shrugged. "The library is burning like a coal mine. By morning every volume is going to be reduced to ash. It will take days to put it out."

Through the open window, over the hearty crackle of flames and the shouts of police officers, Nelson heard sirens.

"I'm not sure what you mean." He pushed himself up and sat on the windowsill.

"As we speak, this university is going up in smoke. It's being reduced before our eyes from one of the great research institutions in North America—perhaps the world—to nothing. Every community college in America is going to be rated higher than us. By noon tomorrow, every professor and graduate student worth her salt is going to be faxing her CV to every institution that still has a library. By midsummer there will be no one left in this department except lecturers, adjuncts, and composition teachers. Mediocrities, in other words, and has-beens and flat-out losers." She looked as if she might smile. "And you."

She rose from her chair, and for the first time in months, this small, slender woman seemed somehow taller and more imposing than he was.

"The point is, Nelson, no one with even the hint of a future in the profession would want to be chair of a department at a university with a gutted library." She smiled at last. "So you're the perfect man for the job."

She looked around the office, half-lit in the glare from the flames below.

"You and I should decide what to tell the police, Nelson." The planes of her face seemed to sharpen in the hellish light. "As I recall, when we woke up, the tower was already burning. I don't recall seeing Vita or . . . anyone else. Isn't that how you recall it?"

"I . . ." Nelson sat on the windowsill with his mouth hanging open. He wasn't sure he believed what he'd seen himself; perhaps he had been hallucinating. He wished he could forget it. He wished he could especially forget the sight of someone lying curled in the corner as he and Victorinix had descended the spiral stair. The memory stung him, and he stood.

"But just now," he said, "diving from the tower, I saw . . . you saw . . ."

"A molten piece of a bell, Nelson. Part of the clockworks."

Nelson licked his parched lips. He opened his mouth but nothing came out. His guilt, he knew, would encompass not only his own actions for the last six months, but the body in the clock tower, the burning of the library, and everything that would follow from it.

"I don't remember . . . much of anything. I guess I was delirious."

Victoria nodded once and turned away.

"You can have all this stuff, Nelson," she said. "I don't want any of it."

She started for the door. Nelson's hand ached horribly, and just taking a step made him wince, but he moved after her.

"Stay," he called out.

Where did that come from? he thought. What am I doing?

Victoria paused in the doorway, a pale figure against the dim outer office.

"We could . . . start over," said Nelson, swallowing. He had no idea where the words were coming from.

"We could . . . build a department from scratch." He took another step toward her, crunching broken glass underfoot. "Think of what we could do here, Victoria. We could build a department that rises above petty politics, that melds the best of both worlds, of traditional scholarship and the best of cutting-edge theory. Even better," he said, warming to his subject, taking another step, "we could combine teaching and research in a whole new way, make them reinforce each other the way they're supposed to. We could turn this department into a real democracy and treat everyone with respect, pay the composition teachers and the adjuncts a living wage and give them benefits, and lure the best teachers and scholars here with the chance to participate in something really revolutionary, a university where pedagogy and scholarship are the same thing, where a good day in class is as exciting as another publication, where . . ."

369

But Victoria was gone. The doorway was empty. Nelson bit his lip against the pain in his hand and stepped into the outer office. The big glass door was swinging slowly shut, and he lunged into the gap, pushing past it with his shoulder. In the dim light of the hallway—lit at this hour only by a single fixture overhead—the elevator door was sliding shut.

"Victoria!" Nelson leaped across the carpet to press the elevator button. Against his expectation, he caught the car; the doors shuddered and opened again, and he rushed into the open doorway, Victoria's name dying on his lips.

The car was empty. He turned, but there was no one behind him in the hall.

"Victoria?" he said again.

She did not answer him, but floating up the elevator shaft, raising the hair on the back of his neck, he heard her voice falling away from him, her laughter pealing like an icy chime.

Chapter One

A year and some months later, on the Monday morning of the second week of classes for the fall semester, Nelson Humboldt—divorced father, single man with cat, chair of the Department of Language Arts at the new Midwestern—awoke from a dream of another morning, from his old life. Except for the fact that his feet never touched the ground, there was nothing surreal or even unusually vivid about the dream. He saw himself in his khakis and button-down shirt and scuffed loafers, floating like a ghost down the stairs of his old town house in married housing, wafting through the living room over stained sofa cushions, shredded pop-up books, and broken dolls. He descended toward the littered breakfast table. There Clara sat in her nightshirt scowling at her scrambled eggs, Abigail knelt in her pajamas on her chair and gleefully hammered kernels of Trix into dust with her spoon, and his beloved Bridget sat with her elbows on the table and her hair awry and bags under her eyes, yawning over a cup of coffee. Nelson had this dream every morning, and every morning hope rose in his sleeping heart that he would make it a little further into the world of his family, that his feet would touch the floor just once, that he would pull back a chair and sit at his place at the table, that his children would squeal, "Daddy!" and that his wife would stifle her yawn and put down her coffee cup and kiss him on the cheek.

It's going to happen, he thought, still sleeping. *I'm going to make it back.* This morning he could not only see and hear his family, he could smell the coffee and taste his toothpaste and feel the edge of the chair against the back of his calves. His heart pounding, he leaned across the table toward his wife, and Bridget leaned across the table toward him. The lapels of her bathrobe parted to reveal the curve of her breast. Her sleepy gaze brimmed with love.

"Darling," she said, and licked him right between the eyes.

"Conrad," muttered Nelson Humboldt, waking. "Damn it."

He opened his eyes and found himself nose to nose with his cat, who stood on Nelson's chest and cried for his breakfast. Conrad had been left anonymously on Nelson's doorstep in a cardboard box last year; Nelson had never figured out by whom. Someone, he thought, taking pity on my loneliness. He had named the kitten after the subject of his dissertation, and now the namesake of the author of *Heart of Darkness* kneaded Nelson's chest with his paws and licked Nelson again between the eyes. Nelson picked Conrad up and set him on the floor next to the bed. As he did every morning, Conrad had woken Nelson precisely ten minutes before the alarm was set to go off. Nelson rolled out of bed with a groan and hit the button on the clock before it had a chance to ring. Then, as Conrad wound purring between his legs, he padded barefoot into the kitchen of his apartment to feed the cat, turn on the radio, and start his coffeemaker.

To the drone of *Morning Edition,* Nelson showered, shaved, and ate a bowl of cereal. Conrad, replete with kibble, slouched off to sleep on Nelson's pillow. It's Not So Bad to Live Alone, was Nelson's daily morning litany, to dull the pain of missing his wife and daughters: It's not so bad to have the bathroom to myself. It's not so bad to drink orange juice from the carton. It's not so bad to stay up as late as I like. At the moment, he still rattled around in the reverberating, nearly empty rooms, but bit by bit he was making a home. Once I get this place fixed up, he told himself as he brushed his teeth, it won't be so bad. Nelson had the whole second floor of an old house—Vita's old apartment, in fact. The chain of events started by the library fire had led, many dominos down the line, to a precipitous drop in rents all over Hamilton Groves, so that Nelson could afford to live within walking distance of campus—which was just as well, since Bridget got the car in the settlement. Every month, after rent, utilities, child support, and alimony, he allowed himself the purchase of one new piece of furniture. Not brand-new, of course—even a chairperson's salary in the newly privatized Midwestern didn't allow indulgence—but new to him. Last month, he had found a nice floor lamp at the Salvation Army store, and this month he had his eye on someone's old easy chair at Goodwill. Next would come bookshelves, so he could get his books up off the floor, then a desk, so he wouldn't have to work at the kitchen table.

A desk would be nice because recently Nelson had started to pursue a new research interest, even though scholarship no longer played any part in advancing his career. His new project was a study of what he called Asshole Lit, a study of the loveable fuck-ups in modern American fiction: Fitzgerald's Gatsby, Bellow's Herzog, Updike's Harry Angstrom, Percy's Binx Bolling, John Cheever's Falconer, Richard Ford's Sportswriter. Nelson was interested in shedding light on all those charismatic, self-indulgent, narcissistic monsters of male American fiction, whom the reader was supposed to love even when the characters behaved like jerks, because underneath all that adolescent charm, they were capable of redemption. Any number of feminist critics, Nelson knew, considered these characters as simply monstrous, and who could blame them? This guy's forty, they seemed to be saying, and he's only now discovering how to behave like a human being? Nelson sometimes wondered if redemption that late in life really counted, even after all the damage that had been done, but it was all he had to cling to under the circumstances.

Still, it didn't help to think too much about what could not be undone, especially on a Monday morning. If he strayed too far, in fact, from It's Not So Bad or Asshole Lit, he would begin the Chain Reaction of Guilt, his other, less comforting morning litany: guilt over his failed marriage, over the loss of his daughters, over the library fire and its effect on a great university. Watching himself in the mirror, he knotted his tie all the way up to his Adam's apple as if he were cinching a noose. The blunt stump where his right index finger used to be no longer shocked him, but he took note of it every day, as his own Mark of Cain. I didn't start the fire, he told himself every day in the mirror, and every day the nine-fingered man in the mirror replied, *You might as well have.*

"The horror," he murmured, stooping to scratch Conrad's head, "the horror." The cat cracked his eye and then closed it again and curled his paw over his muzzle.

"Mistah Conrad, he sleep," said Nelson. He snatched up his briefcase—which held only his lunch and a copy of *David Copperfield*—plucked his Company blazer out of the closet at the top of the stairs, and headed for work.

Victoria Victorinix had been right about the effects of the library fire. The Annex had burned for three days, despite the hundreds of thousands of gallons of Minnesota lake water that the Hamilton Groves Fire Department had pumped through the ruined skylight. The heat from the underground fire cracked the pavement of the Quad, venting smoke and steam; a gray pall, smelling of wet ash and burning chemicals, hung over the campus for weeks. The university, it turned out, had not insured itself for the loss of its library. The chief librarian committed himself to a psychiatric hospital in Minneapolis.

Meanwhile, by Monday morning, most of the senior faculty in Midwest's College of Liberal Arts were on the phone to colleagues all over the world, looking for jobs. Private and departmental fax machines were clogged with CVs; e-mail traffic quintupled, temporarily shutting down the university's servers. When Nelson returned to campus at midweek, his right hand completely mummified in bandages, he found some members of his department already packing up their offices, not even bothering to wait for the end of the semester. Someone taped the poster from the film *Titanic* on the door of the department office; people whistled the love theme from the film in the hallways, or sang "Nearer My God to Thee" just before bursting into hysterical laughter.

The last few weeks of the semester were canceled; seniors were allowed to graduate with a wave of the hand. The remaining undergraduates flooded the Registrar's Office with applications to transfer to other colleges; the Admissions Office was inundated with panic-stricken letters from next year's incoming class, wondering if they could get their deposits back. Lawsuits were filed by angry parents; alumni called for a congressional investigation; the graduate students' employee union disintegrated, as its officers frantically followed their graduate advisers to new schools. A long article in *Lingua Franca* compared the Easter morning fire to the burning of the ancient library of Alexandria.

All sorts of changes, both professional and personal, accumulated in Nelson's life over the following months. He saw Victorinix only once more, in the hallway outside of Sergeant Garrison's office at police headquarters. Nelson had been waiting on a bench to tell his version of their ordeal in the clock tower, and he rose awkwardly and nodded as she came out of the office. Victoria passed him without a glance, her eyes hidden behind the little round lenses of her dark glasses. A week later Nelson was informed that she had accepted a position at an Ivy; he also heard that Gillian was following her there. His last communication from either of them was an e-mail from Gillian some months later that read, "She does too love me."

Meanwhile, Nelson stuck to their agreed upon story, even in the face of the sergeant's skepticism.

"I used to work homicide in the projects in Chicago," said Sergeant Garrison.

374

"I saw less mayhem there in six years on the job than I've seen here in six months."

Nelson only shrugged.

Soon after the library fire, and the loss of his finger, some of the people who had been touched by Nelson's moral authority seemed to wake up as if from a long sleep. The Canadian Lady Novelist stopped bringing him baked goods; before the summer was out, she was lured back to Canada by a university in Toronto, with the promise of a big bonus if she won a Nobel Prize. The Housing Office sent Nelson a letter telling him that his eligibility for university housing had expired. Linda Proserpina started smoking again.

Others remained as Nelson had left them. Stephen Michael Stephens remained awake and moved to Longhorn State University in Lamar, Texas, where he set himself up as a rival to Henry Louis Gates, funding his own successful African-American Studies program with a generous grant from Bill Cosby. Penelope O moved to a new position at Berkeley, where she started doing interdisciplinary pussy readings, broadening her erotics of scholarship to include David Hume, Louis Pasteur, and Saint Teresa, the Little Flower. To Nelson's astonishment, Weissmann followed her to the Bay Area and became the world's oldest house husband, staying home with their infant daughter, who was named after Penelope's favorite characters in literature—Justine Scarlett Weissmann-O.

Nelson remained chair of the department by default; as Victorinix had predicted, no one else wanted the job. By midsummer after the fire Nelson sat alone in his office on the eighth floor of Harbour Hall, presiding over a mostly empty building. Since the dean had other matters on his mind—his own job search foremost among them—Nelson used his de facto carte blanche to promote the entire Composition Department to assistant professorships. Slowly at first, sniffing and blinking like Plato's cave dwellers turning to face the bright sunlight, pale women in their thrift-shop couture came in twos and threes out of the Bomb Shelter and took the elevator higher in Harbour Hall than they had ever been in their lives, bearing before them in cardboard boxes the meager contents of their plasterboard cubes, to claim their new offices. Nelson appointed Linda Proserpina to be his assistant chairperson, and as they stood together in her new office, looking down at the yellow earth-moving equipment on the Quad below scraping up the scorched bricks of the old library, she squinted against the unaccustomed light and pulled out a pack of Camels.

"Can I smoke up here?" she said. She was looking thinner in the face already. "Because if I can't, I'd just as soon keep my old office."

"Nobody will care," said Nelson. "Trust me."

Then, in the middle of the following fall semester, as Nelson and his new department of single women struggled with classes made up of sullen students with low GPAs who weren't able to transfer to other schools, the university was privatized. The new governor of Minnesota, a former professional wrestler, acted with his trademark dispatch and sold Midwest to the Harbridge Corporation, an international publishing conglomerate that was in the process of branding itself as "America's One-Stop Education Resource!" The changes were swift and striking. Overnight the University of the Midwest in Hamilton Groves became simply Midwestern™ A Harbridge Company, and the university's Latin motto, *Sapienta prima stultitia caruisse,* was replaced with "We're Midwestern™—If We Don't Teach It, You Don't Need to Know It." Tenure was abolished by corporate fiat; everyone, including deans and department chairs, was hired on a year-to-year contract. Tenure review was replaced with biannual performance reviews, based entirely on student evaluations.

"We're selling a product," read the blunt memo sent to all Midwestern instructors. "If our customers aren't satisfied, we're not doing our jobs." The use of Harbridge books was "strongly encouraged," while the use of books by other publishers required written permission from the corporate office. The teaching load was five classes a semester, no exceptions. All staff were required to wear a company blazer with the Harbridge logo—a worm with glasses coming out of an apple—over the breast pocket.

Other departments struggled under the new regime; the few remaining professors with any ambition at all jumped to Hamilton Groves Community College. But Nelson and his cadre of classroom-hardened comp teachers found themselves uniquely suited to the new way of doing things. The corporate salary was actually better than the old university salary for comp teachers; year-to-year contracts were better than semester-to-semester; and Harbridge, mirabile dictu, actually provided benefits, sick days, and vacation time. To attract students, the classes were smaller, and Harbridge provided each instructor with brand-new copies of their entire college textbook line. Teachers received a little bump in pay if they assigned Harbridge titles, and there were cash bonuses at the end of every semester for the teachers with the most glowing student evaluations.

"Cash," gasped Linda Proserpina through a cloud of gray smoke, when Nelson asked her if she minded the new system, "is better than tenure."

Professionally Nelson was thriving, but his personal life had disintegrated after the library fire. The morning after the fire, he had let himself in the front door of his town house to find Bridget peering at him as if she'd never seen him before in her life. They stood for a long time just gazing wordlessly at each other, each of them too stricken to speak. The living room was immaculate, decorated in pink-and-yellow crepe paper for Easter morning. Two Easter baskets stood on the coffee table; one, Clara's, was untouched, the other, Abigail's, seemed to have erupted, leaving shards of dyed egg and shreds of paper grass all over the carpet. The sight of the baskets brought tears to Nelson's eyes. He knew what he must look like: pale under a layer of soot, his beautiful clothing stained and torn, his hand crudely wrapped and bleeding. Bridget had reverted overnight from Donna Reed to her old self, rumpled and baggy eyed in her old terrycloth bathrobe, her face lined and gray. He could see in her eyes that she knew about Miranda. In the midst of this awful silence Clara entered, glanced once at her father, and marched past him without a word, her chin thrust defiantly forward. He heard her in the kitchen opening the refrigerator. Abigail appeared a moment later, dragging a mangled Easter bunny by its foot; she wrinkled her nose at her father as she dashed past him into the kitchen, crying, "Lucky Charms! No more eggs benedict!"

As the girls banged about in the kitchen, Bridget broke the silence. "I'm leaving, Nelson. I'm taking the girls to my father's in Chicago."

Nelson swallowed, too guilty to speak.

"I want a divorce," she said. "I don't see any need to waste our time with a separation."

Nelson sniffled, stung to the heart, and Bridget edged past him, pinching shut the lapels of her robe. She hesitated as she passed. "Please clean yourself up," she said. "I don't want your daughters to see you like this."

But instead of going upstairs to the bathroom, Nelson fled to his shabby office in the basement, where he propped his head in his good hand and wept sooty tears all over the top of his battered desk. The furnace sat cold behind him. A little dirty sunlight filtered through the narrow window at the far end of the room. Above the desk, the map of literary England had entirely disintegrated, leaving nothing on the wall but a stain.

377

Now, a year and four months later, Nelson stepped onto Michigan Avenue and joined the stream of students and teachers converging on Midwestern's campus for the morning's classes. He could tell the teachers by their red Company blazers. There was still a summery blush of heat in the air, so he had been carrying his own blazer over his arm; now he shrugged it on. He could have picked the teachers out of the crowd even without the blazers, and undergraduates all looked the same, no matter what their GPAs or SAT scores were, but he did miss seeing haggard graduate students lurching along like the undead under the influence of caffeine and cigarettes. Midwestern no longer had any graduate programs in the liberal arts, with the result that the geography of Michigan Avenue had changed forever. Pandemonium had been replaced by Starbucks, though Nelson had heard that it wasn't doing well: The new undergraduates at Midwestern were mostly minority, working class, or nontraditional, not the sort of people interested in paying four bucks for a latte. The bar and grill Peregrine had gone under as well, replaced by a Wendy's.

Paideia, the scholarly bookstore, was now the U Shop, another Harbridge company, doing an extraordinarily profitable business in Midwestern sweatshirts, caps, beer mugs, toilet seat covers, and football blankets. The only real objection the alumni association had made to the sale of the university had been the potential loss of the football team, so the governor had insisted that Harbridge maintain the team as a condition of the sale. The corporation went the governor one better: Quickly frustrated by the pesky rules and eligibility requirements of the NCAA and Title IX, Harbridge bought an NFL franchise and turned the team pro, giving the university's new recruits the chance to play pro ball right out of high school *and* get a college education, and offering Midwestern's alumni, students, and season ticket holders the annual possibility of a Super Bowl.

"Have you heard the Word today, brother?" someone called after Nelson. "It's the only Word that matters."

Nelson tensed himself and instinctively shuffled sideways as Fu Manchu swung into step alongside him. His old nemesis had not only recovered from his last encounter with Nelson, he had found God. He still had his droopy moustache, but now his World Wrestling Federation physique was stuffed into an off-the-rack suit, in which he was often mistaken for the governor of Minnesota. Whatever he had called himself before, now he went by the name Brother Dennis. At least a couple of mornings every week, he accosted Nelson on the way to class with the same vehemence with which he used to demand spare change.

"For the letter killeth, but the spirit giveth life," bellowed Brother Dennis this morning, shaking a handsome leatherbound Bible at Nelson. "Second Corinthians, chapter three, verse six. Can your library full of books save your soul, Professor? I don't think so!"

"Thanks anyway," Nelson said, walking faster. Did the guy have to talk about libraries and books all the time? Brother Dennis fell behind.

"Okay, then, I'll let you go in sin one more day, brother," declared Brother Dennis, as Nelson, his guilt throbbing like a drum, crossed the street and onto the campus.

"I forgive you!" snarled Brother Dennis. "But I can't speak for God!"

Nelson was just breathing easier when he sensed that someone else was about to call him from behind. Ever since the night of the fire, Nelson had found himself unusually sensitive to his surroundings. This sensitivity was especially acute at night, when he could sense the movements of birds, insects, and small animals all around him. Furthermore, he had developed a taste for very rare meat, and his night vision was remarkable. (For some reason, this early warning system never worked with Brother Dennis.) But even in broad daylight, he always had a half-second's warning when someone was about to call his name.

"Yo, Nelson!"

Nelson smiled to himself and kept walking.

"Yo, Tony!" he answered as Tony Pescecane trotted alongside.

This was the new Pescecane, reborn from his coma as radically changed as Fu Manchu. To Nelson and everyone else's astonishment, he was the only big-name member of the faculty to keep his appointment. To everyone's further surprise, he immediately resigned as chairperson, and, in a frighteningly sincere avowal to Nelson, promised on his mother's grave that he had no designs on the department.

"Fuck that shit," he told Nelson in a conversation in which Nelson himself was too astonished to speak. "All I wanna do is teach."

He had given up the seignorial "Anthony" for "Tony." He had donated his expensive European wardrobe to Goodwill and replaced it with jeans and muscle shirts (though Nelson knew that the jeans were tailored). He had sold his Jaguar (and replaced it, Nelson knew, with a 1964½ Mustang that was worth even more). He had even offered to compensate Miranda DeLaTour for her sexual harassment, but she had dropped the complaint after the fire; there was no point to it anymore.

Most remarkably, though, Tony Pescecane had renounced literary theory and all its works in a high-profile article in *The New York Times Magazine,* complete with a glossy black-and-white photo of a thick-armed Pescecane in jeans, Yankees jersey, and high-top Converse All-Stars. In the article he committed himself for the rest of his life to teaching undergraduates, and only undergraduates, to love the same great, canonical works of literature that had rescued him from the docklands of New Jersey.

"Fuck graduate students," he had told Nelson. "They're ruined already anyway."

Having given up his role as the Michael Corleone of theory, now he wanted to be the Tony Soprano of pedagogy. Today he was wearing jeans and a polo shirt with the collar flipped up; he refused to wear the Company blazer. He gave Nelson a friendly punch in the arm. Nelson repressed a wince and lightly tapped him back.

"So, Nelson, these new fucking syllabi," said Pescecane, "the fuck's up with that?"

The week before classes had begun, the Company had issued new, "recommended" syllabi for the undergraduate language arts curriculum. These new documents were as likely to include graphic novels as they were epic poetry, the works of David E. Kelley as they were the works of William Shakespeare, *Carrie* as well as *Emma.* The university's catalog didn't actually come right out and say it, but clearly Harbridge intended to market Midwestern as the place to come if you wanted to get college credit for reading *Vogue* and *Car and Driver* and watching *Ally McBeal.* The pedagogical excuse given, much to the new Tony Pescecane's embarrassment, was the old Pescecane's theory of literary street cred; the memo cited his infamous MLA address chapter and verse. What made the memo even more embarrassing for poor Tony was that it had been written by Miranda DeLaTour, his (and Nelson's) ex-lover, in her new job as Harbridge's Vice President for Curriculum Development, College Division. But in the unspoken compact of romantically embarrassed men everywhere, neither Nelson nor Tony ever mentioned her by name.

"Well, Tony," Nelson said, "you know how they are up in Corporate. They think only of the shareholders."

"Fuck the shareholders." Tony Pescecane grabbed the crotch of his tight, tailored jeans. "I got your shareholder right here."

"Nobody says you have to use the syllabus," Nelson continued.

"Yeah, but half these bints"—Tony dropped his voice, indicating with a jerk of his chin the former comp teachers hustling toward class in their red blazers— "will do it for the money." The new syllabi came, as did all of Harbridge's "suggestions," with a financial incentive.

"What about the kids, is what I wanna know," Tony went on. "Who gives a fuck about them?"

I, Tony, thought Nelson, *Working Class Hero.* Nelson opened his mouth and shut it again without speaking. He knew that Pescecane didn't need the money he earned teaching; he had a highly lucrative second career on the lecture circuit, where for fifteen thousand dollars a night, plus travel and expenses, he would tearfully replay his *New York Times Magazine* mea culpa before appreciative conservative audiences, at chambers of commerce and economic clubs all across America. The highlight of each speech came when, like Robert MacNamara apologizing to angry veterans for Vietnam, Tony Pescecane offered his personal apology to every novelist, playwright, and poet in North America for the damage he had done to literature. To make up for it, he said, he was not going to rest until every kid in America learned to love literature the way he did. And yet, for all his self-promotion and hyberbole, Nelson had to admit that Pescecane got the best student evaluations of any teacher in the department.

"Well, Tony," Nelson finally managed to say, "I guess you'll just have to show them a better way by your sterling example."

"Ahhh, fuck you." Tony gave Nelson a good-natured rap on the arm and veered away across the Quad. "Later, *paisan.* I gotta go teach these ignorant fucks how to read and write."

"Hey, *paisan!*" Nelson called after him as Pescecane swaggered away through the crowd of shuffling students. "Would it fuckin' kill you to wear the blazer?"

Nelson stopped dead on the Quad and let the thinning crowd move around him. A slender, rather stylish Linda Proserpina waved her cigarette at him in passing, and Nelson felt a twinge of something he hadn't felt since Bridget had left him. He followed Linda's blazer through the crowd with his gaze, admiring the sway of her skirt; a little voice was telling him to go after her and ask her to lunch. But before he could call out to her, a chill came over him: He no longer trusted little voices he heard on the Quad. He looked at his feet and saw that he was standing on the paved-over crack in the Quad where the burning library had vented steam and smoke. He started following the crack through the dwindling crowd, to where it ended in the grass at the edge of the pavement.

Nelson glanced at his watch; it was almost eight o'clock. Students were filtering into the classroom buildings all around. The Quad was empty. Nelson glanced over both shoulders, and even, out of instinct, up at the empty sky where the tower used to be. Then he stepped onto the grass.

To his right was the university's temporary library, a pair of double-wide trailers on the grassy patch where Thornfield Library used to stand. Nelson could hardly bear to look at them. Midwestern's library now consisted mainly of recent issues of general interest magazines; some canonical literature in editions published by the Company; and odd volumes donated by alumni. Most of the books that had been in circulation at the time of the fire had been made off with by the people who had checked them out. The library's sole remaining claim to scholarly interest was its collection of the works of James Hogg—including all three volumes of the rare *Tales of the Wars of Montrose*—the most comprehensive Hogg collection outside of Glasgow and Edinburgh. The Company had promised to build and stock a new library, but the powers-that-be up in Corporate had been making disturbing noises of late about distance learning and the wealth of on-line resources and who-reads-books-anymore-anyway? Nelson suspected that the budget for the library had been spent on the NFL franchise, but it wasn't his place to worry about money.

He stood alone now. At his feet was the grassy, V-shaped declivity where the skylight of the Annex used to be. After the fire had at last gone out, and the cloud of ash had subsided, the university had paid a toxic waste company to pump out the sludge of burnt, sodden wood pulp that used to be one of the great libraries in North America. Then the blackened shell of the old library had been pulled down, its charred bricks bulldozed into the hole, and the entire underground Annex had been buried. The bodies of Vita Deonne and Slobodan Jamisovich were never recovered.

Nelson hardly ever came to this spot, and he came here only during the day. Whenever he stood here, he felt a thrumming through the soles of his shoes, as if something was stirring down below in the Annex. And only when he stood here did he ever feel the ghost of his finger, a staticky tingle without a trace of heat in it. He was faced with the consequences of his use of the finger every day of his life; but only here, on top of six stories of earth and burnt brick, did he allow himself to think about what had happened in the tower that midnight before Easter. And even then, he never came to any conclusions, only unanswerable questions. Was Vita a man or a woman? Was Vita one person or two? These were questions, of course, that Vita herself had raised in her work, questions that she had intended every self-aware living creature to ask itself. Were Vita and Robin Bravetype and the silvery sprite facets of one being? Or was the sprite a separate creature altogether? Was Vita acting under its influence? Was it the sprite who had arranged Nelson's mutilation on the Quad that Halloween noon? Had Nelson only been a conduit for preternatural forces? Or had his desperation and his ambition unleashed something that lived in the tower, not a ghost, but a spirit of chaos, of discord, some spirit of vengeance on behalf of the abandoned authors of the Poole Collection? The sleep of reason, thought Nelson, produces monsters. But he pushed the maxim away, unwilling, even in broad daylight, to follow that line of thought to its logical conclusion. He did not want to know who the monster was.

The Quad was silent now, as silent as the tower had been that night, when the clock stopped. Nelson felt a pang as he realized that, if the tower still stood, the clock would, at this moment, be striking the hour. Still he could not move from the spot. Perhaps Victoria's official version was correct: Everything he saw in the tower was a hallucination brought on by shock and loss of blood. Vita had brought him and Victorinix there; perhaps she had even spoken to them. But in the end, all that happened was that he had woken up in the flaming library and jumped for his life. The streak of silver he had seen falling from the tower at the last moment before its plunge into the Annex had been a piece of molten brass, nothing more.

But that's not true! his imagination protested, and he was certain that Victoria, whatever she said, didn't believe it either. Think of the situation metaphorically, he told himself, recalling the definition of literature he had read in the one book ever published by Professor Blunt, his somnolent graduate advisor at Sooey: "A literary work is any work of imaginative writing—prose, poetry, or drama—that is inherently more *interesting*—rich, complex, mysterious—than anything that could be said *about* it." Think of what happened in the tower, Nelson tried to convince himself, as a living work of literature, my own private, unfathomable literary epiphany, a mystery. It was the best he could come up with.

In the end, he told himself, who, or what, Vita had been simply didn't matter.

She was my friend, he thought, and I betrayed her, and the memory of his betrayal burned him like the flames of the burning tower. On the first anniversary of the fire, he had intended to come out here at midnight and recite Shakespeare's "The Phoenix and the Turtle" in her memory, in the hope that literature could assuage the hurt—Vita brevis, ars longa—but when he arrived on campus late that night, he had seen a security guard making his rounds and lost his nerve. Now, on this autumn morning when he ought to have been in class, he could only remember a few lines from the poem.

"Beauty, truth, and rarity," he murmured, "grace in all simplicity, here enclosed in cinders lie."

He glanced guiltily over his shoulder. The Quad was empty, silent. All the students were at their desks, all the teachers before their classes.

"Truth may seem, but cannot be," he said a little louder. "Beauty brag, but 'tis not she; truth and beauty buried be."

A breeze with a hint of winter in it made Nelson shudder. He felt a pain in his missing finger. He hurried away from the grassy declivity, across the Quad.

He arrived in his classroom a few minutes late. Introduction to Literature was his first class of the day. Far from being a comprehensive review, this class was Nelson's most idiosyncratically designed. Despite the financial incentive to use Harbridge's intro lit text, Nelson based his class on a series of novels, all of them life stories: *David Copperfield, Wuthering Heights, The Great Gatsby, Beloved, Rabbit, Run.* The idea was to provoke his students to consider how their own life stories might be illuminated by literature, but he had a private agenda as well. He had picked *Copperfield* to start with because the book held at least two models for a man's comportment in life: the naive, but decent narrator, capable of mistakes but fundamentally good, and Steerforth, perhaps the most charismatic fuck-up in the English-speaking canon, the great-granddaddy of Asshole Lit.

As he came in, he was greeted only by the various gazes of his waiting students. Some of them were sullen, some bright-eyed, most of them wary. The former University of the Midwest had finally achieved the diversity to which it had long paid lip service; Nelson no longer faced the overindulged, pampered, narcissistic, upper-middle-class white kids who used to make up the university's student body. Now he faced the kids who couldn't have afforded it or met its entrance requirements before: inner-city black kids, Latino kids from farmworker families, poor white kids from dying industrial towns, divorced moms, downsized middle-managers, laid-off factory workers. Many were the first people in their families to go to college; others were starting over in their thirties or forties. Their clothes were not as stylish as the clothes of his old students, their haircuts not as expensive. Taken as a whole, they were both ill prepared and heartbreakingly expectant.

"Good morning," Nelson said, in his heartiest teacher's voice. "I'm sorry I'm late. Let's get right into it."

No one in the class said anything back to him, and Nelson felt his heart twist. He knew he'd never reach the academic empyrean again, that he would never be more than a mediocre scholar, but most of all he knew he would never teach really first-rate students ever again, that he would spend the rest of his life teaching students like these. Yet far from resigning himself to his fate, he embraced it. This was real teaching, he often told himself, the sort of teaching his father had done back in Iowa, introducing literature to those who had never seen it before in their lives. But this morning, rattled by his moment of contemplation and remembrance on the Quad, troubled as always by remorse, he couldn't help but wonder if what he did for a living mattered, not just to him, but to his students. The hard truth was that these new students just weren't as smart as his old ones, or as well educated, or nearly as intellectually curious. They accepted his authority as a simple given, but they scarcely respected him. A lifetime of reflexive contempt from teachers, employers, and police officers had conditioned these students to expect nothing but contempt from Nelson, and they were prepared to meet it in kind. The world was prepared to be disappointed by these people, and prepared them to be disappointed in themselves. As a result, Nelson's students hardly ever asked questions; they often didn't do the homework; and Nelson could count on the fact that out of the twenty people facing him right now, only three or four had even started the novel under discussion, and only one or two had finished it. Often, the one person who most eagerly shot up her hand was the most consistently wrong.

And the odds were against these folks, Nelson thought as he opened his briefcase, even here in this classroom. In fact, the odds were very good that, even with a college education, most of the men and women before him would end up behind the counter in a convenience store, or in the grease pit of an auto repair shop, or, at best, in a little gray cubicle in some vast, fluorescent-lit office. Sometimes he wondered if he was doing them any good at all. Would having read *The*

Great Gatsby raise their pay? Would *Wuthering Heights* lighten the burden of a dead-end job? He looked into his open briefcase and saw only his lunch and his battered old Penguin edition of *Copperfield*. What earthly use was *David Copperfield* to these people? What earthly use was *David Copperfield* to anybody? What earthly use, thought Nelson, has *David Copperfield* ever been to me?

He took out the book and shut the briefcase, and he moved to the lectern. He had brought with him to this class no lecture notes, no commentary, no critical texts. Is this enough? he wondered, staring at the creased paper cover of the Penguin. Is all that these kids need, is a book?

I'll never know, thought Nelson, and that's the hard truth of teaching. It's also, he reminded himself, the glory of it.

He placed the book before him and opened it to the beginning, flattening the cracked old spine with the heel of his palm. It will have to do, he told himself, because it's all I've got to give them. Pressing the four remaining fingers of his right hand against the pages, he lifted his eyes over the heads of his class and spoke from memory.

"Chapter one," said Nelson Humboldt. "I am born."

The Author's Retractions:
Heere Taketh the Makere of This Book His Leve

Now I pray to you who harken to this little story or read it, that if there be anything in it that pleases you, you thank our Lord Jesu Christ, from whom proceedeth all wisdom and all goodness. And if there be anything that displeaseth you, I pray that you lay it to the fault of my skill, and not to my will, that would very gladly have said it better if I had had the cunning. For our book sayeth, "All that is written is written for our instruction," and that is my intent. Wherefore I beseech you meekly, for the mercy of God, that you pray for me and forgive me my sins and especially my many, many quotations from better books and more pious writers, in particular chapter 18, wherein Vita speaks the words of Thomas Hardy, Lewis Carroll, Emily Dickinson, William Shakespeare, John Milton, Terence, Plato, and the King James Bible. I thank our Lord Jesu Christ and His blissful Mother and all the saints of heaven, beseeching them that they henceforth grant my friends, who shed only the light of true piety and understanding on my undertakings, the grace of true penitence, confession, and satisfaction: Keith Taylor, John Marks, Martin Lewis, Gretchen Wahl, Kären Wigen, Margaret Wong, Ross Orr, Miriam Kuznets, Dror Wahrman, Glendon and Mary Hynes, Marcia Kelley, Becky McDermott, and Dean Garrison, the father of Lorraine Alsace. Pray also for the souls of Neil Olson and Peter Steinberg, publishing professionals who yet deserve to ascend into heaven. Bless, O Lord, George Witte and Reagan Arthur for the uncommon virtue of their patience. Pray for the ascension into paradise of Tiger Lily (1983–99) and Mr. Alp (1982–99), simple creatures perhaps, but not soulless. And pray finally for the benign grace of Him that is king of kings and priest over all priests, that redeemed us with the precious blood of His Heart, for Mimi Mayer, who scarcely needs it, being as near as Our Lord allows on this earth to a living saint. May she, and I, be among those at the Day of Judgement that shall be saved. *Qui cum patre et Spiritu Sancto vivit et regnat Deus per omnia secula. Amen.*

Here Is Ended the Book of *the* Lecturers Tale, Compiled *by* James Hynes, of Whos Soule Jhesu Christ Have Mercy. Amen